Michael Scott Rohan was born in Edinburgh, in 1951, of a French father and Scottish mother, and educated at the Edinburgh Academy and St. Edmund Hall, Oxford. He is the author of nine fantasy and science-fiction novels, including the award-winning Winter of the World trilogy, and co-author of three more, as well as several non-fiction books. His books are published in the USA, Japan, Israel and throughout Europe. Besides writing novels he has been a *Times* columnist, edits reference books, reviews CDs, videos and opera for *Classic CD* and other magazines, plays with longbows and computers, drinks beer, eats Oriental food, keeps up with hobbies including archaeology and palaeontology, sings, argues and travels a lot. After many years in Oxford and Yorkshire, he and his American wife Deborah now live in a small village near Cambridge, next to the pub.

Maxie's Demon

Michael Scott Rohan

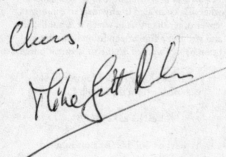

Cheers!

Mike Scott Rohan

ORBIT

An *Orbit* Book

First published in Great Britain by Orbit 1997

A CIP catalogue record for this book
is available from the British Library.

ISBN 1 85723 462 6

Typeset by Solidus (Bristol) Limited
Printed and bound in Great Britain by Clays Ltd, St Ives plc

UK companies, institutions and other organisations wishing
to make bulk purchases of this or any other book
published by Little, Brown should contact their local
bookshop or the special sales department at the address below.
Tel 0171 911 8000. Fax 0171 911 8100.

Orbit
A Division of
Little, Brown and Company (UK)
Brettenham House
Lancaster Place
London WC2E 7EN

To Richard, Colin and Tim

Acknowledgements

To Colin Murray and Tim Holman for editorial support; to the late and sadly missed Richard Evans, for unfailing belief and help; to my wife Deb, for the same, and introducing me to Prague; and to Mike Skelding and the late Pete Bayliss, also much missed, who – in an entirely different context! – came up with the opening line.

CHAPTER ONE

No Right Turn

SEX IS ALL RIGHT, but it's nothing like the real thing.

I pressed my foot down gingerly. I almost jumped at the snarl that answered me, deep enough to feel, not hear. It was the old electric feeling. Suddenly I was lord of limitless power. The bucket seat hugged me in white hide and made me a part of the machine, brain to a bigger, stronger body whose every quiver I felt and controlled. Now I was the strong man, the wild one. I was the one who set the pace.

Out ahead of me they stretched, fat, docile slugs in dotted ranks, and I saw myself weaving and winding a stream of fire between them, leaving a trail of dropping jaws and wet pants. The road stretched out arrow-straight ahead to where it met the sky, and I felt I could just ground the pedal and go shooting off it like a launching ramp, straight into the sunset. But there was all that bloody traffic in the way, taillights flocking like mindless fireflies; and I had to be careful. Didn't want to draw attention to myself, did I? I'd gone carefully this far, light on the throttle, low on the revs. Draw back; rein in. There were cameras and things. Don't stand out. Just another commuter, however sleek the car.

There'd be time enough for thrills, later.

I did an elegant side-swerve, all four-wheel drift, to avoid an unwary citizen in the outer lane, a sardine gaping out of his conventional little can, carved him up neatly on the inside – and swore. I was getting careless already. Leave the plebs alone, boy. Let them gape. Be grey; be glad.

The back of my neck was itching. Cameras and things – why the hell had I moved out on to the motorway? This bitch coked up at low revs. Speed, that was what I'd been thinking of. Stupid, stupid. If I'd only stuck to the back roads.

Maybe I could turn off. I searched my memory feverishly, there was one hell of a junction up ahead, wasn't there? All splits and merges and multiple laning, idiot planning. Cloverleaf hell, as junctions go this was a Venus flytrap.

I could drop out of sight there, altogether. I reached around for my road atlas on the passenger seat, but my hand lit on the hard little box of the scanner radio beside it. Christ, I hadn't even turned it on! I flicked the switch, the array of lights flickered, sweeping up and down the frequencies. A couple of meaningless crackles, and then there was a voice.

'. . . *car checking in – suspect is moving through traffic on the westbound carriageway, I say again westbound, driving recklessly . . .*' I swore, and stared into my mirror. I couldn't see anything, but there was so much traffic. A trickle of sweat ran down behind my ear lobe, and the old urges surfaced, swamping all my cool good sense. Never mind whether they meant me! Get moving, now, fast, get away, get out, run run run run run. All the old primeval rat rose up in me, as the boot stamped down into the sewer mud. I floored the pedal and changed up, and up, and a hard hand pressed down on my chest as the car really took off.

The engine was amidships, behind my head, and the manic bass bellow filled my ears as I was blasted back in my seat. The deep-dish wheel leaped and bucked against my wrists, a battle that hardly had anything to do with direction. It was like wrestling a living will, a maniac writhing any way and all ways. Yet in the midst of it, weaving between citizen cans and rustbucket trucks and trailer units full of freezer-fresh cabbages, fear snatched my eyes back to the mirror and the ice-blue flicker that had awoken in the dusk.

I couldn't hear the sound, I didn't need to. Sickening fear. They were that close, they must have been shadowing me right from the start, practically, waiting so I wouldn't panic and bolt in the commuter traffic, maybe damage the pretty car. Christ, that meant they'd be ahead of me as well! Waiting to drop a stinger in my path, split the tyres and stop me painlessly . . .

We'd bloody well see about that! Cops can't drive worth a damn. I could outrun them in this, I could hardly do anything else. Just one clear stretch—

I wrenched the wheel straight-armed, sliding up and down the gears with featherlight jabs on the brakes, no more. I wove a jagged line of swerves and skids and sudden violent braking, I beat crazy riffs of dents and bangs and ditching as the citizens smacked each other. But not me, not one of them touched me, not one!

Then the balloon burst and fizzled, like all my balloons, always. I hunched behind the wheel, and wailed between my teeth. Why here? Why now? Why me? Why'd they have to be there, the bastards? Why weren't they out catching real crooks?

Look at the dash! The citizen who'd shelled out for this classic had never put more than twelve thou on it. Just used it as a weekend runabout, probably, when he was tired of his Roller. Now *that* was a crime. That was the old man's kind of thing . . .

Sign gantries came sweeping up above me, and batteries of lights – and cameras. I could see them swivelling on their poles, and gave them the finger for their trouble. The flicker was nearer now, though, for all my speed, sweeping blue across the low cockpit roof, filling the mirror. Christ, he was close – how the hell, in a pissy little patrol car? Cops can't drive.

We were just past an exit lane. I swung this way and that to shake him, then bore down hard, spinning the soft leather rim, wrenched the car across the lanes, across the shoulder, the grass – bump, crash, sang the six-figure suspension in a spray of dry soil and weeds – and out, away up the exit slope, leaving Blueballs skidding into the shrubbery. I twisted around in my seat to gloat.

The engine retched. The revs sank. Memory, swift-slashing glass shards – a fuel cutoff, if the car overturned and the driver's weight came off the seat. All Ferraris had them; formula stuff. And I hadn't much weight, so when I shifted . . .

I slammed my backside down hard, but the engine was coughing, misfiring, coking up probably like all these high-revving temperamental—

And suddenly the screen was full of truck, as if someone threw it at me. Big, bigger, bright green, very, with a red light leering. Me – *why bloody well me?*

I slammed on the brakes, I hauled the wheel, I screamed. All very conventional. The car took off. Like a launching ramp. Straight into the sunset. Still screaming.

It landed. I rose and smacked into the roof. It bounced, I sprawled, the gearstick goosed me playfully, the bright-red bullet ran forward on burst tyres and collapsing suspension, howling like a demon. I must have landed on the bloody fuel switch. We were racing across one lane, then another, brakes screeching, cars swerving, blank faces turned to terror-masks whirled by – and I never guessed, then, that they must be mirroring mine. Another lane, a bump, a crash and a screech of sparking metal and now I really saw the sunset, whirling, spiralling as I spilled and tumbled about, knowing I was falling into a pit of fire. The old man's hand came up and cuffed me so hard my eyes went dark and whizzing spots of red filled my head, like the atomic models in the college labs.

And the turning and bouncing went on and on and on.

Why didn't the fire come? Why?

A breathtaking bang, a slithering roll and agony flared as I was flung about like a cat in a spindrier, my knees and elbows and head whirled out into a wild riff of blows. Then, almost sickeningly, stillness and silence, except for the tick and creak of cooling metal. A burning stench filled my nostrils. Something gave, and I slumped down heavily on my neck, my head driven painfully into my chest. I was upside down, knees by my shoulders, showing my usual aspect to the world.

And, it began to dawn on me, I was still alive. I might even be all right. Normally I wasn't too hot on life, but right then it was sunshine and apples and Pimm's No. 1 – how long since I'd tasted that? – and Celia the Snake Dancer and steak and chips all rolled into one.

You think that's improbable? Try hanging arse-upward under about eighty litres of high-octane.

An awful hope and panic billowed up, and I was thrashing and gibbering to get free, seeing the fire-ball blossoming above the seat of my jeans any moment. A leg fell free into emptiness and I did an involuntary backward roll. Suddenly there was open air and grass, and I scrabbled like a maniac on all fours to get away, clutching at the ground in gratitude.

When I ran out of breath I lifted myself on my stinging elbows, and looked around. The car was a mess, crumpled like a beer can in a giant fist, resting upside down on its rollbar in deep grass, wreathed in steam or smoke. Whoever owned this wasn't going to get his toy back. Serve the bastard right.

I was sitting on a garden wall, looking at a row of toy cars, telling two littler kids that my dad worked in the factory that made these, and that if they let me take them tonight I could get copies tomorrow. So they picked out all their favourites, of course. A treat to watch them.

I was looking at the old man's Jaguar, with its wing stove in against the gatepost, feeling my pants wet – oh hell, they were. Somehow in the middle of that lot I'd lost control. I began to shake violently and my stomach just punched up at me. Explosive vomit arched across the grass.

Strangely enough I felt better, as if I'd spewed out my terror. At least the bloody machine hadn't caught. Maybe, I decided with the idiot clarity of the concussed, I ought to get my scanner out; it could be traced to me. I tested one aching knee gingerly, and managed to get to my feet. Then the flare of heat stung my face, and I fell down again. It wasn't a movie-style explosion, more like elephant gas, but it was fierce enough, a greedy, mocking roar that took all the relief out of being alive. It was telling me just how close I'd come. It was crisping up all the cash I'd been looking forward to, that might have made the difference – not that Ahwaz would have paid out anything like a fair price anyway. He'd just shrug and go on about the shipping costs to the Gulf, the way he always did. He didn't even have to get nasty. One of these days . . .

No. I couldn't do anything about Ahwaz. I

couldn't do anything about anything. And my legs and arms hurt, a real wincing pain, and the back of my head. I'd bitten my cheek, and my damp pants were riding up. The cash wouldn't have changed anything. I hugged myself and whimpered.

I looked up abruptly. Somebody was looking at me, and I hated his guts for it. He was standing there quite calmly, about ten yards away, a smallish man, little bigger than me but more heavily built. His face, as far as I could see it in the gathering dusk, was leathery, outdoor, expressionless; he was leaning on some kind of heavy crooked pole. I stood up again, not too shakily. He didn't say anything. I glanced around quickly for ways out. Plenty of those; it was an open field, rich-looking strips of some kind of grain – wheat, probably, heavy heads whispering in the breeze over the rumble of the road.

The car had burst through a low straggly hedge and come to rest in the lush green grass at its edge. Above the hedge, a surprising distance away, I saw the rising strips of bridge and flyover that made up the junction, its lamps a hazy golden curtain in the dusk. I looked nervously for flashing lights at the edge, but there weren't any. Maybe they hadn't even seen me spin off! Maybe nobody had!

But they'd see the fire soon enough, and the scar; I'd crashed like a jet. I'd better get out of here, fast. I looked back; the junction was there too, and its approach roads, glowing beads told endlessly in the dark. And to the other side – Christ, it was all around! This must be a patch in the middle. And yet somehow the junction hadn't ever seemed that big, as I remembered it.

I rubbed the back of my head gingerly. It was all a bit much. The yokel still hadn't said a word, which confirmed everything I'd ever felt about yokels. I looked at him. He looked back, a very ordinary sort of oik in the usual shabby shirt and trousers. Only one thing stood out, a gleam of metal among the grass at the base of that stick; it was a scythe, begod, the huge old-fashioned kind. They still used them on verges, sometimes, but I didn't like the connotations. He made a pretty grim reaper, at that.

'Ferrari,' he said suddenly. 'Ar.'

Well, that about put the situation in a nutshell, I had to admit. Voice like a corncrake, but a bit more reassuring. At least he didn't talk in small capitals. I assumed my best upper-crust self-confidence. 'Yah. Bit of a nasty smash, eh?'

Silence.

I shook my head ruefully. 'I was fond of that car. Still, lucky I'm alive. And nobody's hurt. It's burning itself out, it shouldn't spread to your wheat or whatever it is.'

Silence. I wanted to kick him, but I wasn't feeling too stable right then, and he looked tough. Besides, there was that scythe. Play it natural. 'Look, laddie, I'd better get to a phone, hadn't I? Is there a pub somewhere around?'

He jerked his head backward, at what looked like an oak covert, but was actually something like a windbreak. Now I looked, I could just make out a squat roof behind it, thatched probably. 'Oh.

Right. Well, I'll just – pop over there, then, eh?
Er – right.'

Silence. He stood watching me as I limped off,
first into the grain, then, remembering myself,
around the verge; but he didn't say a damn thing
more. I decided his parents were first cousins.

The last thing I wanted was a phone. I wanted to
get out of there. I needed a ride out, but trying to
thumb one around the junction I'd just spun off
would be about as clever as tapdancing in a mine-
field. But before all that I needed, I really needed, a
drink.

By the time I reached the door I needed it a lot
more. There was a path alongside a fence, and I
found myself hanging on to the wooden rails. The
pub was easy to spot from here, its newish-looking
red brick glowing cheerfully in the greyness beneath
an ornate thatched roof, very high pitched. It had a
sign, but it was swaying in the breeze so much I
couldn't read it – or was it? By the time I reached the
post it was quite still.

The Wheel, it said, with an odd design of an old
carved cartwheel apparently hanging against a starry
sky. *Très, très* quaint, I thought giddily; something
Biblical. Yay for Ezekiel. I shuffled effortlessly
down the path, fumbled with the old-fashioned lever
latch and more or less fell inside.

It was dark as any number of pits, and the resem-
blance didn't stop there. The waft of beer was
pleasant enough, but it carried a wide range of
guest odours, ranging from old locker rooms to a
hint that the landlord kept pigs – lots of them and
very well fed. I was past caring. As my eyes

struggled to adjust, I slumped down on the nearest empty bench I saw, leaned my elbows on the table and sank my head in my hands. The moment my elbows took the weight I yelped and clutched at them, bruised and raw, and sat wincing and swearing. Then I felt a light hand on my shoulder, and realised somebody had said something. I looked up to see a pleasant, plump face, female and quite young, beaming down at me sympathetically through the gloom.

'Had an accident, 'ave yer, moi dear?'

I nodded painfully. 'Came off the road a way back. Into the grassfield behind the trees. Lucky I got thrown out, I suppose.'

The face nodded. 'Oo yer, moi dear. Could do yerself a proper peck o' mischief that-wise. And yer could use a drink, I'll be bound. Just sit yer down there and let Poppy fetch yer a good deep draught. And physic for your sores and scathes, to boot!'

I nodded thankfully, hardly able to speak. God, what a nice girl! More sympathy than I'd have got from the usual tarts I went out with. I blinked gratefully at her – then I half shot to my feet, forgetting aches and pains and everything else. She was wearing some kind of costume – white cap, long skirt, full blouse – full enough, at that. Why tell? Label her 'Tavern Wench' and you've got the essentials.

God, just my luck. One of those bloody tourist traps. Ye Olde Banquet Fayre and that sort of crap; though this one looked more authentic than most, if only because of the gloom. The only light came from the small leaded windows, and that was fading fast, building a great pool of shadow between me and the bar. No cod hanging lanterns or plastic chandeliers – no lamps at all, by the look of it. That might be carrying things a touch far. I wasn't alone, though, that much I could make out. Rough accents grated through the air. They must have stopped talking the moment I came in, but now they were ignoring me again. Fine by me. Within a minute the girl was bouncing her way back with an encouraging smile and a laden tray.

'There now! Get you that down your pipe, and a bite of bread to boot.' She plonked down a great earthenware mug of ale, and a wooden platter with a hunk of brown bread. 'And here's water and salve, moi dear, and a rag or two. If you can't—'

'No, thanks, love, I can manage. Kind of you, though.' I hoisted the mug in a toast, and dimples broke out all round. A born comic's face, kindly, sleepy-looking eyes and tip-tilted nose, an odd upper lip that pursed and pouted around her broad rustic burr and turned her smile into a beaming half-moon. I was almost a bit sorry when she did leave me alone. She unnerved me slightly; maybe I just didn't want her fussing. I was about to ask about Band-aids, but maybe she'd go galloping out for some, or something else embarrassing; she looked the type. Nice, but I didn't need it. The beer I needed.

It was real ale with a vengeance, hoppy as hell and full of bits, but not too strong; and though I prefer white bread, I had to admit this fresh wholemeal stuff set it off nicely. I could have done with some butter, though; stuff this healthy eating lark. Maybe she'd put something in the beer, because after a few minutes I felt strong enough to try the first aid. The water made me want to hop around the ceiling, but the salve – something herbal and greenish, as best I could make out, and smelling strongly of mint – certainly cooled things off quickly enough, and dulled the general ache. For the first time since I'd got behind that bloody wheel things began to calm down a little. I'd still got off pretty lightly, considering. In the shit I might be, but with waterwings.

Or that was what I thought then, anyhow.

A wizened old man came doddering out with a lantern in each hand, and began struggling vainly to loop their handles over little pegs in the beams, while the customers egged him on with ribald suggestions. This was evidently the floor show around here, the local answer to Las Vegas. With much moaning and clanking and Gabby Hayes-type mutterings he managed it eventually and trimmed the wicks. After the gloom even those dim yellow flames made the room stand out as stark as a bank of photofloods.

I blinked, and kept blinking. My God, not just a theme pub. They must be doing Olde English banquets or something, all chicken legs and Charles Laughton. They'd sure as hell overdone the picturesque clientele – as ripe a load of yokels as ever dropped out of a butter commercial, all leathery cheeks and tangled whiskers. A couple of them were even wearing smockfrocks, and one warty character had battered kneebritches and boatlike wooden shoes. Straight out of the casting agency, most likely, and filling in before summer rep.

Not that barmaid Poppy, though. Somehow you couldn't mistake her for anything she wasn't. And come to that, I felt less sure about the others. Those faces, the hard outdoor gloss to their cheeks, the bad teeth, the dirt on their hair and clothes – life and work did that. Not many people lived that way these days, not even gypsies or travellers. Grating-squatters and Cardboard City bums, maybe, but they never look that tough. These grimy tables, the dim walls with painted hangings obscured by smoke and grease, the trodden patina of bare earth, brick and bone chips – this was all just a bit too bloody real for the coach trade, wasn't it? And after a few minutes downwind I could guarantee one thing: this lot had never even heard of a hygiene inspector.

So, underneath all this some very nasty little thoughts indeed seethed up and out.

Like, maybe this was a haunted inn and I was seeing—

Like maybe that yokel with the scythe—

Like maybe I didn't get out of that crash after all—

Frantically I clutched at my wits as they made an excuse and left. I'd never believed in ghosts – not really, anyhow, not much. This beer wasn't off the astral plane, was it? And if they were anything ancient at all, why weren't they more surprised at modern me?

Besides, spooks shouldn't need Lifebuoy this badly.

Then I heard the door open behind me. I always notice that. Not a sound I like much, maybe because all my life I've been waiting for it – the old man or the teachers or the cops or bookie's goons, something like that; but it always makes me look around.

What I saw, though, flooded me right out with relief. A tall man, stooping under the lintel. A modern man, in modern clothes – very modern. He strode past me to the bar and rapped lightly upon the rough planks with a smart walking stick. He would have looked smooth anywhere, but down here among the shit-kickers the hair and the rigout made him almost ridiculous, like something cut out of a lifestyle glossy.

Almost. He looked too sure of himself by half. He took a beer mug – no, a tankard – from the old scrote, and leaned back on the counter, glancing calmly about. A regular, at home here. More than that, maybe; the massed village idiots were all tossing him a wave or knuckling brows and tugging forelocks and whatever. A bit out of character for spooks.

I tried not to feel too relieved. A theme park, it had to be – a stately home, maybe. I could believe Flash Harry was the owner, or the manager at least. Or maybe . . .

A great light dawned. It had to be these recreator types – middle-class pillocks who got their rocks off living out Olde English fantasies down to the nth detail. Even the sackcloth knickers, or total lack of same, and who knows, maybe authentic pet lice called Bill and Shirley. I'd seen them in Civil War gear and Viking armour hanging around railway stations on their way to fight old battles – total prats and proud of it. Being surrounded by them made me itchy, as if I was catching codpiece fever or something. This one probably had his doublet and hose in the car. In a Harrods bag.

I relaxed – too soon. His eyes were fixed on me as surely as bombsights. Reflex suggested I hop up and shoot out the door, but I fought it down, sort of. He had that calm, considering look I kept seeing on people who gave me grief, and when he hoisted himself easily off the bar and strolled over my heart sank. He lowered himself on to a high-backed settle by the wall, propped his stick against it and swung his shoes – pretty good shoes – up on to the bench opposite. I clutched the heavy table, half tempted to tip it over right now and run. But suppose I couldn't? Then he'd have me cold. And he was a big, sleek bastard, not quite young but lean and strong-looking, like a tennis pro. His clothes were casual, cords and a blouson jacket, pricey-looking; they wouldn't slow him up.

He gave a polite half-nod. His voice was surprisingly deep, his accent BBC neutral. 'Evening. You the chap who came off at the junction, are you?' He didn't wait for me to deny it, shaking his head. 'Willum told me you'd come this way. Bad smash, that. You're lucky to be here.'

That was a matter of opinion, but I mumbled something into my beer, trying to look dazed and delicate. I wished he'd take those bloody eyes away, but he just tilted his head back. 'Sad, too. Nice

motor, *very* nice. Ferrari Testarossa, wasn't it? Don't
see too many of those these days. Never ever, in fact,
eh? Worth – God, I don't know, what would you
say? Two hundred big ones at least. At least,' he
repeated.

I tried not to wince, but I could see where every
step was leading. 'Sure. I wouldn't know. It was the
old man's.' It could easily have been, after all. And
I'd probably have screwed it up just the same way.
Too much Testarosterone.

He looked a little surprised, maybe at my accent,
but he didn't give up twisting the screw. 'And the
insurance! A classic boy racer like that, third-party
cover alone'd come to, I don't know, how much? I
mean, even my Morgans cost me into the high
hundreds. Each. Something like that, at least a
couple more big ones a year, whew! You must be a
very lucky guy.'

I ground my teeth. This close I was seeing more
about him, the kind of things I make a habit of
noticing. Casual buckskin shoes, ordinary enough
except there was no maker's mark on the sole, and
the fit was perfect. Casual cord trousers, not new but
heavy and uncreased, with a soft, thick belt, and
above them a casual shirt in a subtle heathery shade
you don't just find in the shops. But it was the
blouson jacket that bugged my eyes; that nubbly
designer Donegal stuff with the coloured flecks
would have cost serious money in wool, but this
was raw silk, thick and close woven. And I'd caught
a glimpse of a hand-painted lining, some kind of
sailing scene.

I knew that kind of stuff. A bit more luck and

sense, and I'd still have been wearing something almost as good. They put this smug son of a bitch in the millionaire class. Even his bloody stick looked like a personality concept, the wood probably something Peruvian or whatever. And extinct.

Not a cop, then; but dangerous. Power. The kind of power that might go with owning that stately home or theme park. Or – sickening thought – owning a Ferrari. He'd certainly identify with the owner; Morgans were pricey enough. Power. One word, one move, and you could bet I'd have all these loyal arsekissers on my back.

'Well,' he remarked, 'since you had the car in the first place I suppose you can afford all that. Lucky, as I said.'

And he was looking at my clothes, too; cheap Levis, leather bomber whose shoddy thinness showed through the tears and scorches, chain-store shirt fraying at the collar, stained trainers. But I wouldn't give him the satisfaction. 'Yah. My people have the cash. Can't take any credit for it – I was born, that was all. Like in *Figaro*. Silver spoon, consider the lilies, that kind of thing.'

That shook him, and so it should. It was near as dammit the truth, and these days I was finding that more and more of a luxury. The eyes narrowed, all the same, and he lounged even further back on the settle.

'There are problems, though, aren't there, with owning a car like that? Like thieves – oh, not just your ordinary joyrider, but the kind of organised thief who steals with a ready resale market in mind. Sometimes to order, even with a target and an information dossier supplied by the dealer. Classic cars for export, to countries where they don't ask too many questions before they register, that kind of thing.'

'Yeah,' I said savagely, 'they keep me awake at nights sometimes. Listen, I'd better go get to a phone, hadn't I? Obviously they don't have one here!'

'Not right now,' he said mildly. 'And my mobile's in the car. Back at the junction, though—'

'I don't want to go that way,' I said, thinking quickly. 'The, uh, the beer – I shouldn't have had that. If they breathalyse me – well, one more spot on the licence and I turn into a pumpkin, eh?'

I was surprised to see something very much like laughter in those implacable eyes, and the twinge of hope was so sudden it hurt. 'Look, er – there wouldn't happen to be another way out of here, would there? Rather, er, unobtrusive. Then I can just blame the crash on a joyrider, and . . .'

He really was laughing now, silently. And there was a disturbing shade of pity in his voice. 'Listen. I'd better explain something to you. I wasn't even going to try, but you – well, you're very well educated, aren't you? A bright lad, for a – never mind. So listen, listen hard and try to use those brains of yours, because you've dropped into something a lot bigger than you can imagine. What do you think of this place?' He waved his hand about. 'Don't bother answering. It's real, isn't it? Completely real. Could be, oh, Elizabethan, seventeenth century, eighteenth, maybe even early nineteenth, where the Industrial Revolution hadn't reached yet.'

I wasn't going to say anything. He was trying to sell me something.

'Well, it isn't. It's all of the above, and a lot more besides. You see, they built it at a crossroads, this inn – logical enough. But then other roads were built, all around this area, and suddenly fewer people stopped here. They drove by, and the trees grew up and hid it, and nobody bothered to cut them back. Roads crossed and recrossed around it, more and more of them, in a little shallow circle. That has an effect, you know, in space and time – junctions, and journeys. Things, places, they recede, they fall away, they become harder to reach, except in certain ways and at certain times. They – drift away, you could call it, not physically, but in time. Away into a wider region, or realm. A strange kind of place some people call the Spiral.'

'Fascinating,' I said. 'And that's where the flying saucers come from, is it?'

I'd worked once as a placeman for a pro psychic, the spoon-bending variety – one of my more reputable jobs. I'd got used to dealing with nutters and true believers of every kind. But it was this character who looked like the sceptic, amused, detached, not unkindly. 'As a matter of fact, no. They're dreamed up by utter nutters. But they may well be out there somewhere all the same, because everything is. Everything man can imagine or dream up, and more.'

I looked amused right back at him. 'Heard that idea before somewhere. Interesting, but, well, it's just philosophy, isn't it? Sort of carrying on from that bloke Giordano Bruno or somebody. They may exist or not, these worlds, but it's never going to make much—'

'Oh, they exist,' he interrupted calmly. 'And they can make quite a lot of difference to us. Though whether we shape them, or they shape us, that's a question. With me, well it sort of went both ways. It may for you, too.'

'Me? Why should I ever—'

'Because you are already. Involved, I mean. There are places where space and time mingle, and this – here, now – this is one of them. You're in it. And the more you know about it, the better. Listen and remember. You don't have to believe, not now – just remember, so you'll know, if . . . When.'

At least it wasn't cop-calling time. I shrugged, and hoped he wouldn't bite me. 'I can't stop you, sunshine.'

'Damn right you can't. Places like this, they're sort of a margin, a borderland – caught on the edge of the Spiral. Its influence reaches out right through them and beyond, right into the everyday world at times – night more than day, and most of all at dawn and evening. And everywhere it touches, things can happen. Pretty strange things. But they also open a gate the other way, these places. OK, you can quote Beaumarchais, but did you ever do any science?'

'Some. Not to college level – that was modern languages. But—'

'Right. Ever hear of Maxwell's Demon?'

I felt a silly sense of panic, the way you do watching a TV quiz with an answer chasing itself around your subconscious. Then it bubbled up. 'Hey . . .

yes. Sort of a paradox, wasn't it? In thermo-dynamics?'

His immaculate eyebrows shifted maybe a milli-metre. 'I'm impressed. Yes, a joke really, by a nineteenth-century boffin called Clerk Maxwell. A discriminating gate that only let molecules through one way – a potential perpetual motion machine, among other things. If it worked, it'd violate entropy; and we still have a hell of a job proving it wouldn't. They hadn't quite got round to computers, so he had it worked by a demon. Well, I often think of the Spiral the same way, only with probabilities instead of molecules. The wilder probabilities pass outward, but they power the centre, which keeps on generating more. And there are lots of gates. They open on to all these ... worlds, realms, regions if you like. You can reach them – a lot too easily, sometimes. You can steer your way between them, if you're the right kind of natural navigator, pass into pasts and futures and times that never were at all. Myths, legends, ideals, dreams, even delusions if they're self-consistent enough – all the shadows cast by our everyday, mundane world.'

He caressed the head of his stick. The lanterns flickered in the draught. 'Everywhere has a shadow of that kind. Every country, every region or city creates its archetype, its shadow self, where its past and present – and future, sometimes – mingle with its mythical existence. Even people cast shadows, the mythical counterparts that grow up around a real person, like Robin Hood, or King Arthur. Or the George Washington who really did throw a dollar across the Potomac – and probably cut down that goddamned cherry tree, for all I know. And out on the Spiral they all come together, these shadow worlds, drifting and shifting around us as if we live at the hub of a wheel.'

He downed an impressive swig of beer, and sighed happily. 'Which is another name for the Spiral, in fact. Hence the name of the inn.'

I shrugged. 'I'd have thought the Pub at the Hub would have been better.' But despite myself, I was impressed. This citizen was the best value since the late Marquis of Bath, an authentic visionary. And he had the money to kit out his own private fantasy, that was evident. I wished I had some of what he smoked.

He shook his head, a little grimly. 'You still don't understand. This isn't the Core – or the Hub – any more. This is the Spiral. And out here the rules are all changed. It's a jungle; it has paths, but there's a pitfall every few feet, and wild things lurking in the bush around. Anything's possible – literally anything you can think of. Even . . . I suppose you'd call it magic. Anywhere in the Spiral, along its margins even – reaching out into our world, as I told you. It can get powerful – horribly powerful. Maybe Maxwell spoke truer than he knew.' He smiled at something, definitely not me, and I didn't like that smile one bit. Then he shrugged. 'Of course you don't believe me. I don't expect you to do that – just to be careful.'

'Thanks, I'm sure. Don't get het up on my account. It's what I'm good at.'

'Is it? Is it really? The best, the safest thing you

could do is head back to that junction, right now. But here's something to think about. When you were standing in that field, by the wreck, didn't the junction look farther away than it should? In every direction?'

'A mere trick of the setting sun—'

Suddenly he looked really dangerous. 'Don't piss me about, boy. How far would you have to have flown in that thing? A hundred yards? Two hundred? Then why didn't the landing reduce you to instant corned beef? Don't waste your snappy answers on me. Save them for yourself. You'll need them.'

'Sure,' I said. Neutrally, because that flash of anger had put the frighteners on me. 'Er – but the other ways—'

'Out the door, turn right and down the village street, straight over the crossroads.'

'Thanks,' I said, trying to get up as if I wasn't running away. Then I remembered something awkward, and fumbled in my pocket. If they were all pretending to be Elizabethan or whatever, would they take my money?

'Don't sweat it,' he grunted, seeing me hesitate. 'I'll pay.'

I almost accepted, as usual. I'd hardly any cash, I might need it all, but something inside me twisted into a tiny knot of defiance. Maybe it was the weary contempt in his voice, maybe it was Poppy's kindness. 'I'd rather,' I said stubbornly, lobbing back the sneer.

He looked up, surprised. 'All right. I'd say a pound would cover it, with a tip.'

'So they take our money in the . . .'

'*On* the Spiral. Here they do; a very good rate, too. Not further in.' He watched me put the money down. 'Since you won't listen to reason, chew on this – a long time back, when I first wandered out on to the Spiral, a very wise friend of mine told me that how you manage out here often seems to depend on how you first get in, good way or bad. I was lucky. You – well, what would you say? I needed help. You may, even more. You can leave word for me here. My name's Steve.'

'Mine's Hugh,' I said, because it isn't. 'Thanks, but I wouldn't hold your breath or anything. And thank the girl for the salve!'

I tried to head for the door at a civilised pace, not bolt. But the sheer relief when I slammed it behind me, and heard the latch drop, was almost dizzying. There was this old eccentric who used to sit in railway carriages, wearing dark glasses and grinning and beckoning at anyone about to come in. Somehow he always got a compartment to himself. And that would be what this citizen had been trying to do to me. Scare me back to the junction, sure – which'd be lousy with blue pointed heads by now, every cop in the county probably, all busy taking statements and causing five-mile tailbacks. Sod that for a game of soldiers! And him pissing himself with laughter at the thought, no doubt. The only safe way for me was the other way, wherever it led.

Last time it had been an open prison, fraudsters and embezzlers for company – a better class of felon, just like the old man's friends. This time it'd be somewhere harder; so there wasn't going to be a this time.

Maxie's word on it, and Maxie is never wrong; well, not since the 3.45 at Kempton Park, anyhow. Odds-on favourite, too.

CHAPTER TWO

Green Light

THE VILLAGE STREET was a misnomer. You've heard of getting into a rut; this was it. In places it was still a path, well trodden and pebble-strewn, meandering away between banks of scrubby grass. Maybe two or three cottages on each side, a few grubby sheds, a couple of farmhouses set well back along even narrower paths.

None of your honeysuckle-round-the-door perfuming the evening air; more like faulty drains. Or no drains at all.

So *this* is Broadway!

At the little crossroads the other streets looked just exactly the same. Handy; saves all that stressful decision-making. It was dusk, but none of the windows were lit; they were probably all in the pub. It did occur to me I might slip in and snap up the odd essential to speed me on my way, but these yokels probably still clapped people in the stocks or the ducking-stool or something. Besides, did I really want some guy's best moleskin leggings? No, the sooner I was out of here the better.

I hurried over the crossroads and on, stubbing my unprotected toes on stones and swearing, and found the path beginning to slope upward through a narrow dell. This countryside didn't go in much for hills, but there seemed to be a rolling stretch beginning here, with what looked like grazing fields behind solid hedges – nice to look at but murder to dodge through. I glanced back hurriedly to see if I was being followed, but the only citizen in sight was a vaguely female form beating the hell out of something in a cottage vegetable patch.

I shivered. I could empathise with weeds; nobody wanted me either. Ahwaz wouldn't, not now I'd blown his biggest single profit this year. Neither would his competitors. So I'd have to find some other scam; but where would I start? The sun rolled down behind a hill, and darkness wrapped itself around me as I walked.

I hobbled up the path, spurning unseen pebbles lurking among the grass tussocks. It hurt, it was getting bloody cold and my feet skidded on the half-frozen mud, but I told myself I didn't care. I was set on getting out of this den of acculturated lunatics and back into the real world I'd just about learned to cope with, even if they couldn't. The high bank on either side, crowned with a rickety rail fence, bulked higher as I approached the rim of the dell, turning the path into a sharp V against the stars. I plodded on, shivering in my jacket. At least my knees weren't aching so badly now; they were numb with cold.

A star – a planet, rather – gleamed golden at the brow. I fixed my eye on that as a guide, tripping now and again over the tussocks and the hardness of the world. Tiredness gave me tunnel vision; it was a little while before I realised that the banks had sunk down again, and I was over the brow. My guide glistened in a vast chilly dome of blue and silver, cloudless and moonless, floored with deep velvet. It was achingly beautiful, and for a moment it held me, not cursing, not caring, not thinking at all, simply drinking it in with the clean air. It was clean, too; it smelt . . .

I didn't know what it smelt like. Inhaling starlight, maybe, needles of it, jagged edges, fire in my lungs; I coughed. It sounded strangely loud, weirdly so, and the darkness swallowed it once it was gone. The chill drove through me, painfully. I thought of the warm fug of a heated car, and looked hungrily around for the road.

I couldn't see it; and I couldn't hear it. Yet I could hear my own soft, rasping breath, desperately loud. There was nothing else, not even the faint background hum that haunts you when you're sitting awake in the small hours, waiting bleakly for the wrong kind of knock on the door. This was madness, this was utter bloody lunacy. They were all around us, the roads. I'd seen them with my own two eyes. I'd dropped off one, for God's sake. I ought to see that same approach ramp looming against the distance now, all three tiers of it, and the grotty concrete landscape that always goes with the things, studded with little token greenery patches and halfdead shrubbery. I could hardly help hearing it; in the field I'd heard it, in the village – there was nothing wrong with my hearing.

That was right. There was nothing. Nothing between the stars and the velvet but a path, two fences and in the middle me. Trees were painted silhouettes around the dome's base, infinitely distant, mere shapes with no solidity. There were no lights of any kind, still or speeding, chained or single. There was nothing except what the stars threw down. There was too much nothing, it became an unbearable pressure. Sheer emptiness pinned me down and stared at me, an insect on a card. It bowed my spine like a ton weight. There was only my breathing, and that was in little short gasps now, and each breath blew a little more of my last warmth out into the nothing, which drank it up. Nothing, and it was wrong.

Almost as if it answered the thought, suddenly there was something. Light blinked, a faint, fragmented gleam through lacing foliage, and one clump of the painted trees sprang into shape and nearness. Not that near, though; and there wasn't a bloody thing comforting about it. It was close to the ground, but not at it; and it was completely still. It might be an upper window, not very large; but it was pale, maybe greenish. There was no warmth in that lonely gleam; the stars seemed warmer, and by being there it only stressed what was missing. This was no world of mine.

The village felt warm and normal by comparison. I didn't know what or where this was, I wasn't even going to wonder about it. I was going to turn right back and walk down between the little houses, not even warm myself at the inn but keep on straight back to the junction and take my chances there.

Warm myself? I hadn't been that cold. I'd crashed into a field of ripe grain, being harvested – a bit early in the year, maybe. It had been a warm evening, with masses of fleecy cloud; it couldn't have turned to this, not so quickly. This was the bleak midwinter, like the carol said, and if frost wasn't making moan it was just drawing a deep breath. I was plain terrified; I wasn't going to walk back, I was going to run like hell. Only before I could turn, I heard it.

It was from the field next to me, a little way behind. It wasn't a human cry, that much I was sure of and no more. If it wasn't human it had to be animal – didn't it? But there I wasn't so sure. High-pitched and hungry, it turned me to an animal myself, hunched and frozen like a rabbit caught in the headlamp beam. But I shook off the paralysis with a single convulsive shudder; then, bruises or no, I was over the further fence in a vault and pumping legs across the barren soil with my breath sobbing in my ears.

A vixen's cry is a shocking thing. I'd heard one, late at night, on a moonless country lane. It had made me jump; it didn't make me run. This wasn't it. This one left me no choice; it gave me a sharp jab right in the basic instincts. And it was somewhere down the slope, between me and the village.

The boot slapped into the sewer; the rat leaped and ran like – well, like me. My ruined jacket squeaked with the effort as my elbows pumped, close to my sides, keeping my balance, wasting no energy, my knees lifting high. I'd been on the school team, but as a distance runner, and this was a sprint, a merciless thing with God knew what on my traces any second. At least I was light-footed enough so my shoes didn't break the frozen crust. I'd been running for a good few minutes before I registered where. I was heading for that light, because it was the only thing to head for; it looked a lot nearer now, but not that much more reassuring, still pallid, still greenish.

I ran headlong into the shadow of the trees, and hung crucified on a hawthorn bush. This is about as comfortable as bonking on barbed wire, but all I could do was hang there and gasp. Then I heard that cry again, only much, much closer. Flailing and panting, I tore myself free, ripping more off my jacket and my hide. Blood ran down my face, twigs tangled irremovably in my hair. Then I was past, pushing through the trees and heading for the house they half concealed.

In good repair and a good light it might have looked better – well, quaint,maybe. But even in the starlight you could see the mangy-looking gaps in the thatch, the flaking half-timbering and the crumbling walls with the wattles standing out like bones in a corpse. It had me peering around for the gingerbread oven.

There were no lights at all in the lower windows; they were heavily shuttered, and the door tight shut. It had an old-fashioned garden-gate type of latch, the kind you can open with a penknife, or a reasonably stiff potato chip for that matter. I tested it gingerly, but it didn't lift. The light came from the upper floor, from a smallish window just below the eaves. It was escaping through a half-closed shutter, it wavered as if people were passing and repassing before it. Somehow it didn't occur to me to knock, at least not at first; but I had to get off the ground, and fast. So, up and let's have a look, then maybe I might risk introducing myself.

There were no drainpipes, but there was a low, shingle-roofed outhouse with a water butt to one side, and I could reach the sill from there. The butt moaned and creaked under me, and something parted with a little flurry of dust, but I was on the roof in seconds, and inching along towards the window. I couldn't see through the casement, though; I'd have to get on to the actual sill itself, and that was narrow. I'd known cat burglars who'd taught me a thing or two and said I should try it; but like the old man always said, never buy into a falling market.

Still, I was only going to look, wasn't I? And it wasn't that far up, and there were bushes to land in. Gingerly I plastered myself to the grimy wall and stretched out a toe. Just as well I didn't have big feet. No sweat; the wood was firm as a doorstep. I took the weight, reached out to snatch the side of the aperture and pulled myself across on shaky fingers. I stood a minute, breathing fast, then very slowly peered around the edge. I could have saved the caution; the mildewed casement wasn't glazed. Its panes were small patches of some thin, streaky plastic, brownish, whitish – mostly opaque. I touched it, and realised it was horn, ground very thin – transparent in places. There was one I could get my eye to, so I leaned that bit further, trying not to breathe too hard.

I sighed gratefully. The light in there was peculiar, but I could see through, in a misty sort of way. Just people. I don't know what else I'd been expecting, but that cry gave you all sorts of ideas.They might even be sane, who knows?

Mind you, I wouldn't have given you odds. The older of the two citizens, the one I could see quite clearly, looked like something you trip over at Grateful Dead disinterments – sorry, revivals. All hair and beard and kaftan, very white, tall and thin – clearly a casualty of Woodstock, or walking wounded, anyhow. The other one had his back to me, but you could tell he was younger, rough-haired, shortish and muscular, with tension in his stance. His hand crooked like a knob-legged spider on the pages of a large book, poised on some kind of lectern. They were both bent over, peering at the floor as if somebody'd dropped a contact lens. The old hippie was prodding at the floor with a long, thin stick.

After a moment I realised they were bobbing, in time to something, a chant maybe. I felt a terrible urge to start clucking and scattering grain. Their shadows against the walls exaggerated the move-ment grotesquely; shadows that showed the light was coming from between them, from the floor. It was green, all right – very green, to show through the dense panes like that, and very bright. If I stretched up to that other transparent bit—

The wood cracked with an explosive pop. My foot skidded. My balance went, and emptiness yawned at my back. I scrabbled at the side, at the pane. Mildew and slime threw off my clutching fingers. Logically I should have just turned a fall into a jump, aiming for the bushes, but at that kind of moment logic is generally in the corridor smoking a cigarette. Fighting for balance I lurched forward, then lost it again and toppled headfirst against the casement.

It gave and exploded inward. I went straight through it with a howl of raw panic and claws of horn and wood scraping at my face and hands, clipped a stack of books and landed in a sort of obscene crouch slap in the middle of the floor. The books toppled, and the table beneath them collapsed in a flurrying snowstorm of paper scraps. I hit something hot; it fell with a clang, green fire streaked along the floor and the most godawful stench hit me. The green light went out, and the room was suddenly black, except for fire-dancing shadows. The old fellow reared up and let out the most amazing screech.

'*The daemon! The daemon!*'

I heard a door flung back and feet go rattling down a stair, punctuated by screeches. I tried to stand up and instead found myself nose to nose with the other man, gibbering and scrabbling on the floor.

'What the hell—' I snarled, and he let out an even worse scream, with a burst of bad breath to boot.

'*Hell?* Oh no, no, most merciful daemon, I do avouch thee no, I am not worthy the taking, I'm but a miserable, misled sinner led astray by men of more schooling and wisdom to speed the satisfaction of their greed for treasure in the search for which we did seek indeed to raise a spirit but would not for the world have disturbed thee—'

About the middle of this stream of apologetic gibberish I became aware that all was not well at my back; to be precise, I was getting more than a little hot. And where was that firelight coming from? And the stench—

My turn to scream, and who wouldn't? I was on fire, my torn jacket was smouldering and singeing my hair. I sprang up, scrabbling at it, bashed my head on a rafter and came down all over said citizen. He broke the local scream record and shot out from underneath me, headfirst down the stairs by the sound of it. I was too busy rolling on the boards trying to put the flame out, and by the time I'd managed it there was only the sound of somebody shrieking in the distance – about half a mile away, I guessed, which meant he was putting up a good speed. Serve the stupid bastard right.

I looked at what I'd knocked over when I landed. A brazier of some kind, full of God alone knew what mess, still sizzling and flaming as it trickled out across the floor. Sulphur I was sure of, stale lard or tallow I guessed at, the rest I didn't want to know. I was half tempted to let it burn the place down, but I wanted some shelter till dawn, so I scooped it back with a stained brass ladle. I righted a low stool, slumped down and sank my face in my hands. More loonies—

My hands came away wet. My face was bleeding from a hundred little scratches. I must be a sight;

what would Poppy make of me now? Smother me in bandages, probably. And take me home to meet her mummy.

A thought struck me, and I looked around. Sure enough, they'd had some other light; there were a couple of candles in crude earthen sticks on the mantel. I lit them – no, not candles, smelly rush dips, but they'd do. I looked around, and found I was standing on masses of chalk and charcoal markings, evidently done with minute care but nonsensical enough to get an Arts Council grant. A panel of letters, one to a box, about a hundred of them, and at the centre ... I could see where I'd landed – slap bang in the middle of a weird-looking circle. Some kind of ritual or ceremony. A magic circle, maybe a pentacle. Yes, there were the points of a star.

Great; I'd interrupted a Satanist Scrabble game.

That gave me pause for thought. I'd come bursting in, howling, landed right in the circle with my face all bloody, with my jacket smouldering and stinking and wreathed in flame – and I'd shouted about Hell, hadn't I? They'd been up to something, those two, with their bobbing and chanting – maybe a guilty something. Maybe they really were ... I felt a slow, evil smirk coming on. No wonder they'd jumped to the wrong conclusion. And now I was snug indoors here, and they were out there with that crying thing, something really worth being afraid of.

I hoped they hadn't left the door open.

I grabbed the dips, and padded very softly and carefully over to the door, listened a while, then went out and down the stairs with my heart thudding in my ears. One creak and I'd be back up them like a rocket. Loonies, the lot of them; witchcraft loonies as well, by the look of it – one as easy as the other, probably. Ten to one they were vegans and anti-smoking as well. Total bloody flakes.

Come to think of it, that howling had probably been another of them out remoulding his masculine self-image by assuming a wolf-style role enhancement, or whatever. He was probably out there lifting his leg on the fence right now.

The thought didn't stop me shivering, though. The floor below was almost empty, one large room from wall to wall with a couple of truckle beds in it, a few books piled up, and a trap to the floor below that. I peered carefully down that, and saw nothing but a crude table and benches on a beaten-earth floor, a wide fireplace with logs laid ready and a dangling stewpot. And the goddamn door was wide open! I almost expected to see a man-shaped hole in it. I hurried down the creaky steps and slammed it shut. The latch was broken; there were slots for a bar, but no bar. There had to be something I could jam through them—

I turned to look, and somebody tapped me lightly on the shoulder.

This, of course, is Nervous Trigger number 13, and I have the complete set. Somehow I wasn't holding the candles any more, and anyhow they were out. The shrieking terrified me even though I knew it was me. I cannoned hard into the table, tipped it over, ran for where I thought the stairs were, connected with my forehead and sat down hard. Somebody, also shrieking, tripped over me and fell headlong. He was down, so I kicked out savagely, and he shrieked all the louder. Well, he was human, and resentment booted terror out of the way. Only one thing to do. I pounced before he could, landed on his back, put a hand on his head and ground it into the floor while I pulled his arm up behind his back.

'Shrsh!' he protested. 'By're lrve, gmtle shr!'

'Move once,' I snarled in his ear, 'and I'll slice out thy chitterlings to have carbonado'd for my nuncheon!' Instant Elizabethan desperado talk; I was a bit proud of that, but maybe it left something to be desired. If anything, it seemed to reassure him. By the handful of hair I had, this was most likely the old fellow, so I relaxed a little and let him speak clearly.

'I perceive by your graciousness, sir, and also by your grasp that you be not the daemon I – eh, ha ha, most unflatteringly thought you. That entirely innocent misprision, enhanced perhaps by your, shall we say, mode of entrance, leads me to ask if there is any fashion by which I may be of service to you? Preferably other than on this commodious floor?'

'We'll see!' I felt for his waist. He'd been wearing some kind of belt or girdle – I found it, pulled it loose and began tying up his hands with it. God, I felt tough. 'Just so there're no tricks – and so I can get some straight answers!'

His voice shook more than this seemed to warrant. 'I would earnestly desire of you, sir, that you not leave me bound, nor abandon me thus! We stand in the gravest danger, both!'

'Danger? How so?'

He hesitated, so I tugged the girdle tighter. 'Sir, we were engaged in – in an inquisition of a purely philosophical nature—'

'An experiment?'

'*Experimentum*, indeed, sir. To this remote and desolate corner of the earth we came, where ancient forces are reputed to be ever present, to conduct it. In a spirit of most innocent enquiry we sought to, ah, summon one of a wholly angelic nature. But around the purest such venture there are ever evil forces hovering, and we, ah . . .'

Pure; innocent. Protesting too much. I knew, I'd been there. 'I just bet. Thought you'd got Someone Else, eh?'

'Our mistake, sir, surely to be forgiven. Your irruption was to say the least unlooked for. But the conjuration was left incomplete, the circle broken! It but hangs fire, an you take my meaning. If not reversed, why, who knows what might—'

There was a sudden low groaning, and the whole house shook.

We both looked up. The boards above our head bowed and creaked. A rough-cut beam moaned and bent. There was a slight waft of a smell I couldn't describe and wouldn't dare, and a wind like a great inhalation lifted all the dust – and there was plenty – in boiling clouds. The old fellow and I looked at one another. Then the beam cracked with a gunshot snap.

I was out that door in two leaps, and only when I collided with a holly bush did I remember I'd left the old bugger in there. Give me credit, I did at least look back, but I needn't have worried. A half-second slower and he'd have left footprints up my back. Hands tied or not, he was out and past me with his robes flapping round his scrawny shins, and the 3.45 favourite should have gone like that. That was all a split second told me, that and the awful pale glare out of that upstairs window. OK, I didn't believe in the supernatural, but I wasn't about to stop and argue the point with that. As natural explanations go, it looked pretty vicious.

So here we were back at the ploughed field again and me running like a maniac, retracing my steps for all I knew. In other circumstances this could have been a bit boring, but just then that didn't bother me at all. Especially when I heard another of those cries, only a lot louder this time, and it came not from the path where I'd left it but from the house. Which meant that whatever our two hairy citizens had been calling up could have been drifting nearer all the time, sort of, just about ready to drop in much as I had. Nice thought. A minute or two later and I might have met it on the doorstep – or the windowsill. But I kept on running. When it found nobody in, it might decide to go home the same way – that was my conscious reason, anyhow. I don't think I could have stopped if I tried.

What brought me up was the fence rail, right across the chest, winding me; and I was flailing at it and sobbing for what felt like eternity, till I calmed down enough to realise what it was. I began to feel a bit stupid, then. After all – an old dump like that, half falling down, probably because nobody could afford to restore it . . .

I should have recognised the type. I'd been in enough of them when I worked in architectural salvage, otherwise known as lifting fireplaces, frames, handles and anything else not nailed down. A place like that, and a pair of superstitious loonies – a man could believe anything. The light? That brazier tipping again, probably. Could burn the place down. Shame, that.

I turned to peer into the dark. And that was when the roof flew off the grim little place, and the light boiled up from within. Out of the cavity, like a decayed tooth, the glare rose up. A mushroom cloud, almost, and for a moment I thought about green glows and silent, invisible death. There wasn't any explosion, though, just a crash of timbers; and the sphere of light lifted long and slow, like a balloon, and hung against the blackness. Then I realised it was moving, forward across the fields. A pale globe of light, with something stirring at its heart. An outline – a figure, striding.

It walked, and the light advanced – but much faster. It strode weightily upon emptiness, maybe fifty feet above the ground; but not upon silence. I could feel every footfall pound through the iron-hard earth beneath, reverberate dully in my roaring ears. Smoke or steam wreathed lazily about it, twisting in the windless air. Did I mention it was coming straight at me?

Don't they always?

I was over that fence in one bunny-hop, sending the rail flying. Then it was along the path, where the

banks should be rising – they weren't. Wrong way!
But I barely managed to make myself turn around.
Only the thought that something worse might lie
ahead made me do it, that and the open ground. At
least the banks were some shelter; but as I reached
the crest the slope to my left suddenly glimmered a
greasy green, and that smoky globe rose like a hellish
moon over the other. I was past, then, chasing my
own faint shadow in that pale light, but utterly
unable to look around.

Now I ran like a cockroach runs, automatically,
with no help from my brain at all. I was in agony, I
thought my heart was going to give up and sit down
for a breather on its own; but there was a bend in the
path, and trees, and suddenly there were those
cottages, with a few lights showing now, and the sign
of the dear, sweet, lovely, hospitable inn. I hit the
post hard enough to rattle the sign, clinging to it like
a sanctuary-seeker to the church knocker and
screaming.

Screaming for Poppy, or meaning to, and I
think the police and Jesus Christ may have been in
there somewhere too, which is pretty funny,
considering. It felt great, here between the houses,
with my arms around that wood, solid and real. I
knew nothing was going to come here, nothing
could get me here. I could hear doors banging
somewhere; soon they'd carry me in and give me
beer and make everything all right again somehow.
Then I looked around.

The trees at the turn stood out like skeleton
fingers against that frosty glare. Imagine a scummy,
algae-streaked, polluted pond frozen solid on a grey

afternoon and you have the colour, and you're welcome. It was swelling as I watched. That did it. I
hauled myself painfully up the post, wavering on my
feet, barely aware that somewhere back there the
sole had half come off one trainer and was flapping
like an idiot mouth.

Where was I? Where do you think?

Half past running time – time to run again. Now,
exhausted, I was swaying from side to side like a
wino, bouncing off fences and bushes and tree
trunks, but the path was level now beneath my feet,
and the air was mild. I could hear the cornfield
whispering in the night, or was that my breath
rasping? Half of it was cut down, and I staggered
over the stubble, yelping as it spiked my bare toes.
And there in the distance, like a vision of heaven,
gleamed the lights of the junction; there was the
burned-out patch around the Ferrari, and I ran
towards it with tears pouring down my face. If it had
been surrounded by cops I think I would have
kissed their great sweaty feet. At the far end of the
strips, in the faint afterglow, I saw a figure stooped
beneath the weight of a huge scythe plodding
patiently off in the other direction.

'That's right!' I shouted. 'You're not getting me
this time! Not yet!'

It stopped, as if looking my way, but I was at the
hedge now and scrabbling through the gap like a
demented badger, down a gritty slope. There was a
ditch, of course, and I fell in it, also of course, but it
was fairly dry. I put my hand out to pull myself up –
and cringed at the godawful roar and the sudden
looming enormity.

I snatched it back with a crazy squeal, and the juggernaut rumbled by. A foot more, and he'd have been keeping me company in the ditch. It wasn't as if there weren't any signs of anything. *No Hard Shoulder*, couldn't they read?

I was on the junction's main outlet road, heading towards the big city. I looked over my shoulder nervously. There wasn't a damn thing there except a ragged hedge with a big bite out of the top, about five feet up, too high for me to see through. No skid marks, nothing. The Ferrari hadn't been touching ground when it came through. So the impact ought to have killed me, right enough. Maybe it had. But a truck stopped when I waved it down, and I had no trouble convincing him I'd had a crash.

'Bugger and a half, too, by the look of yer! Sure you don't want an ambulance?'

'No. No thanks. I'm OK.'

'Well, yer motor . . .'

'Just an old banger.'

'Ho. And not insured? Or taxed? So you're just walkin' away? I dunno, you young lads, think you're bleedin' indestructible. Well, you've had your lesson for today, I reckon. Hop in and I'll drop you in town – Maybury Circus do yer?'

All the way back he gave me fatherly advice till I could have wrung his red neck so hard all his boils popped. He carefully put me down by a phone box. He had a point there. This one took money, not cards. I sorted slowly through my remaining change, swallowed deeply and went in to phone Ahwaz.

The handset practically jumped in my fingers. '*Maxie!* What sort of time do you call this! Where have you got to? Where's the fucking motor?'

I swallowed again. 'I . . . I haven't got it, Ahwaz! I'm sorry—'

'You blew it! I do not, I do not believe you are telling me this! The biggest job I ever set you up on, and you little bastard, you blew it!'

'Look, it wasn't my fault! The cops got on to me somehow, they were after me, they were boxing me in—'

'Of course they got on to you, you fucking idiot, the way you were driving! They had a frigging helicopter on to you – I know, we were listening in to it right here! What do you think I give you that scanner for, huh? So where's the red one – you just ditched it, huh, you crappy little coward?'

'No! I crashed it! I was trying to get away – I was nearly killed, honest—'

'You—' The phone erupted, so loudly I had to hold it away from my ear. Half of it I couldn't understand, but I didn't need to. He was calling me every name under the sun and threatening to rip out my liver. At least he hadn't put the phone down; that might have meant he really was going to rip it out.

The big A was not a gangster or anything of that sort. He was a car dealer, expensive and above, with pukka dealerships in London and Bradford and Manchester and suchlike places. He really did handle the odd legal Ferrari, now and then. He just liked the bigger profit margins on the free variety. Mind you, rumour had it he liked the margin on certain dodgy substances almost as much, and was moving into them in a big way. Certainly he kept some very large lads on the payroll; but I hadn't heard of anyone actually being worked over, at least not too seriously. So didn't I have a right to open my mouth here too?

'Look! I said I was sorry, didn't I? I mean, come off it, this isn't a secure business, is it? Risks of the game, eh? Long odds! You win a few, you lose a few! And this was bloody difficult – I mean, a red Ferrari, you can't exactly hide that in traffic, can you?'

'Difficult? You said you wanted a difficult job, you little shit!'

'I said I wanted a real job, a chance to earn some real money!'

'And I gave you it, didn't I? Didn't I? Job I've been three weeks setting up, customer waiting – real money – I'm too bloody generous, me, I should have known—'

'Oh yeah! Real money! A lousy two grand out of the two hundred you're going to make!'

'More than you'll ever be worth! Me, I'm sorry for you, I take a risk—'

That did it. I'd been through too much. 'You? Just for ringing the chassis numbers and sticking cars in a container? Some fucking risk! Getting ink on your suit duffing the papers?'

'This is an open line, you stupid bastard!'

'Yeah, isn't it! Listen, I got hurt, I got burned, I got the shit scared out of me – you're going to pay me for that, you hear?'

'*Pay* you? Get this, I don't know nothing about

you, who you are, what you're blabbing about – and if I so much as set eyes on you again, I'm going to have to scrape you off my fucking shoe, right? *Right*, you crappy, useless little pimp? Say it! I want to hear you say it, say I'm right, say you're a lousy little pimp—'

I've never been a pimp. Unlike Ahwaz. And I hate pimps. I'd never treat a girl the way they do. I haven't much left, but there's that. I don't know what I was about to do, scream at him down the line, maybe. I'd had too much, I was pretty near a breakdown. And maybe if I had said it, I might have woken up in a plastic sack on the local tip.

Something else happened instead. The whole phonebox lit up in a flare of crackling red light, blasting red that blazed in the veins of my eyeballs and drew lancing streaks of sparks across the glass. The phone itself glared red-hot; I could feel the heat. The handset blazed in my hand, I threw it up and it hung there stiff on its cord for an instant, held by the force of the energies coursing through it. There was the beginning of a startled screech from the earpiece, then only a fearful crackle. The electric chair might sound like that, maybe; from the inside.

But it was gone in the same instant, with a suddenness that left a hole in the air – that's the only way to describe it. Sudden silence on deafened ears, sudden cold on my scorched face. That was just the cool night air blowing around the booth. The handset dropped and swung, rattling against the glass. It was smoking a little. I could feel heat from the phone, but not enough for the colour it had just turned. Gingerly I reached out and touched it. It was about as hot as a dinner plate. But at my faint dab it sagged and fell limply away from the iron back.

A shower of hot coins vomited on to my aching feet.

CHAPTER THREE

Heavy Traffic

THE NEXT DAY I was pretty damn hesitant about going in to work, or anywhere else I'd be recognised. Well, anywhere at all, really.

What had happened on the phone? I didn't know and I didn't want to think about it. But I had hardly any money left, even after the jackpot from the phone. I'd spent most of that on a cab, because I was too shaken to get a bus or a train, and some more on a jacket and trainers. Pre-owned, by a macaque maybe, but Maxies can't be choosers.

My jeans, washed hastily in my cracked little basin, weren't quite dry, but I wriggled into them anyway, shuddering and trying not to strain the seams. It had been the grease holding them together, mostly.

I ought to decamp to Birmingham or somewhere else, fast – but then Birmingham, Alabama, probably wouldn't be far enough, if Ahwaz was really mad.

I'd never heard of him actually bumping anyone

off, true. But then maybe his boys were efficient enough so you didn't hear; and I had heard he was not above breaking a few bones himself in his early days. Anyway, I'd need money, whatever I did. If I could just get through the day unscathed, maybe I could scarper with the takings or part thereof. So there I was, bright and early at ten o'clock, just as Chaddy was unlocking the ten or so separate locks on the steel-panelled door.

'Christ, you look rough!' was his greeting. 'What's all this I hear 'bout you bin up to sumfin'?'

The world probably knew it by now. 'I blew a big job for Ahwaz,' I admitted.

Chaddy guffawed. 'What you doin' 'ere then? Blew more'n that, by all I 'eard—'

'Ah, leave it, Chaddy. Look, if he shows up, give me a shout so I can duck out the back, won't you?'

Chaddy shrugged. 'Do my best. But you better get them booths slopped out firss, hear? An' there's the ashtrays in the girls' room—'

It was always a delight working for Chaddy. Not that this place was his; the owners, once you got back through a chain of holding companies, were apparently Maltese, invisible and scary. Chaddy was just a minder for the minder, but it didn't stop him being a complete little Hitler. I was sure he was paying me half what he put in the books; but if I tried telling anyone, I might just be dead sure.

I mooched on through the shoddy shopfront with its flaking Formica panelling and slather of suggestive posters, unlocking all the windows that weren't painted shut, and Chaddy roared,

'F'Crissake! Born in a fucking barn, were yer?' But I knew he was too lazy to close them himself, and the warm city fug that drifted in was better than the residue of last night's stinks, little boys' room and worse. I clanked around the crudely carpentered booths with my mop and bucket, using the handle to knock out the chewing gum and paper wedges that the johns were forever sticking in to block the little shutters when their coins ran out. It never worked; the mechanisms were too strong, and the shutters just forced the stuff down to make a mess along the bottom rim, for guess who to clean up. I swept them hastily under the seat, along with the dog-ends and tissues; there'd be more along presently.

The door slammed, and I nearly dived under the seat myself. It was only Ellie, one of the girls on this morning. She gave me a friendly wave, the way most of the girls did; not a bad kid, but built like a starving parrot, dyed crest and all. ' 'Allo, Maxie, how'd ya get on lass night? No go? Aw, shame – me, I hadda great time – out wi' Frankie – went t'see the wrestlin 'n' got shitfaced after – gor any coffee?' She trailed on into what was laughingly called the dressing room. I remembered I hadn't emptied the ashtrays, and had to move fast. With her in, they'd be overflowing any minute.

I sidled through the reek of powder and perfume and nicotine and armpits, dodging stray garments and wondering what the hell the punters got out of gawking at Ellie's assortment of bones, sticking out of her skin at odd knobbly angles. Sam, the other girl, breezed in, kissed me on the cheek, said,

'Dahling!' in her idea of a posh accent – she'd got
me to coach her – and flicked Ellie's tights off my
shoulder where they'd somehow settled.

They liked me, the girls, in a sort of mild,
detached way. Some of them even went out with
me, when I had any cash and very occasionally
when they had. They said I knew how to treat
them, which compared to their average boyfriends
wasn't too great a compliment. They weren't all
tarts, professional or amateur. Some were,
including one or two who were bringing up kids,
but a couple even came from fairly stable back-
grounds. Most of them seemed to drift out of a
kind of fearful stratum of low income, low
expectations and low-grade council estates, with
low IQs and domestic violence practically
programmed in. Almost inevitably, unless something got them first, they'd drift back into it
again.

Now my real background . . .

I could keep that secret from men, but the girls
sussed it out at once – or a bit of it, they probably
wouldn't have believed the whole of it. They never
could understand how anyone with the kind of
start I'd had could have sunk so low. Drink or
drugs or gambling, maybe; but though in years past
I'd had a pretty good bash at all three, sometimes at
once, I wasn't an obvious slave to any of them. Not
even to cars, really.

I told the girls I was always asking myself that
same question, but that wasn't true. I'd given up
asking long since. I was just trying to find my
natural level, and maybe I hadn't found it yet.

Sam was holding forth on the latest TV part she hoped to get – two hours' extra work on a cop show – when I heard the door slam with real force. I jumped, but Chaddy hadn't made a sound. So when the dressing room door flew open just as explosively I wasn't prepared, and just stood staring at Ahwaz as he filled the frame.

Of course that bastard Chaddy hadn't sung out, or meant to. He'd phoned Ahwaz the moment I got in, as no doubt he'd been told to. And no doubt he was sitting out there, giggling to himself and hoping Ahwaz wouldn't break the furniture with me, at least not beyond the powers of his tube of glue. I didn't hold out much hope of that, as a meaty fist closed on my jacket and hoisted me on to my toes with straining seams, and the girls ran out squealing. A bandaged fist.

'*Take* – take it easy, Ahw—'

'Why should I? Are you looking at me, you bloody little snot rag? Do you know what you have bloody well gone and done?'

'I couldn't help the car – I've got you others, haven't I? I'll get you more – it was that cutout switch—'

'I am not talking about the frigging Ferrari! Look at me!'

I had been, but I was trying not to, because it made me want to double up with laughter. Instead of his long black tresses, expensively swept back, oiled and curled, he had what was practically a jail-crop crew cut. Yet even that couldn't conceal the fact that the hair along the right side of his head was brownish and frazzled, and his ear and cheeks had a sooty, stained look about them, with little patches of angry red like sunburn. Even his gold earring looked scorched and dull. He looked like a slightly blowtorched phrenologist's dummy.

'Look what you have done! And a hundred-and-fifty-quid shirt *and* a genuine Armani suit *and* a silk tie my brother brought back from Milan! All an absolute fucking ruin! And first I am going to—'

'Wha' happened? It wasn't me, I didn't do anything – *ech!*' That was because his grip kept tightening.

'My bloody dog an' bone exploded, is what has happened! Right there in my own hand, right up against my frigging ear! Up like a fucking bomb! I thought I was gonna be deafened for life!'

'Your – your phone exploded? Yes, mine too, I mean the call-box phone – or something – *uk!* – and I'm very sorry, but how'm I supposed to have done that?'

'It was you I was talking to!'

'Yes, but – *ulk!* – how? I don't know how to do a trick like that! You may, but I don't! And listen, was that your usual phone? That little pocket mobile job?'

He was frowning now, which was a good sign. Anything that didn't involve beating the daylights out of me qualified. 'Sure. Three hundred quid, wafer-thin. So?'

'Well, I mean – *gllk!* – that wraps it up. Don't you see? Cellular radio – no wires – no nothing, it all goes through relay stations – even if I'd connected the line to the mains or something, I couldn't have done that – *uk!* – I'm sure I couldn't have even on an ordinary line, they must have circuit breakers or something. For lightning and that – but even lightning wouldn't blow up a mobile—'

He shook me absent-mindedly. Ahwaz was by no means stupid. 'Then what the hell could have done it? And blown your end too?'

'Don't ask me – have you asked the phone people? And since it wasn't me, could you please put me down? My head's bursting—'

'No more than you deserve for the Ferrari, you little bastard!' He shook me again. 'Next time I need a kiddie's pedal-car, I'll think of you!' He slapped me quickly across the face and back about five times, then threw me at the wall. That would have been a bit more bearable if it hadn't been for his fistful of rings. I pressed back the stinging flap of skin he'd torn from my nose – it always catches the worst, God knows how the French missed Wellington's at Waterloo – wiped the blood from my mouth and picked myself up. Luckily he was more preoccupied with the phone business, and like a lot of people he was in the habit of asking me for intelligent information.

It had got me known as the Prof, for a while; but that suggests some respect. It's the truest nickname that sticks, and for about five years now I'd been Waxie Maxie, aka the Fifth Wheel.

'Something happened,' he said slowly. 'Too strong a signal from the radio station, maybe?'

'I wouldn't think so. Enough radio energy to do that – God, I don't even think a national transmitter'd be enough. And it would have fried the thing, not exploded it. Fried everything in its path, I'd have thought. Something explosive in the phone. The battery, now – there are some weird chemical mixes in those nowadays. Maybe one of those might react wrongly and explode.'

'But it wouldn't hurt the phone at your end – wait a moment, how come you're not burned?'

'Maybe because it was a payphone, and I was just holding the handset. It was the body of the phone that got hot. It didn't explode.'

He shook his head, then winced as his burn-tightened skin cracked a little. 'Beyond me. I suppose I will go and kick ass at the phone company. This phone box of yours, I'll have a look at that too. As for you.' He considered. 'You still want your money?'

Dangerously put. 'Well, I did get the car – it wasn't my fault—'

'Huh! But you have had your uses, true. Maybe I give you a second chance. You know Parker Street corner, along from the showroom? Be there tonight, ten sharp; don't go near the showroom. Dark clothes. Look for a blue Ford van.'

'Er – OK – registration?'

He shrugged. 'Haven't made up the plates yet. Fee is one hundred pounds, flat.'

Not much, but a lot more than I had now. 'OK, but what . . .'

He snorted. 'You think I'm putting announcements in the papers? Ten sharp. Be there or I'll be looking for you. Seriously.'

I swallowed. 'Sure, sure. Ten sharp.'

I watched him lounge out. His minders, who'd been gassing to Chaddy, glanced at me with mild surprise, and as they fell in behind him I saw to my horror that one of them was holding something that looked a lot like a petrol can. No doubt about it, Ahwaz was playing rougher.

'Hey, Mr Lucky!' yelled Chaddy. 'Go make me a coffee, will yer? Three heaped sugars, an' don't go spillin' it all over the bleedin' place!'

I closed my eyes an instant. Take a lesson – never demand coffee from someone you've just dropped in the shit. Sugar is good at concealing tastes, so my revenge really was going to be sweet.

I was a bit dubious about taking up Ahwaz on his evening jaunt, but not too seriously. If he'd really wanted to do me an injury he could have, without all the palaver. I wouldn't be in any more danger on a street corner at ten than I was here. So I got through the rest of the day with as light a heart as you can manage in that sort of place. Towards the evening I was even able to tickle the peepshow takings enough – Chaddy being suddenly seized with a violent stomach upset, and going home in a cab – to take Trace, one of the late-shift girls, for fish and chips, and pick up some suitable clothes.

So at ten of a cloudy night there I was on the corner, well fed, comfortable in a leather motorcycle jacket and intact jeans, and with a couple of pints and a whisky chaser under my belt to keep the wind out. Very comfortable, but I began to regret the pints. No sign of a van, so I nipped around the corner and took advantage of the side of an anonymous parked truck. Until, that is, the door flew open and Ahwaz stuck his head out, and I narrowly missed my right shoe.

'You! What the hell do you think you are doing?' he hissed.

'What's it look like! You said a blue Ford . . .'

'That is our transport!' he snapped. 'Get back out there and watch!'

Fortunately just then the van rolled to a stop, and Ahwaz and one of his minders spilled out of the truck. The other one leaned over and threw the van doors back, and I was bundled in before I could finish zipping up. I made for the front seat; I usually do the driving on this sort of thing. But the gorilla at the wheel didn't make way, and I ended up sandwiched between him and Ahwaz. Around about this point in the movies somebody slips a cheesewire round your collar from behind, but I still felt reasonably safe, the more so as Ahwaz was busily directing the driver, who was in a rebellious mood. I was even brave enough to ask where we were going.

'The seaside,' grunted the ape in the back. 'Bring yer bucket 'n' spade?'

I didn't quite like the sound of that. 'And . . . uh, what's the deal? What've I got to do?'

Ahwaz shrugged. 'Some lifting – real lifting, I mean, not stealing. And keeping your mouth shut and not messing about. Otherwise it will not just be me you are dealing with, but Stifaoin O'Faolain.'

My heart went down through the floor pan and bounced along the road behind. 'What, Stevie Fallon? Christ, you're not getting mixed up with that bugger, are you? He's bad news, he's bloody mad. Used to run dope for the IRA—'

'I know. Shut up.'

'Horse, even – I mean, he's really evil—'

'Shut it, I said. We are picking up a shipment from him, you help load it into this van and transfer it back here, and you do not need to know any more about it. Sit down and enjoy the ride.'

I'd been sussing any chance of jumping out, at a roundabout even, but I was too firmly wedged. It was an unpleasant situation, like Nagasaki. I sat back miserably, caught between the gorilla's armpits and Ahwaz's aftershave – distilled from genuine polecats – and watched the scenery. This sounded like the hard stuff, or at least a big run of hash, and I didn't like that one bit. I hadn't much use for hash since the cancer scare, beyond an occasional puff when it was going around. And I wanted nothing at all to do with the hard stuff, not as pusher, certainly not as user, not even as middle-man. Ahwaz had a nice line in cars already; he needed his head examined going for more, especially this way.

Something occurred to me; from the look of things his goons thought so too. There were tensions flying about in here, none of the usual oafish back-chat, and Ahwaz was visibly fretting and peering at his watch and map all the time. Well, anyone dealing with bastards like Fallon is likely to do that; nobody wants to get deeper into their clutches than they have to. Then a cold light dawned. That would be why they'd brought me along. I was expendable. Fallon could saw my head off and they'd just stand there giggling. Nice thought.

And that was how it turned out. We weren't really going to the seaside proper, just along the Thames Estuary, the kind of little bay smugglers had probably been passing through for hundreds of years, though Ahwaz only grunted when I said that. Moonlight filtered patchily through thin bits of cloud, and the river was a sullen black mirror. You could only see things as highlights against it, and thorn bushes and nettle patches don't have any.

Somewhere out there was a boat, though I never saw it, and coming ashore, barely visible in the gloom, was a very big inflatable, lifeboat style, with a very quiet outboard. It seemed to be riding extremely slowly, and as it drew in to the bleak and miserable patch of marshy shore I was currently sinking into, I realised why. It was towing something, something big and below water that dragged, and could be conveniently cut loose. And sure enough, as it reached the shallows the top of a heavy black plastic sack broke surface like the Loch Ness Monster, bulking high. Not quite high enough, though; you wouldn't go to this much trouble for mere pot. This had to be higher-profit stuff, and that meant nasty. More crystal than a chandelier, probably.

'Right,' muttered Ahwaz, 'you get down there and greet him. Be nice to the man, give him what he eats, but keep your eyes open. Help him get his stuff in. We'll be right back here.'

I swallowed. I knew what Ahwaz had in mind. Go down to the shore all open and above board, and a couple of squirts from a machine-pistol would let Stevie keep his crack and beat it, as you might say. And if you think that's paranoid, it's because you do not deal with the likes of Stevie.

Certainly nobody seemed in any hurry to hop ashore. 'Isn't trust a wonderful bloody thing?' I said to the darkness, and mooched down to the muddy edge, and waved my arms. There was a moment's silence, and then the boat nudged the bank and Fallon himself jumped ashore. I knew him by sight, a lanky thug with a face like a mangy wolf and a grin without a bare ounce of Irish humour. He was looking a bit bulkier, ten to one because there was a flak jacket under his windcheater. Maybe he had some ideas about Ahwaz, too.

'I've seen you about,' he said without enthusiasm. 'Where's the wog?'

I jerked a thumb over my shoulder. 'Back there. With company. I'm supposed to help you unload.'

'OK,' he muttered, gesturing to the other figures in the boat. 'Faster the better. The filth have got the area lousy with radar. You come help drag this lot in.'

A line was passed to him out of the boat, and I glimpsed something that was almost certainly an Armalite barrel. Shuddering, I hauled in the sack. Fallon left me to it, adding a laconic hand only to heave the formidable weight on to the bank, a rustling, multilayered bulk swathed in duct tape. I could feel tight lumps shifting.

'Open it!' came Ahwaz's voice. 'Carefully! And check what's inside!'

Fallon flicked a knife open. It slashed through the tape in a scalpel stroke, though I had the feeling that wasn't what he kept it for. Inside was exactly what I expected, plastic-wrapped parcels of white crystal, twenty-five of them, each about as heavy as a sugar bag. 'Check it!' said Ahwaz.

'You bloody check it!'

'D'you want your money or not?'

'I wouldn't know horse from horseshit! I don't do this sort of stuff!'

Fallon sucked in his breath impatiently. 'Sod this! I'm not hanging around for the filth to zero in on!' He caught me by the scruff of the neck and dug the knife under my chin. 'You check it or he can, but if I haven't got my dosh in five minutes flat, it's you floating face down out there – got it?'

'All right,' said Ahwaz. 'Choose a bag, bring me it. From the bottom of the pile.' But when I tried to hand him the plastic sack, he shook his hands away sharply. 'You hold it!' He unclasped a pearl-handled knife and stabbed it gently, then touched the tip of the blade to his mouth. He tasted, spat and nodded. 'That's it.' The driver produced a briefcase and opened it. 'Give the man this. Bring back the envelope. Then get the others loaded up.'

I reached in for the fat envelope, puzzled. It wasn't just for a middleman Ahwaz wanted me; he would have been safe enough with his goons. And he seemed desperate not to touch anything—

I stopped dead. He wanted me to. I didn't have gloves on. He'd got a bag of heroin back there with my fingerprints on it, and nobody else's. He'd have a few more in this heap. And he'd have me. With that kind of evidence he'd have me by the short and curlies; he could shop me to the cops with a plausible story, do me and get in good with them at the same time. I had a record, not a bad one, but with that kind of form who'd believe me? Chances were I'd go down till I was tripping over my beard. He could turn me in tomorrow, or keep me slaving away for him till doomsday because it would still be a shade better than prison. He could rule my life—

'C'mon, c'mon!' snarled Fallon. I must have frozen where I stood, and Ahwaz knew why, because I could hear him laughing.

I stopped him so fast he nearly choked. It was stupid, I shouldn't have dared; but my blood was roaring in my ears. After what I'd been through these past two days I wasn't half as scared of Ahwaz as I should have been; he didn't glow green, for one thing. I'd been pushed too far. I jumped to the bank's edge and stood there, teetering in the mud, with the envelope held high to fling.

'This'll sink like a bloody stone!' I yelled. I saw the sudden movement in the boat, my blood froze, but I couldn't give in now or they'd kill me anyway. 'Even if you shoot me—'

I knew my mistake the moment I'd said it. Never give people ideas, especially those who don't have too many of their own. Ahwaz was bright enough to hold back, but not Fallon's goons. Somewhere out there two lonely brain cells met and cuddled, and the rifle swung up; I could see it clearly, a faint, dull gleam in the night, and I didn't even have time to be afraid. I heard the shot, deep and strange and hollow, not at all the flat whip crack I'd expected. A wind sang past me, too close; but there was something wrong with it—

I felt nothing. But the rifle barrel flew up and discharged skyward with a shocking crash in that silent night, and the flame danced on the black water like fireworks. Then the rifle tipped down into it with a flat splash, and a bulky outline fell forward as if diving after, but landed writhing on the inflatable's side. Fallon's face, behind his scrubby beard, stood out pale in the shadows, eyes gaping in their deep sockets; but it was past me he was looking. There were no doors there, but it felt as if somebody opened one all the same.

There was another boat. This one you could see, though you wouldn't be too happy about it – not because it had a searchlight or Customs markings, nothing nice and normal like that. You saw it by its own light, just a little, a glimmer, like sea phosphorescence. It was a sailing boat of some kind, not enormous, and it was gliding speedily in to shore with its two sails taut. The trouble was, there was barely a breath of wind. And what there was wasn't blowing in that direction. And there wasn't a soul to be seen on board.

Now at this point, of course, the sensible man gets going, and God knows I'd had plenty of practice only last night. But the moment I tried to move there was a noise like a hippo on heat, and the muck slurped lovingly around my nice new trainers, and I almost fell face down in the clag. I caught my balance, then wished I hadn't. The mud might be safer. There were figures leaping ashore, dimly seen; there were shouts. Any minute now there'd be the helicopter with the searchlight, and the megaphone bellowing, 'Armed police!' They were running straight towards me.

But the sound of those shouts – not nice, respectable cop shouts, not even the Drug Squad. More like Manchester United fans – then suddenly I was covered in mud splatters and the stampede was parting around me and trampling past. Half-seen shapes, dim as ghosts but all too solid, in weird, patchy getups and streaming hair, waving ill-defined objects that glinted with dull menace.

Definitely United.

Fallon's jaw was still dropping, and who could blame him? They *moved*. But his hand was already pulling out of his coat, and it certainly wasn't empty, and there was movement in the boat. I was right in the line of fire – wasn't I always? My knees knocked and I shrank inwards, wishing I could imitate a Flatlander – or the famous Oozelum bird.

The machine-pistol levelled right at the leading figure. But in the fragment of a breath between the aim and the firing he had somehow covered the ground between. There was a cutting flash and a wild yell, some word I didn't catch, and something went up in the air. The pistol jerked and flickered red and yellow snake tongues, but downwards, at random, whipping up the marsh. Fallon wasn't in a position to aim. In fact he'd rather lost his head altogether. The rest of him did a neat little jig step and fell in a gangling heap. The figures jostled around it and reached the boat.

Gorge rising, I heard that cry again, and then there was a shot, not the pistol's popping or the rifle's crisp crack, dull and heavy-sounding. Somebody screamed, abruptly cut off by a very nasty thudding, but I hardly noticed. This time I had heard the word they were crying, I could hear it again, drawn out, impossibly wild and bloodthirsty. They were all shouting it.

'*Maaaxieee!*' roared a rough male voice, as metal rang on metal with a shattering sound.

'*Que viva Maxieeee!*' That was a woman's voice. Something heavy splashed over the side. There was a burst of happy laughter.

'*Maxie! Maxie hoch! Hoch!*' Air hissed out of something with a punctured squeal.

'*Que muera!*'

'*A morte! A vittoria! Viva Maxissime!*'

And those were only the ones I could make out. Beating seven types of whatever out of the dope boys, and shouting my name.

Of course I was just standing there all this time, enjoying the night air, naturally. All this time, I decided afterwards, must have been about ten seconds, maybe fifteen at best. I think I coped pretty well, allowing for shock. I didn't waste time having heart attacks or losing sphincter control or anything like that. No, I had one foot free and was literally taking my first step for flight when I realised everything had suddenly gone very still.

There was a hissing, deflating sound, and from about the same direction a faint bubbling moan that tailed away into nothing. Some way off in the marsh there were frenzied squelching noises, and in a brief glimmer on a muddy pool I glimpsed three figures splashing incontinently through it, making pretty good time for their bulk. Definitely it wasn't Ahwaz's day.

Or maybe it was; he'd got a good start. Like I said, not at all stupid.

That was when I realised I was still holding the envelope.

And then the shadowy crew came flowing back off the inflatable and splattering back through the marsh again. Right at me. They were around me before my foot hit the ground, or what passed for it here.

'Hey, Maxie!' said a harsh voice, and a hand thumped me kindly on the back.

'Maxie *bambino*!' Another woman's voice, and hey, a long arm around my shoulders as I wheezed for breath.

'Maxie! What've they done to you? You OK, lad?'

'Mack-a-sie! Hey, he's OK, huh? He's brave, isn't he not brave?'

They were all around me, poking me in the ribs, thumping me on the back, ruffling my hair and – I hoped this was the women – squeezing my buttocks, and taking my name generally in vain. The last time I had this much attention from anyone I was being beaten up by a Rasta gang, and the sensation wasn't too different.

I fought for breath, caught it and regretted it. It was like ten o'clock in the peep show on a hot night. It even had the marsh lying down gasping. Whatever this lot did for amusement, bathing wasn't part of it. But even as I noticed it, it was gone, and that really did make me look up.

I was surrounded. About eight of them, and at least two female, and that was as much as I could

make out. Apart from the weaponry, and the blood.
Then the moon came out, or maybe my eyes
focused. I've seen more encouraging sights, even
allowing for the mouldy light.

They really were festooned. They were panting,
surprise surprise, and at every breath they rattled.
They were wearing more weapons than clothes.
The guy in front of me, a snaky-looking Oriental
type with wiry hair fanning back from a low
widow's peak, was grinning, but the dagger in his
teeth, threatening his droopy moustache, ruined
the effect. He might have been wearing a few scraps
of black shirt and trousers, paddy-field pyjama
style, but the rest was belts and brassards, and an
interesting pattern of dark stains.

The woman next to him definitely wasn't
wearing a shirt, but instead of one brassard she had
a long whip wound around, with three or four
pistols thrust into the thongs – big, heavy pistols,
flintlocks even. She had some kind of cloth about
her waist, but all I really noticed was the twin
machetes tucked in it. With one in each hand
already, that gave her a lot of edge. OK, she had
earrings, but even those were little daggers, pretty
businesslike ones that clanked against her steel
collar. Her face was OK if you like them high-
boned and hard, with streaks of straight black hair
slathered to it, and flecks of blood to taste. She
grinned, too.

The black guy beside her – he was wearing armour, a breastplate with a belly, and one of those
fore-and-aft helmets like melon rinds, and long
baggy trousers, white in the few bits not claimed by

nasty-looking stains. He was grinning, as well. The night was alive with teeth.

'Hey, Maxie!' he said, in an absurdly high-pitched voice. 'You sure are one lucky guy!'

'Uh?'

'*E vero!*' said the other woman, rounder and curlier, shaking me genially by the shoulder. Rounder, curlier and strong as a horse. 'Look, *signor*, see what we have got for you!' They shuffled hastily back, as if they were showing baby the Christmas tree.

'Erp,' I said. The moon was still pretty grudging, but somehow I could see every little detail. The inflatable, half deflated in the shallows, its floats of reinforced fabric bubbling from half a dozen enthusiastic slashes. One limp arm sprawled over its edge, and a glimpse of a white, still face above, jaw sagging against the shattered stock of a rifle. A boot sticking up on the other side, at an angle that suggested a leg in it; what the leg was attached to, if anything, there was no telling. Another shape floating face down next to it, bobbing gently in the river wash. And on the ground, altogether too near for my liking, there was Fallon – the business end. He was grinning, too. In fact, he was in the pink. The split sack of white packets crackled gently in the faint wind.

'Very nice,' I said weakly. 'Just what I've always wanted.'

Another of my new friends, a blond thug with a ponytail and a great cutlass slung across his back, kicked the sack gently. 'All dis shit,' he grunted Germanically, with an angelic smile. 'All dose bucks. All for you, Maxie. Ain'tcha de lucky bastard?'

'Wow,' I said, hoping the rictus on my face looked like a delighted smile. 'But look, guys, I mean I don't want to hurt your feelings or anything, and gosh, I mean I really appreciate – but me and horse, I mean I never – it just doesn't agree with me – and this much, getting rid of it – I wouldn't know how – and anyhow,' I added, encouraged by the lack of daggers at my throat, 'I – don't really approve of the hard stuff. At all. I mean hardly. Not at all,' I added firmly.

A stunning blow struck me between the shoulder blades. So this was death?

'*Hey!* Dat be truth!'

'Arrr! Dead right, by Jenny's—'

'This is a *hidalgo*, he has principles! *Viva el jefe!*'

'Right on, Maxie!' Somebody kicked the sack, and about fifty very big ones sprayed expensively across the muck. I winced.

More thumps, with roars of idiot enthusiasm. 'Sure, that stuff's poison!'

'Aye! Pitch it i' the tide, me hearties!' They fell on it with howls of moral outrage, ripping the sack apart, punting the packets out into the blackness, whacking them away with their swords like baseball bats, trailing snowy-white comets across the marsh. There were going to be some very happy frogs round here awhile, or maybe they'd just croak.

Whatever I thought about hard drugs, the sight of so much raw money flying away caused me acute physical agony, but I wasn't about to try stopping them any more than I would a runaway bulldozer. I hugged the envelope tight to me.

'A clean lad'ee be, Maxie!' one shouted.

'Sure, no way dat a real man make his pile!' cried another. 'Come avay vith us, baby!'

'*Si, como no?*' laughed one of the women. 'Come away this night, now, share our roving fortunes!'

I don't know what sort of sound I made, but it started out as '*What?*'

'Arr!' roared one of them. 'Away, sail away, sling yer hook for a free life—'

'De vind blowing in your hair—'

'A girl on your arm—'

'*Due fanciulle!* Every day a new one! Every day another place, another story! And a mountain of plunder! Yours to command! Yours if you're our friend!'

'Our brother! Join us!'

'Our señor!' This was a woman, wrapping herself around my arm. 'Join us! Sail with us! You are of noble blood – lead us, and we shall follow!'

'Command us! Join us! We are your strong right arm!'

I carefully lowered my foot into a new patch of mire, trying not to inhale too deeply. With all this dope flying around I must have got a sniff of it. My sight seemed to be going blurry. Lead them? I couldn't even count them. About six I could recognise, including the women, no mistaking *them* ; but there had to be two more, maybe three, because there was always a shifting little knot of them out of sight at the back. It was hard to tell; they buzzed about like hornets. And you couldn't tell by their voices; one woman had a Spanish accent, another something like Italian, there was the School of Schwarzenegger character, but they seemed to come and go.

'Now jus' a moment here!' I managed. 'What's this noble crap? How'd you – I mean, who says so, anyhow? And what do you want me for?'

'You need friend, man!' said one, in a conspiratorial hiss. 'Friend who'll help you get your dues, get back all the world's taken from you—'

'*Si,si!* Friends powerful and cunning and strong, an association of friends who will smooth your passage to riches and position—'

I managed to pin down that voice, a curly-haired creature wearing what was either about twenty lire's worth of rags or something straight off the Milan catwalk. 'Look, you're not anything to do with this Lodge P2 or something, are you? 'Cause if it's Italian politics I don't want to know, right?'

'It is no politics except your own, Maxie!' said the Oriental guy smoothly, tugging his moustaches. 'From here on in what's good for Maxie is good for the world. Or we'll know the reason why!'

The voices had a pull to them you can't imagine, the women's especially as they hung on to my arms and laughed. If I'd been maybe a year or two younger, a bit more impressionable, who knows? It was mad, it was scary – but so was the thought of going back, to Ahwaz and Chaddy and the rest. And if the pitch had been maybe just a bit more modern – like, nobody mentioned fast cars – then . . .

Who knows? I don't. But I did know who I was – five feet and two inches tall, less than ten stone stripped, about as muscular as Aunty Mary's canary and with a beak to match too. And I was supposed to go off and boss this gang of butchers, buccaneers or brigands or whatever?

'Come'ee with us, skipper! Off aboard the lugger, and to our ship! Off to a life like no king's ever dreamed of—'

'Travel and adventure! Strange places and strange musics! Lust and wine and riches—' That was the other woman, the straggle-haired Hispanic type.

'Away from yer crappy little life hereabouts – away from every hurt and humbling—'

'Pleasure and power, and we a sharp sword in your right hand, *para siempre amigos verdaderos* ! To do your every bidding! Come now! Come! Come away, *venid* !'

'Come with you?' I mouthed, appalled. I couldn't make out who that was. 'You must be bloody mad. You *are* bloody mad! What are you, anyhow? Robert frigging Newton?'

'Arhar, Maxie lad?' The one I'd grabbed enquired amiably. I could see the whites of his eyes rolling. 'Bloody mad, if you say so, skipper! Come along now, the lugger be just hereabouts!'

'I'm not your frigging skipper!' I protested. 'And I'm sure as hell not getting aboard any boat of yours!'

'Ah, but skipper—'

'Maxie-eee! *Mi jefe, mi corazon*—'

They were all over me again, promising me this, that and the other. Quite a lot of the other, in fact. They wouldn't take maybe for an answer, let alone no. It felt as if they were about to scoop me up and carry me off. I was cold and wet and terrified and I had half the marsh up my jeans, including some of the wriggly bits, and the last thing I wanted was to be shanghaied off to Nowhere Land aboard this lot's lugger, whatever that was.

'Look!' I shouted, threshing my arms free and trying to pump up my courage. 'Just – leave me alone, will you? Just – just bugger off!'

Slowly, drooping, they let my arms fall and shuffled back, looking like a dog that's been told off. The blond man threw up his hands protestingly.

'Hey, but de skipper—'

'Bugger off!' I was beginning to get bolder the less they responded. And angry, angrier by the moment. Something was sounding little warning bells in the back of my mind; the last time I got this angry, things had exploded. But nothing seemed to be happening here. 'Look,' I erupted, 'you'll do anything I say, will you? Then go on, hop it! Bugger off – or I'll make you do it literally!'

The whipped-cur act again, with noises of protest and disappointed disbelief. 'Ar,' said the rough-voiced one. ''Tis best leave 'im settle his mind awhile, 'tis a mortal big step!' They clustered around again, baying sober agreement.

'So!' said the Oriental type, talking past his knife like a tycoon with his cigar, 'we will go, then. But hearken to this, lord Maxie! You do not believe in us because you do not believe in yourself. We know a born leader when we see one.'

'Arhar! We need you, an' we'll not let 'ee waste thyself thus, no, me bold heart!'

The women, who'd sunk down on their knees by my side, slid gracefully upright. One of them lifted her curly hair high, with a mocking giggle. 'The offer is still open, Maxie. *E altro infortunio*, it brews for you!'

The other one, turning away, shot a glance back over her shoulder. '*Verdad!* And when that trouble boils over, you have but to call, *mi corazon!*' Her eyes glittered in the gloom, and she snapped her long white teeth like a trap. '*Estaremos alla!*'

'*Away!*' said a harsh voice. They trotted towards the water's edge, leaving me swaying, panting, mired deeper than I had been before. Darkness drifted across the water, and in it I suddenly saw the faint outline of the lugger's mastheads as the sails soared up and billowed, and the bows swung out from shore. A distant voice drifted back to me as the shadow shape glided slowly out into the estuary, a shifting sketch in pale chalk on black. 'Trouble comes, remember – and so do we!'

Then there was silence, and the splashing of the waves. Oh yes, and me whimpering.

The mud had eaten one of my trainers, and I had a fine time delving around for it. No sign – and I almost dropped the envelope. Hastily I caught it, and looked inside; and I began to sweat again, though I was freezing. Fifty grand in hundreds, if it was a cent; Ahwaz's fifty grand. He'd seen his big deal bushwhacked, and he'd had to do the runner of all time, and he'd lost his money; and I had it.

I gibbered at the thought. The phone he'd accepted, but this – not a cat in hell's chance, and I'd be the cat.

I hugged the bills to my chest, but newspaper is better insulation. I had to get out of here. Ahwaz might even come back now. But I was miles from anywhere with only one trainer, and for all the big notes I could brandish, I hadn't nearly enough small ones to get back. Try giving a cabbie a hundred; chances are he'll run you straight to the nearest cop shop. Unless he's one of the East London minicab boys, in which case he'll probably roll you on the off-chance there's more.

I swallowed painfully. There was money here, and maybe shoes, too. Wading in could only improve my jeans, so I clambered over the squidgy slickness of the inflatable and its horrid cargo. One I couldn't touch, and anything he'd had would have been spoiled anyway; but the other had a heap of Dutch guilders and about a hundred in English cash, and his trainers were better than mine, though not such a good fit. Then, looking away and making little mewing noises, I managed to rifle some of Fallon's pockets for more.

About five hundred in all, plus more guilders. More money than I'd set eyes on in a few years; but it felt cold and clammy as death in my fingers. There was something else about it, too, but I couldn't think what, and I wasn't about to hang around. I had a long walk ahead, especially as I didn't dare go back to the road where we'd left Ahwaz's van. Maybe I should have hopped that lugger and all, right enough.

And then that nagging thought hit me clearly at last – the brigands or whatever they were, why hadn't *they* rifled their victims? They'd chucked the drugs away. They'd left me the money. They hadn't come for the cash, nor out of sheer public spirit either.

So what had they come for?

Me?

CHAPTER FOUR

Obey Signals

ALL THAT MONEY, though, all that dosh. That was what really got to me, so badly I couldn't worry about much else.

Who'd it belong to? Who wants to know?

I plodded across the marsh, almost blind, brain clacking away like a jet-propelled hamster wheel. Fallon wasn't very likely to come back asking for it; mind you, if he did, he'd get it. No arguments, *at all*.

Ahwaz – well, what I say is, when you run away from a dodgy investment you've got to take your losses. Sooner or later, of course, he'd stop running and start looking around for somebody to blame it on, and he'd probably start with me. Only he'd have to find me first.

Fifty grand can take you a long, long way. He owed me it, too. All those jobs I'd done for him, all those lovely motors lifted – the peanuts he'd paid me. A complete bloody thief, that's what he was – a thief.

And that brought me back to these thugs or bandits or whatever they were. They could have taken the money right out of my hand. Or the hand with it, for two pins. They had a claim, and they were pretty good at getting straight to the point, and the edge too for that matter. I couldn't make them out. Every time I thought about them my head ached and my mind blurred. It must have been the dope floating about. They couldn't really have been the way I saw them. Almost like the ghosts of the old-time smugglers or pirates who'd used the marsh, who'd maybe been sunk in it often enough, by the revenuers or their rivals. Or strung up on lonely marshland gibbets to rot away, bit by bit, tarred so they'd last as a warning, creaking in the icy sea breeze . . .

Actually it was quite warm. I still shivered and looked behind me, not eager to see a dangling silhouette against the baleful skygleam. I didn't, and what's more I didn't see the smelly boghole in front of me either, before it swallowed my foot to the knee and threw me flat in some brambles. It bred a healthy scepticism.

I was being paranoid, that was all. Ten to one they were just a raggedy-arsed gang of wild men, diddy-boys or travellers or something, who'd come in to bust up a big dope deal – for the cash, not the dope, which is risky to market. That would explain why they kicked the stuff around – and got themselves and me an incidental high. I got some crazy ideas, they forgot the money. I didn't; but then I was just a bit saner to start with, maybe. So, tough titty on them. To the victor, the spoils – especially if the victor doesn't leave a forwarding address.

Trouble was, the victor didn't know what to do

next. I couldn't go anywhere like this, not without somewhere to dry off and warm up and get a few hours' rest. I'd be conspicuous, I'd be remembered, leave a trail. Did I dare go home? It was a risk, but then so was anywhere, the way I was now. I was rationalising, the rat heading back to its hole; but I didn't see that at the time.

The envelope was getting battered, so I tucked it inside my shirt, giving myself a chest for a change. All the long way home it crackled and creaked against my heart. It was a bloody long way, too. By the time I got off the marsh, after much slipping and sliding and falling in pools of God knows what, it was nearly two. No buses running, not much traffic, no cabs and no free rides, at least when they stopped and caught the pong of marsh all over me. The Gollum look was not in that year.

For that matter there weren't many shifty little marsh-sodden characters wandering around with a small fortune up their jumper, traces of powdered heroin all over them and four drug-runner corpses some way back along their tracks. It made me feel a tiny bit conspicuous. So I had to be very careful about hitching. I mean, suppose I happened to thumb down a cop car—

It didn't bear thinking about. And I even had to make myself pass up a nice little MG I found down a back road, standing empty suspiciously close to a cosy hay barn. I didn't dare risk getting nicked with this much on me, not to mention the traces of snow, and with my luck I probably would.

Mind you, I was already inside and fiddling for the ignition leads before I thought twice, but that's the force of habit for you. I was strong, though, and left the hayloft lovers to wonder why someone had filled the driver's seat with slime and frogspawn during their little passionate interlude. Another one for the X-Files.

Eventually I slopped and squelched my way to a late-night garage, stuck a coin in the carwash and hopped through it. I came out the other end soaked and foaming at the ears, but at least I didn't smell, except of low-grade car shampoo. I really was Waxie Maxie now.

Wet is pathetic when ponging is not, so a kindly soul gave me a place in the back of a car transporter and eventually dropped me off not five hundred yards from home. Round there five hundred yards could mean about five potential muggers, but it was near four now, probably outside their union hours. Either that, or the Turtle Wax made me look too slippery.

The neighbourhood I was favouring just then wasn't so much the wrong side of the tracks, it practically was the tracks, a railway freight junction embalmed in thick layers of authentic Industrial Revolution soot. By now the roof would have stayed up if you'd taken the actual bricks away, and chances were my landlords had. My street was like that. The local ethnics were always complaining we lowered the property values.

All the same, I got back to my door with only a minimum of ducking and dodging. It wasn't the most welcoming sight, a massive Victorian affair in about the same state as the British Empire and patched up with rough-nailed sheet steel and spray graffiti. If there were ever a name on that sort of door you just knew it would read *Dunlurkin* or *Sticky End*.

Or possibly just *No Fixed Abode*.

I stepped over the usual ammonia-rich body snoring among the dustbins and slunk up to the opulent penthouse apartment I rented, or rather owed rent on. I slid the door to behind me, shot the bolt, turned the key, kicked in the scrap-wood wedge, put my back to it and slid down to the floor, groaning. The floor groaned back. Then I made a wild grab for the envelope, shielded by my leather jacket, and tore at the wodge of notes inside.

Fifty grand it was, new notes but none of them dodgy as far as I could tell. The marsh had got to it, a little, and the carwash too – laundered money, ha ha ha – but it was deep and crisp and even still. I stared at it, giggling feebly. This was luck. This was the break, the moment I'd been praying for. This was the ride out, the getaway. I started cackling like Scrooge. This was the way back. This was – the light went out.

Hastily I shoved another coin in the meter, tore off my trousers and trainers and thrust them into the cracked little handbasin. There was still a lot of mud in there, and car shampoo as well, so they turned into a sort of horrible pink frothing slough. But eventually I hauled them out much cleaner, stuck them on the window line to dry and retreated to bed to keep warm. I couldn't sleep. The sheet and mattress felt cold and clammy, but then so did I, and I was used to that, anyway. The blankets were better, so I rolled up in them as best I could, trying to enjoy the friendly tickle, and dug my head into the pillow to cool my jittering brain. Did the bloody thing always stink of stale vomit? How long since I'd changed it, anyhow?

Fifty grand! My old man would have laughed at that, once. How much had he pulled down? Maybe eight times that a year, maybe nine. Laughing with his hearty City cronies – that was how I remembered him. Laughing with them, scowling at me. Scowling whatever I did, but most of all when it started with the cars. Me standing there shivering in what he called his study, my ears ringing where he'd boxed them, and him stalking back and forth in front of me. *Stealing! A son of mine stealing! What would your poor mother have said if she'd known you'd turn out a common thief! A joke? D'you know just how much keeping this bloody little joke of yours quiet has cost me?* Always the same – the lines, the reproaches, the blunt *Get out!* that finished it. Until the next.

Laughing with his friends – the jolly, avuncular types who dug me in the ribs and slipped me cigars and took me off to clubs on the quiet. *We'll see you OK, Max! College? Well, if you must, but remember, your desk's just waiting! Me and your old man, we're like that, eh? Like that!*

And then the grey days beginning. The vintage Bentley, with that colossal outside handbrake I could hardly work, and getting sent down in my second year, and finding the old man away in the City and all the jolly uncles somehow never around and impossible to reach on the phone. Then the quiet grey men at dawn, tramping all over that precious study, piling the papers high. The arrest, the front pages, the first remand and soon after that, on bail he could barely manage, the massive coronary in the private clinic. On a public ward the resuscitation trolley might have reached him in time; but the old man liked his privacy, and had scared all the nurses away. Maybe deliberately. He had been cheating, all this time, stealing from his clients, his shareholders, finally even his fellow directors. Now he could cheat justice, too. I think he might have liked the idea. After all, he was never a common thief. It was always different, because it was him.

Not that he left me destitute. Far from it. He hadn't provided for me as such; I think he thought he was never going to die, and even his will was mostly a neatly trimmed tax hedge. But he'd got me really well snared up in his highly creative accounting. I found that all this time I'd been owning and selling things I'd never even heard of – stocks, shares, assets, mostly other people's. All along I'd even owned the house he kept threatening to throw me out of. The house and a lot else went in damages and back taxes, of course, and on the bills of his helpful lawyers and his devoted doctors and about half a million agents and fixers and hangers-on. But the lawyers had to leave me something, for the look of the thing, and there was a residue transferred too long ago for the taxmen to repossess; so when the dust settled I had a modest capital.

What do you think I did with it? I don't know. I can barely remember. But one day the bank didn't want to know, and from then on it was the down escalator only. When I came out of jail they stopped even trying to sue me.

So here I was. But for once, just this once, I didn't need to stay.

The trouble was where to go. The further the better, you might say – and the faster. But if I did that, I might just confirm suspicions that I was mixed up in the Mass Murder on the Marshes – I could see the headlines already – or even responsible for it. If they got to Ahwaz he'd try to pin it all on me, for one. And there weren't any safe boltholes in the world any more, not even for villains a lot richer than me. You could even be hauled back from Brazil these days. So should I sit tight, go into work as usual and play Mister Know-nothing? Fine if the cops were after me; not so good if Ahwaz was. Not with Chaddy his usual helpful self; worse if he suspected I had something to do with his mysterious case of the trots.

Funny, that, how effective it had been. A big reaction to a small thing. Like my getting angry on the phone – or afraid out on the marshes. Everything getting out of hand, getting too big for me.

I twisted and turned, feeling more and more nervous and taut. It was as if I was waiting for something, as if I as expecting – a call, or maybe a knock on the door, the wrong kind. I drew my cold knees up and hugged them. Who was I kidding? Nobody called here that I ever wanted to see. Any knock would be the wrong knock.

Finally I sprang out of the creaky bed, picked up the plastic bag my new shirt had come in and wrapped the envelope up in it, very carefully, sealing it tight with some sticky labels I had lying around. I checked the door was locked, though I knew

perfectly well it was. Then, very quietly, I opened
the window, and with my damp jeans brushing my
legs I twisted out and around to a point in the brickwork of the old chimney-stack behind.

That psychic I'd placemanned for had started as a
straight magician, with me as one of his stooges – the
'totally unrehearsed' guy who's called up out of the
audience and sawn in half or vanished from a little
box, that kind of thing. You had to be a pretty good
contortionist for that. Nobody larger or less lithe
than me could twist around enough to even look at
the bricks there, let alone reach them. I tugged out
one I'd carefully loosened a while back, to hold a
few valuables such as the old man's watch, before I'd
decided it was safer in the pawnshop. In slipped the
envelope, and the brick went back neatly, with a
slather of spit and grime from the roof to camouflage
it. I ducked back shivering under the blankets, not
lying down but pulling them up under my chin. That
expectant feeling was growing stronger, building up
to some sort of horrible, sweaty peak.

Then the door popped open. Not burst, not flew,
just popped from shut to ninety degrees like that, as
if there was no such thing as lock or bolt or wedge,
and stopped dead, without a crash or anything.
Light from the bare bulb in the hallway flooded in.
Equally suddenly a face thrust around the door.

Not a face I knew – and yet it was familiar somehow. A man's, lined but not old, and striking –
coarsely handsome, even, despite a wart or two and
the greasy brown hair and beard that framed it. I
yelped, and it gave me an encouraging toothy beam.
'How goes it with you, esquire? Eh?' A soft,

rolling accent, none I could place. In other circumstances there might have been some charm in it, and the twinkling eyes. 'Now tell me if you will, sir, hast had any odd happenings of late?'

I choked. 'You mean – besides this one?' I gaped at the impossible face an instant, then ducked under the blankets. Stress – I was having nightmares, that was it, the kind you get just before waking. When I came out it'd be gone.

Surprisingly, it was. The door was shut, locked and everything as if it had never opened, the stairway light was evidently off. Not a sign of any visitor. I swallowed, barely; my mouth felt like a mummified dog's bum. I levered my shaking legs on to the floor and staggered over to the muddy washbasin. The rusty tap-juice was soothing nectar. I was just tilting back another when the image in the mirror engaged me with a friendly leer, and spoke. Oh yes, and it had somehow sprouted greasy hair.

'Strange events is my meaning, good master! Like maybe visions that come upon you of a sudden, feelings of great exaltation, potencies and powers, as may be?'

The glass burst like a bomb in the gritty bowl. I squealed and whirled around, and there at the window – on the fourth floor, mind – was a face, as well. Only this one was different. This one I did recognise.

At least it was polite. It gave a sort of grave, shy smile, lifted a rather odd skullcap and mouthed at me. A pretty earnest question, by the look of it, and I could just about lipread 'happenings', and maybe also 'curious'. It was the old gink from that horrible house – and come to think of it, the hairy fellow was the other one, the one I'd landed on. Well, wasn't that nice? Practically old mates. I screamed and dived under the bed.

A tidal wave of old beer cans, sweet wrappers and used contraceptives – God, how old were those? Were they mine, even? – shot out the other side, so it wasn't exactly deep concealment. But Christ, it felt better. Until, that is, I opened my eyes again and saw the old man's face peering myopically under the blanket on that side.

'I do most earnestly beg your pardon, my esteemed sir, but I do desire your further acquaintance—'

I squeaked, because my throat was too tight to scream, twisted around and found myself almost nose to nose with the hairy fellow. He had nostril hairs like corkscrews, and a small crop of warts around his nose.

'Begging your pardon, young sir, lest I give you cause for unease! But in the matter of which I enquired but now, namely some degree of strange happening in your life—'

I tried to speak. Nothing came out.

'Some sudden irruption into your daily affairs,' intoned the old apparition from behind me. 'Every-day acts growing unexpectedly potent, perchance? The unexpected arrival of assistance in difficult situations, even?'

I fluttered my lips and nodded weakly. Anything to make them go away.

'Ah*hah* !' said the old fellow in a satisfied kind of way. 'See you now, Brother Edward, the truth of my contentions?'

I looked around. Edward was still there, but his features had crumpled up in deep thought, practically to the point of disappearance. He looked like an abstract arrangement of hair and warts, and believe me, it wasn't an improvement.

'Aye, aye,' his voice muttered, with a much grimmer kind of satisfaction. 'And the agent of this assistance, my master? A ... sturdy fellow, sans doubt?'

I shook my head, and flapped my fingers. He seemed to read the gesture.

'Not one, then? Several?'

'Y-yes,' I managed.

'Ah.' They nodded sagely to one another. 'Well, my good sir,' the older man continued. 'I must pray that patience of you which Elihu counselled unto Job. Although, I trust, your visitations will be less severe. But fear not! At some moment not long distant we shall appear again unto your good self. There we shall unfold unto you the several actions and causes of this unfortunate error!'

'Oh – you don't have to—'

'And we shall offer you a sure and certain release,' he continued relentlessly, bobbing and bowing. 'Until then, good master—'

Blink. He wasn't there. Neither was brother Edward.

I lowered my face weakly on to the floor, and raised it hastily as the dust in the rotten old carpet got up my nose. They say ninety per cent of your household dust is you, and if that was right I'd just inhaled about half of me back. I sneezed, repeatedly, and hit my head on the bedsprings every time, with a sort of spavined twang. The tart downstairs started hammering on the ceiling.

'*Don't ya know there's people tryin' ta fuckin' sleep down 'ere?*'

'Well, that'll make a change!' I shouted back, and heaved myself wearily out from under. Wait a minute – if *she* was trying to sleep, it must be dawn, after six even. Where had the night gone? I was still sneezing, I was still damp, and unless I assumed I'd just had a nightmare, I'd hardly slept a wink. Wonderful. No wonder my eyes felt like pits of rat's pee. I slopped the dust off my face, dodging the broken glass in the bowl, and fell face down in my vomitous pillow.

So they were coming back were they? Just let 'em try.

I drew one deep breath, felt sleep wash over me like comforting layers of black silk – and was jolted by hammering at the downstairs door. I shot up on one elbow and reflexively screamed, '*Piss off!*'

There was a sudden rumbling on the stairs, a scream from the tart cut off by a single barked word. Even the first explosive letter triggered an instant reaction.

'*Police!*'

I was off the bed in an instant, snatching my still wet jeans and trainers off the line and wriggling into them, writhing as the soaking seams squeezed their little trickles down my legs. I was already jamming my feet into the squelchy trainers when the door boomed and bent under a heavy fist.

'*Oi! Open up in there!*'

My instincts were doing all the work. Call it a

conditioned reflex, if you like. The rational Me was wittering with panic. I hadn't expected Plod anything like this soon. Then a thrill of horror trickled down into my crutch, just like the jeans only chillier still. There was a quicker way they could have linked me with the night's doings – information received.

Chaddy, the son of a bitch! Hearing what Ahwaz had told me, knowing Fallon's form as well as I did – he could put the two together when the news hit the grapevine. As it would in less than no time. And wouldn't he enjoy turning a penny on it from his bed of pain – or maybe throne! Too dangerous to grass on Ahwaz directly, of course; but on me, who'd care? And the cop computers could find citizens even quicker than Ahwaz, sometimes.

Isn't reflex amazing? By the time they had the strainer jack across the frame and burst the door open, I was already halfway out of the window with hardly a conscious thought, all driven by sheer stark terror. Beat that, Dr Pavlov!

I was vaguely aware of rushing and shouts at my back, but I was above all that, scrabbling out on to the window ledge in the grey, dank dawn. A little way along an extension roof branched out at ninety degrees into what had been the back garden. I could scramble along, but jump across more easily – I thought. I dithered about making a grab for my money, thought better of it and sprang. Great sausage fingers clawed at my collar, then something seemed to give and I landed with a crash that dislodged several tiles and most of my breath. Clinging on like a monkey, I half expected to see the cop dangling shreds of my shirt, but instead the great oaf was gaping at a handful of what looked like coarse red-brown hair. Maybe I was a monkey.

Then I had something else to worry about. Another thug bulged out on to the ledge and leaped. He reached the ridge too, but the overstrained ridge-tile split beneath his great Doc Ms and he skidded, flailed and slid – both ways at once. His boots shot down the crackling tiles with a shower of ruddy sparks and he landed heavily astride. His eyes bulged, his mouth opened so wide he could have moonlighted as a goldfish, and he sprawled flat along the ridge, conveniently in the others' way. I wasn't hanging around. I reached the end of the roof, clinging like a minor ape and gibbering like one too, and slid down into the gutter among the leaves and dead pigeons. I reached over, grabbed the drainpipe, dislodging a foul old nest, and began trying to shin down it.

That wasn't too easy. I was a floor lower now, but that left three to fall and it looked a lot further than it did on the nice solid stairs. The pipe shifted and creaked at every move I made. I whimpered and hugged it as if it was my only friend in the world, which wasn't too far off the mark right then. Then I heard a cheery shout from below, and felt a great wash of despair. I should have known even the Blue Meanies would have the sense to cover the back yard. Somebody was humorously opening a dustbin and inviting a little turd to drop in.

Who could they possibly mean?

I leaned over to see if I could grab the next pipe. Immediately there was an ominous grating creak and a little trickling rain of mortar as the pipe fasteners pulled out of the wall above me. I wailed horribly, then shrieked in even greater fright. About a million miles below my slipping feet the end of the pipe that was still fastened to the wall exploded outwards in a scarlet flare and snapped off just above the ground. It swung outwards, with me still clinging like the Night Lemur, or Aye-Aye – *aiaiaiaiaiai!*

I saw the rubbish-strewn remnants of the lawn flash by before my eyes. I'd expected my past life, but maybe this was symbolic.

Then the pipe hit the solid old garden wall, and we parted company. There was, as they say, a moment's confusion. Then there was a tremendous thump, a horrible shower of fragments, and an enveloping stench that could have given the marsh lessons.

I threshed feebly in a slimy black sea. Either it was the Styx, or I'd landed with lethal accuracy right in one of the neighbourhood garbage mountains, binbag Vesuviuses that the council trucks passed by hurriedly, presumably in case somebody jumped out and hijacked them to Morocco. Morocco might have been an improvement, mind you; we bred a pretty fierce strain of trash around here.

I struggled upright, wheezing and cursing; a black bag savaged my ankles. I fell down again in a shower of fruit peel and pizza boxes – who was crazy enough to deliver round here? – then sprang up again as a wave of bulky bodies crested the wall behind me like the Rwandan Olympic Hurdles Team (Mountain Gorilla Division).

I took a running start, trailing streams of everything you can imagine but wouldn't want to. How is it deprived areas have so much more to throw out? Especially since we're really hot on recycling our garbage, usually by cooking it. The only consolation was the crashes and cries of disgust behind me. I hadn't noticed yet that I was running the wrong way.

I was that little bit disoriented. Instead of weaving a way through the back alleys, I'd headed straight for the main road. I registered this important fact round about the time I turned the corner and came face to face with three running uniforms and a panda car with its roof-light flashing. I yelped and wheeled, but I hadn't a hope in hell. I whipped back around the corner, and straight into a tangle of strong arms. I threshed and fought. Then I realised they weren't in uniform, those arms; in fact, they were mostly bare, and they didn't smell of Old Spice, either. And they rattled and jangled when they moved.

'Hi dere, Maxie!' said a gruff voice.

My hair bristled, and I had just time to suck in a deep breath and scream, '*No killing!*' That wasn't enough, God alone knew what they might do instead. '*Nothing serious!*'

Then the panda car rounded the turn, and ran straight into the bandits. I half expected to see bodies fly, but a morning-star mace flailed down against one wheel, a tyre burst with a resounding bang and the car screeched around and stopped. A huge cutlass smashed down through the bonnet into the engine, unleashing a fountain of milky coolant; a spear butt starred the windscreen from end to end. The siren bleated, and somebody shot it.

A steel-tipped whip whined across the car roof and caught one of the oncoming coppers around his anoraked chest. He was a huge bugger with a moustache like a yardbrush, but the whip plucked him right off the ground and sent him skidding across the roof, smashing the light.

'Jesus Christ!' he screamed, goggling at the bare-breasted bird hauling him in. 'Get the Vice Squad!'

Another cop flicked out a telescopic baton, only to have a great broadsword take it off an inch above his hand. He stood stupidly for a second, and the brigands piled in on him and the others, more or less barehanded.

'*Don't hurt anyone!*' I screamed. '*That's an order, you hear me?*'

'We hear you, *señor* Maxie!' giggled the brown-skinned girl. She hauled on the whip. Nose-Fungus spun off the roof in a blur and crashed into the garden behind. Then she thrust both arms through the crazed windscreen and bodily yanked out the screaming policewoman at the wheel, considered her an instant, turned her upside down and thrust her back, head down into the footwell and instant *Folies Bergère* above, all suspenders and frilly knickers and very nice too.

The other woman came leaping up the back of the car like a springboard and took off with a whoop, over my head and down on to the cops who'd come over the wall. With a wild scream of '*Maxieee-eee!*' the others went streaming by and flowed over them, while I danced around gibbering.

Sort of a giggle, when you think about it, me screaming not to hurt the Sod Squad. All right, I was doing it out of common humanity and because citizens who raise serious blisters on the Law tend to get into the tabloids – *TOERAG TOFF MAIMS OUR BOYS IN BLUE*, with sentence to match. Not to mention getting these sort of dizzy attacks and falling down the cell steps, sometimes as often as twice a day. Even so, it didn't feel right, somehow. I'd have got blackballed from my clubs, if you could get blackballed from my kind.

I peered cautiously at the groaning heaps the bandits left behind. One had his parka forced down over his arms and his legs jammed up into it, and another was handcuffed into a sort of granny knot, leg over neck. For one sickening instant I thought they'd decapitated the third, but appearances were misleading. The trousers over his head he might have got out of, if he hadn't had his legs down the arms of his jacket and his belt wrapped tight around the package.

'Nothing serious,' I told them over the sound of smashing glass. 'Just youthful high spirits.'

Something clanked against the car, staggered by and rolled over, a dustbin on legs. Naked legs. The abraded boots looked familiar, though. Definitely not his day.

'*You're all under arrest!*' screamed somebody from the centre of a rolling scuffle among the garbage. '*Every bloody one of you! Oh Christ, woman – get off—*' A brief flurry, a pair of trousers flew triumphantly in the air and something like a giant skinned rabbit dived back across the wall – to judge by the wild scream, straight into a nettle patch. Along the path the straggle-haired woman stood beneath one of the few trees left hereabouts, peering up into its lower branches, from which two pairs of naked legs dangled. She was idly stringing a vile pair of boxer shorts on her sword.

'*You friggin' well give those here at once!*' roared a voice. She nodded amiably and poked the sword upwards. There was a sharp squeal, and the leaves shivered.

'*Don't encourage 'er, sarge!*' quavered another voice. '*She ain't bloody human! They're mine, anyhow!*'

Personally I'd have kept quiet about that, but there you are.

It all looked very fine and right and proper, everyone seemed to be getting acquainted, and evidently I was no longer needed here. There was the money, of course, but it was well stashed; I could come back later for that. A lot later. A shame not to be able to say goodbye and thanks, really, but it was getting properly light now; time I was off. I was just tiptoeing away past the squirming parcels of cop when I was caught up in a sudden rush and entangled in a thicket of muscular arms and cheery idiot shouts.

'Hey, Maxie! No sweat, baby! Alla pigs hogtied just fine!'

'Arr, and ne'er so much as a broke bane among 'em! All alongside of yer merciful command, my fine young sir! Aharr!'

Any minute now he'd be calling me *Jim, lad!*

The grins; the voices.

'You think we let them get you 'way from us, Maxie *mi capitan*?'

I was spun around from one to another, and the gathering light showed me them more clearly this time. It hadn't been the dope. They were very much there, and they were just exactly as weird as I remembered them; and ghosts they weren't. The black guy was still grinning, rubbing the protruberant breastplate as if it was his real belly; his jet-black cheeks were ridged with cicatrix marks, but elaborate gold bracelets jangled on his arms. The wild old guy with the Robert Newton voice really did look piratical, and it wasn't just the dirks and cutlasses in his huge belt, or his ragged jerkin and pantaloons and stocking-cap. Over every inch they left bare he sprouted tattoos, some of them the usual mermaid and anchor stuff but others apparently done by a sex-mad Tibetan on bhang, all punctuated by a nice assortment of scars. His grin was gap-toothed, with tobacco juice drooling out of the corners to stain his scrawny beard yellow; his wiry forelock had evidently been smoked the same shade. He looked really vile, and you could tell he just loved it.

There was the lanky Teutonic type, or maybe Scandinavian, with blond-beast looks that stopped short at a vicious-looking slot of a mouth and receding chin beneath, a bodybuilder frame with an adolescent sod-you slouch. I'd seen a couple of killers who looked like that. There the Oriental, twirling his moustache and looking about as inscrutable as a red-hot skewer. He didn't look Chinese – Korean, maybe, or something more exotic, a Burmese Karen maybe, with that great plume of hair. He did look stark raving mad.

There were those bloody women, leaning on one another and giggling manically till their bare brown boobs bounced and their daggers jangled. They were waving their trophies, including a crinkled old jockstrap and those eyewatering shorts (mauve, with dayglo teddy bears). I hated to think what they might have taken instead. There were . . .

A couple of others I still couldn't make out. But they were crowded to the back as the others all came pushing enthusiastically in on me. All told, they were about as reassuring as Attila the Hun's PR team.

'*Listen!*' I panted. 'Look, thanks, thanks a whole heap – I mean thanks very much, *très très* professional and a treat to see and all that – but I really have got to get out of here fast, still – and—'

Me and my big mouth. I was about to ask them to help me get the money down; I should have done that first. I knew how fast they reacted, didn't I?

The next thing I knew I was swept off my feet, right up to shoulder height – and I *really* hoped that hand was a woman's. Then before I could get my breath back they literally ran away with me. The pace was terrific, and they just flowed over anything in their path. When they came to a wall they boosted each other over, and whirled me across from hand to hand, too dazed and winded to call out. It was like one of those races at army shows, with teams of panting squareheads manhandling guns or casualties or something over an obstacle course. This lot could have given them teamwork pointers. They went over a railway fence, barbed wire and all, without so much as breaking stride. Or even looking out for a train.

And every time I sailed past there'd be a friendly

nod and a wink and a slap, a cheery reassurance that made me want to kill them all horribly. I kept having this mental vision of a huge bundle of notes tip-toeing quietly away.

Beyond my flailing feet rose the high walls of the old warehouse district, turning its back alleys into deep shadow canyons that only seemed darker as the first sunbeams slanted across the open streets beyond. We didn't go that way. This lot were adepts at keeping out of sight, and we slipped from shadow to shadow like returning ghosts. All the threshing I could do made no difference, and it was only when they checked, momentarily, in the shadow of a twenty-foot brick wall that I drew enough breath to roar at them. Instantly I was lowered featherlight on to my feet, with hands dusting down my clothes, patting down my hair, and generally smoothing me out.

'Hey, whatsa matter, Maxie?'

'Ees anything amiss?'

'De wall's no sweat, ve can—'

'*No!* I mean, thanks, thanks again, but you shouldn't – run away with me like that! Where're you taking me, anyway? There were . . . things I wanted to go back for first!'

'Possessions? Arr, dross, trash, nothings! What'll ye need o'them when we're a-layin' the bloody world at yer feet? Only come now—'

'*I said* — I mean, I asked, *where're you taking me?*'

'Why, to de sheep, of course!'

'Sheep – Jesus, not again! I don't *want* to go to your sheep – *I mean*—'

Instant groans of hurt and disappointment all round.

'Ya you do! No place safer dan dere! No place you'll find more friend!'

'Those pigs of constables shall not emprise you there, *señor*! Come, be kind, accompany us!'

'Aye, aye, lad, ye'll not be lettin' yer true shipmates down!'

'We shall sail, lord Maxie, far beyond their grasp, to realms of pearls and gold and finest jade, to palaces of fair walks and languid concubines making drowsy music, to sunny pleasure domes with caves of ice—'

I twitched. 'Come again?' The Oriental didn't strike me as the literary type. Kung Fu or Shun Tzu, if anything, not Coleridge.

He twirled his moustache. 'The lord Maxie does not believe me? Behold, and wonder!'

He whisked one of those horrible swords off his back, so fast it whistled. A Japanese sword, not the graceful samurai curve but the straight, vicious ninja blade. That figured. He whirled it in true schlock-film fashion, but fast, so fast it seemed to open a shimmering umbrella of steel before my eyes, drawing them in. And in that hissing circle of light an image formed and grew.

I blinked. A girl, Japanese probably – though the Oriental didn't look that, either. Not your actual geisha, though. They've got this thing about little schoolgirl uniforms there, and that's what she was wearing, more or less, and she was looking pretty cheerful about it. She wasn't just a picture, either. She was smiling, reaching out – to me. She knew I was there. She mouthed my name, and writhed a little. And behind her there was a blonde girl, falling out of an old-fashioned négligé – a bit too top-heavy for my taste. An old-fashioned idea, or an Oriental one – like all those bug-eyed manga heroines, maybe. And a black girl, just as overdeveloped, another, some kind of Polynesian—

I blinked again. My own private Miss World, all clearly longing for little me. Invisible coils of heady fragrance snaked around me, tickling my nose and other sensitive areas. How the hell I noticed what the black guy was doing I can't imagine, but I vaguely saw him upend his helmet above the arc of the blade. Out of it tipped a spill of coins, a stream of gems, strings and sprays and necklaces of many strands, cascading down among the girls as they squealed and giggled and snatched at them.

Abruptly the sword was rock-still before my eyes, mirroring the same image in its glossy greenish metal. The girls were writhing at the foot of a dais below a huge black leather chair, a sort of modern throne, plutocrats and mad dictators for the use of, flanked with macho-looking guards in ducky leather uniforms and brutal machine-guns. It looked as if somebody'd hired Dr No's interior decorator. I half expected Ilya Kuryakin to come abseiling down the chandelier any moment.

To either side men were bowing, men in immaculate suits, men who had the very stamp of tycoons and *zaibatsu* bosses, the kind of characters who looked down on mere millionaires like my father's City friends as they might look down on me, falling to their knees or being forced there by the goon squads. But the casually elegant figure in the chair ignored them and went on tossing riches to his pampered toys . . .

Guess who?

Well, OK. I mean, I know about come-ons, I've been a strip-club barker, and this was strictly for the cheap seats. The guards, for a start. I knew the real me would be more frightened of them than my enemies ever would. I'd go all paranoid and start sleeping on beds floating on mercury pools, like some old Chinese emperor, so the assassins couldn't creep up on me. Mind you, with all that nice mercury vapour they wouldn't need to.

Not that the vision didn't have some effect, especially when I imagined Ahwaz among the kow-towers. Even then, though, my fantasies didn't go much further than a really good boot up his jacksy and a short spell in the snakepit – short, because snakes are sensitive animals and I'd hate to hurt their feelings.

The same went for this lot.

'Yeah, yeah!' I said brightly, easing the sword aside with a gentle finger. 'Really nice, but . . . look, I'm not really into all that, not the type really, I just want to get my mo – my *things*, and, well, settle down for a while and think about—'

'See!' barked Hong Kong Fooey, and tilted the blade about an inch from my eyes, which didn't leave me much alternative. It caught the light with a blinding emerald flash, and another image sprang to life. Drably real this time, pale green official-looking walls lined with paper-strewn desks and filing cabinets, and a large map festooned with concentric circles and arrows of tape, and a couple of mugshots. Hard-faced men in brash casual clothes swigging from plastic cups, sitting on desks talking vigorously to ... other hard-faced men, looking bruised and haggard, and wearing a weird assortment of bits and pieces. One with a yard-brush moustache, and bare legs protruding from under a long mac. I knew him, and I could read that map, and see where the arrows pointed. And the mugshots I knew only too well. I remembered the police photographer being sarky about my noble profile. This was an incident room, centring on the marsh, and the only face in sight was mine.

I whimpered a little. The bandits were oddly quiet.

'Maxie!' whispered one woman urgently. 'Now you must come away wit' us! What choice have you got left?'

Her hand clutched my sleeve. Not hard, and there was nothing but sincerity in her face or voice. I shivered, and let my hand fall. 'Yeah – no choice. OK, fellas! Have it your way!'

They relaxed, with a sigh I could feel – and I plucked my sleeve loose and dived between their legs.

Advertising I can cope with, it's what you expect. But when they pull sincerity out of the bag, I just *know* I'm being sold one.

Tall timber time, kiddies. I rolled on the pavement, sprang up and bolted. OK, they could move like lightly scalded cats, but maybe the surprise ...

I stopped in the sudden sunlight at the street's end, stupidly wondering why I wasn't surrounded by a tangle of brown arms – or jangly blades. It was almost disappointing. I blinked back, mildly irritated, half expecting to see nothing, just a suddenly empty street. But there they stood still, colourless in the grey-green morning shadows, clustered close as if to remind me of the solidarity I was losing.

'*Come back!*' they called, their voices mingling, and they half raised, half spread their arms. For the first time I hesitated. There was a real hunger in those voices, and it struck a chord somewhere. '*Come back, Maxie, come and sail off with us to fortune and happiness! Come, and never know loneliness again! Never know want! Come, and sail the seas of the Spiral!*'

I stopped dead. That name I'd heard before, and I knew where. The inn. The Wheel. That sleek SOB Steve. Somehow it had almost faded from my mind. Now it all came back, all the bloody daft things he'd told me, cresting a bubbling tide of indignation.

The bandits were coming towards me, slowly, as if they too were hesitant.

'Remember, *señor* Maxie!' called one of the girls, her voice sounding oddly fainter the nearer she came. 'So near, so far, we cannot help you. Only in the places where the ways cross and recross, where the wall between the worlds is weakest, only there may we come to you! Yet call on us in your need, and you shall still have what power we can spare! For are we not yours, *señor*, and you bound to us more strongly than with chain or cord?'

'And in the end,' said the Oriental softly, 'does not the proverb say all men are drawn in by the bonds they make for themselves?'

He reached out suddenly, and his fist abruptly swelled and blurred, like an unfocused photo.

I jumped back, around the corner, expecting a rush of feet. But there wasn't a sound. After a moment I very nervously put my nose around the corner, on the theory you can afford to risk what you've got most of. The alley was empty. No noise, no footsteps. They'd just . . . gone. The sun topped the walls at last, and the alley flooded with light. The early morning was silent still, no sound of footsteps or traffic. Except for those sirens—

I hopped like a rabbit. I had to get off the street, out of sight. That incident room vision would still be in the future. This would just be the snatch squad's backup. Even so, anybody wandering around the area at dawn they'd notice and file away in their tiny blue minds for future abuse. Better if I got out of sight somehow. The sirens were getting louder. I ducked into a deep little doorway and did my best to look like a hinge. On the off-chance I tried the handle – well, you do, don't you? It wouldn't budge – but a small panel, a sort of porthole, slid open.

My eyes bugged. A white beard came out and waggled in my face, neatly framing a benign smile in the middle. 'Now, touching upon the nature of these mysterious manifestations, good sir—'

I let out what must have been a sort of strangled castrato squeak, slammed the port shut and, forgetting the sirens, I ran for my life.

The Spiral.

One man had used that word to me before, and that had been the start of my troubles. It was all spilling back to me now, dripping icily down the back of my neck. The sirens came screaming down the main road, and I dived over the wall of an office block forecourt, not an instant too soon. Hunkered down with some miserable miniature conifers tickling the gap between shirt and jeans, I got one thing straight at least. I figured out who I was more afraid of.

Forget the money, forget the getaway, forget everything else till I got these psychos off my back, useful as they sometimes were. I was going back to the Wheel. I was going to talk to Mr Smarmy Steve his own self.

Really talk.

CHAPTER FIVE

Proceed with Caution

THERE WAS JUST one problem with that idea. I couldn't find the bloody place.

I stood high up on the junction's narrow walkway, leaning on the railing, with the wind flinging my hair in and out of my eyes. They were aching with scanning the horrible tangle of concrete tagliatelle spread out below. The traffic flowed under and around and behind me like worms down an endless gut. It was really dispiriting. All those lovely motors, and I couldn't get my hands on any of them.

I couldn't hang around here much longer, either. I was too conspicuous. This wasn't exactly a local beauty spot, more the kind of place people got talked down off, and if the cop cameras spotted me they might assume I was planning the big dive.

Much more of this and they might have a point.

At least I looked respectable, which only goes to prove what they say about appearances. These were the first decent clothes I'd owned since God knows when, paid for by the motley crew of stiffs out on the marshes; luckily I hadn't put their dosh in with the rest. It was only a few hundred, plus the guilders; it wouldn't get me far. I still knew some good outfitters, though, and the big station washrooms had provided shower and shave. So the next thing I needed was some wheels. Well, don't I always?

Of course I had more sense than to go off and nick one of my characteristic high-price jobs. That's just what the cops would be watching for, *modus operandi Maxissime*. So I shivved my way into a nice bland downmarket Toyota instead, the sort thousands of ordinary citizens polish on Saturdays.

Well, what else could I do?

OK, so I wouldn't normally be seen dead in one, but I couldn't buy anything, and a hire place would want my licence. Anyhow, I drove the thing as if it was full of eggs – which it was, actually, having been lifted from a supermarket park. The citizen who polished it would hardly know it had been gone. And I was careful to ditch it somewhere conspicuous, outside Vi's Egganburger, a battered roadside trailer caff that lies in wait to ensnare unwary Eurotruckers and similar innocents. The polishing citizen could pick it up there none the worse. Unless he celebrated with one of Vi's sandwiches, that is – cheese, ham or salmonella? Rumour had it the junction roadbed had been laid on her doughnuts and topped off with her tea.

Besides, I'd left it unlocked with the key in, so with a bit of luck somebody else would nick it, and cop all the blame.

Even that thought didn't cheer me up much. By the time I'd legged it up here I was freezing, and I was even worse now. The heart of the junction was down there, and all I could see in it was a moth-eaten hedge, ruined by these huge machine cutters, and a smallish field inside it. The low light played long shadows across its mangy grass, but you didn't feel they hid anything; they didn't have room. It was just a larger version of the neglected roundabout centre or central reservation – uncut havens for wildlife, otherwise known as roadkill ranches. It was far too small for anything I remembered. I clutched my head and groaned. Had the whole thing been hallucinations, all along?

Yeah. So I was hallucinating the money in my pocket, the clothes on my back and about five thousand rozzers sniffing at my trouser legs. If I didn't do something damn soon, I'd be able to ask them. No, it had happened, and the only one I could think of to tell me the hows and the whys was this Steve character. Complete with an I-told-you-so smirk on that male-model face of his . . .

There was an awful sinking feeling, as if the concrete mountain beneath my feet was suddenly crumbling away. Given what I knew about road contractors – and Vi's doughnuts – it probably was, but that wasn't why. I'd thought the bastard looked familiar, and now I knew why.

Steve, sure, one of the boys. Stephen Fisher, no less, the shipping tycoon. Stephen Fisher, creator of C-Tran, the worldwide automated freight network. Stephen Fisher, the billionaire, one of the biggest in Europe – and the daftest, the man who made Howard Hughes look sociable and Bill Gates . . .

Well, maybe not quite that, but up among the

leaders in the Gates Fruitcake Handicap, for sure. *Hello!* had done a profile of him, while I was in stir; you'll read anything in there, after a while. Not an easy job, they'd claimed, because he was given to disappearing into the wilds for months and months, when he wasn't living in one of his string of castles across Europe. They'd run him to earth in his great Scottish pile, all claymores and banners and open fires, medieval as hell with a helicopter pad on the roof and a cellar full of computer gear. What had really stuck in my mind was shots of his wife, not at all a bad bit of stuff if you liked them keen and athletic, with eyes that could burn through a stone wall. Just the sort of thing you dream about in the slammer, but in real life she'd have scared the shit out of me. She'd been some sort of cop, apparently, so that'd account for it. I remembered thinking he'd have to be several per cent nuts to cope with that babe. The article said they shared a peculiar sense of humour, something along those lines.

Yeah. I could believe it. It fitted all too well, didn't it? A critically rich fruitbat, with a taste for the grandiose, the medieval – and just maybe the practical joke.

Except that some of the things I'd seen nobody could have staged, not outside the SFX department. My own mind, maybe, suitably tampered with – dope, post-hypnotics, mind control. Somebody might well enjoy playing God with those. And I'd be a perfect guinea-pig, a nobody in no position to protest. But I didn't believe it. I could still feel that diamond-hard air in my lungs, hear that cry . . .

I shivered. There was one even worse alternative.

These loony experiences could be true, and him still in charge of them. There was that mysterious character among the bandits, or maybe two of them; I never saw them clearly enough. There was the way everyone at the inn reacted to him. He'd known something would happen if I took that path.

Christ, what did we have here? Some kind of black magic tycoon? I didn't know what to think. The whole thing made me want to puke.

Some dough-faced citizen shouted at me from one of the passing cars – wondering if I was about to jump, or maybe suggesting it. It'd be dark soon; I had to make a move, somehow. Maybe I ought to just go down and poke my way about that hedge. The answers were there, one way or another. And if those weird characters showed up just one more time, the answers might become sort of urgent.

I slouched off down the ramp, wondering if it really would be that bad, going sailing off with the Lost SOBs or whoever they were. Worse than working for Chaddy, or moonlighting for Ahwaz? Worse than slinking back from the stinking peep-show to my stinking little garret?

Worse than just being me?

OK, they played a bit rough. Maybe it was time I started. I flexed my shoulders, enjoying the weight of a proper coat across them. How long since I'd felt that? I'd been born small, I'd lived small. Cars lent me the body I didn't have; cars made my feelings larger, made citizens pay attention to me. So maybe the bandits would do that too. And what they were promising me went a lot further than four wheels. All right, people might get hurt. I'd been hurt, too.

About time I called in my dues. The thought of it gave me a shivery little feeling in my guts and a tautness in the crotch. People would get hurt. The ones who hurt me. Maybe they'd better start forming queues . . .

I stopped, stared, leaned out over the railing so far I really risked a fall. Except that my hands had frozen to the railing, and my spine stiffened to the sudden thrill. The gusts riffled my hair, but it didn't seem cold any more; the chill ran deeper. Across the junction approaches, across an exceptionally scrubby triangle of grass, a finger of reddish sunlight was falling. Two deep furrows suddenly spilled over with scarlet, pointing like an arrow to curving skidmarks on the dusty road, hardly worn at all – broad racing treads, not at all usual. And these in turn pointed to a part of the hedge I'd looked at like the rest; but now the low light highlighted a gap, a notch really, half concealed by the tangled stems. Not the most welcoming effect, that – like a wound, somehow. But it was the first new thing I'd seen for hours; and no ordinary car left those tracks. I leaned back and went padding on down the walkway. After a minute I began to run.

Keeping out from under the cameras wasn't easy, but on foot you could watch them and time your dashes – especially as they tended to follow the heaviest traffic. I'd had lots of practice, but it was still a bit like *1984*. I didn't know what the country was coming to. Cameras on half the city streets now, infringing everybody's civil liberties so you had to creep up to cars on your hands and knees, or just work bloody fast. Totalitarian, that's what I call it.

Maybe that should have made me think, but it was only as I crossed to the island's outer verge, with the red sunlight ahead of me all the way, that I clued up. I was being led.

Here came the traffic, though, and the camera was swinging this way. No going back – and what the hell to, anyhow? I hopped the kerb, hit the hedge and tried to peer through the gap. A sudden glare of scarlet dazzled me, making me hesitate, almost too long. A dinosaur bellowed in the twilight, and the green bulk of the trailer truck swept around the curve, too close in, far too close. The slipstream would pluck me off the verge like a dry leaf out of the ditch. I didn't even think of choices. I jumped, and felt the dry stems rattle about me as the thing swept by, that close. And there I was in the field.

Only it wasn't the one I'd seen from above. And the scarlet gleam was that last spear of sunset striking the detached and unscorched door of the wrecked Ferrari. And there beside it, still leaning on his monstrous scythe, was Willum.

His face hadn't improved; I've seen scarecrows that looked less like turnips, and they *were* turnips. Even the expression was the same. If I hadn't seen him move I'd had sworn he couldn't have. And yet there was a difference in him, somehow. I couldn't place it, but it made me uneasy.

'Arr,' he said.

'Hi, Willum,' I said. 'Look, I'm just going—'

'You'm back, then?'

'Yes,' I said patiently. He wasn't any bigger than me, but the scythe was. 'I'm off to the inn to look for—'

'Could've kill y'sel' in that there,' he said unexpectedly, and spat.

'Don't I know it. Look, I'm just—'

Slowly, very slowly, he shook his head. His unblinking eyes had something of the toad about them, the same awful stillness. 'Cain't pass 'ere. Too many of y'.'

'*What*?' I hunched back into myself. 'Look, wh- what're you on about? There's just me!'

Then I saw what was different – about the same as a bull just looking and a bull that's going to charge. I moved, then. To be precise, I jumped like a rabbit. By the barest split second it was enough. The scythe flashed, no more than that – then glinted right where I'd stood, its tip half buried in the crumpled Ferrari door.

'Are you *crazy*?' I screamed, then dodged again. The scythe would have had me, all the same, if it hadn't been for the door stuck on the end. The result was a construct the Saatchi Collection would have snapped up – Agro/Aggro, something like that, symbolising the rural rebellion against the consumer society, maybe. The wind resistance must have been incredible, let alone the leverage, but that didn't seem to worry him one bit. Me it worried, but I was already off and running in this year's cornfield steeplechase, straight down the middle, trampling the stiff stalks in my path. There's never an art critic around when you need one.

'Yew c'm outa there'n!' screamed Willum in what sounded like genuine outrage, and the sweep of the door-laden scythe ruffled the little hairs on the back of my neck. I didn't waste words, I just screamed and ran faster, across the field, on to the track and around the trees. Somewhere in that lot I saw the door go sailing across the sky like a Frisbee, and knew the handicap had changed. Stark terror on my side evened it up, though, and slightly longer legs. I rounded the corner, and saw a shape I recognised in the front garden of the inn, apparently snipping away at some of the roses.

'*Popp-yy*!' I shrieked. She turned round, as if in mild surprise, and took in the situation at once. I staggered gasping to the rail, and managed to vault it, just.

Faster over the jumps, that's the secret.

'*Willum*!' She came storming down the gravel path towards us, flicking her towel as if it was a serious weapon. 'Willum, you bad, bad boy, you stop that this minute, d'you hear? The very idea – and to this poor gennlemun who's been in his motor accident, too!'

To my astonishment Willum lowered his scythe and stood there looking about as sheepish as he could, which meant if he bleated they'd have sheared him.

'Tain't my fault,' he muttered rebelliously. 'You look at 'im, this'n. You see if there ain't too many round 'im, like. Draws'n, he does. Should've snuffed in that there Ferrari crash. Cain't ave 'im running round—'

'That don't mean you're to go settlin' any accounts, Willum. Gennlemun's got trouble enough without your close shaves!'

Willum flicked the scythe absently back and forth between us. 'Mebbe not, till I'm sikkered,' he said grudgingly. 'But ask 'em – go on, ask 'em—'

'Ask me bloody what?' I panted, dabbing at my forehead with the first non-paper handkerchief I'd owned in five years. 'I don't know anything! That's why I came here – to ask! A guy called Steve said I could—'

'Ah!' exclaimed Poppy, in deep satisfaction. 'Now, you hear that, Willum? Master Stephen said he could come here! Master Stephen himself, mark you! So, now, are you goin' to gainsay him? Eh?'

The effect on Willum was startling. Something like animation flooded into those little piggy eyes, and the heavy mouth worked. 'Uhh,' he mumbled sulkily, and his scythe drooped in disappointment. 'Should've ruddy tole me. Not a flamin' mind-read'r, am I? Bloody gentry 'n' their farty Ferraris ... Still too many on'n ... just doin' my job—' He turned and plodded off, trailing his scythe sullenly, like a naughty child, occasionally decapitating innocent weeds out of sheer spite. He barely had to flick his wrist, and the air was full of flying dandelion heads.

I felt my neck gingerly, in case it had got cut already and was just waiting till I nodded.

Poppy shook her head sadly. 'He don't get no better, that'un. The very idea! An' don't take to heart what he said 'bout that crash. How you got out of it's none of his business, he's just annoyed 'cos the car's still in his field. And what's all this 'bout too many of you?'

She regarded me quizzically. 'Only one that oi can see, an' not too much o'that, neither. Come inside, moi dear, an' we'll stick a bit of weight under your ribs. Mind you,' she added thoughtfully, 'there's a lot Willum can see, more'n most of us. It's gettin' 'im to make any sense out of it that's the struggle. Oi ask you, what's the use of all manner of vision when you can't string one polite word after another – or won't, rather, because you're so cussed? That's Willum all over. But your Master Stephen now, there's ever such a nice man, and so polite too – a little cool, o'course, but him with his responsibilities, too. Still, you ask 'im nicely like, an' he'll tell you all you want to know—'

All this saw me inside before I could get a word in, and seated at the best table under the least smoky lantern with a huge earthenware mug in front of me. There were the usual rustics, apparently nailed in place since I was here last; but nobody else. 'Well, that's, er, very encouraging, Poppy – that you think he'll help me, I mean. D'you expect he'll be in tonight, then?'

She pursed her long upper lip and made a noise like a very reluctant cork being removed. 'Ah, now. That oi really could not say. Sometimes we don't clap eyes on 'im for a year or more – oh, but there's no call to be takin' on so, oi was going to say that he's been in every couple of nights for well nigh a month now. Says he's got business hereabouts, though what that is it's not moi place to enquire, moi dear. So you just drink your good ale now, and oi'll ask in the back, and see if they know, eh?'

It was good, too. So she knew and liked him, then? And trusted him. That was something, definitely. On the other hand, she seemed to like me too, so that was one judgement shot. I wouldn't have me in a gift.

She reappeared, shaking her head. 'No, moi dear. Last night 'e was here, so not tonight, most like. They said 'e seemed worried about something, an' that's most unlike 'is natural self. But you can leave a message with me, if you like, and oi'll see it gets to 'im – and before he comes back 'ere, if we're lucky.'

'You can do that? Poppy, you're a marvel. Sure I can't marry you?'

'Oi think oi might be a bit of an 'andful for you, moi dear. You don't look 'alf fit enough, and oi likes to keep a man busy. Drink up, now, an oi'll get you another. And you'd like some grub, wouldn't you? It's sausages tonight.'

Sausages it was, great fat, cheery Falstaff things with obscene splits, sizzling and spitting on the wooden trencher among mounds of mashed potato and glazed carrots, peas, beans and fried bread.

'You get that down you!' said Poppy severely. 'Then may be we'll be able to see you when you turn sideways, moi dear. Besides that great conk of yours, oi mean.'

'Gee, thanks!' I said, nettled. 'That's aristocratic, my nose. I wonder if they ever gave the Duke of Wellington this kind of trouble?'

'Only when 'e put his hand down my placket, moi dear. Oi said you can put your hands where you likes with your French 'ores, oi said, or Bony himself for that matter, but a freeborn English girl don't appreciate bein' guddled like a trout. At least not without warmin' one's hands, anyhow. Well, don't let the cat run off with it, moi dear. Sing out when you wants more ale.'

Off she trotted, leaving me blinking. The Duke of

Wellington? Well, why not, why not? If I hung around here too long I'd likely be getting my head thatched.

I took her advice and tucked into the sausages. They were coarse-textured but superb, a whole different animal from the soggy greasebags you get these days, like at motorway service stops. Next time anybody palmed those off on me they'd get them right back, Wellington style. And I wouldn't even warm my hands.

'A good evening to you, kind sir,' said a cheerful voice, from behind me. 'I trust nobody fills this place?' I was too busy stuffing my face to look up, and just waved. Somebody plonked down quite hard on the bench beside me. Then for a moment I thought the cat really was after my sausages, as something white and furry snaked across the table.

I choked violently, and sprayed the place with sausage. It was a long white beard.

'Goodness gracious me!' I exclaimed, or something along those lines. Only the bats would have heard it, anyhow. I swung around to bolt, only to find myself nose to nose with that leering mirror face again. Only this time it wasn't in the mirror.

'Ah, be at peace, sir, be!' the other man exclaimed, in an accent so burry I had trouble making out what he was saying. 'Not for all the world would we cause you distress. By your leave, good sir, sit and be contented!'

Nose to nose with me is still quite a way off, but I had empirical proof that this was real. Not even an astral projection could have had breath that bad.

All the same, I was about to head for the tall

timber on general principles, but a large hand clamped on my arm, almost encircling it with finger and thumb. The casual strength of it was startling. When you saw the leer in the flesh it looked more like a friendly smile.

Gingerly I let him pull me down. Just let him relax, though, and – but the oldster was coming in on my other flank, mopping and mowing with creaky politeness. Him I could make out a little better, but was it worth the trouble?

'Why, good sir, you do seem in a moved sort. Do compose yourself, I pray you.' He lowered himself to the bench, leaning on a silver-headed stick, and patted my arm amiably. 'We mean you naught but benison and well-being! True, we may have dis-composed you somewhat by the manifestations of our scrying, true. But naturally we thought that such matters would have become commonplace in your day, as the dawn of centuries saw vulgar suspicions dissolved like ghosts in the sunrise of rational philosophy—'

'He means we thought you'd be well used to such things,' laughed the other man. 'Excuse my learned friend the Doctor, he'll often speak after the manner of his beard, snowy-pure but long in unrolling. We dared to hope that our discoveries would have taken root in your time, and such ways of communication be commonplace. That's all. We'd no intent to, ah, discomfort you with apparitions!'

'Dis-*comfort*?' I bubbled with outrage. At least the sausage in my sinuses was keeping the beer in. I was so furious that I inhaled the lot down again. 'I thought it'd be Care in the Community next! The funny walk and the mumbles! I thought—'

I'd thought they weren't flesh and blood. But here and now, at least they were. OK, even the old fellow was bigger than me, just, and the other had muscles; but I'd seen them both run like bunnikins, and jumped Santa here. That took the starch out of them. And what I could do once . . .

My face must have been the giveaway, or just maybe it was the steam shooting out of my ears. The younger type – brother Edward wasn't it? – hopped hastily back over the bench. The old fellow stayed where he was. That may have been because I was very deliberately winding his beard around my fist.

'Nay, my good sir! Stay, my good sir!' he babbled. 'I beg you, do not allow your just offence to lead you into some rash action—'

'Nay, sirrah, hold!' chipped in the other one. 'Hold your hand!'

'Just as soon as I've stuffed this bogbrush right up—'

'No!' His heavy hands landed on my shoulders and pressed me back down. 'Will you not hear us? Aye, there's been grievous offence done you, but not all of our making. A man might say some of yours also! So will you not grant us the justice of accounting for it?'

I paused, but I didn't let go. Neither did the whiskery type. I could have resisted, just; but those arms didn't seem to be straining too hard. It occurred to me, as it tends to about this point, that I was, after all, not a thug like Ahwaz, and that that was something to be proud of. Besides, I'd just noticed he was wearing a sword.

He cocked his shaggy head on one side, considering, like a speculative thrush eyeing a snail. 'We could perhaps offer some small emollient?'

I eyed him back. 'Exactly *how* small?'

'Why, the benefit of all mankind—'

I tugged the beard idly.

'And f-fair and ample compensation!' chipped in the older man hastily, babbling a bit as I wagged his chin. 'Sir, we offer you both aid to end your present annoyances, and balm for those you have already suffered. Our honour requires it; and by God's grace and the favour of great men we are in a position to offer you both. Material balm!'

'You don't say?' I let go the beard and sat back on the bench, absent-mindedly waving away a sudden smokiness in the air. I was cooling down rapidly, but I'd been pretty angry – almost as angry as I'd been with Ahwaz—

No exploding phones or bandits rushing in to chop people up this time, though. A thought struck me, and I looked down suddenly. The table felt hot beneath my fingers. Where I'd been leaning there was a slight scorched outline on the scrubbed oak planking. It fitted my hand.

I blinked. That wasn't where the smoke had come from, though. The old fellow was making a funny noise. He was frantically trying to straighten out his beard. It had curled up into a tight springy cone, as if somebody had twirled it up in a giant red-hot curling tong.

It smelt like it, too; but that still wasn't where the smoke had come from. An awful thought struck me. I felt my ears gingerly. They were burning; but I don't think it was from being talked about.

Warty Whiskers was warily settling himself back at the table. 'I guess,' he remarked to the older guy, 'that our friendship might prosper better if we made ourselves known to Master, ah, Maxie.'

'Ah, a thought,' nodded the old man, still tugging at his corkscrewed beard in a sort of absent-minded fluster. 'Well, my good sir, at your other hand there sits my younger but still most apt and blessed brother in learning, Sir Edward Talbot Kelley, late a scholar of Worcester College, Oxford, lately created knight of the Holy Roman Empire, and in his thirty-fourth year.' Kelley half rose and bowed. 'And before you sits all that there is of John Dee, *aetatis* two and sixty, with the rank of gentleman esquire and the degree of doctor of philosophy in the most venerable university of Cambridge, now Astrologer Royal to her most puissant majesty the Queen Elizabeth.'

My eyes narrowed. 'The Queen has an astrologer? I know Nancy Reagan did – but the Queen?'

'And consulted most freely by all at the court, from my lord of Walsingham to the lowest groom.'

'Walsingham? Wait a moment – *which* Queen Elizabeth?'

Kelley chortled. 'Why, of England, man, where else? Is there another I haven't had word of?'

'Well,' I said carefully, 'yes, funnily enough. I mean, I'm thinking of the right one, am I? You know, Armada, body-of-a-weak-woman-but-heart-of-etcetera, slept here, Progresses? Good Queen Bess?'

Dee looked over his shoulder. 'I, ah, should not

put it quite so freely,' he muttered. 'Even in this somewhat out-of-the-way place. The intelligencers of the court . . .'

'Oh, great. Hey, you haven't told her she's going to meet any tall, dark strangers, have you?'

The old boy looked uncomfortable. 'Well – ahem! – as chance and the stellar motions would have it—'

Kelley chuckled. 'So? She did encounter my lord Dudley's nephew, the young Earl of Essex—'

'Oh, him. Watch him. He ends up getting played by Errol Flynn.'

'Gracious mercy!' The old boy looked very alarmed for a moment, then confused, then he cheered up. 'Ah well, no matter for the moment, for I am out of her service awhile. Among other concerns, in the quest for you, young sir; and glory be to Heaven above that we found you!'

'Yeah. I almost fainted with delight.'

The man Kelley chuckled again. 'Sir, sir, 'twas not to be helped! We had to get word to you somehow, and it's taken us these five long years since our previous, ah, encounter!'

I blinked. 'Five? Hold on a minute, that was only the night before last!'

Kelley grinned and winked. 'Ah, sir, but that's the way of this strange shadow realm. A night and a night for you; for us, a fistful of years!'

I sat back and stared. Five hundred years or five, they didn't belong in the same time as I did. Or did they? They had accents, they spoke pretty oddly. I'd had trouble understanding them at first, but now I seemed to be getting attuned or something. That was peculiar enough; and yet I believed them, as much as

I believed anything in this weird place. This far, anyhow.

'So how the hell did you find me? Private eyes?'

Dee looked puzzled. 'Eyes? Are they that infernal picture device of your era? No, sir; we cultivated the rare and refined art of scrying. Which, if you have not heard of it, is divination by looking-glass. Although metal or stone polished may also be used, or even the surface of still water, so that it turn an image. Philosophically – that is, hermetically – all such images may be considered identical, or to be more precise universal, so that one has but to attune one's thoughts to—'

Kelley coughed, and the old boy smiled. 'Well, well, it is an art too complex to explain this hour, and besides brother Edward is a greater adept than I.' He patted Kelley's shoulder. 'An art I sinfully envy him! For in all our first researches I saw naught but my own foolish image, whereas very soon he fell entranced and held converse with spirits of light, and looked upon untold wonders, such as I could scarcely credit!'

He wagged his head in innocent wonder, and I looked at Kelley with more interest. He had the kind of bluff, genial manner and rugged, open, rather boyish face that sets all my warning bells jangling.

'Ach, that's nothing!' he laughed modestly. 'A gift, not any doing of mine. And in truth it was of little use then for everyday concerns.'

'Truth!' chuckled Dee. 'For that we had to pursue our researches further, into these strange borderlands of the everyday world, Wheel or Spiral or whatever the pagans here call them. We chanced upon them first by noting that there were places where our experiments seemed always to fare better, where there seemed to be founts of power we could draw upon. So by searching out where the power was strongest, to which end I made a simple device, we pressed further and further across the divide. That was what took us to this little-frequented region of the Welsh Marches in the first place—'

Welsh Marches? We were nowhere near Wales here. But did Dee realise that? It dawned on me that he might not be as clued-up as he seemed about this Spiral business – which would explain some of the cock-ups, anyhow.

'And thence to somewhere better!' said Kelley enthusiastically. 'Better by far! The breadth of Europe we searched out that power, till we found ourselves a place of truly surpassing potential. And one where we may pursue our researches in peace, untroubled by the persecutions of the churches and the ignorant men who stream into them! A place where natural philosophers have an enlightened patron, merciful and generous to those he protects. That we found! And there we pressed our studies to the hilt!'

Dee wagged his beard. 'Aye! Of a glorious sudden, I, I too could discern visions in the glass – although of this world only,' he added a little sadly.

Kelley rubbed his hands. 'Well, there we perfected and refined our rites, beyond those first stumbling essays. There'll be no stumbling this time, I warrant you! And thence we have traced and explored along—'

For a moment they both looked almost embarrassed.

'—along paths mystical and strange. And found that we could pass thus between the interstices of time and space, to wander at will between worlds and ages! In this fashion we have traced you and come to you this very day – and where from, think you?'

He looked at me triumphantly. I shrugged.

'From Bohemia! From the depths of Europe, in a few short hours, by secret ways beneath the earth you could not conceive of!'

So much for travel broadening the mind. I wondered what he'd make of the Channel Tunnel.

'OK, so now you're here,' I said, determinedly unimpressed. 'Mind telling me just what it is you came for? Apart from scaring me half to death, that is?'

Kelley seized my arm and stared earnestly into my face. 'Why, to liberate you, of course! To bear you back thither, and there to lift from you this burden that has fallen to you by ill chance. And to draw blessings from it for all mankind!' He sat back. 'As 'twas we who laid it upon you, though all unwitting, 'tis we who can most safely lift it once again. Is that not so, brother?'

Dee nodded soberly. 'That is so, brother.'

'Well, bully for you!' I said, still playing it very cool. The more they talk about favours, the closer you read the small print. 'Let's get one thing straight, though – before I let you or anyone else lead me up any mystic paths, I'll want to know what's at the end of them! So, spill it – what're you up to? What's all this about?'

Dee looked concerned. 'But have you not already

understood? That is why you came here, was it not?
To seek some friend's counsel? Have you not had . . .
shall we say, curious experiences? Encounters that
are past your power to explain?'

'Apart from you, you mean? Too bloody right I
have. Enough to keep me in nightmares for the rest
of my life!'

'Nightmares?' Kelley opened his mouth to say
something, but Dee ploughed on regardless. 'Surely
not so severe! We imagined you confused and
daunted, perhaps, by what was so suddenly thrust
upon you. The seeing of visions – the conferring of
powers you could scarce control – even, maybe, the
coming of strange and mighty visitants. Is this not
so?'

That rocked me back a bit. 'Well, yes,' I admitted,
'That was it, all right. Only the visions – the visitants
– they really were bloody nightmarish!'

Kelley wasn't laughing now. 'Surely that was only
the – shock? The suddenness?'

'No it frigging was not! Not just, anyhow.'

He sounded concerned. 'But did they . . . threaten
you in any way?'

'Yes – no! Maybe – no! Christ, I don't know what
to think!'

The old man nodded. 'When you tell of a nightmare, it loses its power to frighten, does it not?
Primo, my young sir, we must hear clearly what has
been happening to you. *Secundo*, we may then tell
you how we plan to relieve you of it – and to reward
you as best we can. Young sir, will you not relent,
and place some trust in us?'

He sounded sincere; but then I had a nice line in

that myself once. Still, I was just bursting to tell somebody about all this – somebody who'd credit it, anyhow. 'All right,' I said. 'I'll spill the lot.'

It didn't take long in the telling, but they nodded and hummed as sagely as if I were some distinguished lecturer, only chipping in when I left any detail out. Intelligent questions, too – about the wind that night, the individual bandits, that kind of thing. I had to admit they were an impressive pair, Dee a little woolly but obviously full of knowledge, Kelley sharp and practical. I know brains when I see them, but there was more than that here. You could imagine you were dealing with a theoretical physicist and the engineer who puts his projects into practice. That made things a little uncomfortable for me. I couldn't entirely cover up just what I was and what I'd been doing, no matter how many naked truths I tried to dress up.

Or give them a nattier G-string, anyhow.

Dee shook his head sympathetically and tut-tutted, but I could see him getting sniffier and more high-minded. Kelley just chuckled good-humouredly. When I finally ground to a halt, though, he glanced at Dee with obvious deference.

The old man sighed, and plucked at the corner of his dark garment, gown or whatever it was. 'Well, young sir, I do indeed regret what you have suffered. Again I offer you our apology. Yet more of this trouble has been of your own making than even I suspected. Indeed, you may in a sense be the author of it!'

'The *author*? You mean I dreamed it up? Listen, you crap-headed old hearthrug—'

'Be calm, sir, please!' Dee rapped his stick on the ground. He had more command than I'd have expected. 'I have heard you out! Will you not hear me?'

I subsided, and he nodded. 'Good! I do not seek to mock you. That these . . . encounters happened, I do most firmly believe. Yet I believe also that the understandable terror they inspired has caused you to . . . to paint some aspects in hues darker and more, hmmn, demonic than they merit. Think!' he said, as I opened my mouth to shout. 'Think again of what has truly happened to you, each time! Why, you have received help, have you not? And in answer to even your lightest thought! You were saved. You were most mightily succoured!'

I was tempted to ask if I still was being suckered, but he wouldn't have got it. 'Well, maybe – but Christ, if that's being saved it's nearly as bad as getting caught! Anyhow, it probably wasn't just for me – I mean, who'd bother—'

Dee raised his brows. 'Have you not heard, perhaps, of guardian angels?'

I stared. Then I laughed, dislodging the last scraps of sausage. '*Angels*? Come off it, doc. If those bozos off that boat came from heaven, I don't want to know, right?'

'But I do, Master Maxie,' said Dee, and sat back calmly against the settle. 'I do.'

He smoothed his beard thoughtfully. 'All my long life I have sought and dispensed knowledge, and still sought more. The labour I have spent would have profited me far more in other occupations. Why, ask you? Because I would find some way to breach the boundaries of our mundane world. Some straighter path to the fountainhead of creation, through which the ills of mankind could be overcome and all men live as brothers.'

The same old dream. Only maybe it didn't seem so daft five hundred years back, who knows? Not me. I've always thought the citizen who first said all men are brothers was probably Cain.

Dee was looking out into infinite distances. 'To this end I have delved into every branching of art and philosophy. In the deepest mathematical arts I have found some promise that such a thing might be, and in the writings of such illustrious astrologers as Master Tycho of Denmark. Yet it was only when I looked beyond them, to such savants of bygone years as Masters Ramon Lull and Pico della Mirandola, and beyond them the great Henricus Agrippa and his master Trithemius Abbatus de Spondheim – only then did I begin to see the gateway. But opening it – ah, that had to wait until the coming of my young friend Master Kelley. I said, did I not, that he has from the beginning held converse with other realms?'

No wonder Kelley's face seemed familiar. He'd have made a brilliant double-glazing salesman. Or a pyramid seller. He was smiling modestly now, leaving the talking to Dee.

'You're telling me . . . he really talks to *angels*?'

'Indeed!' The old boy genuinely was sincere, his corkscrew beard wagging up and down with the force of his words.

I blinked. 'Wow. What'd you talk about? The weather? Harp lessons?'

He frowned. 'Best you take such matters less lightly, young sir. You'll needs learn more of them ere we're done. We have had some success. Messages have been received, and guidance. We have been told how to better our lives, that we may deserve such a privilege.' He wagged his head. 'Often in most unexpected ways. Why, would you credit—'

Kelley raised a mildly protesting hand. 'Leave all these deep matters for later. Let it suffice that we undertook a project of awesome moment!'

''Tis so!' said Dee eagerly, tugging at his beard again. 'To summon, by means of a difficult rite, a great angel into our presence! And to establish what might be termed an especial link or sympathy, by which we might call upon some fragment of his awesome powers.'

My hair began to crawl. 'Wait a minute . . . I get it. So you were trying to buy into a franchise? With one of you as local agent or whatever?'

He nodded amiably. 'I had dared to dream that I might have that honour. To wield so amazing a force for good, a wondrous fount of healing for the world!' His eyes brimmed with austere joy. 'But evidently the angels willed that it should fall to another . . .'

Kelley's smile was firmer. 'Should *first* fall to another,' he remarked.

'Oh. So you were holding one of your . . . rituals or whatever it was when I, well, dropped in?'

'Not just one ritual,' said Kelley quietly. '*The* ritual. Dangerous as blackest night, and as impenetrable. It demands the effort of Sisyphus, rolling a boulder up a steep mountain. It may bend minds until their cracking point, like willow twigs. It was progressing as never before. And into the midst of it – you fell.'

'I was scared, that was all! I was looking for somewhere to hide! There was something loose in the fields around there, something that scared the—'

'God willed it,' said Dee, not that humbly. He looked as if he'd picked up the news at some heavenly cocktail hour. 'For his great purposes, no doubt. So by your unlooked-for incursion, the vessel and source for the overflowing might of the angels—' He sighed. 'Is your doubtless worthy but wholly unprepared self.'

He said *unprepar-ed*, Biblical fashion. Somehow that brought it all home.

I wanted to run around the room and gibber. Angels? Believing in things has never been exactly my strong point. Let's face it, even in my short life I've sold too many lines to too many citizens. The magistrate who believed I was caught headfirst through a car window because I wanted to see the time on the clock. The passers-by I pulled in on behalf of a cult to have their subconscious tweaked, at so much per superego. The stripshow punters I promised the ultimate erotic experience. The believers I helped to hoodwink for my spoon-bending psychic. The more they believed, the less I did. And angels – well, you could say they were fairly high up my list.

Devils, now, they were another matter; I mean, you only had to look at the regular crowd down at the Port Mahon any evening. They made anything up to and including the First Circle seem inevitable.

But angels never came in. Not even to the saloon bar.

Yet the man Steve had said all things were possible out here. Now I was beginning to get just how much he might have meant. 'What I've seen didn't look that angelic,' I said slowly.

'Aye,' muttered Dee, disturbed again, 'and I confess that I do not wholly comprehend that. The character of these . . . brigands, these visitants . . .'

'Ah now, and is not that clear as daylight and champagne?' demanded Kelley. 'Should not the human agent focus the angelic light, as 'twere a burning glass? And lend it his own colour, like a window of stained leads? Is that not his purpose, to determine what form it shall take?'

'Ah!' cried Dee, and stamped his cane on the floor again. 'Well reasoned, brother! That must be it indeed! *Primo*, the angelic aid appeared in somewhat irregular form, young sir, because it was not *ab initio* intended for you. *Secundo*, because you were neither expecting it, nor apt to control it. A horse is a gallant aid and grace, but not if you lack bridle and rein, or indeed the very art of riding. *Tertio*, because you were, let it be said . . .'

'Buggering about on dirty business!' grinned Kelley, in a way I somehow minded a lot less than Dee's embarrassed squirming.

'Ah'm, let us be charitable and say . . . somewhat far removed from a state of grace.' Anything rather than admit you were chatting with a self-confessed felon, let alone sitting at the same table.

I thumped a fist on the table. 'Now wait just a bloody moment here,' I spat, feeling the whole rigmarole of reasoning leaping about in my aching head like a rat in a coffee can. 'Let me get this straight. You're telling me that I got all these nightmare goons instead of the robe-and-halo brigade because I wasn't thinking beautiful thoughts?'

'Because you were not about beautiful deeds!' exclaimed Dee. 'Can you not comprehend that? May not angels seem like devils if seen with distorted sight? A spirited horse may seem fair to one who can command it, frightening to another who cannot.'

'Well, maybe,' I protested. 'But you two were ready enough to go for it, weren't you?'

'Ready, aye – but with fear and trembling. To be the rightful vessel of such awesome power requires long discipline and self-purification, such as the art of *magia* already requires. Anyone not so equipped would surely find it a terror indeed – still more, it seems, one who cannot control his evil thoughts. I say not that you are so great a sinner,' he added hastily, tugging at his corkscrewed beard. 'A youth wild and untutored, no doubt. But nevertheless—'

'The power comes to you, lad, as you require it,' said Kelley, more kindly. 'But you're the wrong fellow, with the wrong purposes, and so it comes in wrong forms. It does you good, but by the most frightening means! And as long as you go on like this, you'll be but a blind beggar upon a runaway horse!'

I wondered. It made a nasty kind of sense. There was the pure light or whatever blazing out, and me in the way, as a sort of crap-coloured filter. That was Maxie all over.

And yet I'd never seen myself as the type to blow

up phones and chop citizens into chutney, even types like Fallon. Steal his motor, yes, any day; but the Conan routine wasn't in my line. At least, not consciously. Could I have all that kind of rough stuff racing around in my subconscious? Were all those thugs a reflection of the inner me? Was I a sort of closet Ahwaz? It was an obscurely depressing thought.

The old fellow patted my shoulder in a fatherly sort of way – a bloody patronising father. 'Small wonder it should have filled you with such terror, my poor young fellow. And yet, do you know, I could even envy you it, even that briefest glimpse of power.'

'It may be, too, that the colouring is not all his,' added Kelley. 'We know of our own experience that dangers may hang about any such exploration. It attracts – well, shall we say, opposing forces? It may be that in the unhallowed state of the experiment they gained some entry thereby. It might not be denied them.'

'In which case,' said Dee severely, 'the removal of this power from you becomes a matter of greatest urgency. Else you may risk becoming as Dr Johannes of Wittemburg, who took a demon as his servant and so, although meaning well, did ever ill. Surnamed Faust, I remember.'

'Now him I seem to have heard of,' I said.

'A very sad case,' agreed Dee. 'I met him myself briefly, in Cologne, not long before— Very sad. And hideous.'

'Oh,' I said.

'Then you'll come?' demanded Kelley.

I made a helpless gesture. He thumped the table.

'Look, man! Look upon the world, in your day or ours! Does it delight your eye? You are a man of education, of talent, fallen because fortune turned against you. Would you win back your rightful place? We can alter that, man, and more!'

Then he sat back, and shrugged as well.

'But that you need not credit, if you've no wish to. Suffice it that you can be free of all frights. And you can return to your own time no whit the worse, save for the weight of a rich reward. You need lack nothing the coffers of the Empire of the Romans can provide, and its great lord Rudolph of Habsburg. For it is he who is our patron, he the Holy Emperor of the Romans himself. He commands your presence! We – we do but request. Yet, unless you trust these others, these brigands or whatever, in your shoes I would brook no delay!'

I sat back, staring. I'd desperately wanted the whole thing to make sense, and now it did, after a fashion. OK, it was a hair-raising sort of sense that ditched every standard of rationality and reason I ever had. But what with bandits busting out of the woodwork and Elizabethan sages strolling in for a quick one, they were hanging a bit loose anyhow.

I was getting dizzy. I didn't know what to do, where to go. I wished that man Fisher was here; but then why should I trust him more than these two? After all, he'd steered me right into this in the first place.

And in a way, too, I trusted Dee. A bit pompous, a bit self-important maybe. OK, he really did want to benefit mankind, that I was sure of; but those who care loudest about man in the mass often sell man next door a touch short. They have trouble narrowing the focus.

Still, I couldn't see a likelier solution. I didn't much fancy being a kind of loose connection in the angelic circuit any longer.

'So how long'd all this take, then?' I demanded.

'A day of your life,' shrugged Kelley. 'No more. One simple rite—'

'Say, rather a day or two, brother Edward!' said Dee reprovingly. 'Be not in unseemly haste! We must first cast the nativities, seek out the auguries and make all other preparations, so the rite will be safe this time.'

'Oh, of course, of course,' said Kelley grudgingly. 'Though it will be safe enough in any event. And once done, by the same, ah, mystical pathways we may restore you to this very moment. Come, sirrah, our horses are printing the gravel without. Will you not come, for the good of all? Or risk some visitation more terrible yet? Perhaps here, where the powers you face must surely be stronger?'

I swallowed, suddenly dry, and gulped down the rest of my beer. That decided me. I stood, and shouted for Poppy.

'A moment, moi dear!' came her voice from the kitchen.

'I've got to go, love!' I called. 'But remember that message, won't you?'

'Oi may not be an oliphaunt, moi dear,' she said, waving me goodbye from the kitchen door. 'But 'ave no fear regardless!'

I waved back. Dee and Kelley were already outside, and I heard the soft whinny of horses. Mystic pathways? Well, I was halfway up the mystic garden path anyway, it seemed.

I turned, and plunged out into the dark.

CHAPTER SIX

Slippery Surface

IT WAS INKY black now, beyond the yellow shimmer of the porch lantern. Moths danced fantastic shadow dances over the gravel. Three horses stood there, nodding impatiently and nuzzling at us as we came out. Nothing mystical about these beasts, anyhow – smaller and shaggier than some, I suppose. I couldn't help noticing they smelled a bit stronger, too. 'Will you mount, sir?' enquired Kelley cheerfully, cupping his hands to my stirrup like a groom. I was already checking the girth and leathers, though, and swinging myself into the saddle.

'Ah,' Kelley grinned. 'And there I thought every man of your time would've lost the art equestrian to those fiendish fire-carriages. Yourself most of all!'

I grinned back, finding my seat in the rather lumpy saddle. One thing I'd done a bit of in my teens was riding to hounds, because everyone did – well, everyone in our family. It had never stuck; too exhausting and too cruel. Besides, if you had to kill foxes, I'd sooner shoot them, like pheasants or grouse. Preferably sitting, from behind. In standing corn and out of season, come to that. But I hadn't lost the knack with horses. Mind you, I did keep wanting to shift the gears.

The old fellow laboriously kilted up his gown, revealing leather leggings, and hopped surprisingly nimbly up on to the leading horse. It was Kelley, with his stubbier legs, who heaved and puffed himself up, his rapier clanking against his boots. He buttoned up his soft leather jacket, its fancy tooling shining in even the faint light, and jammed a round embroidered cap down on his unruly hair. He twitched its feather upright, winked at me and jerked a thumb at the doctor. 'Waall, illuztrious measter? Art assur-red? Wilt set uz on ower weay?'

For a moment he sounded like a cartoon hayseed. Had they been doing their best to talk something like modern English? To reassure me, probably. Fat chance. But it felt more as if something else had slipped, momentarily.

Dee nodded, and cast about him like a dog sniffing the night air. Then he clicked his tongue and urged his horse out into the blackness. He didn't hesitate; I did, but Kelley flicked my mount gently forward and fell in behind. Just where I didn't want him, even if he would have needed a really long cheesewire.

The darkness closed around us, without even a star, and though the air was cool I felt as if I was suffocating. As far as I could make out we were turning away from the field, anticlockwise around the pub and along behind the stand of poplars. It was pretty unnerving. For one thing, somewhere out there was Willum.

As my eyes adjusted to the dark I could just about make out cottages along this street. They seemed narrower and more cramped, their listing walls overhanging the path and their unkempt thatch bristling against the faint skyglow. There were no lights in their windows; nothing so much as stirred. We seemed to turn off the main street and along a narrow path which wound among their outbuildings, ramshackle barns and sheds ripe with the musty smell of hay and chickens, the odd whiff of drying apples and an occasional eyewatering presence of pig. Somewhere in the distance I could hear the faint rumble of the junction, and now and again a ramp or flyover would glimmer out of the darkness, veiled in its own hazy yellow glow of lights. They looked unbearably homelike and comforting. And if that doesn't tell you how desperate I was, nothing will.

Before very long the farm buildings vanished, and the ragged walls of fence and hedgerow took their places, with the occasional stooping mass of a tree; but never a leaf rustled in the heavy air. I rode nervously. I hadn't lost my seat over the years, but I hadn't used the muscles much either, those I'd ever had. And I kept expecting a stumble in the blackness, or a sudden sweeping tree branch. Or maybe just one of those all-purpose soggy thuds from up front.

It didn't come, though. I began hearing other things; bubbles, gurgles, and a soft, sinister whispering of water, and beneath it all a dull, earthy pulse, almost a feeling, not a sound. Yet if anything the junction seemed to be getting louder. I peered ahead, but the furthest I could see was Dee – and suddenly he threw up his hand for a halt. He needn't have. I thought I'd ridden into a brick wall. My horse checked and whinnied, I choked and swayed in the saddle. The piggeries had nothing on this.

'Aye, a rare stink!' grinned Kelley from behind me, dabbing at his nose with a cloth. 'A few breaths, though, and 'twill pass.'

'I've a better idea,' I wheezed. 'Why don't we? Pass, I mean?'

'Because this, I fear, is our road,' intoned Dee mildly, lowering himself from the saddle with practised ease. 'Somewhat of a privation, true. But so strange a passage is not achieved lightly. *Per stercoraria in cloaca.*'

'*What* is?' I demanded, peering into the dark and fumbling with my long-dead Latin. *Through* – something – *into the* – something else. What was ahead didn't look archaic. Painfully modern, in fact, all blocky concrete outlines straight at the edges, but with curved things in the centre, and something moving above them, sweeping by with a trickling hiss. Swinging arms, above circular concrete tanks.

'Wait a bloody minute!' I squawked. '*This* is your way back? This is a frigging sewage farm!'

Gdunk gdunk gdunk went the pulse, chugging the brown tides of civilisation through pipes and filters and bacterial beds beneath our feet, leaving nothing but the aroma to curl around the steel-shuttered buildings with their tall ventilator pipes. Even for a place like this it was a bit fierce, ammonia and methane and every little ester that goes with them. The worst of it seemed to be coasting happily down the breeze from straight ahead. Right where Dee was leading his horse.

There was a door ajar there all right. Nothing but blackness behind it, but you could practically see the open air curling up and turning yellow. The stink sidled out with a confiding leer, like a strip-club tout.

'No – I said *wait!* You're not going – you're not getting me—'

Nobody was paying me a blind bit of notice. The aeration tanks with their endlessly circling trickle arms looked like stiffened clocks, as if around here time really had bogged down.

I swung out of the saddle just in time to avoid hitting the lintel, as my beast nosed in after Dee's. I wrapped the reins around my hand, but I couldn't pull its head around. The building was a decrepit pile of decaying concrete, held up mostly by habit and sprouting little sprigs of weed from every crack; the door was jammed open, the lock long ago bent and vandalised. The *gdunk*ing sound echoed around the rust-streaked roof. There wasn't any floor; a darkened ramp sloped off into the depths.

'We must make haste!' said Dee earnestly. 'Foul airs gather here!'

'Oh really? I hadn't noticed.'

He blinked at me. 'Truly? Yours must be a hardy age.' He patted my shoulder again. 'But this goes beyond mere hardihood. To linger is to risk suffocation. Lead your mount, and swiftly.'

I was about to express my opinion of the whole idea, but Dee was already away, and my horse was following his, as horses do – only with my hand still tangled in its reins. The brute pulled me off my feet, and one went over the edge of the uneven ramp, crumbling bits off the crummy concrete. Behind me Kelley's mount was crowding in, and in the dark nobody saw my plight. I couldn't do a damn thing, not even scream – that would have meant drawing a deep breath. So, hopping, wheezing and gibbering, I was shanghaied down into the dark.

The horseshoes echoed on the concrete, and I prayed they wouldn't strike a spark on the mouldy stuff; the methane here would go up like a bomb, and we'd come down over half the Home Counties in a shower of—

Extremely distressing proportions.

Above all I didn't want to hear a splash. That was exactly what I heard, from about three feet ahead. I whimpered.

'Be not so hasty, master Maxie!' Kelley hissed. 'Here we must mount up! Good brother, there's need of a spark!'

'Naught easier!' said Dee's voice, before I could scream. Please God, not a tinderbox or something—'

The glow wasn't like that. Too gradual, too faint, too cool. The first thing I saw by it was Dee, holding his staff, with its silver cap in his other hand; and on the top it had concealed glowed a globe of glass, with something pearly at its heart. The light had the same tinge, and as Dee raised the staff it grew stronger. The ramp ended in a concrete shelf, stained and slimy, and beyond it a greasy brownish tide lapped and bubbled. His horse stood ankle-deep and dejected at its edge, with Dee holding his long legs up in their stirrups to avoid trailing them in the muck.

'Thus it was we traced the sources of power!' he said affably. 'A simple device, but driven by magical power. Light flows through All, even when it is light our eyes cannot detect. It is only necessary to attune it to the limits of our sight by such a device. And when it begins to operate, and gives forth even a faint glow, there the borderlands of the magical realms begin. But where, as here, it shines still brighter – why, then we are within the purlieus of the Great Wheel itself!'

I shivered violently. The old bastard was pretty bright himself. He'd made a Spiral detector. And here we were, not just on the edge but right up to our necks in it. Among other things.

'Now,' he said decisively, 'let us be on our road!'

I let out a light laugh that somehow turned into a hysterical cackle. 'Into the *sewers*? *This* is your frigging strange and mystical path?'

The old man nodded. 'Strange as't may seem, it is.'

'Hey c'mon! There's not much mystery where these lead – look what's coming the other way!'

Dee shook his head chidingly. 'Only be patient, young sir, and you will see. True, it is an ignoble road, through filth to the light. Yet is not that the human condition, even from birth? Why then should this be so very different?'

He had me there. With my lifestyle I ought to feel right at home. Most of my adult life I'd spent in the gutter. Now I was right down the drain. Natural, wasn't it?

The horses were tossing their manes and snorting. 'Me too, chum,' I told mine softly. 'But you didn't leave me much choice, either. And the more I get to know about this Spiral place—'

The sooner I should get shot of it. I mounted up, praying I wouldn't slip. Dee's horse was already moving, hooves skidding slightly in whatever awful slush lay under the turbid surface. Another thought struck me. If daft old Dee had stumbled on some way to alter the wavelength of, say, cosmic radiation to that of visible light; if there were ways to muck around with physics like that . . . It was a blood-chilling idea. That was entropy to hell and gone, just for starters. What else could follow? That bastard Fisher hadn't told me the half of it. Anything, cubed.

Including, for all I knew, coming galloping up through the Piccadilly Circus comfort stations.

We were moving upstream, unlike everything else, along the concrete channel. Here and there, though, older-looking brick archways were opening – in better condition, most of them, though crumbly and fanged with grey nitre. The oldest yet was stoneflagged, its channel deeply eroded, though only a thin yellowish dribble ran into the main. Dee calmly stuck out his hand, and we turned the horses into it. We rode in the channel bed, silently, swaying and cringing to avoid the little stalactites that reached down, or dribbled icy drops down our necks. The air was a little clearer, which wasn't saying much, and neither did we. The hooves plashed and echoed, as did Kelley's rasping cough, but there was no other sound in the sewer behind.

Now and again other openings flanked the old sewer, some of them looking even older, and they blew draughts cold or fetid out at us as we passed. Occasionally one would belch and spout a flood of water or a thick stream of sludge. Into one of these, no different from the rest to my eye, Dee directed us, and almost at once across an open space with a vaulted roof into another, flanked by the remains of rusted old railings and no improvement at all. We rode quietly, my horse following Dee's as he jogged easily onward, sitting very straight and unafraid, never once looking to one side or the other, utterly confident in his road. I became aware of Kelley moving up beside me.

'You're fallen quiet.'

'Christ, what d'you expect from me? Shafts of wit? Among the wafts of sh—'

He chuckled. 'Never fear!' His teeth glinted dully. 'He knows where he's bound, he'll not lead us awry. Not by a step.'

I glared at him. 'Fi— Somebody I spoke to said you had to be a tremendous navigator to get through the Spiral. Instinctive.'

'The Spiral?' Kelley chortled softly. 'I've heard this realm called the Wheel, like yon inn sign, but who knows? Spiral may be apt, or more so. The Doctor'll batten to that.'

There was a sudden scrabbling from behind us,

and a faint, distant chittering, high-pitched. Kelley whirled around with his hand to his swordhilt, then subsided with a cheek-puffing sigh of relief.

'What was that, then? Economy-size rats?'

'No.'

My hair bristled. 'What d'you mean, no? What was it, then?'

'How should I know? Or want to?' He leant closer. Down here you'd think his breath would be gilding the lily, but it still registered. 'Many paths cross here. Most of men; some not. Few of them need concern us, unless we should stray into their midst. Which we shall not.' He jerked his head at Dee. 'See how surely he threads his way. He could do't as well in utter lightlessness, where a common man'd trip at the first step. Times are, I think his very sureness be his strength. Sure, because he's no idea he could fail.'

We jogged uneasily along, turning first this way, then that, through a network of nauseating fluxes that never seemed to find an end. Only the tunnels changed, from brick to concrete to stone and back again, with occasional startling variants. Victorian coloured tiles, ludicrously bright to be stashed away down here – or did they hold little picnic parties to admire them, that sanitation-minded breed?

What looked like seamless ceramic dominated one brief stretch, with far away the faint whining hum of massive engines and, much nearer, passing at speed, a clatter that suggested something with six feet. Heavy metallic feet, and fast. I told myself it could be cleaning machinery, but then I've always been a lying little sod.

Round another bend and, whoops, splishety-splash into a sort of broad storm drain, vast and echoing with a roof of rounded arches; Roman or medieval, maybe. Always it changed, sometimes at every turn. Only the stinking stream beneath our feet stayed the same – the lowest common denominator of man.

And the time that passed, or didn't; and the oppressive silence. It felt like something solid, an unforgiving weight squeezing in on your eardrums, an immense mass of blackness poised over your head. Almost in self-defence we began to talk. Mostly it was Kelley and myself, he eagerly going over and over my experiences, about the twenty-first century, any and every shred of knowledge I could give him. He had charm, despite the buzzard breath, and he used it. Dee didn't bother, but occasionally he would drop a question into the conversation with a kind of genial condescension, like an uncle listening to his favourite nephews chattering. That was how they made you feel, those questions. They told me a lot about him.

I knew the type, only too well. I could even have been one myself, I had quite a few of the qualifications. They didn't live in ivory towers; they *were* ivory towers, tall pieces sweeping across the chessboard, ignoring the halting pawns and acknowledging only their own likenesses. Not the stereotype upper-class twit; they were often bursting with brains and talent. But practically from their cradle everyone had told them that; or worse, let them assume it. They'd just gone gliding along their effortless rails, into anything from the

Civil Service to business, academic life, even the media, and considered it perfectly natural. So they thought just that little bit the worse of everyone who had to *try*.

Oh, they could be philanthropists, idealists, even; they could be kind. *Terribly* kind. But always from the heights to the depths, across a great divide. It was a strength, that isolation, often a frightening one; it could make them good and kind in ways ordinary people never managed. But it could also make them amazingly naïve, especially in human matters. And when they were, there were others down here waiting.

I knew. They'd been waiting for me.

Dee had just that kind of unconscious arrogance. Talking to angels! He would bloody well believe he could do that – or at least that he was entitled to, and never mind why anyone else couldn't. He'd be the last one to think of it as overambitious, as hubris; he probably thought of himself as humble. He probably was humble – at least until you pricked his basic assumptions.

Prison visitors and other intellectual do-gooders of one kind or another, always ready to pronounce on equality of opportunity and social justice over tea and cucumber sandwiches in the back garden – only if the cucumber wasn't sliced thin enough, God help the au pair. To do them justice, they'd invite a paroled axe murderer along, if only he could talk. They'd invite me, provided I sounded proley enough; my real accent would never have done.

Talk was what they respected, I found. They

assumed, consciously or unconsciously, that no-body could talk properly without a couple of letters after their name. So when they picked up some streetwise villain with a good line in patter and a bit of second-hand erudition, they decided he was a rough-diamond intellectual *manqué*, and fell all over him. They were so secure in their own rightness that they couldn't really appreciate just how wrong others could be. I knew one upper-crust female barrister who'd hopped into bed with a string of no-nos – well, me included – and finally married one appalling thug with a body count into two figures, though they'd only got him for one. A fallen angel, she'd called him.

Dee thought he could speak to angels.

Kelley I was less sure of. He was a lot more friendly, all crinkly charm and bushy whiskers, but it was harder to see what was going on underneath. When I asked him questions for a change, the answers I got were pretty general, and beyond the fact that he was born at Worcester and went to Oxford, I learned little about him. About his studies with Dee he was quite ready to talk, but it sounded like gibberish. The most I could make of it was that it was a mixture of mathematics, astrology, all kinds of elaborate summoning of higher powers, and the kind of thing comic strips used to show with a stream of daggers coming out of your eyes.

This scrying number seemed to be something like good old traditional crystal-gazing – in fact, they used a crystal ball, among other props. I didn't try telling him the whole crystal ball bit started with Roger Bacon's attempt to describe a primitive lens, any more than I'd tell a modern tea-leaf gazer that it should only work with *Chinese* tea leaves forming the patterns of the *I Ching*. Never argue with an idiot, the Vikings used to say; you have more to lose than he has.

Mind you, they'd scryed me out across four hundred years and God knows how many miles, and here I was; so who was the idiot now?

Things floated by. Some of them I recognised. Some I wouldn't want to. One or two seemed to be moving under their own steam, and mercifully we weren't close enough to enquire. Now and again there were more scufflings and cheepings, and in one long, low place, while we were ducking under corroded girders and a brick ceiling, there was a sudden swift, rush and splash, as if a heavy body launched itself in. If it did, it never came near the light.

More than once there were the sounds of sploshing feet; very faint and distant, once or twice, there were voices. But only once in all that ride did I see another person. This was passing through a fairly modern-looking stretch, where the flow would have been ankle-deep – a heavy-set figure enveloped in dark hat and heavy overcoat, quite ordinary. He ducked purposefully out of one tunnel and into another, without appearing to notice us, and was gone. That was all; but there were splashes and shouts echoing out after him, as if many others were running in pursuit. It set me thinking. I didn't like what I could see. I asked Dee if we were getting near the journey's end now.

He smiled indulgently. 'Aye indeed! We have

come a long few leagues in a brief compass, and the greatest step is behind us.'

'So we could have about reached, say, Vienna now?'

He stared. 'Why, beneath its very streets. How came you to know that?'

I stole a surreptitious glance at my watch. You could almost hear the zithers. Any moment . . .

The sound shivered across the low roof, jarring and explosive but still recognisable as a single gunshot. I shrugged, though my back was chilled. 'Just asking.'

A realm of legends. All right!

I was still brooding over it when Dee's horse halted suddenly. Luckily mine stopped too, because I was in the original brown study. Well, where better?

The stonework around us was rough but fairly solid, a narrow tunnel like most of the others, with an even lower one leading into it. Water flowed somewhere nearby, faster and stronger than any sewer, and clear droplets trickled down the mossy walls. 'We are arrived, by all good graces!' said Dee happily. 'An old cistern by the river, latterly pierced to take the flows from the street kennels, and near forgotten. We must lead the beasts out. Happily 'tis dry enough, for now.'

I lowered myself gingerly down, my thigh muscles creaking and protesting, but not as much as I'd feared. We could only have been on horseback an hour or two, though it had felt like centuries. The ground beneath was slimy, but I managed not to fall over, and the side tunnel, sloping sharply upward, was dry as Dee had said. The ceiling was very low, though, and it took some persuading to get the horses along it; the saddles scraped the roof, and Dee had to bend far down, blocking his light. Blackness swallowed us. Suddenly, though, rubble rolled underfoot, and the ceiling wasn't there any more. I could dimly make out ruined walls, low heaps of debris with clumps of fireweed thrusting up between them, and tangles of snarly thorn-bushes. I felt the play of air about my head, and the first breeze for a while that didn't smell like a pub cellar with the barrels being changed. It did smell of something, strongly – coal-smoke. But nothing like industrial strength, and it was clean, clean, clean. Muddy cobbles squeaked beneath my feet, and the horseshoes clinked. The horses were snorting happily.

Kelley chuckled, spat and clapped me on the shoulder. 'Well rid, good master! Here's the end of our noisome road!'

He tilted my chin up. Dee's light was dimmed. I could see the sky!

Just a narrow strip of it between looming build-ings; but after those tunnels it seemed to glow. It was dark, clear and starry, though streaky veils of cloud sailed past the rooftops. They looked weird and archaic, tall, thin peaks topped with spikes or crosses or long knobbly bars, ending in high, crazy-looking gables that seemed to lean over and peer down through their blank little windows on to the narrow street below. It wound and kinked away on either side as if to avoid them, only to come under the shadow of more looming walls as it went, upslope but up and down like a miniature fairground ride. At every turn dark, narrow alley mouths and dank little pools gleamed under the sinking moon. A high spear-topped gable stood out against its quarter-disc. A cat slunk along it in silhouette, hissing and spitting at something down below. You half expected to see a broomstick fly past.

'Gee, great!' I said, a little unsteadily. Dee waved his hand and led the horses quietly forward down the street. In places it was so narrow that the upper storeys of the houses, outthrust on heavy beams, seemed almost to meet above our heads. There were carvings on those beams, painted once; fragments of what might be gold leaf caught the moonlight in places, but now they were crumbling and weird. There were no lights, except here and there a wan candle shivering behind a slatted shutter, usually, when you peered through, in front of the faded image of some saint or other. But then, quite suddenly, the street opened out like a cramped man stretching. Beyond a bare, stony expanse of rutted earth the moonlight gleamed on the rushing water I had heard – a river, wide and fast-running, black and choppy and cold. Ahead of us, high over the bank, a gatetower rose with chisel-pointed roof, and between it and its twin on the bank opposite, in stony contradiction to the fierce-flowing energy beneath, ran a massive bridge.

'The Charles Bridge,' whispered Kelley. 'Stood already more than an hundred year, and good for an hundred more at the least. The guards will be asleep a' this hour, for all the curfew.'

I didn't like the sound of that. 'Listen, I thought I was supposed to be some sort of guest of this emperor!'

'Aye, so, and we also,' muttered Kelley, slightly embarrassed. 'But better he shouldn't know our every coming and going. Nor that we've hidden ways out of his walls!'

'He is a most benign and kindly patron,' said Dee in tones of gentle reproof. 'True, he may seem somewhat dominated by worldly concerns. Who shall blame him if his most immediate interest is in the baser fruits of alchemy – the nourishing of wealth, the prolonging of life and, um, manly vigour, the confounding of his enemies' stratagems, and suchlike minor matters? Still he never ceases to seek for wisdom, among the Jews even, with an ever-open mind and a generous right hand. Oh, true, he's harsh and wrathful when he is crossed, aye! But if you do but use him with proper respect, why, he is meek as a lamb. And he has periods of great melancholy, when the troubles of the world weigh upon his head, but equally others of great exaltation, when one may speak with him almost as an equal. But he is a patron of the arts, a prince of pleasures, a lord of learning! Would that all great rulers would hold scholars in such honour as he does us! A most great and meritorious monarch!'

I nodded, but not for the reasons Dee assumed. If I wasn't mistaken, I'd just heard a fair description of a greedy, lecherous, sensual, paranoid, superstitious and quite possibly manic-depressive son of a bitch. A spoilt brat who'd fawn on you all right as long as you kept up the posterior osculation – Dee was catching – but hell on wheels the moment you gave him the slightest annoyance. You heard the same kind of bull about the Kray twins and the other East End bosses from the old villains who remembered them. I wondered what Kelley made of him.

The hefty man shrugged. 'Truth, his favour is like the sun's.'

'Too hot for comfort, and always clouding over?'

I could see his grin even in the shadows of the gate. 'A fellow after my own mind, I wager. Aye! And so when dealing with His Majesty, the wise man wears a cloak!'

I hadn't been looking around much till now, so as we started out into the muddy centre of the bridge the view caught me by surprise. This was a city of hills, and we were at their feet. Its skyline welled up all around us in rising waves of rooftops, a jagged row of gothic teeth, spires and towers and turrets like charcoal scratches on the sky. Hardly any two rooftops the same, sometimes bowed and concave, like little old men leaning on their sticks; sometimes domed and majestic, or high-peaked and chisel-tipped, with the pointed spires spearing up between them. Up the waves mounted ahead of us to a lowering shadow at the crest, a great sprawling mass of castle, with high cathedral spires topping it like stony lace, stark against the veiled sky. Here and there moonlight glimmering on patterned grey tiles threw a roof into three dimensions, but mostly they just looked like a backdrop out of pantomime, or a Disney movie – one of the scarier ones.

It didn't look solid, it seemed to shift and change with every fleeting wisp of cloud. My eyes were chasing glimmers of light among the tangled gables, lights that swam in and out of focus. But it was only when I looked down at the river that they made sense for a moment, in the choppy reflection. It was as if there was another building there in the background behind the hunchback housetops, something larger, square-walled, upright, a glittering tower chequered with glowing windows. A tower of glass . . . Strange how fairytale that sounds, when our cities are littered with them. For a moment it stood out there, clear in the water; but when I looked up there was nothing but the faint, elusive lights and the rushing music of the water against the pillars. My sanity did a quick soft-shoe shuffle. One of the lights still winked; and in one of those windows, as always, the fluorescent tube had been flickering.

You could believe in magic a lot more easily here. A whole hell of a lot.

Then a branch of memory drifted by, and I clung on to it, hard. Suddenly, I was almost heartbreakingly grateful to Stephen Fisher.

I realized Dee and Kelley were looking at me. So were the horses. Maybe I'd been gibbering. Dee made an understanding noise. 'Perchance you saw something, some vision that does not belong?' He looked back. 'Some glimpse out of another age, perhaps? Aye, indeed. We have, also, a'times; and I confess I do not wholly comprehend it. As if the city in all its ages and forms still exists behind the Prague of this day—'

'Shadows in the Spiral,' I said, echoing the quietly certain voice in my ears. 'Cast in time by the living city. Shadows of yesterday's Prague, and today's, and tomorrow's, all mingled to make up a greater Prague, Prague the legend. It's waiting for us around every bloody corner.'

Dee's bushy brows headed for his hairline. 'You are a philosopher, sir? How is it that you seem to comprehend—'

'I'm getting more frigging philosophical by the moment! 'Cos the only alternative is going stark raving bloody bonkers! Somebody told me about this, that's all. And he said it could be dangerous.'

'That may be,' Dee said calmly. 'For no doubt it is the worst times will leave the strongest legends. But what good thing was ever won without risk? And we are on the work of angels.'

'OK, fine by me. Just so long as they don't insist I join them, right?'

As we reached the further tower I looked back. I could still see them, those lights between the house roofs. They seemed redder now, though, and flickering more. That could just have been the air; but I thought of the campfires of besieging armies, the blazing rooftrees of looted farms. Hadn't the Mongols got this far – or was it the Ottoman Turks? One of the rape-and-pillage specialists, anyhow. What if their legends were stalking the night out there?

Among the darkened streets on the far side nothing stirred. We moved beneath dark casements, holding our horses on the shortest lead-reins they'd tolerate. A low, mournful note broke the silence, a horn of some kind, and a voice chanting tunelessly. Kelley looked sharply to Dee. He shook his head. 'The nightwatch. A long way off.'

Kelley grunted. 'Cannot be far enough for me. Austrian mercenaries, the most of them,' he explained to me. 'Like the Imperial Guard, and a mightier pack of whoreson dogs you'll travel far to find.'

'You should see some of the Serious Crimes Squad. All arse and no forehead.'

What was it the man said – when Greek meets Greek, they smile?

We were climbing still, closer to the castle. Suddenly across the city, out of sequence, clocks began to strike the hour. Deep in the very shadow of the walls a seam of red fire opened and spilled across the cobbles. Dee and Kelley exchanged pleased noises and hurried on. The clocks clanged, the ruptured-sounding horn echoed along the street, the chant echoed off the walls. How anybody got any sleep around here was beyond me.

The red light came from an archway in the wall ahead, like a red tongue lolling across the road. It was falling through the narrow gap of a double door, and it dimmed as if somebody was continually peering out. Kelley, too, went ahead to look before we crossed the street, both ways, quickly; then he gestured sharply at the door, and led us across the cobbles, fast. The door creaked back as he did so, and I barely managed to get an impression of the street, but I saw that the gateway was in the front of a tall, narrow house, one in a row, all alike in shape but differently decorated. Tall as they were, though, they backed on to a still taller wall of huge grey stonework, roughly dressed. It gave me a sudden shiver; it was the base of that enormous castle, and the house, for all its height, seemed to crouch beneath it.

In we went, through the centre of the arch, along the red light carpet, and the door creaked quickly shut at our backs. We entered a pool of flame, the flaring light of a single torch. The horses snorted softly and nodded, glad to be home. A bolt clanked to, hard enough to be heard. Somebody sighed gustily: Kelley.

Dee was already dismounting; I followed, rather creakily, but managed to keep my dignity. Kelley puffed and swore luridly at the fellow helping him, a groom, presumably. He and a couple of others gathered up the horses and led them off, speaking to them in a strange, spiky tongue I guessed was Czech. Dee called softly in the same language; they touched their caps, and other figures came scurrying, dim shadows in the red glare. Kelley came bustling up, took me by the arm, and steered me around, more firmly than I liked. 'Come, sirrah, best we get you within—'

Suddenly Dee made a very silly clucking sound. 'Ah, you see, my jennet, my little jade? Am I not returned upon the very hour I foretold?' He turned to us. 'Be not so very hasty, brother! Shall we not spare a moment for our own homecoming, aye, and make our guest known to our gracious ladies?'

We stood in an open space under the vaulted arch, a sort of extended gateway opening on to a slightly wider court beyond, where my nose told me the stables were. To one side of the arch there was a door open now, a rectangle of light with two figures silhouetted against it. One of them held up a candlestick, and things got brighter in any number of ways.

The women were quite a contrast. The older one was a homely enough body, a sort of loose round-ness tied vaguely into her clothes, with straggles of long brown hair escaping all round the cap she wore. Her face was just about as shapeless, an amiable potato, but lit up by a pleasant, placid smile. She looked not too bright, but immensely genial and accepting – just the sort of homebody to warm an old scholar's bed. But the other was something else.

Straight out of one of those Elizabethan paint-ings, green gown falling away from high breasts, the lot. Those wide eyes, just as green, but sleepy and modestly downcast, framed in blonde curls above strong cheekbones and full, sensual lips. OK, they had different standards of beauty then. She might not look quite so pretty to them, but that was their problem. By my standards she was stun-ning, and she couldn't be much older than me. And she had that kind of sexual magnetism which adds up to a lot more than looks. Even just the way she stood radiated it, even the polished glide with which she stepped down to meet us. Trust that smooth bastard Kelley! And she didn't look too overjoyed to see him back.

Dee spread his arms wide. 'Come clip me now and tell me where are all your foolish fears found now, hey my little frosling? *Buc-buc-buc-bawk!*'

And blow me if the one who tripped forward for a hug and another bout of chicken impressions wasn't the blonde.

The potato undulated cheerfully towards Kelley, who gave her a casual squeeze, a peck on the cheek and a pat on the backside. Dee put a fatherly arm about her shoulders and ushered both of them forward. 'Come, my dears, and greet Master Maxie, come from afar to aid us in this great work! Ask him no more for now, but take him to your bosom as our honoured guest!'

Now that, I decided, I could just about stand.

'Master Maxie, I present to you our lady wives – good Mistress Joan Kelley, and mine own, by baptism Jane, and virtuous and devoted beyond my deserts!'

Well, there was a facer for you. Luckily I had actually learned how to bow, a long time back, or I'd have just stood there with my jaw hanging out. If that old beanpole could keep up with a little goer like this, there might be something to this magic lark, after all. She did me an aristocratic little curtsey, revealing just a hint of cleavage, and then tilted her cheek up to be kissed.

My instant reaction died as I saw the frozen look on her face. A formality, no more; not much welcome here. This close I saw shadows under those eyes, and little tremors at the corners of her lips. She looked strained and cold, and she said nothing at all. Maybe Dee wasn't coping so well, after all.

There was certainly an atmosphere about. It was totally blown away by Joan Kelley, who rolled over to be kissed as well, chattering so cheerfully in a ripe burr that I only got about one word in three. As they included welcome, pull up chair and burnt wine, mind you, they sounded pretty good. Maybe Kelley had the best of it, at that.

Off she bundled me, with Jane Dee sweeping in front with the candlestick, up the steps and into a wide room, a hall really, dominated by the immense arched fireplace set in the far wall, surrounded by benches and chairs. Down the middle of it ran a colossal table, under a horrendous litter of books and papers and slates and weird apparatus. I'd done a little work in the old scientific instruments racket, helping a friend of mine to put the odd extra century on astrolabes and that sort of thing, so I could guess the kind of price some of this stuff might fetch.

The weirdest of all, though, had a table to itself at one side, an extraordinary affair of linked-up tubes and cans and glass globes full of nasty-looking liquids, bowls of powder and brass braziers overflowing with ashes. It had a kind of cranky, unstable, explosive look about it, supported by suggestive scorch marks on the faded wall-hangings behind and the metal sheet beneath. Kelley propelled me past it just a shade too fast, and I made a mental note that it might be worth some attention. Instead I just sort of idly picked up one nice little piece, what looked like some kind of ethnic hand mirror in polished black stone. It caught the light beautifully, and I looked up to see the two men staring at me.

'Oh, sorry—' I began, before I realised it wasn't that kind of stare.

'There now, brother Edward!' breathed the old man. 'Did I not tell you? Has he not lit upon the true gem?'

'I told him naught o'that, I'll allow!' said Kelley shortly. You could practically see the wheels spinning. 'Know you what you hold there, my – young sir?'

I shrugged and made as if to put it down, but Dee held up a hand. 'No need, no need! Do you see aught?'

'Just my face. Much the same as usual.'

'I bid you look again,' said Dee earnestly. 'For that is the first of all my scrying devices ever to yield ready results. It comes from the New World, a sacred mirror of the Mexican heathen made from some stone of great strength. That you should have seized upon it is . . . interesting.'

'I think it's obsidian,' I said, peering at it. 'A sort of glass that forms in volcanoes.'

Dee raised his bushy brows, pleased. 'Really? Is that so? A fit beginning, then, in the fires of creation! Still seeing naught? Keep it by you in the house, nevertheless. Gaze in it often, when you have leisure. Strive to see, as you would over great distances. Who knows, we may make a scryer of you yet! Not that all men have the art inborn in them. I myself began to see in it only when we came here. Before that there was a fellow called Saul who professed to perceive much therein, but I see now 'twas all invention. I had some hopes of my son Arthur, but only when brother Edward was sent to me did we achieve true communion with the angelic realms!'

One or two things were rapidly becoming clearer. 'So . . . it's mostly through him they speak?' I enquired innocently, tilting the stone this way and that.

'It is,' Dee answered, waving us to cushioned benches by the fire. 'Although with my humble help in the rites that open the ways, and with the reading of their meaning. For much of what these noble beings say is too high and lofty for our comprehension, and their dictates, though noble, are often passing strange. Why, figure you that—'

'Need our friend be bothered with such deep compacts so soon?' Kelley chipped in, so slickly the bells jangled again. 'They might perhaps disturb one who has as yet no deep grounding of knowledge—'

'But why conceal anything,' I demanded gently, 'when one day soon all men shall hear the angelic word?'

'True!' exclaimed Dee, greatly struck. 'Know then that they have commanded a new order upon the Earth, in which all men shall recapture the innocence of Eden and live as brothers. All are to labour for the common good,' he added excitedly, 'and all things are to be held in common for the good of all.'

I couldn't resist it. 'What – you mean, from each according to his ability, to each according to his needs? Something like that?'

Dee stared delightedly. 'Aptly put, young sir! He is surely ripe for enlightenment, is he not, brother

Edward? Well, the seraphim in their might have dictated that we shall set an example, he and I—'

'And others!' chipped in Kelley, with the faint relief of somebody turning the stampede at the last moment. What was he trying to stop Dee saying? It must be an absolute lulu. 'But we must not rest here too long, my friend. The rite that'll free you we cannot carry out in this house, where eyes and ears may pry and the Spiral is still not at its strongest. We have found a hilltop beyond the walls that is a most mighty nexus, at dawn and dusk especially. If we're to reach the gates before daybreak and the hill while the light's yet low, best we set out as soon as may—'

'By no means!' exclaimed Dee. 'Brother, do not let your natural zeal to free our friend carry you on too much apace! This is no small matter, to take the swiftest course with. We must be some days, even, in preparation, lest it miscarry and place all in deep peril — mots of all the brave Master Maxie!'

'Look, I'm all for speed, but what's this peril business? I'm not *that* bloody brave!'

'Casting nativities, fastings, prayers and purifications,' Dee ploughed on like a runaway icebreaker. 'Orientations, ascensions, declensions, recensions – oh, the peril? I should not concern yourself too much. There are aspects of the rite which are capable of miscarrying. Always there are hostile forces hanging about us, as about any human activity. But the angels have assured us they will ward us faithfully. So if you are truly in haste—'

Joan Kelley began handing around platters of

bread and scrambled eggs, and wooden mugs of steaming mulled ale. I took a deep swallow from mine. 'Yeah. Well, that's very, um, reassuring. But just you go ahead and take all the precautions you want. Er, angels help those who help themselves, that sort of thing, eh?'

Dee sighed. 'Ah yes – the Emperor himself said as much, when we tried to bring their word to him.'

'I can imagine, somehow. You were hoping he'd be one of the brothers, eh?'

'Oh yes!' exclaimed Dee. 'We did our best to explain to him that the panacea for all the ills of his realms lay in its lords abandoning all base concerns and submitting themselves to the angelic behest. But he seemed curiously uninterested.'

'Wow. Fancy that!'

'Aye, 'tis hard to credit. The Papal Legate, too. One would think that he of all people would appreciate that the clergy should live by strict Christian principles, but no! When we passed on the angels' word to that effect, he did but threaten to have us put out of the window! Which is a common barbarity in palaces here.'

'Sounds a bit undignified, sure.'

'His receiving chamber was on the fourth floor,' said Kelley grimly. 'As is also common.'

'Oh. Still—'

'No, young sir!' exclaimed Dee indignantly, wagging a long finger. The ale was putting a flush in his cheeks. 'All men should be able to subdue their base passions – and can, at need! Why, have not brother Edward and I had to do so? And in a most unusual fashion—'

'Aye!' interrupted Kelley hastily, positively blazing with visionary zeal. 'As one in the Angelic Brotherhood, owning no exclusivity in life nor any conflict, but sharing a common will—'

'Aye! Sharing all!' There was no shutting Dee up now. 'Even those matters most commonly the object of mankind's most ignoble jealousies!'

I boggled. God, he couldn't mean . . .

Couldn't he?

'Aye, even the most sacred property of all!' cried Dee fervently. 'All we must practise in common, even to wedlock. All we must hold as one – even our most dear possessions, our lady wives! And though it has been hard— Is aught amiss, Master Maxie?'

'No, no, nothing!' I said hastily. 'Just . . . saw something in the stone. Thought I did, anyhow. Maybe a glimpse. But it's gone now.'

I was telling the truth. Jane Dee, leaning over me to top up my ale from a steaming earthenware cruche. Jane Dee reflected, rigid in the flickering firelight. In the dark mirror our eyes met, and she hastily looked away. But not before I'd understood a bit more about Master Edward Kelley.

'Oh, wonderful!' Dee chortled. 'I beg you, try again! As often as you may. As I was saying, it has been hard for us – though not without some benefits I would not have looked for, I admit. Yet this subjugation of our base instincts we achieved, brother Edward and I. And if we two, why not all men?'

'And all ladies?' I enquired. Jane Dee had finished pouring and offered me the cup with both hands, courteously, no hint in her demure face of what I'd read there.

'Oh, yes, yes, they also,' he added a little absently. 'In an ideal commonwealth there shall be room for all—'

I let him run on. Apparently even women and servants could be admitted, though exactly why they'd go on being servants seemed to have escaped him. 'If only we can convey the angelic word to more of mankind, I shall gladly consider it fair use for the talents I one day return to my master – eh, brother?'

Kelley had been sitting very still, a watchful stillness. Now that I wasn't roaring with laughter at Dee's revelation, or otherwise throwing a wobbly, I could see him relax. That stone really did have its uses. 'I'm impressed,' I said, and meant it.

Dee beamed; but I wasn't talking about him. The black stone had given me a revelation of a sort, after all. And an idea.

'Who know? Who knows?' said Dee cheerfully. 'One day, perhaps, you also, young sir, may hear the word. Let us see what your nativity says—'

'High time that we do!' agreed Kelley cheerfully. 'Ere we read Master Maxie any homilies, we must keep faith ourselves. If we're to take all these pre-cautions, needful or no, best we make a start!'

'True, true, brother!' agreed Dee. He sat back and smoothed out his beard, which was rapidly recovering from its forcible curling. Not surprising, really; that sewer air would have straightened out anything, except possibly me.

'We have had a sleepless night and a trying

journey; but it will not pain me, I think, to draw a nativity now. Is that the astrolabe I see over by your hand, brother? And a slate and chalk – we shall pen it out fair later on. Now, young sir, to commence with, your natal date, and perhaps also the time of day, if you are – what? Why, bless my soul! No easy task casting the nativity for a man born some four hundred years hence, eh, hah-hah? But the motions of the heavens do not change, the mighty clockwork is ever wound, hah? And the place of birth? I see, I see . . .'

He was worse than a station sergeant with a charge sheet. Not just your usual Gypsy Lee's The Stars & Your Sex Life sort of routine, but enough dates to choke a camel.

Date of birth – place – family – father's and mother's birthdates and death dates – grandparents likewise – you name it, in it went, into a sort of stellar Irish stew, with Dee muttering and screeching away with the chalk in a way that sent shivers down my spine. It was like being back in kindergarten.

Kelley bustled about, fetching and carrying books and weird instruments. I wasn't bored; I sat and salivated. I could have shifted that gear for a small fortune down Petticoat Lane. What he was thinking, there was as usual no telling, but he seemed to be in a good mood again. Maybe he thought I'd missed the point of Dee's revelation, or had just taken it for a formality; but I knew better.

Suddenly the frenzied chalking stopped dead. 'I'faith!' muttered Dee. 'Mercury in the houses of Jupiter and Venus? An ill marriage, that mingles thiefdom and whoredom at the behest of lust!'

Oops. I've never had any time for astrology, but somebody up there had me pretty well to rights.

'Read rather,' said Kelley hastily, 'that wit is at the service of power and beauty – no bad thing in a young fellow, after all.' He grinned at me over the top of Dee's dome.

'True, true,' said the old man. 'One must make allowances. But how then would one read Mars opposing, in the sign of the Crab? And eke Saturn, standing today by the Goat? Does that not mark valour and wisdom in great part confounded?'

Oh, bugger. That's Maxie you're talking about, lads.

'A man of peace, shall we say?' intoned Kelley solemnly. 'Although not fated to be a scholar?'

Dee looked ready to shed a tear over such a sad trick of fate. 'And in the sign of the Water-Bearer, yes, the impatience, with authority—'

And so it went on. You could have called it a sort of piecemeal character assassination, except that my character was terminated with extreme prejudice long ago.

Kelley kept on twisting the readings round to a better interpretation, so obviously anyone less brilliant than Dee would have cottoned on. Evidently he thought he was doing me a favour; actually he was getting on my wick, and other areas. I know I'm a toerag, but at least that's me and not some assemblage of excuses. What's more, I'd got a pretty clear idea of what he was, too. And I didn't like the way he was trying to rope me in.

Mentally I took my hat off to the clever bastard,

of course. Not much mystery about how it had happened. Old Dee hanging on every word from his angelic sponsors, the luscious Jane within reach – just too good an opportunity. Con artists always try something like that, pushing their marks to new limits. Something to do with keeping their contempt alive, maybe, because contempt is what they're really feeding on.

All villains do, to some extent; I don't want my own Ferrari, I want *yours*. And if I get it, peace upon you – from a great height.

The trouble was that here I couldn't quite summon up the old cynical grin. I liked Dee, arrogant old twit that he was. And I recognised Kelley's brand of twinkly charm, all too well. Some things don't change. It was the kind that turns up on an old lady's doorstep, claiming he's come to fix the phone or get his parakeet off the roof. It's the kind of charm that not only persuades a girl out on to the street, but gets her back to give *him* the proceeds. On me it was already wearing thin. I knew patter and lines when I heard them; I had quite a few myself.

And what about Jane Dee? She looked, well, nice. Not just to slaver over – nice. A foul word, OK, but the best I could manage. Nice, it suited her. What about her? Not a scrap of expression on her face; that said quite a lot in itself. I was beginning to get highly pissed off again.

Suddenly's Dee's lump of chalk screeched across the slate, with cringe-making effect. The sudden booming had made us all jump.

'What the devil?' demanded Kelley, his eyes

flickering from side to side in the familiar con-man's reflex, acquired in years of looking for the exits. Maybe mine were doing the same. It was Dee who strode to the door and down the archway steps, to where the servants were already pulling back the bars. Padding along behind, I made a note of that; there was somebody they'd open up to without waiting to ask the master, and I could guess who. They were locals. I could practically feel my eyeballs swivelling madly.

Outside the gate there were only glitters in the grey light, vague clonks and clinks and the thump of heavy feet on cobbles. Only one figure marched in. He was so thoroughly swathed in armour, head to foot, that they might as well have included an opening ring. No mistaking what he was, all the same. The Universal Sergeant turned to us as we came out of the hall door, clanked gauntlet to helmet, and spat a stream of German at Kelley. Kelley spread his arms helplessly, and pointed to Dee. So Kelley didn't speak German? But Dee did, very well. They pitched it back and forth for a minute, then the old man turned to us. 'It seems we are greatly honoured,' he said cheerfully. 'The Emperor himself requires our presence at his levee – with our new guest.'

'And just how's he know of *that*?' demanded Kelley, while I struggled not to start whimpering.

Dee shrugged, unconcerned, but I was surprised Kelley had to ask. There'd be a servant in the house, maybe all the servants, well paid or terrorised to send word to the blackened ramparts so close above.

I fought down the urge to scream and run. The swiftest way into the Imperial poky, that. So far Dee and Kelley had managed to stay out of one. Better rely on them – or if pushed, sell them as far down the river as I could. They'd got me into this, after all.

'You cannot go thus meanly attired!' Dee was exclaiming.

'Meanly? This get-up cost me a fortune – and the ride hasn't done it much good, either! And what's His Nibs going to want with me, anyhow?'

Dee, as usual, wasn't listening. 'No robe of mine would be to your measure. Ah, brother Edward, a gown of yours, the green one perhaps. And a cap—'

To my surprise the outfit fitted me pretty well, probably better than it did bulky brother Edward, a rich affair heavily embroidered in gold thread. 'Tell him not I told you this much,' chuckled Dee in an undertone as he helped me into an incredibly scratchy ruff, 'but Edward purchas'd it from the players.'

'The players?'

'Aye, the King's Men! You see, men of quality oft-times bequeath their best apparel not to their fellows, who would scorn to wear it, but to their servants, whom it would scarcely become. So they sell it to the players for a shilling or two, for their stage dress. But sometimes, when times grow hard and the theatres close, they'll sell it again to gentlemen of lesser means! So step proudly, for you may perhaps wear Julius Caesar's gown! Or King Herod's!' It was a harmless little joke, and Dee enjoyed it hugely – so much so I suspected it was his way of letting off unconscious steam at 'brother Edward'. And perhaps of encouraging me, too.

As we passed the table on our way out I saw the slate lying there, with one great scratch of chalk across it. Evidently as far as the stars were concerned, all bets were off.

Sergeant Sardine bowed, then snapped to attention. 'Ve goh! I lead!'

'A churl of some wit,' commented Dee quietly, as he wheeled about and clanked out of the gate. 'I warn you, few speak any English here, the Emperor included. The soldiers often do, though, from having Scotch mercenaries in their ranks.'

With the women watching anxiously we were politely escorted out of the gate and into the street. I would have expected horses, but apparently going on foot was usual, with the castle so close. Our procession turned heads as it passed, one tinned lobster in front with a torch and the rest clonking along behind. Dee led the way with immense and leisurely dignity, magnificent in black fur-trimmed college robes, skullcap and wide-brimmed cap, leaning on his silver-topped staff. Was I imagining the glow that seemed to come and go beneath his fingers?

Even before sunrise the streets were getting busy, and the coal-smoke was growing from a tang to an eyewatering cloud that could equal any modern rush-hour. I looked around curiously, but I'd have seen more if Kelley's cap hadn't kept falling over my eyes. The torch wasn't ceremonial; you'd have missed potholes without it, and worse.

Still and all, the streets were cleaner than you'd expect from the history books – though this was the better part of town, of course – and the people, on the whole, well fed and healthy-looking. The horses were pretty well fed, too, hence the street problem. And they had better teeth.

All in all, apart from a slight lack of wheels to lift – and I could always turn to horses – it didn't feel nearly as outlandish as you might expect, not much more so than any foreign city. People were people, anywhere, anytime. But it did feel like a hell of a long way from home.

Never more so than when we marched up a long flight of steps towards the castle gate, with an oily great portcullis dangling overhead and what looked like rows of shrivelled turnips on spikes around the top. It took me just about this long to realise what they really were.

'Fear not!' Kelley hissed encouragingly in my ear. 'The Emperor'll not bite your head off. The mannikin's monstrously athirst for aught with magic or alchemy in it, and liberal to those who wield such skills! Even to shielding the damned Jews, would you credit it? Why, they are let free to leave their own filthy quarter and wander around like Christian souls in the city, the court even, during daylight hours! All for their blaspheming rabbis and their Kabala, God's wounds!'

'Amazing,' I said carefully. 'Need shielding, do they?'

'Need it?' Kelley chuckled. 'If it wasn't for him there's stout fellows in this city would sweep it clean in a night, bitches and brats and all! 'Twould be a pity to foul the good river Moldau, and that's all!'

'I guess it would be,' I said, still very carefully. Making all the allowances you like for his time, I was still getting just a bit tired of brother Edward. At least I forgot to be scared, though.

Until we got into the castle, anyhow.

It was huge. Not just a single building, but a sort of miniature town occupying a whole rocky plateau, with that cathedral down one end but maybe four or five palaces surrounding it, plus a gaggle of smaller buildings from convents, barracks and stable-blocks right down to streets of cottages, all hemmed in by grim towered walls. There was just as much bustle as down below, but more purposeful, with soldiers everywhere you looked. This place spelt power, a kind of power no king or president could have in my world. The Kremlin might have been like this before I was born, maybe, but nowhere else. You couldn't forget there was one man at the head of all this; and we were off to see him now.

I'd have taken the Wizard any day. The Wicked Witch of the West, even.

'His Majesty receives in the Vladislav Hall today,' said Dee, as we headed into a huge, echoing stone-flagged corridor, and climbed a great flight of stone steps. 'Were the weather more clement, it might have been in his summer palace or even his gardens, which are among the most pleasant in the world. Although I will allow the roaring of beasts in his Menagerie can be a trifle daunting . . .'

'He keeps them hungry,' said Kelley wryly. We

were brought up short on a high landing, a sort of antechamber with hot and cold running lackeys. It was clearly designed to impress, this chamber. Probably not the way I was impressed, though. Rich bullion-embroidered hangings, carved furniture, silver lamps dangling from the high ceiling, paintings – it started the old saliva running again. If I could only get one small furniture truck up here – well, forget Petticoat Lane market, you could take on Sotheby's with this stuff.

Clearly he knew how to live, this Rudolph. Just a couple of these chairs would have set me up pretty well – after a little guy I know had worked them up into four more 'restorations', anyhow. Or any of the paintings, though they were definitely not for the Impressionist punters. The style of the times seemed to be anything from the highly artificial to the downright weird, as witness a couple of smallish portraits that flanked the high inner doors.

'Ah, yes,' nodded Dee, seeing me boggle. 'By Messer Arcimboldo, one of His Majesty's favourite court limners, though why I confess escapes me. Those are his likenesses of their Imperial Majesties.'

'Likenesses? They're made of bloody fruit and vegetables!' Apples for the cheeks, a melon for the forehead, bunches of grapes and asparagus for the hair, peapod eyelids, cherries, plums, eggplants, gherkins, you name it. The more you stared, though, the clearer the faces became. I'd know Rudolph from that, and a cheery son of a bitch he looked with those bulging apple cheeks; but they also narrowed the eyes above, and about those I wasn't so sure.

'Just as well they aren't full length,' I remarked. Kelley almost doubled up; Dee looked puzzled.

'There's another less often seen,' whispered Kelley, tapping his nose with a finger. 'Shown me in secret by a chamberlain. Arcimboldo used not fruit, but the bodies of fair women – reclining for the brows, one bent for the nose, so, with the buttocks – you follow?' He chuckled. 'A living likeness, indeed!'

The doors boomed back. A lackey bellowed something in my ear, and we were being more or less shoved forward into the open space beyond.

It was enormous, bigger than the huge hallway, built of some warm yellowish stone with a high, rib-vaulted ceiling, the kind you expect clouds to form in, and vast areas of glass to light it. The sound of our steps on the heavy flagstones echoed away into the distance. All it needed was a voice announcing the departure of the 8.15 to Philadelphia Suburban. With courtiers, lackeys, ladies and hangers-on, including the local equivalent of peanut and popcorn vendors, it was just about as crowded as Grand Central Station or St Pancras. Probably not a lot safer, either.

But here the crowds parted swiftly before us, and fell in behind. They gave the impression that they weren't paying any particular attention to us, or to the great carved and canopied chair beneath the tall window at the end. But the moment I saw its occupant I knew they were faking it. Or rather, the moment he saw me.

It was about then I remembered to be scared again. Funny how it all comes flooding back.

It was quite a tribute to this Arcimboldo citizen. For a moment I almost did see a heap of green-grocery, he'd caught the look so exactly. Even without the portrait, though, I'd have known who it was sitting there, or rather perching. No crown, no jewels, nothing ceremonial; in fact he was the only person there who hadn't even bothered to get dressed. He was a short-arse, maybe a little taller than me, wearing a grey robe whose gold embroidery was at war with a subtle pattern of food and grease-stains. The heavy silk nightshirt beneath, also stained, was escaping in all directions, and I didn't blame it. Unkempt sandy-grey hair stuck out from beneath a purple silk nightcap, and his bushy beard and bristling moustaches were stained purple with wine, to match his pendulous lower lip. He sprawled comfortably across the throne cushions, with one leg draped over the arm, leaning on one hand, scratching bits of himself with the other, and surveying the world through those pouchy, alert eyes.

His actual expression was like the portrait, genial, jolly even. It looked as if his barometer was set to mildly manic today, no worse; but it was the eyes that pinned me. There was nothing very penetrating about that look, but it still put the fear of God into me about as surely as the magistrate in my first juvenile court. It was sussing me up, not as a human being but a potential receiving end – what of, would come later.

Dee and Kelley went into a sort of contortionist

act. I managed a pretty reasonable bow, and left it at that. Rudolph acknowledged Dee with a polite nod, but he had an altogether different sort of look for Kelley, less respectful, more interested. He rubbed his thin hands over the carvings on the chair, caressing their curves.

'*Also, Magister! Ihr ist ein neuer Gast gekommen! Mach'ihn dann mir bekannt!*'

Dee did the bogging and twisting bit again. 'My noble and most puissant lord, permit your humble servant to make known to you my esteemed colleague the Master Maxie, a young but accomplished student of philosophy who is but this morning arrived from England to assist us in our labours on your behalf!'

At least that's the gist; German is even better for gassing than English, and Dee just ran away with the ball. Rudolph listened the way you would to a football commentary, absent-mindedly caressing the carvings in a clutching sort of way. They were the only part of the chair polished bright.

When Dee ran down, he simply said, '*Ach so!*' in such a dry voice the contrast was hysterical. He hoisted himself on the throne and gave his backside a long and loving scratch, with grunting. Then he turned to me. '*Sei gegrusst, im Gottes Name!*'

I bowed again. '*Ich danke Sie, Durchlaucht! Es ist mir der grosseste Ehre, in ihre Dienst zu eintreten!*'

Kelley had been standing there like a dumb animal, but now I saw him really taken aback. Dee beamed. The Emperor's eyes opened a little wider; they were a kind of cold green, and bloodshot. He smacked his full lips. '*Gut, gut!* Not yet perfect, though. You have the strangest accent – like a Netherlander or a Frisian, almost.'

He was hearing the twenty-first century. 'I hope to improve it by acquaintance, Highness,' I said, gravely.

He nodded, chasing an itch around the neck of his robe. 'You're welcome, and not only as these learned fellows' colleague.' He was still squinting at me. 'You are nobly born? You have the look. But no title?'

I was impressed. My grandmother was a Bavarian countess. 'A younger son, Highness. In England we inherit nothing, neither land nor title.'

He sniffed petulantly, and wiped his nose with a thumb. 'Would that it were so here. I would not have so many princelings under my feet! So you have become a scholar. But you are yet young. Do you in truth have the art to assist these gentlemen in their *magnum operem* ?'

Testing my Latin? But Maxie's still the lad. I was quite enjoying myself. I'd been taught court manners as a child, but you don't get that many chances to use them, even in modern prisons. I bowed again. 'A great work indeed, Highness. But few could say more truly than I that I have looked upon another world.'

He snorted evilly and clawed at his groin. 'Ach, the speaking to angels! All very well, no doubt! But have they told you aught more of worth to *Ritter* Edward's project? Have they taught you the device of mating the Red Man with the Fair White Woman?'

My jaw dropped, but not, for once, because I didn't understand. I understood only too well, and not from my days down at the peepshow, either. The old swine hadn't been talking about just any great work – it was *the* Great Work. Alchemy – and I could guess just what kind would interest him most. And that, of course, explained Kelley's Heath Robinson machine.

'Indeed, I know of a certain technique for its success, Highness.' *All you're going to need is a small particle accelerator ...*

That bastard Kelley had promised to make him gold.

Dee was looking at me in restrained surprise; Kelley's face was poker-blank but tense. I ignored them, and coughed deprecatingly. 'The, er, achievement is making it in viable quantities.'

The fleshy cheeks puffed out. 'Hmph! Exactly what Master Kelley is forever telling me. Still, I must say he has kept his word, and given me ample proof of his ability.'

Proof?

Those chilly eyes gleamed. 'I could hardly have believed it, if I had not operated the engine myself. If I had not passed in those lumps of base metal with my own hands! And to see the precious particles appear within the cauldron of water—' He gave a luxurious little shiver. It didn't stop him taking a second to scratch one armpit. Then those eyes nailed me again, and the manic needle began to climb.

'Perfect me that process, whether by the angelic wits or any's, and you will not lack for any reward I can provide! I have estates and provinces enough in my gift already, but with such a resource I shall be able to dispose of thrones, if I wish. Remember that! And remember something else. Another learned alchemist, a man of Greece, swore he would make me the elixir of life. What he offered me, I put to the test – upon his own young daughter. The maid fell into an envenomed fever, from which she is unlikely to wake. He is presently reconsidering his studies within a private apartment with few if any distractions. Remember that also!' He fumbled obscenely inside his robe a moment. He had me worried, but what he pulled out was a small purse.

He tossed it to me. 'An earnest of what is to come! Now go about your business, and fail not!'

Getting out involved infinite bowing and scraping, but if I'd had any choice they wouldn't have seen my arse for dust.

Proof! I glared at Kelley's backside as he bobbed up and down in front of me, restraining the urge to boot it, hard. Just one more little game he was playing – and he'd sucked me into this one, too.

CHAPTER SEVEN

Objects in Mirror
may Appear

THE CLANK-AND-CLATTER boys escorted us back. An honour, of course, but the kind that keeps you thinking. Dee strode along just as regally as before, but I could tell he was practically skipping like a kid let out of school. Any minute now he'd be twirling his staff majorette-style. When the soldiers left us at our gate he startled me by clapping my shoulder.

'Well, young sir! You have acquitted yourself well before His Highness! Has he not, Brother Edward?'

Kelley was as genial as ever, and as opaque. 'Oh aye, very modest, demure as a girl! But he's a close-handed fellow indeed. Had he but thought to share what he was saying with us—'

Dee chuckled benevolently. 'And whose fault's that, dear brother? Have I not urged you to learn more of the indigenous tongue? You can tattle with the angelic host, yet scarce command an alejack from mine host!' Another of Dee's little jokes. I produced a dutiful smirk. No wonder Shakespeare's clowns went down big.

'Anyhow, you had no cause to fear,' he added.

'Master Maxie said naught but in proper support of our efforts, in most politic fashion.'

'They spoke of *my* efforts,' he riposted. 'That much was clear.'

'Of course they did!' said Dee. 'And Master Maxie vowed his help. For which you shall know our lasting gratitude, sir!' He put a fatherly arm round my shoulder and led us in. 'You know now what our purpose is, and why we said you would be well rewarded. If we are to establish the new angelic order, we shall have need of temporal power – for the guidance of others, of course. To this the Emperor is our key! But alas, the key to his purposes is gold. With that he can withstand the power of corrupt Rome, of obdurate Greece and savage Muscovy, and launch his new crusades across the world. So, we must swink to give it him.'

He tapped Kelley's homage to Rube Goldberg as we passed. 'Our efforts have staled of late. We need new guidance, and perhaps 'tis through you, sir, we are destined to find it. Think upon that!'

'Aye, but not over long!' said Kelley, slightly less genially. 'The burden you bear may bring us the wisdom we lack. The sooner we lift it from you, the better for all our sakes!' He stumped over to the fire and began poking it fiercely.

'*Festina lente, festina lente!*' said Dee in gentle reproof. 'I agree, Brother, naturally. Yet still we must not stint our precautions, and take solemn auguries and observations to choose a propitious hour.' He contemplated the ruined notes on his slate. 'The wisdom of the stars seem a little obscure, for now. Perhaps we should seek a few hours of rest before we recommence.'

I failed to stifle a yawn. 'I could use that.' I slumped down in the best chair at the fireside, kicked off my shoes and set my feet to toast.

Kelley picked up the obsidian mirror. 'Maybe. But what if the best, perhaps the only time soon were this coming eve? We should have no time to prepare. I am not so weary I could not still turn my hand and mind to some scrying.'

'Noble of you, brother!' exclaimed Dee. 'There's much in what you say, alas! But Master Maxie seemed close to some revelation earlier, and it is for him the rite's to be held. Perhaps, if he be not too weary, he should be the first to seek what he may see.'

Right then I felt I'd seen more than I ever wanted to; but I could guess what kind of answer that sly bastard Kelley would summon up. I had to have a go first, if only to keep said bastard off my back. He was as genial as ever, but there'd been a dig to that little business about my speaking German – the equivalent of a tantrum, maybe, in somebody less controlled. I'd nettled him. And I knew damn well why.

He was running the old gold potato routine – as old as the *Canterbury Tales*, at least. Of course, back here that was a lot younger. They do the modern variation with diamonds sometimes, or, if you're really sophisticated, designer drugs, but the basic principles are the same. Cheap stuff in one end, pricey stuff out the other by the mysterious process in between.

The Spiral, of course, could make things happen,

and we were close enough to it here; I remembered
the light from Dee's staff. So could Kelley really
have had some luck? Probably he'd tried. He must
have had a hell of a shock when he found that his
scrying trick actually worked hereabouts; so maybe
he'd confidently assumed that his transmutation
scam would, as well. But somehow I didn't think it
had. The same old question applied, the one the
marks never ask – the one Rudolph evidently hadn't,
not yet. Namely, if this process has even a hope in
hell of working, why the blazes is this guy bothering
to sell it to me?

If Kelley could ever whip up gold to order, he
wouldn't be sitting around wooing Rudolph, angelic
order or no. But that wouldn't occur to His Majesty.
He'd be convinced because he wanted to be convinced. That's the secret with born marks; they do
half the work themselves. Your job is to soothe them
along and get some kind of down-payment. Once
they've paid out for something, they're hooked;
they've got a stake too. They'll defend you because
they're defending their own judgement, bolstering
their dreams. Ask any adman. Hair restorers, beauty
aids, mysterious hifi enhancements – you think they
work because you've paid for them.

No, dollars to doughnuts this was the classic
scam. It had all the hallmarks – such as getting
Rudolph to work the process himself. That's one of
the advanced variations, because it gives the mark a
big kick and he thinks it proves something.

No it don't. Have the gold potato gizmo
inspected or sealed or witnessed or anything else the
mark wants, no matter. All you need to be is a

moderate sleight-of-hand man, and able to keep the process nice and complex and scientific-looking. You stand over the mark muttering about how it's dangerous and doesn't always work; you show him how to use the tongs, or 'save' him from spilling molten metal, or blind everyone with a bit of magnesium in the furnace, any one of a thousand conjuror's distractions. And presto! a pinch of dust or a couple of molten-looking nodules get slipped into the works for the mark to crow over. There are all sorts of wrinkles, such as coating the stuff in low-temperature alloy which looks remarkably like lead but melts off in boiling water under the guise of 'cooling'. Every generation discovers new ones, but the game's the same.

Once again, a tip of the hat to Brother Edward. I slumped back comfortably in the inglenook, toasting my toes and contemplating Destiny, and wondering whether there wasn't anything *I* could try selling His Itchiness. Double-glazing, maybe, or aluminium siding – the Hradcany Castle would account for a lot of that . . .

Then an awful sinking feeling set in. There's one big drawback to bunco routines of all kinds. The same old principles of action and reaction apply. The deeper the mark hooks himself, the worse it hurts when he finds out. It makes him ten times meaner when the scam's shown up, because all the guilt and shame and stupidity he feels, he's going to offload on to you. That's hairy enough at the best of times; almost any mark worth taking is going to have a certain amount of influence. But when he's an absolute ruler and an even more absolute son of a bitch, with his own personal dungeons and no doubt monogrammed torture chamber as well . . .

It's absolutely bloody suicidal. You'd have to be a thicko to try it.

I looked at Kelley, with his perpetual air of armour-plated good nature. Oh, shit.

A thicko – or an ego. Now I really recognised his type, one I knew a little too well. A clever dick, a bit of a lad, thought the sun shone out of his exhaust pipe, no doubt. Too damn pleased with himself by half, fooling all these brilliant, powerful people, all of the time. He'd never heard the other half of that one, though, because Lincoln hadn't said it yet. It just wouldn't occur to him. Things like that didn't happen to him, period. When they did begin to slip it wouldn't be his fault; it would be Dee's, mine, anybody's.

And by the same kind of almost psychopathic blindness he'd be just the lad to risk fiddling around with dubious forces like these brigand creatures, or whatever was behind them. He'd be like a moth round a candle flame at the prospect of power. Risks were something that happened to other people. Kelley would always win through.

He wouldn't like rivals, either. I found myself thinking about that poor little Greek alchemist, and who might have put him up to offering the Emperor an untried potion. Maybe there was something more to this hurry of Kelley's. Maybe he did want me to come to harm, to be sure the power stayed his . . .

I made up my mind to have a talk with Dee, the first chance I got. A long talk, and in private. But how the hell could I get him to believe me?

I picked up the black stone mirror. 'I'll have another stab at it.'

Dee beamed. 'Splendid!'

'Should we not first turn to the orb?' insisted Kelley, and now there was a definite distrustful edge to his voice. 'I've ever had the best results with the orb, as you know!'

Dee shook his head firmly. 'It was with this looking-glass, or stone rather, we had our first successes here. It may be better suited to a novice. There is great virtue in glasses. With them I made my first essays, after the passages in Pliny, and later with the surfaces of water, wine and other liquids, as related in the *Ars scintillia* of Artephius. Now Psellus—'

Kelley's shrug could have said a lot of things. I damped down Dee's discourse, and I was grateful for that at least. I angled the mirror this way and that. It was well polished in the centre, but the halo of light scratches around the rim gave its reflections a cloudy, suspended look. Probably easy enough to imagine you saw things in there. 'What do I do?'

Dee was chalking notes on another tablet. 'What you do now, only with all your mind and soul concentrated upon the truth. Look into the stone as you would into a great distance. Strive to make clear the smallest flicker. For a simple inquisition such as this we need no great rites of invocation, at least not yet. But let us not neglect a brief prayer for our success.'

Dee's idea of brief and mine were different. I began to get bored long before he'd finished. All I saw in the stone was my reflection, and I wasn't too hot on staring at myself. I saw too much.

What's worse, there was an annoying tickle in my

ear, a buzz almost, as if some kind of insect had got
in – not one of Rudolph's, I hoped. More like a hair;
I fidgeted at it with a finger, but that only made it
worse. Some kind of tinnitus – maybe this coal-
ridden air was giving me catarrh. Lovely; all this, and
extra snot.

It was maddening, almost like an insistent
whisper. The only thing to do was pay no attention
and hope it would go away. To distract myself I
started looking around the room. Through an open
door I caught a glimpse of the wives, stopping to
listen as they passed by. Joan had a tolerant smile on
her doughy face, like when hubby has his cronies
round to watch the big game, but Jane Dee's looked
pinched and nervy. There was nothing much else
interesting, and as the prayer wound down to an
amen I let the mirror settle back on my knee. The
buzz was still there, louder even and irregular, as if
there were shapes in the sound. I was aware of Dee
and Kelley looking over my shoulder.

'I thought—' began Kelley in a portentous voice,
then he stopped suddenly. Dee exclaimed. My jaw
dropped in astonishment, but what came out was
more like a scream. I jumped up and more or less
flung the mirror down as if it had bitten my fingers.
Dee squeaked in horror, but luckily it clattered
down among the papers on the table. On what
happened next I'm not too clear, though I remember
the floor beneath me slowly welling up and sinking
like a very slow wave. I don't think I fainted, but
the surf roaring in my ears was my heartbeat, and I
was somehow huddled down on a bench, shivering.
Dee shook my shoulder gently. 'Why, what's amiss,

sir! Whence this fright and alarum?'

I drew a deep breath. I'd been too dismissive. I'd forgotten that whatever else Kelley was faking, the scrying worked. I just hadn't realised it would for me, too. 'Didn't you bloody *see*?'

'Aye indeed!' said Dee paternally. 'Truly one might well recoil from such an awesome sight, but there was no need.'

'There wasn't?'

'Why, never so! Did it not speak? No? Ah, well, 'tis my case also. Many times have I been vouchsafed that glorious sight, but 'tis with Brother Edward alone the angelic beings will converse—'

'Wait a minute,' I managed to break in. '*That* was an angel?'

He looked at me wonderingly. 'Why, what else? The fair form, the radiant clouds, the high and noble features—' He wittered off dreamily.

I was still vibrating with shock. Whatever he'd seen, it pretty clearly wasn't what I had. But Kelley? His smile gave away exactly nothing. 'A sight of wonder, as ever. And ere the link was untimely severed, it spoke clearly, to me at all events. Decreeing that we should hold the rites without delay, this very eventide.'

Dee looked troubled. 'Brother, are you certain? There was only that momentary vision. We should enquire further.'

Kelley considered. 'No doubt you're right, Brother. Perhaps Master Maxie's vision was distorted by weariness and ill-preparation.'

Dee exclaimed with relief. 'That will be it, indeed! My young sir, I owe you an apology. In my zeal I'd forgotten you have had many days of travail and sleeplessness ere this. Wife, is our friend's chamber prepared? Then do you light him to it, with our grace. Fear no evil intrusion; I have shielded this house against it. You shall sleep as long as you will, Master Maxie, and in safety, and with your awakening we shall seek clearer counsel.'

It could only have been midmorning, but the prospect of bed was like being sandbagged with a blanket. My limbs went laden, and the idea of just stretching out and thinking of sod all seemed irresistible. I mumbled my goodbyes, and let Jane Dee, candle in hand, lead me up the narrow, shadowy stair to the upper rooms, where a door stood open. Her manner was as cool and aloof as ever, but there was something else in it. She kept glancing at me, as if she was hovering on the edge of a question. The room looked bare, with nothing but a carved wooden press, a bench and a narrow bed with posts and heavy curtains; but right then anything short of an antheap would have looked inviting. She set the candle down on the table and began to draw back the curtains, but hesitated, twisting her hand nervously in the heavy fabric.

'Gentle zur—' Her accent sounded far broader than the mens'.

'Yes, er . . . my lady?'

'May I ask of thee . . . wast truly an angel thou sawst?'

'I don't know, my lady. Since you ask – I don't think so.'

'Yet my 'usband and Maisteer Kelley—'

'Perhaps your husband saw something else.'

'And Maisteer Kelley? To him it spoke, did it nowt?'

'Well . . . I heard something that might have been a voice, or voices. But that too—'

'No angelic likeness?'

It still made me shiver. I avoided her eye. 'I . . . can't say.'

She looked at me properly for the first time. 'I thank thee ne'er the less, good sir. Rest and be 'ealed of thine affright.' She did me a deep curtsey, then turned away before I could say anything else. She strode out with smooth dignity, her wide skirt sweeping the threshold, and closed the door softly. There was something lithe in her walk that suggested good legs underneath. Ah well, chalk up one more mystery Maxie would never solve.

Whose bed would she go to? Brother Bastard Kelley's? Or did they share – no, that was about more than I could stand to imagine. His type – his bloody type. I knew my moment of terror had loused up my great idea, but I was too exhausted to care. I stripped down to my new silk underwear and dived between the coarse linen sheets, sinking into the feather mattress like a fat aunt's embrace. It felt good, and sleep came racing up on me like a train. But behind it there was a restless, feverish feeling. Suddenly I had the leisure to realise just how far from home I was, out of my time, out of my place, surrounded by menaces, very much alone. In every sense. And the train had a shrieking whistle—

I woke up sharply, instantly, with my fists clenched. Somebody had said something, not loudly, but clearly, about an inch from my ear. I couldn't remember what. I pulled back the curtains, but the room was empty. The sun shadow on the wall had hardly shifted. I must have been asleep for minutes at the most. Breathing hard, I sank back again. And back, and back . . .

Falling through the bolster, through the moulded mass of feathers and down into blackness. What I did best, wasn't it? Falling. I'd been doing it all my life. Images came crowding in – the chilly cling of the school bed sheets as I lay awake the night I'd been expelled, afraid of my father coming to get me next morning. The gloating face of the teacher who hated 'my type'. The jeering cops pulling me out of my first car wreck. The ripping sound as my wrist tore the neckline of my first girlfriend's party dress. The prison warders suddenly laying into me on the last night of my trial, spitting with class hatred. The stink of my first cellmate, a crop-headed type who mugged pensioners and amused himself putting the frighteners on me. Slopping out next morning – every morning. The muck and chill of the gutter on my first night out, picked up puking drunk by a tart and ripped off for everything I carried. Hopeless, dragging job interviews, where they started staring out of the window. The stocks I'd been sold crashing to junk values, the horses that narrowly missed a place; the one outsider that made a killing, and the bookie's goons mugging me when I came to collect. The blank-faced bank adviser telling me my last cash had been swallowed up by all sorts of peculiar charges, and the overdrafts were being called in. Suddenly even the horrible hot dampness of my pants at kindergarten and the voice of my nanny, the vicious old bitch.

Where the hell was all this coming from? It didn't feel like anything I was doing. More as if somebody'd run a line into my unconscious and started fishing for all the really juicy humiliations they could. I struggled to fight clear of them, and sink free into the black oblivion of proper sleep. But that began to feel worse and worse, because the blackness seemed to take on a glassy glimmer like that bloody mirror. It scared me shitless, in case that thing appeared again.

It had come and gone in a moment. It could just have been one of those little half-erotic daydreams you get, a coincidence of shape and colour somewhere in the reflection that suggested the shapes of two women, naked, seen from behind, lying languorously stretched out foot to foot as if one was the other's mirror image, forming a wide flattened V. An olivey Mediterranean glow to their skins, their black curls streaming out into darkness, suggested the women from the bandit gang. But the image lingered that instant longer. Nothing actually changed; but the greenish glow of their skin seemed more intense, the serpentine shadow of their spines became blacker against it and with really horrible suddenness the women were suddenly slanted, glaring eyes. Eyes without a face, like glowing slashes in a dark curtain; but feral, hungry eyes, fearfully aware, aware of me.

So I yelped, and I chucked down the mirror. But here it was, the surface of my sleep rising to meet me, and mirrored in it was that growing glare. Suspended between waking and nightmare, I struggled and threshed with limbs that felt manacled. Women. It was women I saw, not eyes; make it women . . .

Women it was – a woman. The whip artist, smirking all over her predatory face, drawing the black tongue luxuriously across her breasts.

Whips aren't exactly my thing at the best of times, least of all now. Not her! Some other woman. Trace. Maddy the Table Dancer. Red-haired Georgina. Any; all. No good, I couldn't summon up a single one, not even Lyd who worked in the Jaguar dealership with all the leather upholstery and drove an original E-type. The E-type I could get, the upholstery even, but no Lyd.

Somebody else, somebody more recent. That barmaid Poppy, all cheery dairymaid curves, wholesome as wholemeal. She was just a blank. What I got instead, and vividly, was Jane Dee, with that lush shape and haunted eyes. A real woman, the kind I'd never had a chance with. And that bastard Kelley . . .

Fire spurted in the school roof suddenly, that teacher vanished under a rain of tiles; the party dress tore wider, and spilled her breasts into my hands. My fist sank into that lousy tyke's face, and the warders bobbed and cringed away from the new hard man; I splashed the slop pail at them, and the other cons cheered. Bank managers grovelled and paid damages, the bookie's goons were swept aside as by a rushing wind and I had him by the astrakhan collar and flicked the little knife open right under his red-veined nose. Then that thieving bitch and her pimp, next, the tearing sound, the scream choked off . . .

Me?

The bellowing impact as the car revved back out of the ditch, smashing into the cops and spilling them this way and that across the road . . .

Me?

This wasn't me. I'd never shivved anything more serious than a BMW's window trim, and never wanted to. I didn't care that much about avenging the past, just shaking free of it. But whoever was digging this crap out of my mind wouldn't let me. I felt as if I was literally entangled, like a swimmer drowning in weeds, thrashing and tearing at the slippery black coils around me. It was that bloody whip! Not leather, though; silky, glossy, more like plaited hair . . .

She bent over me, smiling slowly, and her eyes were very green. 'I always thought it was me you liked the best, *mio Maxie*—' The blackness behind her was swirling and smoky, and her face seemed to fill the sky. Her hand touched my face, and it was rough and hot, like a claw.

The next moment I was wide awake and out of that bed. Under it, actually, shivering uncontrollably on the bare boards and whimpering. I had to make myself stop that, though. It was echoing eerily in the silver chamberpot.

Fear no evil intrusion, ha bloody ha!

It was dark now, the room full of heavy shadow, and only the faintest skyglow from the little window. Eventually I summoned up enough nerve to climb back up, pull the heavy counterpane over my head and collapse, groaning. About five minutes later something seized me by the shoulder, and I shot up with a yelp.

'Awake, young sir!' said Kelley with brusque cheerfulness. I forced my gummy lids open to glare at him. 'Well slept, I trust! A day and a night, whole. But slugabed no more, we must be up and about our business. The Doctor is now agreed with me that since your first scrying so disconcerted you, I should question the angels on your behalf!'

He couldn't resist springing that one on me. That was why he'd let me sleep; to work on Dee, at which he'd had years of experience. Now he thought he had me. For a moment I felt totally despairing, but only a moment. Down there with the echo chamber I'd had some time to think, and I hadn't forgotten it.

The brigands, or whoever else was digging up all those memories, had a purpose – maybe to make me more vulnerable mentally, maybe to make me hungry for revenge, so hungry I might just chip in with the brigands for the sake of that power. It seemed they couldn't find me here; maybe the Doctor's precautions worked that much. So they were trying to corrupt me instead. All they'd done, though, was make me want to stop it happening again. My idea was spoiled; but maybe I could still improvise.

I pulled on Kelley's robe, because it was warmer than my jacket, and the morning air was biting. Besides, it would probably annoy him. Downstairs there was breakfast waiting, bread and buttered eggs and bacon. By rights, given the sanitation and so on, it ought to have been foul, but actually it tasted great, especially compared to my usual stale corn-flakes. I wasn't too hot on the mulled lager, flat, with spices, but sooner that than the water – sooner *any-*

thing. What I really needed was coffee, Turkish-strength, in quantity, preferably on a drip-feed. Dee spouted great heaps of gibberish about his philosophy – the Seven Ensigns of Creation and the Invocation of the Thirty Arts were the least of it. After the night I'd just had, I could cheerfully have invoked a couple of things myself, but I forced the most intelligent smile I could. I was going to need him on my side. Today, it seemed, we were going for the full Monty.

Kelley was already bossing the women about, clearing the great table of its heaps of books and scrolls and slates and parchment scraps, uncovering a hummock draped in an embroidered cloth. Dee patted it paternally. 'The principle of the mirror is reflectivity. That is to say, it returns the onlooker's sight upon himself, and that is very sound. For as Man the Microcosm is himself a glass, reflecting the All, so all truths are within him. Beyond that, though, lies the principle of infinite distance, at which the *bona spirita* may be found, and for that both reflectivity and transparency be requisite. Psellus – did I not mention Psellus yestre'en? – now he sought to extend this principle, I believe, to the invoking of spirits aerial by the means of water in a wide-necked jar, which doth both mirror and give sight. Master Paracelsus, though, makes interesting mention of the possibilities of crystal and jewels in his *Ars beryllistica*, and that recalled to me' – he pulled off the cover with slow reverence – 'the crystal orb of Master Roger Bacon.'

It wasn't as big as I'd expected; most of the height was an ornate stand, a sort of miniature table with a gold mount in the form of naked swirling figures at the centre. And it wasn't exactly clear, more like a light bottle green with a cloudy core. 'Clarity has always been the problem,' admitted Dee. 'Rock crystal of sufficient purity is rare. But as fortune would have it, here in Prague is made some of the finest crystal glass anywhere, and I had them shape me several trial pieces before settling on a method and a formulae. Can they manage better in your time?'

I hummed and hawed tactfully. The average Gypsy Lee model looked better than this. 'They can? All the more mystery why scrying is still not in common use. Now, Brother Edward and I shall carry out the rite, but do you watch and listen and assist us with your prayers.'

I put on my very best if-you-please-sir simper. 'If it wouldn't put you out, could I do something too?'

Kelley's geniality darkened. 'We must have no more wild affrays, lest they offend our celestial mentors. That will endanger all our purposes.'

Butter wouldn't melt, honestly. 'Oh, I don't mean take part or anything. Just sort of shadow the process – with the mirror again, maybe. I'd be more ready, this time. And I might experiment a little. I mean, for example, has anyone ever tried reflecting the crystal in the mirror?'

Dee stared, a little taken aback. 'I know not, upon my troth! Have we ever mirrored the crystal, Brother Edward?'

'We have not,' said Kelley shortly. 'And better Master Maxie content himself with watching, than so mingle himself in matters he does not understand!'

'Oh peace, brother, peace,' said Dee reprovingly. 'You are too harsh. Was I not just as shocked at my first true sighting? And so were you, as I recall!'

I'll bet, I thought.

'Besides, his question is a good one. Aye, young sir, seek as you will, during our rite! Be not afraid, whatever may pass; for in the *Clavicula Solomonis* this is firmly declared the most licit of theurgy! Brother Edward?'

Kelley, dour-faced, lifted the crystal. Dee reverently oriented the little stand against what I realised was a crude compass set in its centre, then spread out the scarlet cloth back over it, carefully arranging its gold-embroidered symbols. 'Behold the *Sigillum Dei Aemeth!* These are the signs revealed unto me of the great archangels of the four quarters, for even they are subject to the power of the stone, in the hands of godly men! And those mighty ones I now invoke!'

I'd expected Kelley to be the showman, but he wasn't. He set the ball down carefully and sat back in his chair, steepling his fingers reverently. Dee was the one who did all the work, and very impressively. Why not? He believed in it. Just like Rudolph, he was doing most of the work himself.

Pretty well, too. The women draped a black silk robe over his shoulders, put his staff in his hand, set down the freshly wiped tablet and chalk beside him, and retreated to the hearth, watching intently. Dee raised his hands over the table, spreading his arms wide, and launched into a spiel so elaborate I didn't immediately realise it was a prayer, of sorts.

With his long beard streaming he looked like so

much Cecil B. de Mille. His normally rather high voice seemed to sink about an octave, and rich, burry words positively rolled out across the room. For the first time I heard what the King James Bible was supposed to sound like. He certainly wasn't making any concessions, and yet I could understand it clearly. Had he and Kelley really been trying to sound halfway modern all this time – or had I been becoming attuned to them somehow? Maybe that was possible around the Spiral, too.

The prayer was certainly pretty flowery, not to mention interminable and full of gibberish Dee called 'mystical names', by which he was invoking God's aid in a way that was more like issuing orders. Religious I'm not, but I somehow didn't think God would only answer his secret Internet addresses, which is what these sounded like. Dee worked his way on to a whole slew of Good Angels. And he made the whole thing sound as petty legalistic as a double-glazing contract.

'. . . and by these mystic names of our God which have special command and potency upon thee, oh AIAOAI and OIIIT, I absolutely require and confidently desire you, individually and severally, to appear obediently to me, the said JOHN, peacefully, content and visible. And consenting to show yourself friendly to me, the aforesaid JOHN, that you agree to fulfil and complete truly, perfectly, clearly, evidently and absolutely, all and each of my requests that concern and involve your skill in transformations, knowledge and power, such as are required and requested by me, the aforesaid JOHN, of each, some or all of you—'

There was more of it. Oh God, there was more.

Much, much more, in English and Latin, while the fire burned down in the fireplace and the grey smoky air invaded the room. All of it in the same bloody do-this, do-that vein. If I'd been God, which for some strange reason I'm not, I'd have given it the bird. And if angels have names like Keyboard Fault #33, I don't want to know.

I pretended to study the obsidian mirror while Dee droned on, tilting it this way and that. I did try mirroring the crystal a couple of times, but only very quickly. Seeing anything more was just what I didn't want. There was that buzzing in my ear again, but I carefully ignored it. Mostly I stole sly peeps at Jane Dee.

Kelley, too, was sitting there looking like a man about to drop off during the sermon. Suddenly, though, he began to twist and twitch uncomfortably. Who could blame him? But when it got worse I began to wonder if he'd picked up some of Rudolph's little passengers. Then his head lolled suddenly, his jaw dropped, and he let out a slow, anguished moan. If boredom had been his problem, I'd have sympathised; but somehow I didn't think so. Dee let his prayers drop and stretched out his arms towards the groaning figure.

'Speak, spirit! By the Divine names communicated unto us, I conjure thee! Show unto these, thy lesser brothers in the angelic orders, all manner of things within the glass, that we may work out thy purpose, nor hold back aught of thy full meaning!'

Kelley's eyes flicked open, wider than I'd ever seen them. Still moaning faintly, he hauled himself up, staring fixedly at the green glass ball. Dee leaned over towards me.

'Now the spirit takes hold of him!' he whispered excitedly. 'And have you been vouchsafed any revelation, thus far?'

I tilted the mirror judiciously away from his wife, and confronted myself, all beak and scattered straw-coloured locks. It showed me one thing – in Kelley's green-gold finery I looked a lot like an exotic parakeet. If that was a revelation, you could keep it.

And yet that dark mirror did add a sort of dream-like quality to what it showed, especially round the edges where the flickering firelight made it shiver. It showed me a different sort of face, though how different I couldn't quite sort out. One thing, though – at least it didn't have an expression like Kelley's.

'Something a bit strange. Nothing definite. What difference does the spirit make, anyhow?'

'Ah, subtly questioned! What takes shape in the crystal, we can both see – aye, and you also, it seems. But only with Brother Edward does it find its voice.'

It figured. I was quite prepared for what came next, and it was just as well. The voice came, not from Brother Edward but from the crystal, and it was dark and sepulchral, quite unlike his, but blurry and quavering.

'*ABNO!*' it declaimed, like a haunted speak-your-weight machine. '*NAOCO! OCANM! SHAL!*'

'The great Angels of the Four Quarters!' whispered Dee gleefully. 'They favour us with their counsel!'

'*Behold!*' cried the voice. '*And harken!*'

But what to, we never did find out. The crystal ball burst out in a sudden shrill fluting, a whistling, warbling sound like some unearthly bird. Kelley stared, aghast, and well he might. It was a handy little number, ventriloquism; but I'd learned my set of tricks four centuries later than him.

That was my cue. I leaped to my feet, but solemnly, as if answering some mighty command, and held the mirror up high, catching the firelight and reflecting it on to the crystal, awakening glittering rubies in the bubbled glass.

'I hear, oh Radiant Ones!' I cried. 'Speak to me directly, I beg you!'

And the crystal spoke with a different voice, higher and eerier.

'*Yea, I am the Walrus! I am the Eggman! Behold, verily, I am the Fool upon the Hill who seeth the sun in its going down and whose eyes behold the world in its turnings around!*'

Dee gaped. 'The what? The Fool – is not some such symbol in the Tarot? – I mean, I charge you, spirit, speak! Give us some earnest of what thou art and whence thou comest, of thy truth and goodness!'

'Aye!' roared Kelley, mysteriously restored to himself. 'And that thou art not a false and deceiving son of a – son of Abomination! Prove it, or be damned!'

'*I am the Man of a Thousand Voices speaking perfectly loud! Earnest shall I give thee of the truths I speak. Take up thy tablet, and write thereon, as I commandeth!*'

Not bad. I was getting the hang of this stuff. This was the nervous-making bit, though. If we'd had pencil and paper I would have been safe enough, or even a modern chalk stick. That lump wasn't quite long enough. Still, here goes.

'*On the face turned from all sight but thine, write any name thou willst, however secret, however holy, the most that has been revealed unto thee! Write it fair and with respect, and I shall tell it unto thee, straight!*'

The pair of them boggled beautifully. Over by the fire the women had leaped up and were watching, wide-eyed and wondering. Like a man in a dream Dee picked up the tablet, holding it close to his chest, and slowly, with long strokes, scratched a short name.

'*Thou hast written ORO!*'

Dee's jaw dropped. 'The first of the Twelve Names of God! 'Tis so!'

Kelley snatched the slate. 'I credit it not! Thou'rt but a deceiving demon!'

'Nay, nay, brother!' breathed the old man. ''Tis so!'

'Then read thou this!' snarled Kelley, and slashed a rapid pattern of letters across the slate with wincing squeals of chalk.

'*Thou writest ill, thou man of little faith! But hear this, and be corrected. LLZACA thou daredst to name!*'

Kelley's eyes flickered. Looking for the doors again, eh?

'The Divine Title of the Angelic Summoning in the East!' said Dee, in shaky delight. 'Oh Brother, doubt no longer! Master Maxie, did I not foretell it? Some new revelation is made unto us today!'

Written fair and with respect – that meant long, clear hand actions I could follow. It's better with a long pencil or pen, when you can see the end wiggling; but I'd watched Dee write on the slate already. It's an old routine, but it worked for Victorian spiritualists, it worked for Houdini and it still worked for my late employer, before they found the videotapes of those private hypnotherapy sessions, that is. He'd taught me a few basic skills to make me a better stooge – basically kiddie-party conjuring, but to black belt level, and streets ahead of anything they'd heard of here.

Kelley was simmering. He knew it was ventriloquism, all right. But he couldn't so much as hint at the possibility without pointing an even bigger digit at himself. 'Well, maybe, Brother John, maybe. But remember, once, when you doubted a command I conveyed, the angels vouchsafed me the favour of a written mandate upon the purest parchment, that came floating down to us from on high. Can we not ask such an earnest again?'

Sod. Released by a thread from the rafters, no doubt. But I'd been half expecting trouble, and a good conjuror's stooge can think on his feet.

'*Oh ye who would see a sign! Yet it shall be given thee. Yea, it shall be traced out in thy sight! Take virgin parchment*' – now I knew how they pronounced it – '*and inscribe it after this fashion —*'

A few minutes later we were staring at a broad sheet of parchment with a circle of letters on it. And I was asking Dee what this could be all about, and he was shaking his head mournfully. 'Nay, 'tis all new to me. The angels have shown us strange methods of picking letters from the cross-row and suchlike schemes and patterns. It was thus they gave us knowledge of those divine and angelic names you heard, and of their arcane tongue.' I'd guessed as much. The cross-row was how the Elizabethans often laid out the alphabet, and the names sounded like that kind of random gibberish. But this would be something they hadn't tried.

Jane Dee appeared, carrying an elegant little crystal goblet. ''Tis the best we have,' she said doubtfully.

'Then it must surely serve, wife!' said Dee cheerfully, upending it in the centre of the circle as the fluty voice had directed. 'Now, brother!'

Kelley's infernal good humour had all but evaporated – a great relief. Grumpily he settled himself down opposite. 'This I like not,' he grumbled. 'Cannot we seek guidance by the tried and trusted ways?'

Yes, and I knew damn well what they'd been about to say. To my surprise Dee turned unusually testy. 'I remind you, Brother, it was to seek new communications we launched upon this whole enterprise! Did you not many times counsel me to open my mind and have faith? Do likewise now!'

He stuck a finger on the base of the glass. I added mine, and under Dee's stern eye Kelley reluctantly plonked a horny fingernail alongside.

'A brief prayer?' I suggested to Dee, with malice aforethought.

Quarter of an hour later Kelley's saintly smile was

wearing pretty thin. Fine by me; the more tired his finger was, the better.

Suddenly Joan Kelley, watching with Jane, gave a breathy little squeak. Slowly the glass was beginning to move. They all stared at it like a snake as it slowly circled the ring – and stopped, at the letter F. Kelley snatched away his finger as if he'd touched a snake, but Dee seized it and, surprisingly, was able to force it back. Again the glass circled; again it stopped, at the letter R. 'Who does this thing?' demanded Kelley, his weathered features turning a curious grey. 'I'll swear 'tis bewitched!'

'Blaspheme not, brother!' warned Dee sternly. 'Have you not looked upon marvels as great? No man's hands propels the glass, that I can see or feel!'

He was right, in a way. The ouija-board effect is just a matter of tensions. A single humorist can start or stop the glass moving with the faintest of efforts, then use all the other shifting finger pressures to keep it that way. That's how it worked, anyhow, as it spelled out the word *res*.

'In Latin!' breathed Dee. 'Meaning – but here it starts anew!' Kelley gulped and muttered as under our fingers the glass spelled out *ipsa* and *loqvitvr*. I was ready in case he tried to hijack it, but he was too unnerved by the eerie glide.

'The matter may speak for itself!' translated Dee, astonished. 'What now? *Fidete*, it readeth, as if to say *trust*!'

I was a bit chuffed with the *vs* for *us*; that gave it a nice old-fashioned look. Not that I knew much Latin, really, but I'd picked up quite a few legal tags – what with one thing and another, and another –

and they sounded suitably vague and impressive.

'*Fidete – cvm – amicvs* . . . trust as friend, aye, aye!' nodded Dee excitedly. '*Fratercvlvmque* – and as . . . younger brother – *in fraternam – et in omnis* . . . in brotherhood and in everything. Ah . . . er, *brotherhood*?'

A long silence. One of *those* silences. Dee was tugging at his beard, which seemed to have corkscrewed again. Kelley's face still wore its genial smile, but slightly lopsided; his real expression was his whole body, taut as a spring, heavy fists clenched. If looks could kill, that one would have burned me at the stake and jumped up and down on the ashes.

He was ninety per cent sure I was a fake – but so was he. If he tried to expose me, he'd be exposing himself too. And suppose I wasn't a fake? Suppose that I'd somehow managed to tap the currents of real magic that were flowing around here? Where would that leave him? His only chance of getting what he evidently longed for was through me. Either way, he didn't dare say a word against me. Any such thing would get him first.

I blinked trustfully at Dee. 'Sir, do not distress yourself. I am sure I am unworthy.'

'*In omnis* . . .' muttered the old man, all his bounce departed. 'No, no, I see much worth in you already. 'Tis not that I doubt that, or the command. No, it only comes hard upon me, to subdue my baser self – harder even than before, for Master Kelley and I had laboured together for many fruitful years. Still, still, I can see the justice of it, Master Maxie, and the benefit.' He patted me on the shoulder. 'If we are to gain from you, why should you not take a full share in all we have – eh, brother Edward?'

I blinked innocently at Brother Edward. As I had expected, he had enough sense not to protest, in case it brought his own little house of cards tumbling down. He muttered something I chose to take as a blessing, and I rose and bowed to him politely. It didn't seem to cheer him up.

'So be it,' sighed Dee, wagging his head unhappily. 'There are solemn rites of brotherhood, to which we will introduce you this afternoon-tide. But first the ladies must be informed.' He drew a deep breath, as if he wasn't looking forward to something. 'Oh, there you are, my dears! Wonderful news, wonderful, you must hear it at once—'

They'd heard, all right. Mrs Kelley simply beamed and bobbed a curtsey, putting her plump, floury cheek up for a chaste kiss. Jane Dee stood like stone, and her cheek when I kissed it was cold, then flamed suddenly crimson. Her eyes met mine for a second, and they had an extraordinary look in them. Ever seen an animal cornered in a trap?

I haven't; but I've been one.

I knew the imprint of that look from inside the skin, and it goes deep, I can tell you. Anger and pain and humiliation and a wild flailing behind the walls of bone, the kind of panic that might make a fox chew off its own leg to be free.

'Hold, brothers,' I said suddenly, and quickly. 'It seems . . . it seems as if a voice speaks to me. As if—'

I was desperately trying to hedge, kicking myself mentally, telling myself not to be such a bloody fool and get something I wanted for once in this life. God knows I was working hard enough for it. But the words kept on spilling out, and maybe the tension lent some life to them. 'I hear!'

I was tempted to try the fluty voice again, but this would be better coming from me. 'To join the Angelic Brotherhood, yes – to share everything alike, great, OK, it's a wrap. My wife shall be yours, er, just as soon as I have one, that is. But I think I am being allowed to understand the angels' orders better than you did. This whole business of sharing, it's a symbolic union, isn't it? I mean, yes, you haven't been doing anything wrong, it can be – er – consummated without sin, sure.'

'Beyond question!' exclaimed Dee, wonderingly. 'What follows?'

'Well – suppose you *can* – only you *don't*? All the more virtue in not, uh, doing it. See?' Dee was listening with intent wonder. Jane I couldn't look at. 'I mean – because OK, you're allowed to, uh, sleep with your brother's wife, it's OK and moral and permissible and everything. *Well* – doesn't that make it much more virtuous *not* to do it? To just stick to your own wife, like before. Couldn't that be a magically potent sort of act? A moral kickstart?'

Kelley was staring at me, utterly transfixed. Well, that might be a good start. His face looked more like a cheese than ever – one of the smellier breeds. Dee gaped like a fish, and Jane even more so, her cheeks fiery smudges against bloodless white. Even Joan Kelley was nodding thoughtfully to herself.

Then suddenly Dee surged to his feet in a torrent of robe, and his skinny fist crashed on the table. 'O philosopher, philosopher, hast come to this, that a child scarce out of the cradle can so correct you? Nay, brother, I wrong you, you are but a conduit for celestial wisdom, and blessed in it! Brother Edward, Brother Edward, did I not think myself unworthy for my doubts of th'angelic word? And here is all made clear at last! Come, Maxie, truest brother, let me clip you to my heart, for you have lightened it a thousandfold this day!'

'And I!' I dimly heard Jane Dee exclaim, half laughing, half crying. 'And I!' Dimly, because I was being suffocated in great folds of silk and wool, not overly clean.

It was as sincere a hug as I'd ever had from any woman. OK, it reminded me a bit too forcibly of the chance I'd just kicked out the window, but that was some consolation.

So was the look on Brother Edward's face when I turned and said, 'Let's not forget you too, Brother,' and kissed him on both cheeks, General de Gaulle fashion.

I'd remembered you could just about get away with that in Elizabethan times. If I hadn't known he was the controlled type, I'd never have risked it. As it was he seemed to have a slight breathing problem, and the veins in his temples ballooned up beautifully. Always the same, these anal-retentives. With any luck he'd give himself a stroke. Joan Kelley just beamed and turned the other cheek.

And that, folks, is why that afternoon Waxie Maxie was solemnly admitted to the ranks of the Angelic Brotherhood. And felt he deserved it, too, for resisting temptation. Mind you, it was a good thing Jane Dee didn't have wheels.

What took place I can't reveal. Not because of all the solemn oaths I took, but because the ceremony was such an incredible brain-bending, bollock-aching bore. I got some sour amusement out of Kelley, who evidently found it just as bad. He, of course, had dreamed the whole crappy rigmarole up, courtesy of his Angelic web site, to impress Dee. He'd probably never imagined he'd have to sit through it all again. Doing it for me only made matters worse.

Dee never noticed; he was in his element, high as a kite on the sound of his own mellow voice. Much as I liked the old bugger, I could cheerfully have bound and gagged him all over again.

When it was done at last, though, we had a ceremonial feast, and pretty good it was. I suspected Jane Dee had gone to a lot of extra trouble. My plate was never allowed to become empty; my glass neither, and it was wine we were drinking now, a pretty fair dry white with a sort of tongue-prickling tang. The result was that even Kelley cheered up a bit, and we ended singing what Dee called catches and rounds, some of them thoroughly bawdy. At last I staggered up the winding stairs again with Jane Dee lighting my way. The candlelight kept giving little leaps as she hiccupped. I swayed over to the bed in a mellow mood, all last night's nasty moments forgotten, ready for sweet dreams.

Some hope.

I lay back happily enough. They'd swallowed it like babes, all of them. I could make my fortune here. Kiddie-party conjuring – I ought to develop it – make up some props, the double-layered hood, maybe, and the jointed rope, the table drop. Definitely not the sawing-in-half routine, though, or the sword cabinet. They did things like that for real back here. No point giving them ideas . . .

Something jerked me awake instantly, like a cat. A draught bulged the bed-curtains, then hinges squeaked softly and they settled. The latch clicked gently, and the bolt I should have remembered rasped slowly home. I lay frozen, trying to calm my noisy breathing, watching the curtains, expecting them to part suddenly – or would they just sprout a rapier blade?

The temptation to ask, 'Who's there?' was overwhelming, like in the vampire films – and I certainly wished I hadn't thought of *that*. This city looked like a sort of Hammer holiday camp.

More likely Edward Kelley than Christopher Lee, though, and bad enough. Coming to settle accounts, no doubt, and clear the way to the power he wanted. Floorboards creaked, and I wished to hell I knew how to call on it right now. Another creak. Swift, heavy breathing. The curtains twitched, I bunched what was laughingly called my fist and gathered myself to jump for it.

There was a stifled hiccup in the dark.

'?' was about all I could manage.

'*Sss – hic! – ssh!* '

A soft finger touched my lips. 'Hush, hush, good Master Maxie! Wilt betray – *hic*! – me?'

Something like an electrified rodent scuttled up my spine. 'Mrs Dee? N-never—'

The bed creaked gently beside me. A feather of cool breath touched my cheek. 'Say naught, then.

You have been my truest friend, and a younger brother to my poor husband, great as he is in spirit and scholarship, and least, dear soul, in worldly wisdom, where you seem greatest. And much as he pleases me in other wise, he waxes old now and is – *hic*! – little enough to my content!'

'Oh. Sorry.'

She rounded on me. 'But do not think, even so, that anything less than my lord's command would have had me bed with the man Kelley! Man, fie! He's a beast – *hic*! – a very beastly beast, a filthy-handed ape who'll not lave himself but by the quarterday and compels ... compels all manner of gross practices from me! Fie! Me, who has been lady to Her Majesty! A monster. A satyr. And you are my Saint George that has delivered me from him.'

She hiccupped, and sniffled a little. I could smell her. She wore a heavy sort of perfume – oil of roses, probably, with maybe a touch of musk – but it didn't mask her own scent. Definitely she didn't wash enough by modern standards, but it was a healthy, animalistic smell. Her voice went very little-girly. 'A true brother ... and the angels say there's no sin in it with a brother—'

Delicate fingers brushed my bare arm, then seized my hand. 'Thou'st touched my heart already. So, bring it to the board then, and let it drink!' She crushed it to her breast, literally. If they'd had mains then, she could just as well have plugged me in.

One layer of linen nightdress stressed in short order what else wasn't there, and what was. Her breast nuzzled my palm. Shrinking violet I am not, normally; but with her I couldn't move. Her other hand stroked my hair back from my brow, slid down my neck and flattened on my chest. She laughed softly. 'So thin! A true scholar. For sure you've no wife to care for you! Poor Maxie!' Her hand slid downward, closed and rocked. 'Poor Maxie!'

I leaned forward, hypnotised. Her hand moved steadily. A soft blend of wine and flowers blew in my face, and her lips were hot, a little dry, very soft. I couldn't believe it. I really was in another world now. I prised her lips apart with my tongue and chased hers, until she hiccuped and giggled and laid her burning cheek against my shoulder. 'A-ha-ha, no virgin thou, for all thy simplicity!'

Half dreaming, I wrapped my arms around her, and ran my hands up and down her spine, mostly down, ruffling around in that damn nightdress. How could you lose something that important? Then I happened upon it, and she writhed against me, with a soft, exhaling groan.

My oh my, in spades. She had quite a grip, and she wasn't hanging around. I still couldn't quite believe this was happening, or why, or who I was exactly, but by then it was a bit late. She had her legs around my waist, ankles locked, and the bed wobbled and sang a creaky little song as we ground our way down into the feather mattress, grabbing at one another. I did have one moment's misgivings that somebody would hear, but then we were over the jumps and into the final straight, she was giving slow, tearing whimpers in my ear and who else existed anyhow?

The threshing slowed down gradually. Panting, sweaty, face-down and half suffocating with my mouth full of linen and feathers, I found myself wondering if I'd rather be bombing down a long, bare stretch of six-lane blacktop in a Porsche Targa belonging to somebody I didn't like – Ahwaz, say.

Yes, I decided.

But only just.

I rolled aside, feeling the drying sweat and stickiness contracting on my skin, and drew a deep, happy breath. A hand stroked my cheek. 'Ah, good Maxie! Thou'rt a nimble knave, and deft of thy hands.'

'Mmm. You drive me to it. We rushed at it a bit too much, though.'

'Wicked Maxie. What more could we have—'

I demonstrated. 'Oh,' she said, several times, and one thing led to yet another. When the feathers settled on that she was a warm, agreeable weight on my chest, nibbling my ear and hiccupping. I massaged her behind and wished there was some light in here. I seemed to remember they had different ideas about the female figure in the past, but from the brief silhouette I'd glimpsed bouncing against the dim window light, Jane was pretty modern. She ran her tongue around the inside of my ear.

'Maxie, my sweetest dove, my sugar mouse—'

'First time anybody's called me that.'

'Those gross practices—'

'Well, I was just—'

A little while later the covers were on the floor and us halfway after them in a tangled heap. I kissed her between the shoulder blades and manoeuvred myself creakily back up. All good things come to an end, and I felt I was in danger of just that.

She remained leaning on her elbows, and wagged her feet idly in the air. 'Thou hast the right of it, dearest Maxie. Faith, who'd have thought it so different? 'Tis not the practice, but the person.' She sighed dreamily. 'A proper Cleopatra thou'lt make me, riggish without shame—'

I reached out to help her up, but instead she cascaded gently among the tangled covers and swung back up on her knees. 'And thou? How wilt thou think of me henceforth? A faithless wife, a light woman, a street whore to pleasure and pass by!'

I stroked her hair. 'I want to go home. To my own place and time. I can't stay, you can't come. But you I could never forget.'

'You have loved many women, that I know. How should I be different?'

I didn't miss the sudden shift from *thou* to *you*. 'Loved? You must be joking. Don't imagine any of them thought me worth loving, either. With you – yeah, it might have been different. But we can't let it be, can we?'

'No, indeed!' She sounded almost relieved. I might have been insulted, but I understood. 'Tonight we have, and then – not forgetting.'

'I won't forget in a hurry, believe me. I've had the time of my life.'

'I also. But we have hours yet to make more memories.' Her hair tickled my navel.

'What? You have got to be—'

She wasn't.

First light was no greyer than I felt. I am not normally a record-breaker, and I can't claim credit for that night's worth. I looked at Jane, stretched out along the bed humming quietly to herself, with some awe.

Once I'd half-inched a classic Mini Cooper – a demure little package, but the moment you blipped that throttle, mighty forces were unleashed. It nearly had me up a lamppost; and I wasn't much better right now.

I hoped she wouldn't try some of those moves on Dee; at his age he didn't look as if he could stand it. On the other hand, maybe she already had. Maybe he was really my age. By now I was just about his.

She sat up, stretched and ran her fingers idly through her hair. "Tis time. He wakes with cock-crow, oft-times enough. And sin or no, I would have this our secret.'

'Me too. I haven't got that many secrets I like.'

She leaned down over me. 'You weigh yourself short, good my lord. There's more within you than appears.'

I groaned. 'You don't know the half of it. That's what Kelley and your husband want from me. Some kind of ... power they meant for themselves, but gave me by mistake. OK, they can have it, but there's ways and ways, some dangerous for me. Guess which Brother Edward's rooting for?'

She placed a delicate hand on my chest. 'Something precious? Then little enough my lord will see of it, if Kelley has his way. That is a man of evil, and I have cause to know it. He'll preserve the forms of decency thus far only, and then let all masks fall and seize what he will for himself.' She swung herself to her feet, and stooped, with slow grace, to retrieve her nightgown from the feather-strewn floor. She did have beautiful legs. 'I must begone, my Maxie. Angels attend thee in truth, and speed thee happily to thy home.'

I watched her glide out of the door, a momentary silhouette against the thin light, then nothing. Like a vampire, maybe, one of the Ingrid Pitt variety; and leaving me about as thoroughly drained.

The dead hand of exhaustion flattened me back in the bed. Her scent filled the room. So did mattress feathers, and it wasn't surprising. One more bout and I'd have been a dead man, through spontaneous combustion, probably, or just blowing a gasket. As it was, bits of me glowed with friction burn. What I really needed now – yet again – was a good, long, restful sleep with no more interruptions. And of course, the moment I closed my eyes, I was in trouble again.

Half past vision time – time to viz again. My past was back, not so much flashing past my eyes as putting on a leisurely strip-show, with laser effects. The same old run of humiliations, with some new ones I'd actually managed to forget – and then the same icy rewrites, with revenge topping. I curled up in a ball. But I wasn't as shattered as the first time round. Jane had done me a lot of good; I was emotionally drained now, and a touch uplifted too. I could almost feel a bit proud of myself. Whoever was doing this could stuff it. Anyhow, they had to run out of material eventually. Some time . . .

Almost as if somebody heard me, the visions faded. That quickly; and that did unnerve me, because something took their place. Or nothing, rather. Not a sight, not a sound; just a sense of waiting. Like the overlong silence when you pick the phone up, just before the heavy breathing starts. Something was supposed to happen; and it would.

'You have not let me speak,' said a quiet voice in my ear. The room was empty. I twisted feverishly over on my face and wrapped the mangled bolster around my ears. It smelled strongly of Jane. 'You have not given me a chance. Any more than the others.'

Quite, matter-of-fact, reasonable. Baritonal, but slightly female; it might have had a faint accent, like the bandit women, but none of their flamboyance. The pillow didn't stop it at all. I'd no doubt what it must be, though what the 'it' really was I didn't want to imagine. Why was it speaking to me so directly? Something had changed. Its estimate of my intelligence, maybe; or my character.

'What of what *I* want? I want a master. As do we all. Without a master we, for all our power, we have no direction. We have no purpose. We come to you once again. We will be yours, and all the success and power you can command. Do you want to do good with us? You can. Will you leave us in the hands of another who might do worse?'

I relaxed my grip on the pillow. A hell of a promise; a fair point. A pretty clever way of combining seduction and threat. Jane's name hovered unspoken in the air. Those characters wouldn't have to ask Kelley twice; he'd practically take their hands off. Then, with that kind of power, power that burned out of your very hands at the slightest provocation – what would happen to Jane then? And Dee? I caught myself whimpering and plucking at the sheet.

Not pretty clever. Devilishly clever. Demonaic.

'There will be no bargains, no penalties, no barriers lowered, nothing. You have but to command, and we will obey. We will find you, and very soon.'

Booming thunder rolled across the sky. I sat up with a screech, sending the pillow flying, and headed for the underside of the bed again. Avoiding a nasty accident with the pot, used since my last visit, gave me time to realise that I was awake and really hearing the thunder. Also that it wasn't thunder.

It was something booming on the outer door – a pike haft, I guessed, as I got to the window and saw the Imperial guardsman clank into the yard. Dee was hurrying across to meet him, tying up his flapping gown. The armoured man touched his helmet with a piece of paper, and handed it to Dee, who broke the seal with a great show of reverence. He blinked along a line or two, then looking up saw me at the window and waved me down urgently. I arrived still hopping into my shoes.

'From the Lord Chamberlain to His Imperial Majesty!' said Dee anxiously. 'Concerning a submission from the State Police. Their agents report that mysterious foreigners have been espied within the city this past evening. Asking after one of your name and aspect, young sir! Enquiring in all taverns, lodging houses and, ah, low resorts. A man and a woman, says one; or perchance two women. Of most formidable aspect.'

He raised an eyebrow. I swallowed, and shrugged.

'If so, it relates, they are creatures most lawless and dangerous. Attempts to apprehend such a pair were met with – bless my soul! – fierce resistance in arms, and, for the nonce, as it says, their escape. His lordship advises you, Master Maxie, to look well to your own security.' He paused. 'And if you have aught of value to tell which may assist the agents of His Imperial Majesty, to render an account of the same. At once.'

CHAPTER EIGHT

Czech Speed Now

NOW THAT IS the original rude awakening, calculated to send your laundry bills soaring. Just to add to my joys Kelley had heard it all, too. There he was in his nightshirt between me and the stairs, eyes screwed up, voice triumphant.

'You see, sirrah? Spoke I not the truth? As soon cling to a dagger by its tip as to this power ne'er meant for you. And that you can no more hope to wield—'

I brushed past him. He didn't look as if he'd slept much, either. He caught me by the arm, painfully hard, and pulled me aside. He dropped his voice so that Dee couldn't hear.

'Enough of disguise and fooling! You've seen fit to thwart my will in every way since your first coming. And spent this last night ploughing the furrow I cleared for myself! D'you think me a slack fool, to suffer this quietly? D'you dream I'd let you go unchecked, with such a prize in my grasp?' His ham hand shook me at every spitting word. 'A shallow, shiftless cozening guttersnipe like you? You're as far out of your reckoning as your right time!'

'Piss off!' I panted. 'Dee's near enough getting your number!'

He snorted. 'Is he, then? I've had his measure long since, boy, and yours to boot. Can he shield you from these hunters for ever? The power seeks its own way out, as I guessed it would. In this place, in this time, it grows stronger, and you – what are you, you weakling trash from an enfeebled age? Let it overtake you now, and it'll command you, not you it! So, then. You will relinquish it now, without delay, to me for whom it was truly destined, or I'll spill it from your throat!' He laughed softly. 'Or would you rather I let fall a word to these strange seekers?'

'Jesus, d'you think I *want* this going on all the time? Far as I'm concerned you can take it and stuff it up your jacksy!'

He grinned like a dog. 'Spare me your protests, you mewling little kite's turd! You'd have me believe *you* would ever spurn such a cup? As you pretended to with Jane, no doubt! Small chance!'

'I mean it! You've never met these . . . creatures! What makes you think you could handle them any better?'

'Strength, brat. Because I'm strong, and I'm not afraid.'

Dee, padding off back upstairs, saw his two Brothers having a friendly chat and nodded benignly. I opened my mouth, but Kelley expertly tightened his grip. The bones in my arm grated agonisingly. The flesh felt ready to burst like a grape. I gasped with the pain. Still, it saved me from what I'd been about to say. Defying this thug now would be about the stupidest thing I could do.

'All right!' I whimpered, and that was no effort at all. 'I'll do it! I'll do it! Hold the ceremony when you like! I said it's what I want, didn't I—'

His grin broadened. 'Ah, there's reason at last, my bawchuck!' He clenched his grip a little, the bastard, then released it sharply. I fell gasping across the table, clutching my arm. 'Well, well, I too can be accommodating. Dawn is upon us, so we'll wait for twilight, and prepare at leisure. I'll take your word to Brother John.'

'What, no preparations at all? Not even fasting and keeping vigil and all that crap?' I said bitterly, trying to massage the pain away.

He smiled nastily. 'Your night's dancing the shaking of the sheets, and with another man's wife – what braver vigil d'you need? Go, content yourself again for all I care, but make no attempt to leave this house! The servants are in my fee, all, and they will prevent you.'

That I doubted. They were mostly local, he spoke only a few words of German and Czech, and they no more English. They probably wouldn't lift a finger for him; more likely at him, the sod. But I'd only get one chance to find out.

Kelley read my face, and chuckled. 'Aye, and what then? Flee away to your time, brave the turnings of the Wheel alone and unguided? With those hunters in full cry at your back? Know yourself, mannikin, and be wise. I'll spare you a reward still. A hundred such will soon be nothing to me!'

He rolled cheerfully away, beaming at the world.

I glared at his back. Oh yes, I knew his type. From my very expensive school, the liberal kind; from my youth detention centre, the brutal kind. Both the same dog-eat-dog society uncontrolled kids will always create, without even the rub-along restraint of an adult jail; and at the top of both dungheaps the crowing cocks like Kelley, the bullies, the sadists, the manipulators, the psychos. At the top or in the gutter – always at the extremes or headed there. And always violent, or the reason violence is. Some of them grow out of it, some sublimate it; but the real psychos just learn to paper over the cracks. Even without Jane's warning his sudden shift to force wouldn't have been any surprise. But I'd counted on a bit more time. What to do now?

The bastard was right, unfortunately. I'd been a bloody fool to trust Dee and come here in the first place. Even if Dee's precautions worked, those bandits would track down the physical me soon enough. I couldn't persuade Dee to guide me home; I knew I wouldn't be able to convince him about Kelley, not yet. So what could I do? Not just slope off across the Spiral, unguided – I'd all the navigational instinct of a homing slug.

Could I remember some of Dee's landmarks? Maybe, but I'd be a bloody fool to risk it if there was any other choice. No, there had to be. I had one ally in this godforsaken place, and I was going to use her.

'I'll do as you ask, sweet sir, and gladly!' Jane leaned over me to pour me out more eggs, which was pleasant, and kept her voice to a whisper. 'So that no harm comes to my husband, as you promise. For me 'tis a trifle, but for you – 'tis a wise act, but have a care! This is a perilous ford – one single slip and you overset yourself!'

'Tell me about it!' I whispered back. The only reason I'd resort to a stunt like this was that all the alternatives scared me even more – and giving that bastard Kelley what he wanted, most of all.

When he told Dee I'd agreed to go ahead, the old fellow was surprised and concerned. He did his level best to persuade me to wait. But I told him, truthfully enough, that these searchers, wherever they came from, were the absolute last straw; and, very reluctantly, he agreed. 'Though I believe they mean you no ill, they may intend for the good of all to daunt you into agreement. It may be better that you choose of your own free will first. So be it! I shall go about my preparations upon the instant, and this very even we shall set you free. Meanwhile I suggest that you meditate and seek guidance – eh, Brother Edward?'

'Aye, Brother John. In this chamber, I'd counsel,' grinned Kelley. With his triumph in sight his façade was slipping a little, his good nature showing sudden vulpine flashes. He knew my room didn't have a streetward window, so I couldn't even try the knotted-sheets bit.

'Rest and quiet, the very place!' nodded Dee. 'I'll send up bread and ale for your nuncheon.'

'Well thought on!' agreed Kelley, the mask back in place. 'And forget not that you're ever in our thoughts, young sir. We shall be watching over you – upon that you may depend!'

I didn't mind being alone. It gave me a chance to think, to work back through my memories, scribble the odd note to myself on a parchment scrap. Jane had left me what I wanted, and when she appeared with my lunch I began to feel almost confident again – the more so for a quick squeeze or two in passing. Then there was nothing but to lie back and doze and think again; about the sewers, and the alchemist, and Kelley's gold-making machine. No wonder he was in such a hurry. Rudolph would be getting itchier than ever now I'd appeared. Expecting that endless stream of gold potatoes to start any moment . . .

The door opened. Kelley stood there, dark-cloaked, carrying another over his arm. It was surprising to see how grey the window looked all of a sudden. Maybe I'd been asleep, maybe just drifting; but there hadn't been any more visions. As I thought of it, though, I realised there'd been something else, and still was. There was a heavy, windless stillness about the air, like some huge creature holding its breath. Kelley tossed me the cloak. 'I'll have my gown back, sirrah. You'll not need court clothes under this.'

I shrugged. 'Suits me. She was right, you know, you should try washing once in a while. Might help your little problem with women. One more twenty-first-century discovery—' He just grunted, but I was learning to read that impassive face. I draped the cloak over my twenty-first-century raincoat and followed him downstairs. Jane Dee was there, with Mrs Kelley, and our eyes met as we passed. Hers sparkled, and I felt a great cold thrill.

I'd done what I could, and so had she. If it would only work fast enough . . .

Dee gathered me up. 'Have no fear, young Brother mine! I stand for you in this, as in all else now, as steadfast as our Brother Edward. Even though you have chosen the hastier course, you run little risk. The rite is perfected now, the transition shall be brief, the rewards swift – eh? And then back to your own day and age once more, if you so choose. Although I confess we shall be loth to let you go, the ladies and I, eh, my dears?' He sighed. 'Ah, well. To horse, brothers. Mankind's great day opens as this one closes.'

Silently we filed out into the grey afternoon, and mounted up. As the gate creaked open I did my best not to look too expectant. With any luck—

My luck was out. It took long lunch hours. There was only the usual bustle, passers-by who spared us little attention. A small gaggle of geese padded by with ill-tempered honks. I sympathised. If Brother Edward had his way, I was going to get stuffed too.

I noticed he took the lead as the horses clopped slowly out. The slower the better, as far as I was concerned. I cast about urgently in the smoky winter light, but there wasn't any sight or sign of what I was waiting for. I muttered curses; maybe when we got to the gates—

My saddle became one mass of electric icicles. In looking so frantically for one thing I'd forgotten another.

Out of an alley mouth at street's end two tall figures stepped, casting about as obviously as I'd been. Like everyone else they were wrapped in cloaks against the freezing afternoon; but just for a second these brushed against the narrow alley walls, and there was no mistaking the outlines. They were women. But there was no mistaking the self-confident swing of their strides, either; and least of all the long swords at their sides. How many women wore those even in this day and age?

And even as that hit me I saw their cowled heads swing around sharply, simultaneously, towards me, like hawks to a lure.

You can't be a good car-lifter without pretty sharp reflexes and right then my adrenaline glands were on a short fuse. I didn't stop to think. I just leaned right forward in my stirrups, and goosed Kelley's mount with my metal rein-tips, right under the tail.

I was a bit sorry for the poor beast, but the effect was pretty satisfying by any standards. Up shot its heels as I shrank back, up went its hocks. Up even higher went Brother Ed, like Batman on springs, right out of the stirrups, over the ears and headfirst down into a smelly vegetable stall.

By the time he touched base among the brassicas I was out of my own stirrups and sliding down among the crowd scurrying to see what all the fuss was about. Behind me I heard old Dee bleating something about Brother come back. I was a bit sorry for him, too, but no way would I risk it. Plan A hadn't come through in time, and now the searchers had turned up. I had to make a break for it, Dee or no Dee.

And if I ever did get back to my own time I was bloody well going to find somewhere the Spiral couldn't reach and never, never set foot out of it ever again.

Leaving places unobtrusively and at high speed – one of my specialities. Kelley might have trampled the crowd, but I knew Dee wouldn't be able to ride fast through the crush. All I had to do was keep my head down and push my way against the flow, towards the shadow of the castle wall. I wasn't as well hidden as I would have been in a modern crowd, but there were enough taller folk to overshadow me. Away in the background I could hear Kelley's voice swearing blue murder, and somebody equally indignant letting fly in German – the stallkeeper, I guessed. A soggy thud suggested a cabbage connecting with somebody's cranium. A roar from the crowd confirmed it.

I looked back, and swore a bit myself. Dee was making better progress than I'd expected. The proles were obviously well conditioned to get out of a gentleman's way, probably by the judicious application of hoofprints and whips.

I scuttled crabwise along the wall, looking for a doorway or something to duck into. What I found was a heavy postern gate, part of the castle, evidently, and not likely to be unlocked. All I could do was pull my cloak around me and hunker down into the shadows, hoping not to be noticed.

The door creaked open behind me. A white hand caught me by the shoulder and tugged me urgently in. The door thudded softly shut, and I found myself looking into a pair of blazing dark eyes.

'They are looking for you?' the woman demanded, in awkward German.

'Er – yes. Thanks for—'

'You would have led them to me. There are not so many places to hide here.' Not the woman, the girl. Maybe just a teenager, assuming they'd invented such things then. Not at all bad-looking, if you like the dark, strong-featured type, and a bit taller than me. Her face was pale, but even in the gloom she seemed to crackle with vitality. As my eyes adjusted I realised she wasn't overdressed, either – just a short shift of some kind, a nightdress maybe. This sort of thing never happened back home.

'Finished staring?' she snapped. 'A truly grateful gentleman would lend me his cloak!'

'Er—' Automatically I twitched it off and wrapped it around her. She swirled it experimentally, with a satisfied twist of her wide mouth. 'And what do they call you?'

She considered a moment. 'All right! Elina.'

That wasn't a Czech name; it sounded more . . . 'Greek! You're . . . whatsisname, the alchemist! His daughter!'

She sighed. '*Pater hemon*, yes, tell the world. Elina, daughter of Hieronymos Makropoulos, *Iatros*. Orphan, rather.'

'Oh Christ. You mean Rudolph—'

'No. My father tried that muck on himself this time. Only he changed the formula. He shouldn't have. I'm still here.' She sighed, and shrugged. 'Rudolf decided to keep me around, to see whether I show any signs of immortality. I didn't like his ideas for keeping me busy meantime, the evil old

Scheisskerl. So I climbed across a couple of roofs, wriggled through a grille and here I am, waiting for twilight. How do you know all this, anyhow?'

'I think Rudolph may be warming up your father's spot for me. And there's this bastard Kelley trying to set me up.'

She gave that lopsided smile again. 'Oh, him! You're another wizard, then.'

'Wise enough to wish I'd never come here! I'm headed back to my own . . . country.'

'I also.' She cocked her head at me, considering. 'Too bad we can't go together, but you'd be a handicap. You can't pay your way as I can.' She glared at my expression. 'I meant by singing. I'm a very good singer. Thanks for the cloak!'

And as slick as that she whisked herself out the door and was gone. I sprang after her, but stopped. The cloak wouldn't give me that much advantage after dark. Anyway, I wouldn't have just whipped it back off her – and you can bet the little bitch was counting on that. Well, probably I wouldn't. Besides, she was bigger than me.

I eased open the door and peered out. The cold streets bustled much as before. The row had died down, and of Dee and Kelley there was no sign. I belted my coat tight to look as much as possible like the usual tunic, and stepped back out on to the cobbles. Nobody gave me a second glance, except maybe because I wasn't wearing a hat; I solved that by swiping a greasy leather cap from behind a stall. Probably its owner would go off and pinch someone else's, and so on, spreading thefts out across the city like ripples in a pond.

A bad deed goes round the world, and generally ends up socking me in the back of the neck. One more reason I'm not in the insurance business, where the respectable crooks go.

I knew I had to cross town and that damn bridge before it got really dark, and time for curfew. I didn't need any incentive to keep moving. The wind dug into my ribs like a blunt knife, the slimy cobbles froze my feet, and I shook with terror every time somebody came up behind me. Are you or have you ever been a practising paranoid? Why not turn pro – in one easy lesson.

It wasn't that difficult, though. A lot of people had the same idea. The rush-hour isn't a modern invention. I was swept along in a torrent of lower-class types, hurrying back to their hovels, God knows why. A lot of them were streetsellers who'd evidently lingered in search of one last sale, and I managed to pick up a few quick snacks from passing baskets, black bread, sausage-ends and so on – well, it would only have gone bad. Or rather worse, so it served them right. Besides, I nearly bust a tooth on the bread.

From the bridge on it was plain sailing. I took the odd wrong turn, but I had the river to orient myself by, and when I got nearer my destination, the smell as well, which was pretty outstanding even by sixteenth-century standards. No wonder nobody lived here. Yet after my first little excursion I'd greeted it as clean air. That said something about what was down there; and it was waiting for me again. For some unknown reason I hesitated a moment.

Almost one too many. A horse whinnied, and so did old Dee, clambering across the rubble and waving. Of course he hadn't bothered to follow; he'd just gone to the only place I could be going. And so, of course, would Kelley. I swore, and bolted, down into the cracked floor of the cistern, down towards the drain and the dark.

It only occurred to me a moment later, as I slipped and scrambled down the rubble-filled slope, landing heavily on my backside, that Kelley might be in here already. A moment after that, as water splashed around my ankles – at least I hoped it was water – it dawned on me that I didn't have Dee's staff to light the place, either. Nor was there any of that nice convenient luminous lichen they always find in books. Not even any phosphorescent fish-heads, which you might reasonably expect. They probably couldn't stand the competition.

It was blackness complete and absolute. I blundered valiantly for about thirty feet, hit a wall quite hard, and narrowly avoided sitting down in the awfulness below. Somewhere not too far away echoed Dee's distracted wittering, and the darkness bloomed. Not too near me; that was good. Near enough to see by, though; that was better. I skipped lightly off towards what looked like an opening I remembered. But as night closed around me again, and something slithered out from under my feet, I realised there was something else of Dee's I definitely didn't have – his sense of direction.

I was fairly sure there were two channels forking ahead. I was a lot more sure I didn't remember any such thing. And here came the light. I could take the old twit easily enough, snaffle his staff. For some reason I didn't want to. Maybe if I just ducked down the left-hand fork for a few yards . . .

About twenty minutes later, totally disoriented, I went blundering towards the first grey glimmer of light. Dee or no Dee, anything visible looked like a picture of Heaven. But it wasn't Dee, it was something better, a tall shaft with iron rungs set in solid masonry, and a blessed draught of clean air filtering down through a grille. Blue sky, even! All the same, I climbed up warily, and peered up through the bars before heaving them impatiently out of the way. I scrambled frantically up on to – *yes*! – a modern tarred road, cool in morning sunlight. Tall buildings, Victorian stone frontages, flagged pavements, streetlights, white lines – the most beautiful things I'd ever seen. A bike clattered by in the next street, strangely loud. Flowerbeds and fat glossy shrubs glowed through shinning railings that stretched around the corner – Paradise.

I giggled deliriously. This was my own time. Wherever the hell this was, it was home.

After a moment, though, it looked a little less familiar. There were streetcar rails and cables, which we didn't have; but no streetcars. No traffic at all, in sight, and the barest background hum, far less than you'd expect. No pedestrians either; nobody. Well, Sunday morning early, maybe. But the buildings looked odd, and the road signs. All consonants, and enough Zs to give a Scrabble player nightmares—

Sod it, I was still in Prague. Oh well, there were

worse places, even without a passport. At least they wouldn't point out the lack with rubber hoses and battery terminals in sensitive orifices, as they did back in Communist days. I could fake amnesia, plead the headaches or something; sooner or later they'd send me home. Hell, I could tell them the truth. Instant breakdown.

Unless of course . . . *Back* in Communist days . . .

There was just a hint of that coal-smoke in the air. Everything looked just a bit old-fashioned, old-style. No TV aerials. And the road signs weren't Euro-standard . . . I began to whimper a little.

And then there was the most godawful bang.

Another, and the whistle of flying debris that clanged against the railings. And voices screaming, and a loud popping chatter I didn't realise was automatic gunfire, punctuated with deeper pops, like heavier weapons. The air zinged like bees, the shrubbery shook and tore, the flowerbeds disintegrated in sprays of petals. Three men came charging round the corner, men in rough, shabby clothes and caps pulled down over their faces. For an instant I was looking down the barrels of the guns they held, big revolvers and maybe Stenguns, still smoking. I was staring at distorted faces, wide-eyed, snarl-mouthed, unshaven and streaked with sweat and smutches and one great streak of blood. Then they were running past, around the corner, their footsteps clattering into a sidestreet where the rails didn't go.

More footsteps, and suddenly the world was full of gun muzzle again, black and nasty, but not half as bad as the sweat-shining grimace behind it.

Framed in a black steel helmet, it could have modelled for Mr Squarehead 1939. Mind you, it was the twin white zigzag S-runes on the shield badge that really burned in the comic-book icon.

Luckily years of study had programmed in the right reaction. I cowered, screamed and pointed wildly. *'Nein, mir nicht! Dahin, drei Tschechischer mit Pistolen! Dahin!'*

The complete *Untermensch*, that's Maxie.

The SS guard hesitated angrily. I wasn't one of the men he'd been chasing. Worse, I might be a Sudeten German he wasn't allowed to shoot out of hand. Suddenly a black Mercedes roared around the corner, its flanks scorched and dented and spattered with red to match the ragged bonnet pennant, limp arms dangling over the doors. It figured. I could guess who one of them was, now. Other black uniforms came clattering along the pavement.

'He da!' screamed the guard. *'Halten Sie mir dieser! Im Strengarret! Ihr andere, folgen!'* He went pounding off, and I was suddenly submerged in black uniforms and shiny leather overcoats.

'Hey!' said a high, breathy voice. 'Don't *you* get yourself into some real hot shit, huh?'

'Ar! Ever in broils, that's a bold Maxie!'

'But like to suffer de questioning—'

A coiled whip tilted my chin. 'And who can aid you, *señor*, but we?'

I initiated emergency strategy, which was to close my eyes and wail.

When I opened them again the all too familiar faces were crowded even closer round me, cutting off the light with their peaked caps, so close I could have felt their hot breath on my cheeks. Only I didn't. Eyes glittered, teeth shone – closer still, suffocatingly close. The rat had left the sewer, and the hounds were on it.

I never did like blood sports.

'*Cease!*' The voice was high and querulous, but it carried a startling authority. '*Stand back!* Whatever your purpose, this man is but a weak sinner. Why should such as you seek to have your way through fear? I abjure you in brotherly love, stand back!'

And astonishingly, they did – or rather the crush parted like a curtain. There, still in his swirling robes, stood Dee, staff outstretched, lined face anxious but firm. One of the women laughed. Somehow it sounded hollower than before.

I'm not the one to waste a good exit. I heard Dee shout my name, but I was across that road in two leaps. May 27th, 1943, was not a time to hang around most places. Least of all Prague, where the Czech resistance had just sold one Reinhard Heydrich, aka the Blond Beast or the Butcher to his friends, if any, some internal air-conditioning. Triggering off still more butchery, including the whole village of Lidice. That would cast a shadow, if anything would. But how the hell did my little bandit friends fit in? The grating lay open before me; and I damn near jumped.

Splash, splish, splup, unpleasantly back the way I'd come. It had to be – didn't it? There was just that one channel, the flow went the same way, eventually, after about an hour, the floor began to slope up again. All of which didn't explain the inconvenient door I ran into. Maybe I'd just gone past it or something; maybe it hadn't been closed then. Maybe the Pope would have triplets.

Tentatively I tried it. The latch was rusted stiff, creaked like a bastard but it turned. There were no angry shouts from the other side, just faint, peculiar gurgles and there were enough of those back here anyhow. Light seamed the crack. Eagerly I pushed it wider, poked my head around and stared into a long, low vault lined with . . .

Barrels, great fat things gurgling cheerfully in their bellies and letting loose some pretty sewery stinks themselves. I resisted the temptation to just accidentally tap the odd bung, and tiptoed through. They might keep bottles further on.

They didn't; but there were a couple of windows of a sort, narrow, dirty slots at gutter level, their tiny bubble panes barred with iron bars. There were voices out there, what sounded like massed voices singing, harsh and monotonous, and the tramp of feet. Beyond them was a wooden stair and a solid trapdoor, with a bolt I had to coax back. I clambered nervously into light, pretty dim but after sewer and cellar it was blinding. Another long, low vaulted room, empty, this time with tables and bottles and jugs, and all sorts of sausages and things hanging from the rafters by the big fireplace. A tavern of some kind; things were improving. Above the fireplace was some kind of inscription painted on the smoke-stained breast, big German letters – *fraktur* – but all those consonants again. Back in Prague, about the time I'd left, by the look of things. Well, too bad. I'd just

have to start again. At least I could pick up a couple
of candles this time.

I rummaged around as quietly as I could, but all I
could find were small earthenware pot lamps smeared
with puddles of burnt-out suet, maybe, and nothing
to light them with. I sidled to the big door and
listened. It sounded like the open air out there, with
all those voices chanting some kind of hymn or psalm.
I rubbed my hands. Nice, gentle God-fearing types,
always that bit more ready to give you the benefit of
the doubt. I waited till it slackened a bit, then tugged
the door open. A street all right, creaky old Prague-
type rooftops, but fuller than Trafalgar Square at New
Year or Times Square in the convention season. It
looked like a thousand people, mostly on their knees
in the clag, gazing raptly up at some bozo in black
robe and tatty ruffle haranguing them. Others were
just kibitzing, bunches of soldiers hanging about,
scratching under their breastplates, and commanders
on horseback under bright banners, looking bored.
Come to that, a lot of the worshippers were carrying
weapons, and some of them lethal-looking flails and
scythes that made me think of Willum. A young
fellow, leaning against the wall watching, turned to
me in surprise. I smiled sickeningly and switched on
the German again.

'*Entschuldigen Sie mir, bitte, aber haben Sie—*'

I didn't expect the killing glare I got. '*Nemecku?
Jsi speher Zikmundov?*' Hands came from everywhere, hauled me bodily out, and this time I was
looking down a dagger blade. The conventicle or
whatever it was ran down, and just about everybody and his wife came pressing in around me,

pointing and muttering darkly, '*Speher! Speher!* '

Of course, you can't rely on the way words sound between languages. Ask any Frenchman confronted with the word 'con-trick', or any Anglo with the German road signs *Einfahrt* and *Ausfahrt*. Or anyone who heard the howl that went up when they paged some poor Austrian at the airport – 'Will Herr Prick please go to Gate 26?' There're some words that do sound a lot alike, though. Like for example *speher – espion – spione*. Spy.

'*Hej*!' screamed the young twerp. '*Hejtmany! Speher Zikmundov, uz je to jiste!* '

The crowd all started shouting, then fell back as orders were bellowed and a knot of soldiers came through, pushing them back with their pike staves. Plated leather gauntlets clamped round my arms and hauled me roughly along. A hard-faced bunch, with great greasy beards like moulting yaks; unlikely they'd be the charitable type. Soldiers meant questions, and questions, since they hadn't discovered electricity or rubber hoses yet, meant toenails, or teeth. Or worse. And I didn't even know who the hell Zigmund was.

They dragged me off through the jeering crowd. I was shouting, '*Kein Spione! Bin Englander!* ' but I suspected England didn't actually show up much on their mental horizons. We were heading for the guys on horseback. OK, maybe the officers might be better educated. I tore myself free, which wasn't too hard since the guard was about to throw me, anyhow, and threw myself on my knees before the tallest horse, a massive carthorse sort of thing.

'Mercy, my lord! I'm no spy, but a man of

honour! Strayed far from his homeland—'

'Well, at least you get one out of two right, huh, Maxie?'

I stared in horror at the ferocious grin that glittered down at me. That bloody Oriental type fitted in here about as well as a branch of McDonald's, but nobody else seemed to notice, least of all the louts who'd grabbed me. They didn't even blink when another mount swung around, and there in cap-a-pie sardine suit was the other woman, dark curls crammed untidily in around the visor. 'You are not strayed, *signor*! Nor are you in any danger, if only you will throw in your lot with us. Where we are, you are lord and master, if you will only have us—'

A pike prodded me in the ribs. 'Why you kneel in de dirt? You like it?' I really did gape then. There in the armour of the noncom type who'd nabbed me stood the Dutch thug or whatever he was. Only a second ago it had been somebody else's face sticking out. 'Get you nowhere fast. Dey fight a war here, holy war, any minute. Dere's no time for tittle-tat trial stuff – if you lucky, they just string you up, if not – well, shit, you bedder pray we here to help, Maxie!' I tried to jump up, and another pike caught me below the breastbone. The crowd screamed encouragement. From the next helmet along leered the Robert Newton clone.

'If 'tweren't us here you'd be spitted by now, lad! An' you may yet be, twixt one heartbeat and the next!'

A holy war? I remembered reading about some of those round here, religion and nationalism mixed. It was the Middle East of its day, with some types called Hussites bashing and being bashed, the odd burning at the stake, that kind of thing. I could see how that would cast shadows in the Spiral. The crowd was a growling animal at my back. Maybe this was something that really had happened, some poor sod speaking German out of turn and getting lynched for it. These bandits, they'd injected themselves into the situation somehow, taking over whatever roles they needed. The moment they pulled back, the faces would change, the drama would play itself on out. All over me.

'What – what d'you want me to do?'

The hard-faced woman smiled very slowly. Her teeth looked long and sharp. 'Anything that comes to mind, Maxie. Just like on the phone. One thought, and you could clean this whole shitheap up!'

Somehow her voice didn't sound quite the same, as if there was an echo to it, and less accent. I blinked, bewildered. This mob howling for my blood – I could bring fire and thunderbolts down on their heads. But did I want to? Maybe they had troubles enough. I could imagine Londoners in the Blitz acting a bit like that, if they thought they'd found a spy, or Brits in Napoleon's time. All I had to do was think – that was the problem. I was fighting *not* to think. Ever tried that?

The flowers will turn to gold at sunset, but *only* if you don't think of a blue monkey.

'Oh, shit,' I wailed, trying not to suit the action to the word. Thought's not just free, it's about as hard to restrain as a cat in a dog pound. I was scared stiff, I wanted out, and any moment I was going to burn my way clear, I couldn't help it. Burn through hundreds of people—

They were all there now, even the other woman and the black guy, and he really did stick out. The locals didn't seem to notice any of them. Their smiles were as cold as their armour, and they didn't look that persuasive now.

The high voice echoed over the spitting buzz of the onlookers. '*Vzhuru! Vzhuru! Krizaci prebodili Vltava!*' and then, in German, 'Arise! The crusaders have crossed the Danube!'

There was a sudden blaring trumpet, and then everything swirled into motion. If somebody had pulled a plug that square couldn't have emptied faster. There was a massed furious roar, and the whole huge crowd surged away in a sort of human riptide, brandishing their weapons, with even the dogs barking at their heels. They forgot about me, but the brigands, in their armour, didn't stand a chance. They were swept up and away in the flow of brotherhood, visible only for a second and then submerged. Voices died away, shouting, singing something harsh and thudding. There were just two figures left in that square, myself, and, at the inn door, Dr Dee.

'History carries them away,' he said, a little sadly, coming towards me. I backed off. 'They go to rout the knights of the Holy Roman Emperor Sigismund, in the name of their prophet Jan Hus. They will. For a brief while.'

I nodded. In his day Rudolph was back in the saddle. So much for revolutions. 'History's carrying me away, too. Thanks for bailing me out, but I

just want to get away. These creatures, these bandits—'

He looked troubled. 'There is something amiss,
clearly. But if you would only stand and seek
explanation—'

'Explanation? D'you know what they almost
made me *do*?'

'Perhaps they are but testing you – given your,
ah, propensities—'

'Balls! Who thought up that one – Brother
Edward? Yeah, thought so!'

'If you will but swallow your distrust of him—'

'After what you've been swallowing— *Look out!
They're coming back!* '

He swallowed that one too. I was past him and
through the inn door while he was still casting
about, and slamming the great bar across it. I heard
him beating on it and bleating feebly, while I
rummaged frantically for a light. Luckily some
provident type had heaped the fireplace ashes for
rekindling, and there were some sticks still glowing. I could hear Dee's muffled pleas as I ducked
back down through the trap, carefully shielding the
stinking little lamp in my cupped hand.

'Brother Maxie! Shall you open this door or
must I grow sinfully wrathful?'

I smiled, imagining an enraged sheep. Then there
was a fearful bang, and I ducked down just in time
as something whizzed by over my head and
crashed against the wall. It was the door, bar, hinges
and all. I scuttled down the ladder, ignoring the
bolt. No point in having that door come after me as
well. I remembered too late about charging rams;

and Dee was certainly wearing horns. I'd have to be a bit more careful in future.

The sewer scent – Canal No.5 – got up and hit me as I reached the door, but I steeled myself. At least I had some light now; without that I'd just been led, that was obvious, into suitably dangerous situations. Now I'd lead myself. Even if I could only make Vienna in 1946, that'd be something; if there was room for Harry Lime, there ought to be an opening for me. The Spiral wasn't going to get me this time!

Well, maybe it wasn't. All I could do was flounder down one stinking tunnel after another, so turned around no memory would have got me out. The lamp was a comfort of sorts, though it kept sputtering and popping as it ignited little wisps of mephitic gas. And all it actually showed me was how much one lot of dodgy masonry looks like another, especially caked solid with nitre, lichen and worse. Now I could see what was flowing down the centre of the channel, too, I spent a lot of the time walking in a sort of wide-legged Chaplin waddle astride it, in case it ate my shoes.

I had to admit I was getting nowhere, and not even that fast. Until, that was, I came across a tunnel mouth that looked like all the rest – except that its crumbling rim had been supported with a frame of new-looking steel, enamelled black and bolted together. Nuts and bolts and enamel – industrial products, so whatever was up there ought to be reasonably modern. OK, it might be the Nazis again, but this time I'd watch out.

It wasn't long before I found more modern

metalwork, a proper ladder leading up to a very
ordinary-looking manhole cover. Leaving the lamp
on a ledge, I prodded the cover up gingerly – just in
case it was in the middle of an intersection with the
lights about to change, you understand. It wasn't.
It was concreted into cobbles, and it was about the
only thing modern in a rickety little switchback of
a street. It could have been the one outside the
cistern – except that it was dark overhead, and there
were nice bright streetlamps. The coal smell was
stronger, too. Late evening, it felt like, with rain in
the air. I could just make out the outline of the
Hradcany Palace against the clouds, looking much
the same as in Rudolph's day. Bright coloured posters spattered a billboard just above me. Now that
looked modern enough.

Nervously I scrambled out and peered around.
Nobody in sight; no cars, either, but I could hear
one or two in the distance. I slunk over to peer at
the posters. They were mostly a sort of Art Deco,
very nice. Thirties revival – or just Thirties? Sod it,
you couldn't tell. Not even from the products –
Pilsener beer, cigarettes, an opera poster with a
dishy-looking brunette in pseudo-Chinese rig,
Emilia Marty na 'Turandot'. Bet the *prima donna*
didn't really look like that – though I seemed to
recognise this one from somewhere. Ah well, this
wasn't getting us anywhere. Wherever I was, I
needed information, and food, and maybe a
flashlight or two. There were some promising-
looking windows nearby, so I tippytoed over to the
nearest and had a good peer around. Aren't historic
buildings nice? So hard to fit proper locks, let alone

real alarms. No sign of either here—

A hand jerked my collar, violently. I was probably immune to heart attacks by now, but I did my best. A voice hissed in my ear.

Czech again. I nearly garrotted myself trying to shake my head. The voice switched to German. '*Was machen Sie da, Putz?*'

'Nothing!' I gurgled, or tried to. 'Just – looking—'

'*O ja!*' agreed the voice sarcastically. 'I'll bet! And up out of a manhole, too. Come on, I know your kind of looking!' He sounded young and cocky and cool. I twisted around, protesting feebly. That was what he was, all right – younger than me, maybe, but a lot taller and stronger, a lanky guy with a lean, intelligent face and intense, deepset eyes. Jewish, at a guess; he looked a lot like a lawyer I ran into once. Bent his BMW, in fact. And he didn't look any easier to fool.

That wasn't my only problem, either, at least unless some kind of retro fashion had hit Prague. Oiled hair, wing collar, string tie, short bumfreezer jacket – late Twenties, early Thirties, maybe. He was looking at my clothes just as curiously. 'So that's what burglars're wearing these days, is it? Well, I suppose it's you little cockroaches that keep me in business – insurance, you know – but … *Hej! Polizei her! Polizei!*'

From somewhere maybe a street or two away came an answering shout, and the blast of a whistle. I hate insurance people. And I hate roaches, and people who call cop. 'You've got a bloody nerve!' I snarled. 'Insurance? You're the biggest bunch of cons unhung! Me a sodding cockroach? *What about you?* '

There was a sort of nasty raspberry noise, and the streetlamps dimmed. Some other light flooded the street, a red meteoric flash that passed and left me tingling. Suddenly there wasn't a hand on my collar any more. I looked down and let out a wail, but it got wedged in my throat. I hate roaches, and never more than the six-foot stinking monster that sprawled at my feet, waving its little legs in the air. I shrank back against the streetlamp, ready to climb it, hardly hearing the running feet on the cobbles.

A hard hand with heavy uniform cuffs thumped down on my shoulder in the classic gesture.

The skin was black. 'Now *that*,' said a high-pitched voice in the darkness, 'is what I call neat, baby!'

The uniform was greenish in the streetlights, semi-military, slightly old-fashioned – a bit comic opera, except for the huge revolver at his side.

'Hey, *si*!' agreed another voice from the darkness, just as familiar. 'He surely learns, *no*?'

'Boy, I bet dat was fun! Whatta say, Maxie? You like, huh?'

Out of the shadows they came one by one, grinning. All in the same uniform. I didn't know it, but I didn't need to. A cop uniform anywhere makes me itch. Only there sure as hell weren't cops in these ones.

'What the fuck are you on about?' I gibbered. 'Christ, I didn't do that! I don't know how, I just— You did it! *You!* '

Dark eyes sparkled, but so does broken glass.

'Then, *caro mio signor*, surely we could remedy it, and none other. Yet you can, and shall if you but wish. If you do not, then we will not, either.'

''S'easy,' giggled the black guy. 'All yo' gotta do is—'

I was already stretching out my hand over the feeble kicking thing, struggling hard to keep my stomach down.

Not a thing. A man, there was a man in there. A man—

No denying it this time. I felt myself do it, as if my fingertips burst open and spurted blood. Light burned beneath my skin, blazed out red at the joints. Every bone in my wrist glowed like coals in a fire. Furnaces blazed up through my fingernails and spilled out on to the cobbles. Another sickly, slimy rasp, and a man grovelled on the cobbles, waving his long arms helplessly.

He rolled over, gaped at me in blank horror, then at the ring of bandits in their uniforms, laughing hilariously. He hunched himself awkwardly to his feet, half cringing back as I tried to help him, and stood shakily. Then he let out a sort of thin, pressured shriek, like escaping steam, burst through the ring and ran wildly off, headlong down the road, skidding on cobbles, hitting walls, limbs flailing in crazy efforts not to fall, as if nothing could be more important.

I found myself wondering vaguely what being a cockroach felt like. Then I stopped myself hastily. Too many thoughts were happening round here as it was.

Oh well, he'd work it out somehow, I told

myself. In fact I had this feeling I remembered – but I'd got troubles enough of my own. They were still laughing at me.

'Big fun, huh? Big yocks! An' you can do that any time you like!'

'Dat or anyt'ing!'

'Scatter yer foes, win yer friends, sweep aside all as stands in yer path!'

The women whooped suddenly. 'Oh! See! Here's one you would be free of, would you not?'

'A millstone! An ass!'

'No, an ox with horns!' She made the two-handed Latin gesture. 'Make an ox of this one, *señor* !'

The men laughed raucously and they stepped aside with mocking bows to show me Dee, skullcap askew, clambering laboriously out of the manhole. He blinked around at them, astonished. I didn't blame him. They were sounding less and less like angels. And if they were false, then what else might be? But I could guess he wasn't ready to face that, not yet – maybe never.

And meanwhile he'd go on doing Kelley's work for him, till it was just too late. Innocent he might be, but he was deadly dangerous. And for the first time I had a way to deal with dangers. And if he disappeared, and Kelley, there was Jane Dee . . .

I raised my hands, palm out, and felt the light boil down my arms. Dee's jaw dropped as a corona of fire leaped between them.

'If I can do something like that,' I grated, 'then I can send you bastards hopping first!' I swung round at the bandits, expecting some kind of counterblast.

But the light blazed again in a shimmering film, like an iridescent soap bubble mirroring a fire, and they stepped back from me, one step, two. I gasped with relief and excitement, and poured out more power. Their green uniforms shone suddenly luminous, tingeing their faces with the colour. It grew into a misty, muddy green glow, and they threw their arms wide as if enjoying a shower.

The dark women giggled. 'Play with it as you will, *caro mio Maxie!* You do but return to us what is ours!'

'What is ourselves! What can be you! What cannot hurt us!'

The moustachioed man nodded. 'Feels good, huh, Maxie? Go on – use it, enjoy it, get the feel of it!'

'Get to like it!'

'And when ye be a-ready, my lad—'

'*We'll be there!*'

For a minute the red glow and the green seemed to meet and merge like whirling oil films, then blackness bulged up through them. The shadows were drained of presence. They'd buggered off.

I felt – I didn't know what. Uncomfortable. Itchy. Weak. For a minute there I'd been eight feet tall – no, twenty. And untouchable. God, it *was* just like dope, the best, the purest. And now the rush had set in. Only dope's never much use for making you really do anything; you just think you're doing it. That makes keeping off the stuff a lot easier, for me. A freaked-out hijack driver's a self-solving problem. But this was something else. Frightening when I couldn't control it – but maybe now I was learning . . .

I hadn't needed Dee, this time, anyhow. There he stood, alone under the streetlamps, weirdly out of place against the made-up face looking down on him. And he was between me and the manhole.

'Shift, Doc,' I said. 'I don't want to hurt you.'

'Why must you forever flee me?' the old man demanded. He looked anxious but stern. 'Ever and again you have agreed to let us assist you, and we mean you naught but good!'

'Oh yeah. *You* mean, you mean! But who's asking you?'

He stepped back, affronted. 'I know not what you say! But if you will not confide in me, at least respect the angelic forces that also pursue you! The hounds of Heaven in quest of a human soul!'

'Hounds, yes! But Heaven's?'

He blinked. 'But whose else?'

'You tell me. Or go ask Brother Edward. If he isn't half breaking somebody's arm, the way he got me to agree to the ceremony. Ask him why the power they give me just let me turn a man into something horrible. Ask him why they stood around and laughed!'

'Laughed? I find that hard to credit.'

I sighed. 'Yes, you do, don't you? And that's why I'm not sticking around with you. So stop tailing me, or . . .' I raised my hands, and the red glare grew in them. It danced on the old man's beard, but he didn't move a step. Breathing hard, I forced them down again. I *really* didn't like this. 'See that? That's the angelic power. That's what Brother Edward wants to pick up at this ceremony. It scares me, it really fucking scares me. But what scares me most is the feeling that *he'd* be right at home— Are you going to move?'

He just stood there, obstinately. I took a step towards him, ready to rush. He stood fast, lifted his staff slightly. Fear and anger bubbled up together. Red and green sparks crackled at my fingertips. Enough of this shit! I'd never need to run from anyone, ever again.

That's what I did, though. The last Derby favourite should have left the tape that fast. I liked the old bugger, couldn't help it, angry or not; and one giant cockroach was enough for one night, and more. Better just to find another manhole cover.

Only there didn't seem to be any. Not one. Maybe I was just looking down the wrong streets, or maybe there was something more to it. I wandered around those winding little streets for what felt like hours, trying to orient myself by the shadow of the castle. Then drizzle came on and I lost that, too. There were plenty of people about, some of them spoke German, but you try to ask your way after you've been strolling around in the sewers for a few hours. Everywhere I showed up, conversations faltered, folk suddenly crossed the street and back again, when I did too.

It made me almost glad of the rain. When I found myself back at the river, I felt like taking a swim; I couldn't have been much wetter. There was another bridge here, and across on the far bank a huge ritzy building, brightly lit and hung about with those gaudy posters, with folk in penguin suits and long dresses streaming out into waiting limos and horse-drawn carriages. Old World elegance, before the

First World War blew it away; and I could have modelled for the other side of that particular coin. I felt fit for the gutter; hell, I felt *like* the gutter, with water coming down my neck and out my trouser leg.

Then a deeper chill took the same route in reverse, and it wasn't the water. I started across the bridge, staring, ignoring the hurrying figures with umbrellas who swerved suddenly out of my way. The same posters, the same face staring out of them; and behind the Art Deco convention and the pseudo-Chinese make-up, I knew it only too well.

There was a stage door round the side, surrounded by a whole load of exquisites with wilted flowers. When I pushed through them, though, they stepped aside with silent respect, brushing hastily at their tailcoats. Inside the door was guarded by the usual crusty old oaf behind a little window, who leaned out with moustache bristling, then jerked back hastily as I grinned at him, and hit his head. By the time he got out I was past him and scuttling down the backstage corridors. What I was after should be easy to find, made to be. It was. It was all the red velvet around the door, and the neat little name card. *Mme Marty*.

I went straight in, without knocking. There was a squeak of horror as a startled maid sprang up; but it wasn't her I was looking at. 'You owe me a cloak,' I said.

She stood up, slowly. She was wearing about the same as when I last saw her, or maybe less. But it was a lot fancier, all silk and lace and *La Vie Parisienne*; and she was used to being looked at that way, you could tell. But outwardly, at least, she hadn't changed. Not one bit.

'Do I know you?' she demanded. The maid was staring in terror, with her handkerchief to her nose. She must have thought I was some kind of maniac.

'You said you sang well, Elina. Got to admit, you had it right.'

'My name is Em . . .' She stopped, and stared, and nodded, quite calmly. 'So, wizard. You too?'

'No. I came by a different route. We met just this morning.'

She nodded at that, too. Completely cold, completely unsurprised. 'The cloak was useful – *shut up that whimpering, girl!* So what do you want? Blackmail? You're welcome to see who would believe you.'

'No. Just help. Nothing very much.' She shrugged, and reached for her purse on the dressing table. 'Not money,' I said.

'Well, what then? I am expecting a gentleman caller soon.'

'I want—' I paused. What would they have, in these times? 'I want a change of clothes, dry ones, decent ones. I want a pair of rubber boots, and some kind of lantern or flashlight. I want some food, something I can carry. And I suppose this theatre's got some sort of connections to the sewer systems. I want to know where those are.'

She let out a sudden raucous laugh – pure Melina Mercouri, very Greek. I got the idea it wasn't something she did very often. Her face was smooth and unlined, except for little dimples of bad temper

flanking her mouth. '*Christos Soter!* Well, each to
their own. Marie – *Marie*! Telephone down to
wardrobe for a good suit and overcoat to fit this . . .
gentleman. Something practical, a hunting outfit,
perhaps? Very good. And to the bar for some sandwiches. Then ask Josef to bring up boots, not too
large, and a lantern, at once. And tell the Baron he
must wait. And before you go – open a window.
Well, wizard?'

'Very well, El . . . Emilia.' She shrugged again,
sprawled inelegantly on a couch, lit up a long black
cigarette and exhaled the smoke around her face.
In that graceless pose she exposed about as much
as the peepshow girls, and clearly cared even less.
She didn't seem to have any more questions. She
adapted fast; but then I guessed she'd had plenty of
practice.

I felt weirdly alone. It was like sharing a room
with a Martian.

'Well, Emilia,' I said conversationally, 'how's it
feel to have been – what? fifteen? – for three hundred years?'

And I wished I hadn't asked, because she told
me, all in the same quietly unemotional tone. Just
as well the maid came back when she did, with
Moustache Josef in tow. I might have been ready to
leap out of the window otherwise, into the river.

Josef bristled when he saw me. Evidently he'd
have quite cheerfully built a flight of steps for the
sheer pleasure of throwing me down them. But he
took his orders from Elina/Emilia without so much
as a word, evidently as enthralled by her icy magnetism as the maid. It was beginning to get to me,

too. It was almost purely sexual, but refined to a point as sharp and cold as a needle. You had the idea she'd do almost anything, and do it superbly, and with the same vast indifference as anything else. If she could project that off a stage, no wonder she was so big around here.

She watched while I changed, with the unblinking interest of a crocodile, but said nothing – not until I was tying an extraordinary string tie. Then she said suddenly, 'I gave one or two people the formula. Most did not survive it. Do you want it?'

That really made me hesitate. Even if I didn't want it myself . . . If she still had the recipe for that stuff, we could clean up the health-store business, for a start. They'd go nuts.

But five minutes of listening to her had had its effect. And there'd be all those lawsuits for the ones that didn't survive. 'N . . . no. No thanks!'

'As you please. A friend has it for now, anyway. Or rather his heirs. Are you ready now?'

I surveyed myself in her mirrors. Loden coat and leather plus fours, tucked into stiff rubber-coated riding boots, a trace large. 'Fine. Thanks, Emilia.'

'Hardly worth it. Josef will see you out. But before you go—'

I heard a new note in her voice, almost like interest. 'Yes?'

'You are from a time to come, it seems. Am I still famous, then?'

'In opera? You could be, for all I know. Not my thing. But I'll look out for you, if I ever get back. Maybe come and see you.'

She shrugged. 'Of course. Come by a different route, though.'

'OK, OK. And thanks.'

That was as emotional as the leavetaking got. It was almost a relief to encounter the warm human hatred of Josef, as he took me down endless stairs into the bowels of the building. No vacancies for phantoms here; this was quite a new building, and very well planned. Josef was absolutely fanatical about every detail; clearly he thought he owned it, as these college-porter types commonly do. And he turned out to be a positive enthusiast about the sewers, and warmed to my evident interest.

'Yes, yes, we've had them here since the house was built, in 1881 – it burned down before opening, you know, and we rebuilt it! The sewers, yes – we were the first in this quarter to get them, though they're extending them out to the east of the New Town, where I live.' He puffed out his beard. 'Eventually. In about fifty years, maybe. Or a hundred!'

'Sounds about right – can you show me which way the latest stuff is? Out that way and along?'

I congratulated myself on the idea, as I plished and ploshed along, turning my nice new electric lamp at the ceiling to avoid seeing what squished underfoot. I'd let myself be thrown by the Spiral, but now I was determined to sort this crap out logically. I'd go and find the latest, the very latest stretch of sewer open today; and then look for a still newer extension. One, you see, that wasn't built today; and so that would be bound to come up a lot nearer my time. And, strange as it may seem, that's exactly what I found. It was newish brickwork, leading off from about where Josef said the sewers ended; and it had arrows and numbers painted on the walls, and – *yes*! – great chunky masses of cables sprouting out of the walls here and there, as one system crossed another. If I didn't go grabbing at the first spot of light, but took this as far as it went – and surfaced very, very carefully . . .

I was so delighted I took one incautious step. What I stood on you don't want to know, but one foot skidded sharply out from under me on the newer, slimier surface. I staggered, waved my arms wildly, desperate not to lose my footing and fall – anything but fall. In those stiff boots it wasn't easy. I suppose it must have looked like one of the wilder folk dances – the Sewerman's Reel, the Shitkickers, or whatever.

And just as I caught my balance the lamp flew out of my fingers, clanked off the ceiling and bounced down into the centre of that awful channel, which swallowed it greedily. There was an instant's yellowish glow under the scummy surface, and then it went out. I could swear the damn stuff burped.

Darkness descended. I said a word, very loudly. Down there it could have been a comment, a definition, an invocation even or just a sort of general description. As a swearword it didn't seem anything like adequate.

In fact, I was stuck for one that did; so I had to calm down and do a bit of thinking instead. No way was I going to go delving around after the lamp. Even if it wasn't broken, it had probably begun to corrode already – or been digested.

Just creeping forward, though, seemed harder than ever. OK, I'd seen which way I was going – or thought I did. I'd been had that way before. But what choice was there? I couldn't just—

Couldn't I, though?

I looked down at where I thought my fingernails ought to be. They weren't; but a few inches over a sort of feeble firefly glimmer registered against nothingness. I thought of Kelley, and suddenly ten ghostly fingers were outlined in writhing fire. It looked spooky as hell, but I concentrated and the glow grew. Slowly the tunnel outlined itself around me, in starker shadows than before, looking like an antechamber of hell. Only – was that the same entrance, or had I got turned around somehow in all that folk dancing?

Even as the thought formed, the light swelled and swept forward, picking out the painted numbers I'd seen, and the cable trunking. Wild. Was it showing me the right way? Could it show me the way out, to my own time, or something like it?

A fat spark sizzled in the air. Light speared down the sewer tunnels, stabbing at the distant roof. Somewhere down there? Well, where else had I to go? I plodded on, more carefully now. The bias of the light stayed the same. Excitedly I pressed on, and on. An outflow opened, but the light seemed to avoid it, still pointing further ahead. Well, why not? All I needed now was Tinkerbell.

Hastily I cancelled *that*, and hurried on. If wishes were horses, beggars would have a hell of a feed bill.

It didn't seem to be any time at all before the light positively played on something ahead, a yellow steel-caged ladder, with all sorts of little safety symbols all over it – hard hats, protective clothing, that kind of thing, just so you didn't come down here in a ball gown and tiara. Signs of the times, if ever I saw them.

I splashed forward excitedly. Even that God-awful vomit yellow looked so fresh and cheerful after the basic brown décor down here, with snot-green embellishments. I had to fight down an urge to hug it and burst into tears. Instead I climbed, swiftly, feeling as if long, stinking years of history were trickling off my boots. At the top there was a heavy steel trap, very modern-looking. And locked, but that couldn't stop me now. A needle of fire spat from one fingernail and the lock dropped away into the depths with a long, nasty splish. Still cautious, though, I levered the trap up gently, and saw paving stones, a big glass shop window full of books. Slowly, savouring the moment, I tipped the trap back with a clang and clambered stiffly out.

Mild airs blew around me, and probably regretted it. A wide, quiet street under the gentle blanket of a spring evening, a tree-lined boulevard with brightly painted bus shelters, power lines, TV aerials, a couple of parked cars, the odd hoarding—

Still Prague, evidently. The book titles looked like alphabet soup. I didn't mind that anymore. This would do. This would do nicely, thank you.

Now to find the cops, and the British Consulate. I had bashed my head enough times to raise a few lumps, and I probably smelt like the vultures' cage at the zoo. Clearly I was a respectable British tourist who'd been robbed, beaten and thrown down a sewer, was understandably a bit confused, and needed to be flown home and tucked up in a nice hospital with hot and cold running nurses.

I took a deep breath. And then all I had to do was get as far as possible from the Spiral, and never, ever even dream of using that power again . . .

Only I'd used it to get here, hadn't I? Oops. But only briefly. I'd already known roughly where I was going. They couldn't have led me here—

Where was everyone?

There was a godawful rumble, a bellowing snarl that echoed between the high buildings. I know how engines sound, but this one was new, sounding like a kingsize bulldozer over-revving, with a blatting exhaust note. Only bulldozers don't generally come with shouts and screams attached.

It was like a monster movie the way the crowd came around the corner, running and looking back at the same time. But what came after them wasn't a giant tarantula or the Beast from 20,000 Fathoms, it was a huge dirty green tank.

It roared like a Beast, though, and its treads tore up the tarmac. One of them went over a parked car as it turned and flattened it into a sardine tin in one instant of screaming metal and popping glass. It glanced against a fine tall tree and the trunk bent and snapped explosively. A couple of stragglers stopped to shout and wave their fists. Its machine-gun hammered the tarmac into a spray, and they ran wildly on.

The crowd whirled past me like a shoal before a

shark, some of them plucking at my sleeve and shouting at me to run – you didn't need to know the word. I just stood there with my face hanging out, full of a sort of dazed unreality. Then I saw the tank's turret, with its big red star, swivel, the huge gun barrel bounce and sway in my general direction. That was enough. I turned and bolted with the rest.

Behind me there was one thunderous bang, an instant's whirring whistle and the bus shelter ahead erupted in a flare of light. A great warm breath smacked me up and stung me with fragments and smashed me on to the ground. Trees and sky flew by as I rolled, stunned, among a pattering rain of hot fragments. I came to rest, winded and helpless, my ears ringing, unable to move. The only thing in my mind was jumbled relief I hadn't been closer. I could see a couple who had, one a youngish-looking woman, not that I could see her face; they sprawled on the street ahead, unmoving, among spreading spatters of darkness. Bitter smoke drifted across the road.

Behind me the roaring grew louder. Wheezing, stunned, I struggled to suck in air, to force numbed limbs to obey me. Maybe I'd been torn open too, and just couldn't feel it for shock. All I could manage was to flail myself over on my side, kicking feebly, and that didn't help a bit. The grey-green bulk seemed to fill the world, creaking, grinding, its still smoking cannon rearing upward as if to shatter the sky and drop it on me. Less than a hundred yards away, the great metal links whirring down over the wheels to bite and scar the very road that carried them, coming straight for me. Panic let me feel them chew at my skin, feel the appalling weight press down my chest and grow and press and press while the whirling metal ripped my ribs apart—

With my first full breath I screamed. And the tracks slowed suddenly, and stopped, maybe four feet from my face.

I fought to get up, at least to drag myself aside. I managed to struggle up on my arms, then slump back. No good. Above me somewhere I heard the clang of a turret, the clatter of boots on metal.

'So what do we have here?' enquired a guttural voice. 'Another enemy of the people, no doubt.'

'Look at his extravagant clothes,' said another, female. 'An agent of imperialism, sent to delude the people into opposition to the lawful forces of the mutual self-defence agreement.'

Otherwise known as the Warsaw Pact, I reflected dizzily. I'd really picked it this time. Prague, 1968 – still more than ten years before I was born, when Russian and East German tanks smashed even the first faint smile off the Eastern Bloc's face. Their pretext had been rooting out Western agents and counter-revolutionaries. Which meant I'd come as a gift. The moment they found I was a Brit they'd start warming up the rubber hoses and crocodile clips in earnest.

'He might perhaps be persuaded to join the people's cause, nevertheless,' said another voice. My ears were clearing, and my head. I almost recognised it. And did even East Germans ever really talk like that, outside the agitprop stuff?

There was a thump as somebody jumped down off the tank. Boots and combat fatigues filled my vision, and the crude-cut stock of an AK-47 swung around as they hunkered down beside me. A long brown hand stroked my hair, and bits of bus shelter tinkled out. *'Buon giorno, mio signor Maxie!'* said the long-haired woman.

I hauled myself up again, and vomited ceremonially into the road. *'Why* – why the hell won't you leave me alone?'

The two women hauled me up by my armpits, leaning me against the tank. 'Not us, *señor*. You inflict these torments upon yourself. You need never suffer any such things again.'

My head was beginning to clear, and there didn't seem to be any major leaks anywhere. 'Oh yeah!' I riposted feebly. 'I wouldn't bloody well *be* here if it wasn't for you! Christ, why do you want me so much? I don't want *you*! There must be a million idiots who'd suit you better. That maniac Kelley's just slavering for the chance—'

'Oh, him!' The Oriental, sitting dangling his legs from the tank's prow, laughed his buzz-saw laugh. 'Him we would use up, suck the pith out of in no time. You, now, you are something a little more special.'

'Sure, dat is true,' said the blond brigand with the Schwarzenegger accent, lounging on the turret hatch. A bunch of soldiers clomped by, shepherding a little knot of demonstrators. They darted quick glances at me, full of fear and sympathy. 'You, you have somet'ing, Maxie. Somet'ing we can use. Dat's what first called to us 'bout you. Dat is what made us lure you in.'

'Lure—'

The Spanish woman laughed gently. 'Well, let say we did point you i' the right quarter. To see your face, good sir, as the pantechnicon swung in front of you—'

'The truck!' I half screamed. 'You did that? You drove me off the road? You dumped me right up to my neck in – that field, and the path, and that bloody inn – you lured me in all the way! And afterwards, at my room—'

The black man giggled. 'Your fear did the luring, Maxie. All we had to do was, say, chivvy things along just a tad. See, we seldom come so far into the borderlands of the Spiral. Why should we? But they called us, those two.'

'And what then?' sighed the Spanish woman languidly. 'The closer we came, the more we saw, the less we liked. A stiff old booklouse with too many scruples. A sorry thug and trickster puffed up with his own cleverness. What fun would they be to serve? What excitement? So we cast our nets as wide as we could, in that twilight hour, to ensnare any better one who might drive by.'

The truth dug its way home, ugly and humiliating like all the truths I'd been told. 'A poor berk you could dominate! Somebody you and your master, whoever he is, wouldn't have to obey!'

The women laughed. 'No, no, Maxie, not so! Do you imagine we could not dominate that imbecile Kelley in an instant? Whereas you, *caro signor* —'

I tasted the bilious aftertaste of vomit. 'Beg pardon? I mean, this is me we're talking about. I know me, remember!'

'That is just what you do not do, *señor* Maxie.

Consider the you that is behind the wheel of a fast automobile – the you that weaves through the lesser citizens in your path, overtaking all, stopping for none. That is your satisfaction, *si, como no?*'

'Yes. OK, I've never found—'

'But that is because you have power over cars, is it not? Cars only. Cars you can take from those who lord it over you. But what if you had such power in all other walks of life?'

I stared. For the first time they seemed to be talking something almost like sense.

The other woman's hard fingers traced down my cheek. 'Let us be your auto, *señor* – and drive us through your world, as you will. Then no truck will stop you, and no cop catch you, however hard they chase!'

'That's the kind we'll follow!' laughed the black man.

'Ar!' agreed the piratical type. 'Some'un as knows he's been born, take my meanin'?'

'Someone,' agreed the Oriental smoothly, 'who has enough wits to take hold of life – however little use they have made of them, until now. Someone through whom we can live again, as once we did in our turn. Someone who will drain the winecups dry for us once more.'

I stared at him. 'You've changed. You've all bloody changed. You sound – more intelligent. More persuasive. As if you know more about me . . .' A thought shivered through me. 'It's me, isn't it? You're getting it from me! The closer you get to me, the weaker I am, the more you can – what? Read my mind?'

The curly-haired woman shrugged. '*Si, como no?*
Is that so bad? That we hold up a mirror to show
you are better than you think? We have lived our
lives, long, long lives – and there is only so much
living any one mind can do, even with the power
we have gained. But with that power you can live
like a comet, blazing across the years, and us
through you. As you can through others, when
your day too has turned to weariness.'

It was tempting as hell. It made an awful kind of
sense. I thought of Elina, of Emilia, and the horrible emptiness in her voice, the centuries like an
empty, echoing vault around her, every human
experience blending into sameness.

'Like the girl Elina – yes!' snapped the Spanish
type. 'Why else should we have led you to her? To
show you a fate that need not be yours. You can
live as long, longer, but taste life to the full! And
then live again!'

'A thing not all may do,' nodded the Oriental.
'Not Kelley, not much. We could ride him for a
while, his crude cravings, his petty desires, as if he
were a beast of burden. Dee perhaps, but he is old
and withered. But you, Maxie . . . you can. You
will! You need surrender nothing but the privacy of
your thoughts – and what is that but the ultimate
loneliness of man? You need never be aware of us,
unless you wish to; but when you need us, there we
shall be. You need never be lonely again.'

I shook my head a little, bewildered, sick. There
had to be something more to it than that, but I
couldn't get my thoughts straight . . .

The blond type leaned down off the tank. 'You

think we take advantage of you? 'Cause you sick?' He snapped his fingers in front of my face. 'You don't need to be. Not ever again. Heal yous'self!'

A red spark flashed between his fingers. Gingerly I raised a hand and copied him. Another spark, a spark that seemed to burst like a firework. Flame raced down my arm and flooded into my chest, filled my stomach, burst into my other arm and down my legs, chasing pain and weakness before it, tingling along my nerves, thudding through my veins and last of all bubbling up into my aching neck, filling my mouth and nose and blossoming like a flower into my brain. I felt my hair had to be standing on end, writhing, sparking with the power that filled me.

It seemed to inflate me, stiffen me like a sagging tyre. Or a wilting flower watered with strong fertiliser. Suddenly I was fitter, stronger than I'd ever felt, clearer-headed, more decisive, more in control of my own destiny. I could feel every inch of my body, awash with the healing fire.

They watched me, all of them, avidly. It was the most powerful argument they could have made. They knew it; and I was close to my choice.

'There's just one thing,' I said, and my voice sounded oddly more resonant in my own ears. 'If I'm to join you, I'd like to see you – all of you, all together. There's more of you, aren't there? A few, always at the back, always shadows – I don't know how many . . .'

'Dey are older guys,' shrugged the thug. 'Less of dem to see. Dey fade closer back to de centre, become more like unity. Dat's all.'

'Yeah, the centre,' I mimicked him. 'What's that, then? Or should I say who? There's someone in charge, isn't there? Someone who runs you all – who'd run me, too. Like a bloody puppet . . .'

The women touched my arms. 'But Maxie . . .'

I shook them off. 'I'm not joining anybody, not blind like that. Not without seeing you all. You can go find some other idiot.'

The Oriental smiled. 'You are the best we have found for many a day, Maxie. Few others could live as you could. So at last we have you – and we are not intending, not now, to let you go.'

The women's hands closed again, and clamped tight. I was hurled flat on my back, pinned down on the dusty road. Their hair flew, their eyes glittered down on me. Over their heads the other bandit faces appeared, shaking their heads ruefully. The Oriental bowed slightly. 'You wish to see all of us? That may present difficulties.'

'I don't care! Do it, anything you need to, or sod off and leave me alone!'

The women's eyes sparkled. 'As you wish – so be it!'

The tank engines bellowed and hammered, shattering the air with explosive violence. Bitter diesel smoke, half burned, rolled over me, catching at eyes and nose and throat. The bandits, Oriental, buccaneer, thug and women, all had vanished somehow, like bursting bubbles, yet I was still pinned down. Slowly, infinitely slowly, the tracks clanked into motion, the massive metal mountain ground forward towards me, on top of me, blotting out the light as if it reared up over some invisible obstacle, to come crashing down on me in instant, tearing obliteration. The hand I tore free looked ridiculous against it.

'So be it!' hissed the Oriental in my ear. 'We grow weary of the chase!'

'Join with us!' whispered the straggle-haired woman. 'Be one with us!'

'See with our eyes!' growled the buccaneer.

'Feel wit' our hands!' rumbled the blond giant. 'Flex our arms!'

'Remember our memories!' murmured the black man. 'Breathe our breath!'

'Throw yourself upon the waters of our minds!' said the Oriental quietly. 'Swim as we do, one to another! Dwell where you will, in one or many!'

'Your heart falters!' cried the women. 'Your breath draws thin! Your past is ours, our present yours! See us, *señor* Maxie! *We are here!*'

The motors thundered, the treads cascaded down like steel waterfalls. The roaring bulk lurched forward. I screamed—

And just as suddenly I was sitting up, staring at blackness. It took me a moment to realise it was Dee's robe, that had swept across my face like an outstretched wing. He stood between me and the tank, arms raised like a great bat, looking twice his height. The tank engine faded to a sinister, idling throb.

'Did I ever call you angels?' he demanded, quite softly. 'Did I ever reverence you, or seek to understand? Pursuit, coercion, terror and deceit, to the frustration of free will and open choice – is that not how demons should behave? Yet whatever you are,

I counsel you now – if you take the guise of evil, you must also bear its punishment!'

From somewhere or other the bandits were back, clinging to the turret sides, and they laughed down at him like fierce animals, snarling, predatory. The long-haired woman cracked her whip around Dee's staff, and he staggered.

Then there was a bang, a popping explosion and a sudden wash of stinging fire on the road. Another, and this time I saw it, a bottle with a flame at its spout, a petrol bomb sailing through the air. This time it hit the tank directly, and the bandits whirled around, startled, as the fire lashed about them. The road seemed to be full of young people, shouting, gesturing, singing – the same harsh song I'd heard five centuries before. It was a long time afterwards I found out what the words meant.

Slyste, sylste, rytieri bozi!
Pripravtese jiz k boji!

Hear ye, hear ye, knights of God!
Prepare yourself for battle!

The tank roared this way and that on its treads, like a baited bull. Of bandits, of Dee, there wasn't a sign.

I took my chance, scrambled up and ran. There was the bookshop, the window shattered by the concussion, the bright books scattered about like dead butterflies. There was the manhole. I dived for it, missed the ladder and fell screaming into the dark.

'Well,' I thought, 'bugger this for a game of soldiers.'

Save yourself —

Light flared. I hung there in the blackness, cradled in the light that still shone through me, glowing like a beacon out of hands, feet, every inch of skin and bone I could see. It was amazing, Maxie the human Christmas tree. The whole of my ragged ensemble lit up like something really bizarre in home electrics, a glow bursting through every tear and rent, even the toes of my shoes. A thought struck me, and I investigated. Wow. I was sorry I couldn't show it to Jane Dee. Luminous condoms had nothing on this. Then I wished I hadn't thought about Jane, because I had trouble zipping up again.

I felt inspired. I felt as if I'd had six months at a health farm with a gourmet restaurant. I rubbed what passed for my chin and discovered I'd grown a neat beard in the last six seconds. Pity I hadn't grown a chin, too—

That was another I hastily cancelled. You could carry that sort of thing too far. The glow dimmed suddenly; it was because the rents in my clothes had closed up. They were clean, too, even my shoes, intact soles and all. As brand new as ever. Well, whee. The only trouble was I had to go tramping back into that muck down there all over again.

Or did I? Power was a wonderful thing. I could do what I wanted. Let there be light, for a start; and there was. It smelt terrible – OK, let's have something nicer. Roses, the obvious thing; but in that concentration they smelt nearly as bad. I tried frying onions, Armagnac – then settled for Aramis aftershave. There was frenzied squeaking below. The rats didn't seem to approve.

Me, I was having a ball. Did I even have to trail through the sewers at all?

I waved a commanding hand. 'Home, James!'

In the barest instant the light swelled, wheeled, whirled about me like a hurricane spout. I floated in a vortex of fearful energy, untouched, giddy with sheer delight.

I hardly even registered the mocking little voices at the back of my mind, the merest memories of a darkened street.

Use it. Enjoy it. Get the feel of it. Get to like it. And when you're ready—

We'll be there.

Blackness.

CHAPTER NINE

Exit Closed

BLACKNESS, and silence.

Except for the faint ringing in my ears, that was, and my panting breath. I was standing on something solid, and that was as much as I could say. The gloom that closed in around me was more than physical. I knew the feeling only too well. I was sliding down off the foamy crest into the black trough, from the manic springboard into the depressive deep end. Sweaty, drained, slightly unnerved by the memory of that synthetic rush, and yet hungry to dive back into it again – just the same feeling. Only this time it wasn't anything chemical; it was power, pure power. It wasn't something that just exploded inside my skull and left the world outside the same as ever. This had really happened – hadn't it? *Home*, I'd told it, and it had taken me . . . where?

No home I remembered. Not unless it had gone too far, and taken me back to the womb. I wished I hadn't thought of that. OK, I wanted a fresh start, but you could end up *really* neurotic that way. Talk about birth trauma . . .

I quietened my breath, and listened. There was the sound of a fat droplet plopping into water; and a suffocating wave of Aramis. Oh, great; still in the sewers, then. Maybe they were my natural home. Maybe it was the rat genes showing through.

They were one place you didn't take a step without meaning it, though. I hovered there uneasily, leaking exhilaration, trying to get my bearings. After a while I realised there was just a little light filtering down from above, enough to show me the profile of yet another arch of rough masonry, a rubble slope. That didn't look too promising, but I couldn't stand here for ever. I decided I might as well begin to climb.

Then I stopped and swore, aloud and heartfelt. Bitterness gurgled up out of my own personal sewer. Screwed again, Maxie.

That power. I'd never really been using it myself. They'd just handed me it to play with, like a kid, while they kept an unseen finger on it. Home I'd wanted, home I'd got – the home that suited them. That scuffed slot in the slope, that and the imprint above it. That was where I'd slipped coming down here. I was right back where I'd started.

I should have known. I could do almost anything, as long as it suited them. I could shuffle the pack as much as I liked, I'd still only be playing the hands they dealt me. I could have any colour I wanted, as long as it was black.

It was like being God Almighty, with trainer wheels.

They couldn't afford to let me lose myself in my own time, far from the Spiral. They'd rather have me here, alone and helpless. Where they had more power – and I'd have to depend on it. And if that didn't draw me in, there was always Kelley.

Thinking of that cued in something I'd been hearing for a minute or two – the slight scuffling above, the sound of somebody trying to move slowly and quietly. I shrank back into the shadows, looking up at the dim little patch of light. Another pebble came bounding down the slope, a little fall of gravel – and a silhouette there was no mistaking. Tally-ho, there goes the bastard now.

He'd made the same deduction as Dee, of course, and come to look for me here – figuring, probably, that I wouldn't get very far, and would come back. Or maybe he'd tried scrying. Either way, you could see he'd come to a pretty firm conclusion. The needle gleam in his hand was his drawn rapier.

He seemed to be hesitating at the top of the slope, casting around very carefully, as if he was listening. I heard him sniffing; the aftershave had evidently disconcerted him. And alerted him, maybe, to what I might be able to do. I struggled to muffle my breath, wondering why he didn't come down. Most likely he was afraid I'd give him the slip in the dark; and that was not at all a bad idea. Unless – unless I just waved a hand and plastered him halfway across Prague, in a very thin layer.

It was tempting. God, it was tempting. He'd have done it, in a moment; and maybe that was what stopped me, long enough. I caught myself flexing my fingers with the sheer, shivering delight of the idea. Just to know you could do that, all at once, explosively, or just slowly – this was being Alive!

Better than sex, than cars, even—

I bit my lip, hard. I really had gone too far. Who was this talking? Not me. Not even the me that drives like hell. I never really wanted to hurt anyone, not even cops. Well, not seriously.

I just am not the type. So what was making me do this? Sewers full of Aramis, for God's sake! What would I be like if I really had that much power to play with, on impulse? How far from aftershave in a sewer to hot lead in somebody's veins?

Not as far as you'd think. Do that once, and you'd never be the same person again. And that would be just what they wanted. That was why they'd dragged me back – to confront me with Kelley. Giving me enough rein. So I'd use the power. And the more freely I used it, the more I'd be tempted to go for the easy, the complete, the final solution. The moment I let go enough to kill, they'd have me.

It made me sick. The idea I'd ever touched their power was Huey and Ralph material. The aftershave aroma curling around me seemed like a bad joke. Honest crap would smell better – well, maybe not, but it wouldn't remind me of how I'd given in. I'd change it back. I flexed my fingers so hard the joints cracked, and a corona of sparks crackled between them, sending a spurt of white light across the dark slope.

'Ah-*hah*!' snarled Kelley, and sprang forward, sword raised. I gestured frantically, and the loose slope loosened a bit further. The earth creaked and groaned beneath him, and he began to slide. Out of control, arms flailing, he skidded down, right past me, hit a rock, bounced and flipped right over the edge and into the newly stinking sludge beyond.

Not far enough, unfortunately; and he still had his sword. He reared up like somebody Dante *really* disliked, and slashed at my legs as I tried to climb the slope. He didn't quite reach me, and I scrabbled up towards the light.

Scrabbled like Moley on speed, but not fast enough. His sword thrashed the dirt behind my heels. I wasn't going to get clear of him – not without help.

I burst out into the clean air – not that clean, any more – and bolted across the rubble, hell for leather, through the scrubby bushes that had taken root there. Behind me Kelley exploded out like a raging bull, screaming for me in his fury. Whimpering, I bounded on over the wreckage, searching for any kind of bolthole. But there wasn't much light, and nothing ahead but a substantial wall, pretty solid. If I could get over that, maybe . . .

There weren't any convenient piles of rubble. Needs must, when you-know-who's in the driving seat. I took a deep breath, swore it would be the last time and summoned up the light again.

Nothing happened. I could hear Kelley rampaging through the stones, slashing at the bushes, getting nearer all the time. Still nothing – yet we had to be near enough the Spiral, didn't we?

Then, sickeningly, I understood. This was their trap. They wanted me to confront Kelley. They wanted me to kill him, probably. They wanted that change in me. If I resisted the temptation, they couldn't be sure of me; so no more power. They'd rather have him, then; and if he killed me, he could just cast his spell all over again. They'd like that.

Though Dee would be suspicious now, to put it mildly. Probably he could manage without Dee this time – or force him to help? I doubted that. Unless he threatened Jane.

I really hated that idea.

I resented it, and the resentment swelled all my other resentments. Right now Kelley stood for most of them. My lips trembled, and I thought of that telephone. I could just give him a scorching – no. The cutoff inside me was absolute, as certain as a voice in my ear. No kill, no power. And he was coming, now.

I put my back to the wall. I remembered the bone-grating pain in my arm. I thought of how he'd conned Dee, and Jane. He deserved all he'd get. If that's what I had to do . . .

I imagined the heaviest slamming, crushing blow I could. I saw the force of my will hammering down on Kelley, right in front of me, crushing him to a smear on the stones. I felt the power come. I saw it, as if I had eyes in the back of my head, a red wave rising on a tide of laughter. And beyond it, that face with the eyes like the bodies of women, the features that writhed.

With a snarling shout of triumph a crap-coated Kelley burst through the bushes.

I ducked my head suddenly and glared at the ground beneath me. The wave broke, the power surged out of me. Light burst out under my shoes, and I went up like a rocket – action and reaction, nothing like it. Kelley's lunge thrust his sword where I'd stood, and it was struck from his hand and flattened to a smear of thin metal in an instant.

Curses – foiled again!

Almost at once the power vanished, but I was already fifteen feet up the wall and dangling from the top. I heaved myself up and looked over. Another street; a reasonable drop. I looked back, raised a single finger in the air, American fashion. If Kelley saw it, that was fine by me; but it was meant for someone else. Then I swung across, splayed my legs as the catburglar had taught me, and dropped lightly.

I hit solid ground, steadied myself against the wall and caught my breath. It could never have been part of that old building at all. It looked much newer; though many of the stones could have been taken from the ruin. The street facing the wall – and that was odd, like Berlin in the divided days – looked even older and shabbier than the rest, a row of crazy old crook-roofed buildings that leaned to meet one another like a witch's nose and chin. Here and there, though, much taller roofs stood out, some of them really large affairs, neatly tiled with rows of windows underneath, new and gleaming, and high decorated gables. Others were being built, thrusting out of the little old shacks around them like new spring shoots, assertive and strong. The road was just trodden earth and stones, but that too was remarkably clean compared to the rest of town. From here the contrast really hit you; something had been triggered here, a rush of money, maybe, or confidence. Except it was all behind a wall.

It didn't add up, but I had more urgent things to worry about. I padded hastily off, listening for

Kelley clambering after me, but I didn't hear a thing. He might be feeling a bit shocked, and serve the sod right. I'd saved his life. I'd taken a big risk to do it. And probably used up my one chance of conning them that way. They'd be on their guard now. All to save Kelley, little though I wanted it. Still less though he'd appreciate it. Ain't life ironic?

Chances were he'd have some explaining to do to Brother Dee, now; and after that Dee might be more inclined to help me. But for the time being I'd better manage to stay out of the way – except how did I do that, four centuries before I was born, barely speaking the language, and, most importantly, broke? Fat chance. I needed more help – only how did I find that, four centuries – etcetera, etcetera?

Appeal to the Emp? Chancy, with chips. Fairness, as far as he was concerned, was fair him. I considered running the psychic scam over him, but Rudolph might be a bit sour on that right now. If I'd only known a touch more history I might have offered to predict the future for him, but I couldn't remember a bloody bit of detail about these times.

I walked briskly now, not at all sure where I was going. No, there was nowhere. Come daylight I'd sneak back down to the Perfumed Grotto, hope Kelley had gone, make another hopeless stab at tracing my way. I shivered in despair. All that effort, gone to nothing. Ten to one I'd never get back now; and who'd care? Who'd even give it a second thought?

Haven't seen Waxie Maxie around lately.

Yuh. Good riddance.

Yuh.

Epitaph and all. Probably they'd assume Ahwaz had revenged his instant coiffure.

I walked into a wall, and yelped. It hadn't been there a minute ago. Not a wall – a pillar, carved and rubbly, almost wide enough to block the narrow street. A great cold clamp fastened around my neck, and lifted me lightly off the ground.

'Urrk!' I protested, kicking and strangling and clawing at the cold collar around my neck. It was being lifted by a huge man, and my blood ran cold. The hidden man, the brigands' real master – he'd given up on me, and come for me. I was dangling in front of a shadowed face, and I could guess what it would be, the face of my dream. Any minute now those slanted eyes would open—

The moon came out. '*Let me go!*' I screamed, or rather gargled. Pretty stupid, but excusable, I think. It was a monstrous face, framed beneath a great matted thatch of stiff, straight hair; but it wasn't the one I'd seen. The features were blunt, forbidding, brutal, yet with a look of lurking intelligence; and the eyes were open, all right. I didn't think they could ever close; they were blank carved surfaces, like all the rest. It was the face of a statue.

A day or two back that sight might have finished me, but I'd seen – well, nothing actually worse, but pretty stiff competition. Then I did see worse.

That light wasn't the moon; it was green, and it was coming from behind me. I twisted around, and saw, out of the corner of my eye, a green glow swelling behind the wall, rising and growing stronger with every second, like a hunter closing on a quarry. Frantically I redoubled my clawing at the collar. Only it wasn't a collar, it was a stony thumb and index finger. I started screaming in German, '*Lass mich los!! Ich will nicht, ich kann es nicht – bin kein' Morderer—*'

A calm voice spoke from somewhere around my knees. I was dimly aware of a small figure in dark robes who had appeared from around the thing that clutched me. He held up something, a flat tablet, and pronounced a phrase or two in a tongue that wasn't German or Czech; the voice was squeaky and unimpressive, but the words rolled awesomely out into the air. The green glow washed over the tablet for a moment, rippling. Shadow threw the jagged characters incised across it into sudden sharpness. Then the glow shrank with the suddenness of a scream, vanishing like a TV picture turned off. The great arm suddenly let me down until my feet touched the ground, just, but it didn't let go.

'So,' said the dry little voice in very guttural German. 'Now that that's out of the way, how about you tell my friend and me just what kind of a murderer you're not – eh?'

I couldn't see him now, but he didn't sound as if he was being funny. 'Something following me . . .' I croaked. 'Something . . . evil. Like demons . . .'

The unseen man made a strange noise somewhere around his sinuses. 'You tell me? They aren't following you now. So talk!' He said something quietly, and the fingers unclamped, just. I sagged like a leaky balloon, and to my horror I began to cry; I couldn't control it. Then I shied violently; a hand had patted my shoulder.

'*Geh, geh!* You are touched by evil, yes. But it does not have mastery over you, not yet. Be a man, and come.'

I managed to stand up and stop sobbing, more or less. This close I could see a bit more of him in the dimness – hardly impressive, shorter than me even, and slightly stooped, wearing a dark robe with a circle on the back and some kind of round hat. He was looking me up and down with bright eyes, the way a suspicious bird inspects you. In fact he looked a lot like a bird. 'Yes, the smell of trouble clings about you – among others, *feh*!' He was right. Some of the sewer miasma still clung. At least I hoped it was that. 'For indeed, if I am not armed with the wisdom of Schelomo – you would call him Solomonus, yes! – in these matters, well, at least I have the nose!'

He certainly had, and tapped it proudly. His long curls wagged like a spaniel's ears. He was ridiculously reassuring. I found myself grinning at him. 'Me too. I've been sticking it into some very unpleasant places. Maybe I shouldn't risk getting you into anything—'

The little man shook his head firmly. 'You have already done so; and that is my business. Any such force as this loose within these walls is my concern. Besides, you are evidently a stranger and in need of help and hospitality, and that is a sacred duty. I am named Jakob son of David, with the taken name of Loew, and I have the honour to be a scholar, a teacher and a *reb* – you know what that is? – here within the Jewish quarter.'

'The – so this is the ghetto, then?'

'The what? Is that an Italian word? I am afraid I have never heard it. But this is where the tribe of Israel may rest awhile from their wanderings, by gracious permission of the Christian Emperor. It is forbidden to those of your faith; but you are in need. You shall come home with me and drink a glass of wine, and tell me of this trouble.'

I looked at him, all the more reluctant. 'This isn't any danger to anyone else that I know of. Well, not directly. It's my problem. It's sheer luck I came upon you.'

He made that snuffling noise again, like a goat with catarrh. 'Luck? Small chance of that, boy. Did not my auguries tell me there was something wicked abroad? Some new trick of our Christian neighbours, I supposed. Of which there are too many! Sometimes merely robbers and thieves in search of prizes that carry little risk or shame. Many times rapists, the same. Sometimes' – he gestured expressively – 'worse. Fanatics, sowers of riot. But now, heh, and while I am alive, they have to reckon with the terror that walks by night!'

He patted the giant arm affectionately. It had not moved an inch since it put me down, still hovering like an immovable tree limb behind my neck. 'Come! He will do you no harm.' He stepped past the huge form. Gingerly I ducked under the arm, and followed him.

My nerves weren't too good right about then, but I'd probably have screamed anyway. As I passed the huge shape wheeled around ponderously on stiff legs and came clumping after us. The little rabbi laughed. 'Go, take his hand!'

I didn't want to offend – who, I wasn't quite sure. Gingerly I stretched out my fingertips, and quailed as another set twice the size touched mine and slid across my palm, closing smoothly and with just the right pressure. They felt really strange. Stone – but not the sort you trip over. Rough, powdery, porous. It brought back memories of school, art classes, clumsy thumb-shaped pots – 'Like clay,' I said. 'Unfired clay. But it moves!'

'Moist within, as are we!' nodded the rabbi. 'Of such the good Lord made Adam, and so that is his name also.'

'Adam,' I repeated, and the huge shape bowed low over me. The blank eyes were hidden, but the sense of watchfulness seemed far greater. I let the hand go, and it remained as it was an instant, then sank slowly to its side. Like a machine; but this was no machine. I wished I could say I didn't believe this; but after the last day or two I'd hardly have blinked if the Easter Bunny or the Tooth Fairy dropped by. 'And . . . *you* made this?'

The small man smiled ruefully. 'By my hands given form, indeed; but according to an ancient wisdom of our ancestors and the will of almighty God. I did only what any craftsman does – used knowledge to lend strength to weak hands. Unusual knowledge, of course; but the times were mortally hard, and we needed a champion. My hands it were that kneaded him out of a shapeless mass of clay, a *golem*. But it was the Lord of Israel alone who sent a mighty spirit of old to dwell within those limbs, for a time, bound by the sign of great power on his forehead.' The rabbi's voice turned suddenly harsh and vehement. 'In this, his own place, where the ancient wisdom is strong, and in the night, his own time, not all the Emperor's guard could outface him!' He chuckled. 'And the Emperor has seen him, and knows!'

'I wish I'd been a fly on the wall then!'

The rabbi chuckled, and looped his arm through mine. 'Amusingly put, but you do not! For it was through the wall that Adam bar-Jakob entered! Come, come, my home is but at the street's end, and there we may talk at leisure!'

It was an extraordinary little house. There were several of the high new houses along the street, apparently merchants' and moneylenders' homes, and a still higher roof Loew pointed out with some amusement, a new and showy synagogue built by the mayor. Loew's synagogue, where he directed the Talmud school, was smaller but no less dignified, not least because it looked immeasurably old. His house, practically leaning up against it, had the same air. The smoke-yellowed walls of its central room were so bowed out with age it felt more like a cave or a burrow, and it was nearly as sparsely furnished, with a long, age-polished table and benches, a couple of tall fireside chairs and a few chests and boxes. But above the table was a great rack of shelves crowned with a *menorah* and other vessels and stuff in worn-looking silver, piles and sheaves of scrolls, and a fair number of books – a lot, probably, for these times. The rabbi's round shoulders and bent back seemed to fit the walls, as if they had shaped him, and his shadow raced up and down them in the drowsy candlelight as he bustled about, fetching me bread and wine.

The monstrous Adam had clumped down an out-side stair into some kind of cellar, which suited me right down; he was an unnerving creature – or what-ever. Now he was gone I felt calm and secure here, more so than I had for what could have been a life-time. But I also felt very alien, and not only from my own era. I'd never thought much about the Jews I knew. A terrible load of gonophs some were; the spirit of the brothers Kray hadn't entirely left the East End. Just as many were nice guys, like Joe from the deli who was always generous with his salt beef and gefilte fish when I was really down on my luck. All in all, they about balanced out with the rest of the human race, in my book, with maybe a few brains extra. But here was the ancient culture alive and formidable, and with the power of the Spiral bringing its shadow to awesome life. I looked at the *menorah* and the *shofars*, and thought of prophets and judges, Joshua and Elijah, and the thing called Adam in the darkness below my feet, and shivered a little.

Rabbi Loew caught me looking as he set down wine and rye bread before me, with a small dish of salt. 'They are not much,' he smiled, 'but they are old – from the land of Spain, some of them, if you know where that is. Some of the scrolls also, from the cities of Toledo and Santiago in the time of the Moors, many hundreds of years past. A kindlier time, in some ways.' He hesitated, and for the first time I noticed the circle on his robe was yellow. 'You will excuse me if I do not—' He didn't want a Gentile touching them, even a friendly one.

'Of course, yes. I wouldn't want to, anyway. You see – I'm a thief.'

He cocked his head reflectively. 'Well, that's more than any other thief I know will admit; and thieves run thicker than rats in this city. It suggests you're thinking better of it. If not, you should go try your fellow *goyim* across the wall. They've about cleaned us out anyhow, those who can't afford lock and guard.'

'No. I wasn't out to steal anything. Just to save myself – my soul, if you like. It was stealing that got me into this.'

He waved a surprisingly long, slim hand. 'Then tell. My wife and family are well abed, and I need little sleep. Wake me if I nod, though. The ears of the righteous should never be closed to a plea, but the eyes may sometimes droop a little.'

He was not really that old a man, though at first I'd thought of him as venerable. He was probably only fifty-five-ish, though that was older in these times; the hair that straggled from under his skullcap was more black than white. Nor was he as frail as he looked, I guessed; the fingers he steepled against his nose were a worker's, calloused and wiry. I told him what I could, and he sat unmoving. He never showed the least sign of sleep, though. Only the lamp flame made the shadow slump on the wall behind him, and his bright eyes caught the glow.

I watched it as I talked, and at the back of my mind I thought of that bastard Fisher again, and how people cast shadows into the Spiral, shadows of legend. I wondered which I was talking to, a man or his shadow; and I wondered what separated them.

Could they ever meet? That would be like a *doppelgänger* – and I remembered *The Student of Prague*. Prague, where the Spiral was so strong. What sort of shadow would I cast in the night?

My tale trickled away into nothingness, and I sat silent, feeling like about tuppence-worth of Kelley-coating. The rabbi also sat silent, and I squirmed inwardly. I'd been too truthful. Probably now he thought I was a total flake. Suddenly he sat up, and spoke.

'So, you are truly determined to resist these creatures, these demonic servants and whatever lies behind them? Even with the power they offer?'

I sagged with relief. Of course I'd been forgetting that a man with a home-made *golem* in his basement has reasons to take a liberal line on magic and suchlike. 'Power? God, you don't know what it's like. Like dabbling your feet in a flood. It keeps trying to whirl me away, suck me down ... No, I want to cut loose. At all costs! Whatever I might've ... No matter what! Anything!' I hugged myself, shivering.

The rabbi stared at the floor. 'This, this *Spirale* of yours – of such a matter I have heard, yes, though under other names. It does not altogether accord with the tenets of our faith, though according to the *Zohar* of de Leon some aspects of the kabalistic belief, the *Sephiroth* ... But to travel in time, as upon a river – upstream this day, downstream yesterday, maybe no day if you don't paddle fast enough, *ai*! No matter. I cannot say yea or nay. Suffice it that in these parts the art magical is stronger than else-where, whatever the reason, and so many scholars flock here. That much I can accept.' He stroked his beard, and nodded.

'And thence, one thing I am sure of. These things that pursue you are very wicked indeed, yes. But they are not demons as we understand them – nor, as I believe, your faith also. They have too much of a flavour of humanity. Men who have made themselves into the image of demons, perhaps; yet they command too much power for that, and move with too single a purpose. You fear for your soul, you say. Whatever is to fear from them, I do not think it is *Sheol* – to you, Hell.'

I glared at him. 'You haven't seen them! You haven't felt—'

'No. And I did not say there was nothing to fear.'

'Then . . . You. You're some kind of magician, a powerful one. Can I ask you to help me, somehow? I can't trust old Dee – he means well, sure, but if he tries this ceremony of his I just bet Kelley will skew it somehow. Dee trusts him too much. What'd happen to me then – it wouldn't be good. Kelley'll see to that.' My mouth felt very dry. 'And besides . . .'

'Yes?'

'If Kelley gets that power, in the state he is now, I think an awful lot of people might get hurt. And even if it passes to Dee, well, who knows? Even old scholars can get corrupted. What if these creatures fasten on him?'

Rabbi Loew looked sternly at me. 'It seems you do not trust anyone with such power. You judge all others by your own low standards.'

'Well . . . OK, I do. I've seen a lot of people,

the way I live. Maybe the wrong sort of people, all right; but I look at a whole lot of respectable types, politicians, stuffed shirts, you name it, and I see them act just the same way as low-lifes, a lot of the time – what's the big joke?'

Loew was making that peculiar snorting chuckle, and his thin beard wagged. 'I am sorry! Stuffed shirts, hehhehheh, that is good, very good!' He slapped his thigh.

'Look, it's not original, OK? My father – he thought he was a pillar of the business world, but he was a bigger bloody thief than I'll ever be. I don't trust *anybody*! Not that much. Not a millionth part.'

The rabbi was still smiling. 'Then evidently you have gained some understanding. Of course these creatures would seek a master to serve, for that would be how they gain their ascendancy. What is a little service to them, if with every move they draw you deeper into their web? Seeking to live again through you! They spoke the truth, because that is the strongest lie. Ruling you by your own urges, always bolstering you where you are weakest, until you can do nothing at all any longer without their aid and are little more than their creature. Then the servant is the master indeed! Your life would be theirs. They would absorb you, consume you, draw you into their central will. The *vrkolak* that the Germans call *vampir* could not do worse.'

My throat felt suddenly full of broken glass, so dry I couldn't speak. He was putting into words exactly what I'd felt. He moved his hand a little, and his firelight shadow made a gesture of sweeping power. 'Probably that is how they were ensnared in their turns. I can imagine them as you describe them – weak, resentful men, aye, and women, who found in that central will, whatever it was, the chance to become what they believed they ought to be. Petty criminals – you will forgive me? – often see themselves as daring, romantic bandits. Romantic to them, anyhow.'

I winced. I could understand that all too easily. I had the updated version, so I could only believe in it behind the wheel of a car; and by a mercy those bandits had never caught me there, since the first time.

'Yes,' said Loew thoughtfully. 'This Kelley. A rascal, but how much worse would he be if he had no fear or weakness to restrain him? And which of us shall be exempt? Is it not merciful that the powers I have found lie in the hands of a weak old man with few ambitions left in this world? You have done well to resist, young fellow.'

'Then . . . you'll help me?'

Loew was silent a moment, and my heart sank. 'Here, now, yes, I can defend you. Evil things do not cross this threshold. But this link that has been forged, this tether that draws this power to you – I know of nothing to sever that. It is in my case best that he who creates such a bond is also the one to break it. There are what you would call rites of exorcism in my faith, but they are not for Gentiles.'

I began to feel the panic climbing up my trouser leg again. 'Yes, look, but I'm not much of a Christian, really – I'm, what's the bloody word, ecumenical, that's it—'

Loew's smile was as firm as a frown. 'I do not doubt it. But no. And this ceremony of your Dr Dee, it cannot but be a Christian ceremony, can it? As *reb* I can have nothing to do with that.'

I sagged. Back to the sewers again, boys. Might as well go down fighting – though down in something else would have suited me better.

Loew was still smiling. 'However,' he added in a kindly voice, and my spine snapped me bolt upright, 'I *can* seek to banish evil with prayer from any gathering of any kind. That is always lawful. Indeed, it is my duty. I do not have to pay too much attention to whatever other gabble is also going on, do I? So, if your Dr Dee will have me—'

I shot out of my chair and grabbed his hand. 'Oh, he will, he will! He's a good man too, he'll understand! He'd bloody well better, anyway – if he wants me, he'll have to! Thank you, I can't say – I'll never be able to repay—'

He shook his head, and now he did look stern, under the cloak of that shadow, straight now against the wall and very tall. 'Ah, ah yes, you can repay me, indeed. In advance, if you like. Richly. You see, times have been hard for us, for so long, in so many lands. And now, here, they seem to be growing a little easier. Rudolph is a better master than any other Christian monarch alive – not least because he values our money. We begin to prosper as nowhere else. And yet his protection extends only so far – not into the hearts and wills of his subjects, or most of them. So we live still behind walls, and bear a yellow badge of shame, and yet— Hope is like a limb long unused, painful to stir. Dare I ask—' He looked down, and for the first time he seemed nervous. 'You who comes walking out of years that are yet to be, you can tell me—'

'Yes?' I prompted him, for he looked as anguished as I must have a moment back.

'You can tell me – what is to be the fate of my people?'

I must have just stared at him stupidly for a second. My brain was boiling. Pogroms; emigrations; deportations; America; Auschwitz; the Rothschilds; Stalin; lampshades; Israel; the furnaces; fundamentalists; Sobibor; the Six-Day War, all struggling to the fore.

I drew a deep breath. '*Well* . . .' I began.

I slept that night on the hearth, warmed by the dying fire. The rabbi had only beds for himself and his family; but the straw mattress he hauled out was a lot more comfortable than your average trendy futon, and the blankets were more than enough. The lamp had guttered and gone out before I'd finished my potted history, leaving us in near darkness. But the firelight still showed me the play of expression across Loew's narrow features, and the way he tugged at his beard sometimes. Just once he struck his brow, hard; and it wasn't when I might have expected it. I guess I probably didn't tell it well; but at the end he didn't speak for quite a while, and when he did, it was of bed, and of prayer.

The next morning I was awakened by Loew's womenfolk, wife and daughter-in-law and granddaughter, much amused but very polite, though only the young girl spoke much German. A nice cheery trio, who could have got off a bus in Golders Green any day, except for those yellow circles. Loew and his son, also a Talmudic teacher, had apparently gone out to the school, and to send some kind of message, and when he came back, alone, he was still in a very reflective mood. About what I'd told him he said nothing; but I got the feeling he was ringing like a bell. Also, he seemed to be waiting for something; and around midday it came, with a knock on the door.

A young man stooped under the lintel, elaborately curled locks swinging beneath his broad floppy hat, a yellow circle ingeniously embroidered into his elegant doublet. I could guess where he fitted in by the granddaughter's reaction, instantly suppressed, and the way he glared suspiciously at me. He exchanged a quick word with the rabbi, who nodded to me. 'They are here!'

They? I stepped back as two others strode hastily in, muffled in yellow-circled cloaks despite the mild sun. One struck his head on a beam, but made only a noise of dignified expostulation. The other—

I didn't need to be told who. There was this faint, lingering pong . . .

I glared at Loew. '*He* wasn't supposed to be here!'

Dee threw back his hood, blinking around him with the air of a duke in a public men's room for the first time. 'I would not come without Brother Edward. He has a right to his voice in this matter.'

I backed behind a convenient table. 'Has he? He was after me with a sword last night! And he's been conning you – I mean, cozening you, all this time. You, the Emperor, J— everyone!'

Kelley didn't bother to uncloak. He took one step towards me, grabbing at his waist, then froze with the dagger hilt in his hand. The young man's dagger was already drawn, a lot longer, and poised just under Kelley's breastbone. He grinned with satisfaction at my cowardly reaction.

The rabbi nodded. 'My future grandson-in-law, Nathan. Wants to be a scholar. He should be so quick with his pen. Welcome to my home, gentlemen – and behave in it as you would in your own, *Herr Ritter* Kelley. Will you not sit down? Leah, some wine!'

Dee settled gingerly into the rabbi's best chair, glancing about – uneasily, but curiously, at the manuscripts especially. Kelley hawked and was about to spit on the bench, then remembered the dagger and sat down with a thud, hunched up and glowering from under the hood. They were squirming like Bible-Belters in a gay bar, afraid to so much as touch the furniture in case it contaminated them. I realised suddenly that my entire attitude had probably told Loew more about the future than any of my garbled history.

Again, though, Dee surprised me. He hesitated only a little when Loew poured him wine, and as he took it – well, you couldn't call it a bow, but he unstarched his neck just a fraction. 'I – ah – am aware of your name and reputation, sir,' he said, with almost no effort. 'I read Hebrew, although I do not speak it, and ... Whatever the – ah – popular prejudice, I have never been one to undervalue the scholarship of your people, or the virtues of their philosophy.'

'Ah, exactly how I have always felt about yours,' twinkled Loew. 'Whatever the popular prejudice. And there is no denying your accomplishments, sir – as Master Maxie here demonstrates. I am grateful to you especially, Master Kelley, for sending him to me. But dispatching him home now, that is the trick, is it not?'

'Home and free!' I snapped. 'Without this bloody link you've landed me with – and without the power going to Brother Edward here. Or to you yourself, Doc, or anyone ever again. Whatever we're dealing with, it sure as hell isn't angels. Even you saw that for yourself.'

'Folly!' growled Kelley. 'Did I not make all clear to you, as it was made to me? This is a thief, a coward, a liar and lecher, a thing of the lowest vice! Small wonder the angels took an unseemly form to vent their wrath upon him!'

Dee looked deeply troubled. 'That alone would not explain what I saw,' he said quietly. 'Surely even the flaming sword before the Garden must be a thing of grace as well as terror. I saw and felt otherwise. And against this I have only—'

'You have the angelic word!' said Kelley sharply.

'Aye,' said Dee miserably. 'But through you, Brother. As for so many things. And why should that be so? If I may stand before these creatures, why have they never spoken to me directly, even when the art of scrying came to me at last?'

'That's always the way with mediums,' I thrust in. 'Why should something that's true just happen to operate like a conjuror's trick? And to the conjuror's benefit!'

Dee went white. Kelley – talk about body language. His was saying a mouthful.

Rabbi Loew's gaze flickered about, and he stroked his ratty beard. 'Until now, sirs, I have only seen you through Master Maxie's eyes. As he himself admits, he is not unspotted; but I do not believe he lies. That channel of power is a false and perilous one, and should be cut off altogether.'

Kelley exploded, but subsided as suddenly. Not because of the dagger, but because Dee motioned him silent. The old man's mouth was working, but he spoke steadily enough. 'What then do you counsel, Loew?'

Loew rose, and put his hand on my shoulder. 'What this young fellow requests. That you, learned sir and doctor, conduct your rite of exorcism; and that you, Master Kelley, take no part. And that I stand aside to ... guard the ground, as it were. Against intrusions.'

'You?' Dee's brows shot up. 'But this is a sacred rite!'

Loew shrugged. 'Is it, sir? I know of inquisitors who would not agree. And your pyre would stand somewhat higher than mine, as the world reckons. For myself, it does not matter, I believe, as long as the intent is good, and I take no actual part. Save against any evil that appears.'

Dee looked like a disappointed baby – which in many ways he was. All sorts of feelings chased across his face; but after only a moment he raised his hand.

'A golden prospect!' howled Kelley, nearly apoplectic. 'You're just tossing it away!'

Dee looked down at him with something suspiciously like pity. 'He who can do such a thing at need is truly free. We shall proceed as you advise, masters.'

CHAPTER TEN

Emergency Braking

EVENING WAS GATHERING as we passed through the city gates, Dee and myself together. It appeared that Jews still had more of a problem with suspicious activities like entering and leaving, and Loew was taking another route, a secret one probably. We were headed back to Dee's preferred launchpad, the hill-top outside the walls we'd been bound for when I'd tipped Brother Ed into the brassicas; and I didn't like that one bit, because it meant he knew the place. Dee had insisted that there was nowhere else remotely suitable, so free from prying eyes. And besides, why should Master Kelley interfere? Had he not given his solemn pledge—

It was easier to go along with the old fellow. At least we ought to be able to see trouble coming. Probably there was a twentieth-century tourist hotel up there, but right now it was stark and isolated, home to nothing except a wide clump of bushes and a few trees, stunted and windblown. They looked incredibly sinister against the grey clouds. I imagined a brigand lurking behind each one, about to jump out and yell *SURPRISE*!

We dismounted and tethered the horses at the foot, and made our way up the grassy slope. It wasn't that steep, but Dee was old and I was puffing and wheezing under his enormous bag of para- phernalia. 'Christ, what've you brought, the bloody kitchen' – I remembered they hadn't really invented sinks – 'table?'

'Nay, sir,' Dee answered seriously. 'Only the Holy Table of my art, and the frame that bears it. I trust it will endure being thus carried.'

'Great. What about me?'

'Great effort is purifying,' said Dee serenely, digging in his staff. 'It will help to shrive you somewhat for the ceremony.'

I was about to say something that would set my shriving back maybe a year, but he uncapped his staff. In the bleak dusk the head gleamed with a strong pearly light, far stronger than it had been even in the sewers. 'You see? This engirdling realm you call the Spiral must impinge here most forcibly.'

'I thought it had to be crossroads. Or something.' I couldn't manage a longer sentence.

'And so this is,' said Dee, pointing his staff at a litter of white stones beneath the bushes. 'In Roman times – and perhaps before, who knows? – there was a watchtower here, overlooking the conjunctions of road and river, and the commerce and conquest that flowed along them. This was their nexus. There may be other forces at work also, in the clouds perhaps. From this height I have seen visions there, things of which I can say little, but may be known in your day. Great wheels and discs of light—'

'Oh. Wouldn't happen to mean flying saucers, would you?'

Dee chuckled. 'An apt enough description. You have a pretty wit at times, young sir. And what is known of these?'

'Not a lot. Meet a bloke called Fisher, ask what he thinks. Can I rest a moment, please?'

'Oh, 'tis but a few steps now.'

'Urrg.'

Eventually I staggered through the bushes and collapsed in the middle of a slight grassy dip, enclosed by the crumbled walls. Dee lifted the bag off my back and began setting up his paraphernalia, while I lay gurgling on my face, utterly and totally shriven.

There was that bloody table, in a padlocked case swathed in all those embroidered drapes. They revealed a white-painted surface about three feet square, surrounded by a thick gilt border painted with clusters of what looked like Hebrew characters. In the centre was a great six-pointed star formed of two gilt triangles, what Dee called the Hexagram, with a square at the centre, divided into twelve smaller squares, each with its own character in blue and white and gilt. Like the embroideries, it was beautiful, and it must have cost a fortune. Dee liked to do his enchanting in style.

Muttering to himself, occasionally chanting a line, and every so often pausing to bob and bow to what I guessed were the four quarters of the compass, he bustled around setting his scene, or whatever he called it. I figured the supernatural powers were in for a pretty good show.

He unfolded what I thought would be the table-cloth, but turned out to be a wide square of light canvas, painted with black lines and letters, like a crossword with no blank spaces. I crawled back hastily as he spread it out diamondwise on the grass; I hadn't forgotten the green-lit pattern on that lonely farmhouse floor. He set up the table, propping up the legs with what I thought were wedges, but were actually other padlocked boxes, apparently containing magical seals. Bob bob, bow bow, mumble mumble all the while.

Then, prodding me gently out of the way again, he produced a jumble of sticks which bolted together to form an enormous pair of compasses. Putting one end carefully in the centre of the Table, he scribed a huge circle in the grass around the dell, marking it in places with a chunk of stone and filling in the line with powdered chalk. This took him a while, because he kept genuflecting and muttering. Once he dropped the chalk and vanished in a sort of personal white-out, sneezing violently.

Then, resetting the compasses and using his staff as a ruler, he extended another six-pointed star into the circle, marking the lines with strips of gold brocade ribbon. Every so often he waved the compasses above his head, with gestures. Mutter mutter, mop and mow; now he was really getting into his stride. He took up the stones marking the circle, and replaced them with low bowls, into which he poured a sort of thick, smelly sludge from a flask. 'Mummy!' he exclaimed as I retreated hastily.

'Sorry?'

'Mummy paste – brought at great cost from the

deserts of Egypt, and ground by I myself. A very fine piece, nearly a whole arm still enwrapped, with many rare balsams and spices. Sovereign for the rheumatics and many other complaints, but also of passing potency in various formulae. As here, with sulphur and naptha and verdigris, myrrh, bitumen and many other substances—'

'Hi, Rameses,' I murmured, trying not to gag. Dee sniffed the stuff lovingly, coughed violently – sending a plume of chalk leaping from his beard – and stoppered the flask decisively.

'I wish you were able to assist,' he said sadly, 'or that Brother Edw— It takes much longer thus alone; but we are now prepared and fit to commence our ceremony. Indeed, we should, without delay.' He looked up. The sun was falling now, a cool disc behind rushing plumes of grey smoke, beginning to be tinged with pink. I hauled myself up, and peered around. There was no sign at all of the Rabbi.

Dee exclaimed testily, 'Well, well. A few minutes more, perhaps. But we really should make the preliminary Invocation as soon as we may, or there will be no time before sunset.' Carefully he lifted one bowl off the circle's rim and stepped inside, replacing it behind him.

'Er – shouldn't I be in there too?'

'On no account!' he exclaimed, horrified. 'To be in such an enclave of power would be most perilous for you, leaving you exposed to whatever force may be summoned therein. That is how you first incurred this link, dropping from above on to the Hexagram without breaking the outer ring, which would have dissipated the spell. Cross it not nor break it, at your deathly peril! Is there no sign of your friend the Jew yet?'

It was ridiculous, but I felt somehow exposed and chilly outside that circle, as if Dee was safe in some way I wasn't. 'Nobody,' I said, pacing around the bushes. 'You don't think something could have . . .'

Dee sniffed, the way some people shrug. He was beginning to look petulant, and if he was feeling as cold as I was, I didn't really blame him. A chilly breeze whispered aimlessly about the trees. Suddenly Dee exclaimed impatiently, 'Enough! I really must make my beginnings now. My feet grow frozen.'

And, ignoring my protest, he fished out a tinder-box, struck a light and lit a long wax taper. As this flamed up in the grey twilight he carried it over to the first bowl and lit the mess inside. The green flame that spurted up was all too familiar, though it burned lower and less bright as he hastily clapped a perforated lid on to it. Swiftly but with ceremony he lit the others, and was just touching the flame to the last one when a sudden icy gust swirled around me out of God knows where and blew it out.

Then, hard on its heels, came an even stronger blast, and out went the others, in streaks of bitter smoke that made me choke. The bushes bent, even the leafless trees bent and creaked. The chalk puffed up, the brocade strips bulged and lifted as if small scurrying things raced beneath the flattened grass. The cover lifted off one bowl and rolled tinkling across the grass.

'Recover it!' yelled Dee, as his beard blew up into

his eyes. He grabbed at his paraphernalia as the wind plucked and pushed at it, one foot on the ribbons, one hand on the Holy Table. Riffles like ocean waves rolled across the dense grass, lifting like a cat's hackles. I grabbed the cover, burned my fingers, danced around swearing, and only Dee's anguished shout warned me I was on the margin of the circle, teetering against the impossible wind that felt like so many hands pushing me over.

Then against the reddening skyline a shabby little figure struggled into view, in a ballooning gown that threatened to whisk him off skyward like a ragged kite, still clutching at his absurd hat. He waved cheerfully, or that was what it looked like. All at once the gown sank down as if somebody had deflated him, the boiling motion faded from the grass, the trees relaxed and I managed to get my balance. The Rabbi leaned across the bushes. 'Good evening! A little restless, perhaps.'

Dee was plastering down his wispy hair under his skullcap, which had almost blown off. 'Ah'm! A certain . . . disturbance. Not altogether unknown. I confess I was unprepared for a manifestation of such strength, alone as I am. I am grateful for your assistance. The – ah – *claviculum Solomonis?*'

The Rabbi smiled, hefting what looked like an earthenware tablet in his hand. '*Idem*. I also am surprised. But it underlines, does it not, the truth of what our young friend claims?'

'It does,' admitted Dee sadly. 'The sooner Master Maxie is freed of this, the better. Who knows what next may manifest itself through him?'

I stared. 'Hold on – what's this *through me* stuff?'

The Rabbi blinked. 'Were you not aware of it? But of course, you would not see so clearly as I did. The grass, the trees – you were the source of that demon's wind, my son. From whatever shadows it was summoned, it blew through you. There is enough of them in you to be its conduit. Well, I must not linger here. I have preparations of my own to make.'

'Guard yourself as well as Master Maxie,' said Dee unhappily. 'If ... what you suspect be true, there may be more to fear, and as much from man's hand as beyond nature.' I began to protest, but he shook his head firmly. 'Hold you here upon this spot now, young sir! Upon your peril do not move, or speak, or do aught without I command you.'

Dee carefully smoothed out his brocade strips and cloths, retrieved the bowl cover and began relighting the bowls, this time without incident. The Rabbi, with an amiable nod to us, retreated to the edge of the trees, and kneeling down among the stones, he began to trace figures of his own on the ground. I could just hear him singing under his breath, a high, keening sound that suggested things eastern. Dee, meanwhile, had begun to stride around the circle with his staff held in one hand, pointing to each smoky bowl in turn and chanting, bowing slowly and deeply now. It was Latin, I realised, as my ears grew used to the sound – very slow and sonorous. I caught about one word in three, but enough to know it wasn't ordinary book-Latin – probably what they called monastic, with a style and a vocabulary of its own, the sort that survived in church services, plainchant, that kind of thing. At first the Rabbi's nasal singsong made a daft sort of obbligato to Dee's rolling grandeur, but after a few minutes that seemed to fade away, and when I glanced around he was wandering off, leaving only his scratchings in the turf.

It was cold and it was boring, and I was beginning to want a leak rather seriously. Dee droned on, and I didn't dare interrupt him. And then, after a while, I began to realise that the wind was back; only this time it was blowing from a definite direction, across the city from the east, and in the last faint glow of the sunken sun black clouds were riding it. Ragged hagtatters, they raced together, trailing thin veils of misty drizzle around the spiky spires, and advanced upon the hill. The gusts flicked nastily at Dee's robes, and whistled their way under my coat and into all my remaining nooks of warmth. I stamped and swore – under my breath, in case it got into Dee's spell.

It was as if I'd aroused a sleeping beast. Underneath my foot the ground heaved and sent me staggering, almost to the circle's edge. The bushes rattled their dry stems warningly, and the grass in the dell convulsed, not in windrows now but in great pulsating shivers that shook the earth and sent stones rattling. Voices groaned under the ground, moans of tortured stone. I stumbled this way and that, struggling to keep my feet; but though puffs of chalk were jolted from the circle's rim, nothing moved inside. Dee and his bowls and table stood firm, while his words rolled out into the whipping air.

The rain came and went in brief, fierce flurries.

One moment there were the steep city roof peaks, gleaming blackly in the last low rays, then a grey wing beat across our eyes with stinging force and everything vanished. Within the cloud lights moved, faint marsh-gas glows leaping overhead from side to side, and long, shimmering shadows that loomed up like grotesque stiltwalkers and were instantly gone, and the rain after them, spattering and trickling off the drenched leaves. It had become hard to breathe, suddenly, and I panted. Dee never missed a word, that I could hear. There was an instant's lull, and then another gust, a worse one, with a howl that could have come from an open mouth. The ground still shuddered, not all at once but suddenly, just as you relaxed, and I heard stones tumble from the ruined walls.

Then the rain seemed to lift, literally, like a curtain. I found myself looking up at Edward Kelley. He was standing on the top of the walls, wrapped in the green robe he had lent me; but across his shoulder ran a broad sash of some fine material, painted, like Dee's cloth, with signs in squares. Across his other shoulder lay something heavy and grey, a sack maybe; and he too carried a staff, a great cudgel-headed thing with a band of yellow metal about it. His face was a grim mask, expressionless as I'd first seen it, but even his stance showed me the fury that burst inside him as he saw me.

He was fast, as always. In one brutal wrench he hauled the heavy mass from his shoulder and swung it high above his head, with a sweep of his burly arm that set it spinning; and then, like a sling, he let it go. Out into the air it sailed, and as it flew it spun and opened out like some kind of jellyfish. Down over my head it settled, and with the last of its momentum whirled me off my feet. I fell sprawling, clawing and scrabbling at the imprisoning thing. It hardly seemed substantial, yet it bit into my fingers and wouldn't tear. It was a net, gauze-fine but made of silk, I guessed, with weights around the rim so it could be flung like a bolo.

But why? I'd be out of it in half a second.

It was then I saw the markings painted on it, and realised why it was circular. The border, the triangles, the characters – the same as that bloody table. He'd trapped me right in the centre of a Hexagram; and abruptly the air was full of green light.

I screamed and struggled with the entangling threads, but they clung tight around me, sucking down against my face with every breath. Dimly I saw Kelley spring down from his perch and stride towards me over the heaving ground, staff outstretched.

'*Redidendum est!*' he screamed. '*In loco sacrificium sacrificatus est! Venite, venite, potentissime, recipite, redone, refulgete!*'

'*Help!*' I disagreed. Something like that, anyway. The silk billowed above me, and suddenly that ring of faces was leering down at me again, all too familiar – the dark-eyed women, the moustached Oriental, the crag-faced pirate type, the black guy and the rest. Now, though, their faces were all I could see, hanging in the brightening glare. With every pulse of it they changed, shifting and blurring into goggling gargoyle caricatures of themselves, eyes rolling, mouths working as one. The livid lips smirked back over dripping teeth no longer human, no longer animal even, jagged, filthy, terrifying things. Out of those gaping, bodiless throats came the same cold cry that had terrified me that night in the empty fields, hungry, dismal, devouring. Around me they spun, the wailing faces, faster and faster into a dizzying blur. I threshed against the net, but it was useless. Above me stood Kelley, straddling me with his staff upraised, crowing deep in his throat.

'*Refulgete! Redite! Unto your true master!*'

The staff swept down.

And flew apart. It broke like a rotten stick against the massive hand that thrust into its path. Kelley screamed hoarsely as it clutched the scruff of his robe and lifted him screaming from the ground. The blur tightened and dwindled in an instant, shooting back and shrinking into an infinite glaring distance – or depth. Then with colliding suddenness there was darkness, hot and shimmery, and deep within it a glare erupted, shifting from sickly green to boiling crimson and back again. The eyes of my nightmare flicked open.

Now for the first time their raging light was so strong it lit up the rest of that face more clearly, hairy, bestial, with an outthrust wolfish muzzle and licking, slavering tongue. Yet beneath that scanty pelt the outlines of the writhing features held a deeper horror still, for they were a nightmare compound of shapes half dissolved yet still recognisable.

Later, when the nightmares came back, I remembered Arcimboldo's portrait, and the other one, the secret one Kelley had seen; and I wondered just where he'd been getting his ideas.

Those slanting eyes were made of women's bodies, naked, twisted into cruel arcs; the light blazed out through their milky skin. The nose, the cheekbones were the bent bodies of men. It was their pale flesh that formed the face before me, their billowing hair that pelt. No part of that face that was not made up of them, splayed and tormented into unlikely shapes; and, worst of all, there were suggestions, a stray arm here, a half-hidden curve of thigh filling a gap elsewhere, that there were other figures hidden beneath. They writhed, like fretful sleepers, and the expression changed. The snout lifted in a triumphant leer, a tongue lolled out that was a woman's body, barely recognisable under the wash of slime. The steaming jaws spread wide to devour me.

Thud.

A massive toeless foot stamped on the net an inch from my head. Another huge hand closed over its edge. A deafening howl of rage echoed between earth and sky, but the hand plucked up the net with an effortless ripping force that shot me right out of it and spun me over in the wet grass.

I didn't mind. I was laughing hysterically. I managed to stop, though, tilting my aching head back into the coolness. I looked up at Kelley, kicking frantically some eight feet in the twilit air, as immovably clamped as I had been. The net lay crumpled and torn at my side, and the vision had gone with it. Thunder crackled in the distance, and blue flickers lit the clouds.

'Thanks, Adam,' I said. And the damn thing ducked its head, as if to say, 'You're welcome, I'm sure.'

I don't remember very much for the next few minutes. When my head cleared I was on the ground still, but sitting up, with the rasp of cheap spirit on my tongue. Rabbi Loew was looking at me and nodding sympathetically; while behind him Dee and Kelley were exchanging words. Pretty hard ones, too. When an insistently calm man gets angry, he doesn't know how to handle it. Dee was weeping and shouting simultaneously, and shaking his fist in his brother's face, when he wasn't spraying it with saliva. Kelley, his head down between his shoulders like a bull about to charge, was roaring and bunching his free fist as if to thump the Doctor; but every time he raised his fist the huge hand jerked him back by his other arm, ignoring his streams of profanity.

'So you're back with the living, eh?' demanded the Rabbi.

'Sort of,' I admitted grudgingly. 'Oh God. God, that was close, wasn't it?'

'Some. He had assistance, some very low sorts of hireling, and it took a moment for Adam to deal with them. They are sleeping peacefully back there on the hill; and I do not think anyone need trouble to awake them again, unless it be this forgiving Nazarene of yours.'

A few spots of rain were falling again, more gently. I swigged greedily at the stuff – peach brandy, maybe. 'And – is that it?'

The Rabbi considered. 'Most likely it is. They are not destroyed, those creatures; that would take a greater strength than mine, far greater. But, yes, the link is broken, certainly. They cannot now tempt you with their power, nor stretch their arms out to pursue you. Here you are barred to them. And once back in your own time how shall they ever find you again? Here, drink some more of this. Then we must part your Brothers – *Adam*!'

Dee had actually socked Kelley a beauty, right in the eye. I cheered. Before Adam could grab him he landed another, with his staff this time, on Kelley's unprotected head, and a fine follow-through to the nose. Adam caught his free hand and stood there like a gigantic nanny with two squalling toddlers.

Rabbi Loew's quick glance to heaven summed it all up. 'Do you feel well enough to walk? I would have Adam carry you, but—' He shrugged. 'In any event we must leave before the rain comes, and with discretion. There has been enough light on this hill already to attract the attention of His Majesty's guard. Not to mention his witchfinders.'

There was a fresh outbreak of snarling. 'Compose yourself, gentlemen! Or must you be tied into your saddles against our return?' He left them dangling and went to tidy up his own paraphernalia. After a moment I did my shaky best to pack up Dee's for him. He was silent now, head hanging, utterly despondent.

'I shall leave this place,' he said. 'Leave, and in shame. If all my researches have been follies—'

'Oh no you don't!' snarled Kelley. 'His pissant Majesty isn't going to let you, believe me! You're going to stay – and you're going to help me, you hear?'

'Oh no he isn't!' I said, and I relished it with every fibre of my being. This bastard had strained most of them, anyway. 'He's finished with you. In fact, you scabby son of a bitch, we're all fucking finished with you, and you are completely washed up. The wipe. The cleaners. The workover. Two rinses and the bloody starch! Zat clear?'

Man, I was enjoying this. 'The Doctor and I are going back to the city. And he's going to show me all the way home again – aren't you, Doc?'

Dee nodded silently, still hanging his head. 'Right!' I crowed. 'And *you* are going back with Adam and the Rabbi here, and if you're very, very good he's going to turn you loose somewhere along the way. Outside the walls, of course, and if you know what's good for you, you won't try and get back in. That's the only deal on the table, and you can thank the Rabbi on your bended knees. If it were me pushing Adam's buttons he'd just put you down right here and sit on you, but then I'm not religious.'

'You get of a spavined sow!' snarled Kelley. 'Had you not come crashing your way in—'

'You'd have been in my shoes, sure. And you'd have deserved it. Believe me, nobody's ever done you a bigger favour.'

Kelley snarled something pretty remarkable.

'Have it your own way,' I told him. 'Next time I smell a sewer, baby, I'll think of you.'

And so we parted, for the moment. Give Dee his due, he bowed to the Rabbi, properly, and made a nice little speech. Loew went equally solemn on him, made just as nice a speech, then cheerfully ruined the effect with a little *mazel tov* gesture to me. Then off he went into the gathering rain, with the clay giant shaking the hillside at his heels, Kelley tucked neatly under its arm. We headed back to our horses, with Dee still shaking his head and sighing.

'Poor Edward! Poor Edward! So precipitate a man, you know. So eager to have such things be true. I am sure that must be what made him—'

I stopped him. 'No you don't, Doc. Next minute you'll be saying he's just a dreamer who deluded himself. That's always the con-man's last defence line, in my day. It isn't true. They're just lying bastards.'

Walter Mittys, they always called themselves – or their mouthpieces did. But Mitty didn't try to sell anyone *his* dreams.

'No, no, Master Maxie—'

I bridled. 'Look, take it from me. I *am* one.'

For the first time that night Dee looked amused. 'No, Master Maxie. That you are not. Were it so, you would have taken Edward's part from the beginning, or those creatures. Instead you have liberated me from, yes, a most monstrous imposture. As a coney-catcher, young sir, you are an utter failure. Indeed, I detect that you are sickening for honesty.'

'Oh,' I said. 'Well, there aren't any cars around here.'

'Are you sure you wish to go home, then?'

'Yes. God, any time – right now! Sort of. I mean . . . *Shit!*'

'You may reconsider. My son is too young, and shows little disposition to aid me in my studies. I have no assistant now. Nor brother. Nor has my lady Jane.'

And if I told you that didn't start me thinking, I really would be a lying bastard.

She was waiting back at the house, her and Joan Kelley. That gave me a nasty moment, till they started dancing around as they saw us come back. Yes, *they*. Mistress Kelley as well; and she rushed just as avidly to greet Dee. And when he told them they would be going home . . .

'Her too?' I asked Jane Dee as she bustled joyously about, organising a huge feast of a dinner, bossing the maids about in dreadful hog-German.

'Aye, aye, poor lass!' sighed Jane, pausing in her whirl of tablecloths to fan her glowing cheeks. 'Hadst not known? She was main unhappy with that wretch, and cordially he hated her. Always he said it was the angels had made him marry her – aye, the golden angels in her purse, he meant! Now she'll back to England with my John and me, and keep house with us together, for she's a mighty fine mistress of a kitchen – finer than I, who was bred to court only.'

So that was one more weight off my mind. But it wasn't the only surprise I had coming from Joan Kelley. I still felt I ought to say something to her, but when I tried I was enveloped in an overwhelming hug. 'Wronged me?' was what I managed to get out of her broad dialect. 'Nay, never say that! You are my brave gentleman who has freed me from a monstrous dirty beast! The angels this and the angels that, and scarce a finger he'd lay upon me, for all he was so ready upon my lady Jane, stale upon his head!' She chuckled conspiratorially. 'Yet never a patch he was on good Doctor John, for all his years!'

It hadn't occurred to me that a swap went both ways. 'You mean . . . you and *Dee*?'

She gave a tremendously dirty giggle, and suddenly she didn't look nearly so much like a potato. 'Oo, there be a thing to ask!' She dug me in the ribs. 'But never I could refuse you nothing, young sir. Oh, a fine man that is, for all his years. Very hot in the blood, aye; very upstanding. And my poor dear lady Jane, she so cold and thin and dignityfied, she's never been much good to him. 'Tis a sound frame that sets him a-riggish, I can tell you. And now we'll be free to sport at will, and my worthless husband go shake his ears about the world. But mark you, dear young sir, not a word to my lady! Not a word!'

I don't think I could have said anything if you paid me. And for me, that's *serious*.

Ah well – *chacun à son gout*, as the old maid said when she kissed the cat. Clearly it was time to be getting home, all right. I couldn't keep up with these people.

There were things to be done first, though, obligations to be fulfilled. You didn't just slink off from an emperor's court. Dee, as head of the party, would have to go get his leave. That would take a little time, but somehow I didn't think he would have much difficulty, not now. In the meantime he would see me back through the sewers, and return on his own. But first we both had another call to make, a lot less illustrious but even more of an obligation.

The evening after it found us hooded and cloaked again, coming back from the Jewish Quarter. Dee had given me money to buy the Rabbi a gift, though he agreed with me it would probably find its way to the poor soon enough; and he had added a rare manuscript from his own library. I was coming to like the old bugger a lot more lately.

We were chatting quite cheerfully as we turned back down the street to Dee's gate, wondering what we could possibly have bought Adam – about a ton of clay and a model of the Venus de Milo? – when another figure sprang out in our path. Right in our path – and sprang is maybe the wrong word. He slunk, but the way a starving leopard slinks. He slunk; and he stunk, worse than ever, still in his rich robe, now somewhat thorn-tattered, with his hose encrusted up to the thighs.

'Well,' I said thoughtfully, contemplating the knife he was holding. 'We know which way you got back in, don't we?'

Kelley snarled. 'Away out so late, masters? I've been watching hereabouts, waiting. There's some folk on their way down to see you, by the look of it. Shall we not wait till they come?'

And just then, indeed, I heard the familiar rattle and clank of the Imperial guard, bashing hell out of the cobbles. Dee and I looked at one another, drew a deep breath, hastily regretted it, and stepped back a pace or two. The pikemen were already rounding the corner.

'Perhaps I should have called upon His Highness sooner . . .' muttered Dee.

'Guards!' shouted Kelley. 'Over here! Here!'

They came marching right up to us without a break in step, and halted with an epic clank.

'You!' raved Kelley to their captain. 'I know you, you understand some English, don't you? Arrest me these two dangerous sorcerers who are hindering me making the Emperor his gold! It's been their fault all along—'

The captain's feet tormented the cobbles some more. 'By authority of His Imperial Majesty, you are to be held under house arrest. You will please to enter the gate at once.'

The last time I saw a grin like Kelley's it was feeding time and it had stripes. Dee and I looked at one another and shrugged. The captain cleared his throat thunderously, and the pikemen trailed their weapons. Dee sighed and rapped on the gate. It swung open at the first blow, with never a servant in sight. I began to get a really nasty feeling, but there wasn't a lot I could do about it – not in company, anyway.

I pushed the door wide, and we went in, with the soldiers clinking along behind. The captain motioned us into the main chamber, and as I climbed the steps I saw Jane and Joan Kelley standing at the far wall. They looked tearful and uneasy, but this turned to outright alarm when they saw us. They didn't say anything, but their eyes swivelled frantically to one side. I followed them, and nearly had a nasty accident.

Sitting there behind Kelley's contraption, flanked by two guardsmen, inspecting it as if he owned the place – which he did – was the Emperor himself, still scratching.

The soldiers remained outside, but the captain clanked in behind us. Rudolph got up, twitching his whiskers in a genial smile, but he didn't say a word. He sprawled back in Dee's best chair, and waved to the captain.

The tinned officer made another of those thunderous throat-clearings, fixed his eyes upon the air above our heads, and recited in a high, singsong voice, 'Excellencies, your pardon! The morning before last a mysterious missive, in poor German but on fine parchment, was delivered to the High Chancellor by an unknown woman, hooded and cloaked, destined, it was said, for the hand and eye of the Emperor only. In due course the parchment aforesaid did duly reach the Emperor's sight. Whereupon it was discovered to be entitled *The Quickness of the Hand Deceives the Eye*, and to treat of the exposure of certain sleights of hand which may be practised upon the credulous, in the guise of sorcery and operations alchemical. Therefore the Emperor thinks it best that to refute such slanders, unfounded though they be, Sir Edward Kelley should once again and at once publicly demonstrate the operation of his most marvellous invention, exactly as before. And to be sure that there is no defect, Master Maxie shall oversee the operation. Will you please inform Sir Edward accordingly?'

It was a treat to watch the grin wiped off Kelley's face as Dee translated this, and the blood drain slowly out of his cheeks. 'Of course, Highness,' he said hoarsely. 'In only a day or two – tomorrow, even – I shall be in a position to—'

'Once again!' snapped the captain. 'And at once! Here, and now, as His Highness commands!'

Rudolph just beamed impartially and scratched himself.

'But – but – the materials – the process – it will take time to assemble them—'

Rudolph raised his eyebrows. The captain tapped Kelley on the chest, sharply. 'After all the money you have had from His Highness, and all the labours you have told him of, you have not got a store of all you need to hand?'

When Kelley got that he went pure gorgonzola colour, all pale with blue veins. It matched the pong. 'Of course, of course,' he muttered. 'It is that I have used so much, I may have but a little left— I'll essay, I'll essay—'

'His Excellency remembers the process most clearly,' said the captain. 'If you like, he will assist you to determine how much remains . . .'

'No need,' mumbled Kelley, diving for the cabinets beneath his device. 'Grateful, grateful – but soon see—'

By a curious coincidence there seemed to be enough of everything. Kelley protested, Kelley pleaded, Kelley did everything but stand on his head and dance the hula. It looked as if he really was losing his grip. Dee had moved over to stand with the women, holding their hands and looking even more anxious; but he didn't contribute a word to help Kelley, even when the man appealed to him directly. The more he kept it up, the worse it looked; and at last he seemed to sense this. He shot me one long, smoking glare, but I'd seen a lot worse than that lately. Then, slowly, very slowly, Kelley set to work.

To be honest, which is a bit of a strain, I wasn't much happier. It's one thing preaching confidently about spotting sleight of hand, it's another having to spot it – first time around, anyhow. You have to watch two hands at once, maybe even feet too –

magicians and mediums are often contortionists, and can use their feet nearly as well as their hands. It didn't help that Kelley insisted on closing the shutters and stoking up a series of hot little braziers at points along his apparatus, whose bright flames threw the rest into shadow. Up and down the tangle of piping and retorts Kelley bustled, pouring in coloured liquids that steamed, powders that fizzed and spat fumes that smelt worse than he did. I was glad he had the servants lay in water-buckets, in this wooden firetrap of a room. Every so often he would throw up his hands in sudden impassioned prayer, and in this religious age everybody's head bent instinctively – except mine. At other times he hunched, muttering incantations and invocations, squinting over a fire that turned his coarsely handsome features into a lined gargoyle with malevolent glittering eyes. You found yourself watching the eyes, and not the hands.

I had to admit it was a hell of a good performance, especially for a man who'd been through what he had. He had it down pat, though, and to me it showed; sometimes he moved almost automatically, like a choreographed dancer. His machine was good, too; and that was what worried me most. It was a complex of twisting pipes in brass and copper and cast iron, into which liquids and powders fed from glass retorts, doubling and twisting, going through cooling troughs only to be heated again. The lead was melting in a crucible at one end, and as he tipped it into a funnel mouth, you could actually see its shimmer of heat pass along the pipes.

No wonder Rudolph had insisted on a demonstration; this was a closed system, and not nearly as easy to gimmick as I'd expected – especially with molten metal. That might mean that the switch would come right at the end, when the tube debouched into the last cooling trough, under the surface of the water. Clouds of steam, the now solid and manageable lead concealed somehow and the pre-melted gold slipped in – that would be perfect. That had to be it.

I was so sure of that I almost found myself relying on it – until I caught something in Kelley's expression. A touch, a gleam, it was hard to say what; maybe it was just the furious energy in his features. A chill hit me among all that heat. For all his protestations, he was enjoying himself. Maybe he always had been; that was why he'd overdone the protestations, to sabotage people's expectations. They'd feel all the worse when he pulled it off. If he was that confident – he must have had the machine prepared for something like this, primed and ready. I would have. And he might just have arranged that obvious cooling trough, too, a plant for anybody suspicious to fasten their attention on. There's nobody easier to fool than the man who think's he spotted the trick . . .

Which meant that he'd be working the switch with the molten metal, as nobody would expect he could. So there had to be somewhere else it would come from—

'Ah!' he shouted, and Rudolph wouldn't have needed to understand the words to hear the relief and excitement in his voice. 'By the mass, it's taken! It's turned, it flows!'

I was barely in time. I must have pounced. Everybody jumped, Rudolph included. Kelley was reaching over the machine to feed the last brazier, his hand nowhere near the tubes. It was the other hand, momentarily shielded by his body and the brazier glare, that I swatted away. Rudolph sprang up, Kelley positively screamed and swung at me, as if to knock me all over the apparatus – but the captain, moving with startling speed under all that tin, grabbed his arm and held him, not too easily. He was genuinely foaming at the mouth now.

'*You've despoiled it, you little whoreson, you son of a punk*—'

I grabbed one of the water buckets and dashed it over that part of the machine. 'You bet I have, sunshine! You see it, sun – er, Highness?' I panted, as the steam cleared and the tubes contracted with sudden violent poppings. 'Where it's steaming, there, nowhere near the brazier? That's where he's just diverted the molten lead, with this sliding bit here! It's a tap, a spigot! Like a beer keg!'

It was carefully concealed among the twists of the other piping. I'd never have spotted it if he hadn't led me to it, but once you knew you could see it stuck out, like an appendix in a digestive system, a dead end to drain something off the main system. A carefully measured something.

'But it steams here also!' muttered Rudolph dubiously, dabbing nervously at another branch of the piping, also away from the fire. It didn't occur to me then it was the first time he had actually spoken.

'That's where he brings the gold in!' I traced the short iron pipe back, burning my finger in the process. 'Ow! To this brazier here – there must be a crucible inside, and the gold just flows down once the pipe gets hot enough. If it isn't, nothing comes through, so you'd never spot it otherwise. And with that shout he expects everyone to be looking at the trough!'

'Where nothing should appear,' said Dee quietly. 'Yet something – there!'

Molten metal hissed down into the water, and I nearly had heart failure. But as the distorted nodules sank hissing to the floor of the trough, there was no mistaking that dull sheen. Rudolph plunged his hand in, and caught up the still steaming metal. I held out my hand, and he tipped it into my palm. It was heavy.

'Lead!' said Dee, bitterly, leaning over. 'But a mere tenth part of what was put in. I recall there was always some lead still among the gold that emerged. You remember, do you not, Edward? I thought that so convincing, that the transformation should not yet be entire . . .'

With a sudden, savage gesture Rudolph drew his dagger and smashed at the iron pipe with the hilt. The abrupt cooling had probably cracked it anyway. Glinting gold rolled in lacy fragments across the floor.

I smashed the bucket down on the appendix pipe, which sagged and broke off. I stooped after it.

'Well?' demanded Rudolph.

I fumbled it up, and showed him the open end. The tube was clogged with the same dull leaden gleam.

The Holy Roman Emperor spat out something so unholy it even amazed me. Then he waved a hand to the captain, who dropped Kelley and saluted. Rudolph turned on his heel and stalked out, the alarmed pikemen fluttering out of his path like electroplated pigeons.

The captain made a noise like a bomb in a bucket of phlegm.

'A-*hem*! The aforesaid demonstration has not been carried out to the satisfaction of His Imperial Majesty's inspecting officer, namely myself. The practice is therefore deemed to be illegal, corrupt and unholy. I am therefore commanded to escort any persons suspected of such illegal activities to the palace, at once. Of course this could not possibly involve His Excellency the Doctor Dee, who is above suspicion and has in any case never made any material claims. Your Excellency Master Maxie—'

He fixed me with the beady eye all cops everywhere seem to develop just for me. But then he bowed.

'—is but newly arrived, and has given meritorious service. Therefore, the Emperor bids me present his compliments to you, and will you please to inform His Excellency Sir Edward Kelley that he is to accompany us without delay?'

Kelley did the classic pale-to-purple bit.

'*Me?*' he screamed. 'Have you lost your iron-skulled wits? I've never—'

He looked about frantically for a way out, as the pikemen closed in. 'I'm innocent! It would have worked—'

The captain's eye turned even beadier. '*Du ist mich instantlich mit comingk! Oder ist your arsch oot o'the windae! Zu Befehl!*'

Clearly a bright lad, this, though no grammarian. And maybe overinfluenced by those Scots mercenaries.

Would have worked?

Shaky with released tension, I leaned on the table. The broken pipe, heavy with the weight of metal inside, was still burning my palm, and maybe I deserved it, just a little. I was still dizzy with the speed I'd had to react, not once but twice, and with the thought of what might have happened. It brought me out in the mother of all cold sweats.

If Rudolph had thought to look closer . . . But he was already humiliated enough.

If Kelley had thought to look closer . . .

But then he'd never really believed his machine worked, or ever could. I contemplated the stringy gobbets of lead the Emperor had spilled from the trough. The Romans had used those to tell fortunes, once; and they'd certainly told mine. It was lucky I'd been able to palm enough of them to press into the open end of the appendix pipe.

Enough to cover up what it was really full of.

Not that Kelley knew. He hadn't even bothered to look, or demand a closer examination. Lead was what he'd expected me to find. But this once, just this once, his little gadget had only served to divert the evidence that would have vindicated him, and left us well and truly screwed. Royally, you might say.

This once the transformation had come through. He really had made gold.

There he was, shouting about his innocence. He'd conned everyone, but he'd ended up conning himself. And then I'd had to con him, too.

The quickness of the hand deceives the eye. Well, OK.

Why had it worked? It never had before, that was obvious. It couldn't have, or Kelley would have found out when he melted the metal back out of the appendix. Maybe he'd managed to tap the power of the Spiral at long last – through the extra excitement and intensity of working under pressure, perhaps. But there was a nastier possibility. Could somebody else have started to feed him power, as they had me with the phone? Maybe that aborted ritual had left him some kind of link, after all. One that could liberate him, just as it had me. If this went any further the dung could really hit the windmill . . .

The captain bowed again. 'Please to inform His Excellency that he will be still given every opportunity to prove the worth of his process. An apartment is to be provided in the quietest tower of a remote castle, well furnished with all his apparatus, where nothing else at all may distract His Excellency's labours. Until, of course, in the fullness of time His Excellency is crowned with success. Please to inform him of that.'

A remote castle. Far away from Prague, far away from the margins of the Spiral, no doubt. Where nothing really could reach him.

Nothing at all.

'Captain,' I said, and bent a bit myself, 'it's going to be a positive pleasure.'

CHAPTER ELEVEN

Dip in Road

THE THUDDING SOUND grew louder as the ponies splashed on.

'In truth,' apologised Dee for about the thousandth time, 'I am sorry to convey you home with such scanty honour. No carriage, no escort even.'

I laughed. 'I've told you. I don't need those!' The last time I had an escort, I'd been handcuffed to him.

Dee's beard wagged. 'You are kind, sir! And certainly it befits a scholar to make no undue display on his travels. I had thought, perhaps, if our endeavours had been successful, to travel homeward in great style, but I am chastened for that. Now I shall have only what is necessary for my poor Lady Jane and me. No more than a few carriages – four, perhaps, even three. A train of wagons for our modest baggage, a dozen or so outriders, a few men at arms that we shall hire by stages. The world will scarcely see us pass. Poor Edward! Poor Edward!'

'Well,' I said, trying to derail that particular train of thought, 'a carriage and cavalry escort wouldn't fit in very well, down here. Might cause a nasty blockage, in fact.'

'Aye, that is so,' he answered, quite seriously. Almost without thinking he turned his mount's head under a low mould-grown arch I would probably have missed. The note of the splashing changed, and the throbbing grew louder still. 'Know you, I mean to petition Her Gracious Majesty Queen Elizabeth that she shall recover poor Edward from Rudolph's grasp.'

'You know,' I said very carefully, 'he did play you a couple of nasty turns. And he could have gotten you in shit a lot deeper than this with old Rudolph.'

'Oh aye, I know it well. You have been a true friend to me in uncovering it, though a painful one. But I cannot abandon him thus, poor, misguided fellow, not after so many years of labouring in my vineyard. Much of what he did was in frustration at our failures, I am sure, and in expectation of pleasing me. Her Majesty will surely not refuse to ransom a man of such qualities. I shall write him so, often, that he lose not hope.'

I gave up. Kelley was part of Dee's world, the world where angels talked to him and he passed on their messages to respectful kings and statesmen. The fact that Kelley had mostly been planting vines of his own, and nasty ones too, seemed to have passed him by. Endlessly forgiving people is the easy way out, so much easier than facing the facts about them; and about yourself. The Kelleys of this world know that. So do the Maxies, come to that, but we're not so good at milking it.

Still, by all accounts old Bessie was an even

tougher nut than Rudolph, a real brick-in-the-handbag artist. She might like Dee, but she wouldn't lift more than the odd finger for Kelley. As Kelley was probably well aware; and banged up in the middle of nowhere, with no hope but screeds of encouraging bleatings from Dee, might just be a heavier punishment than the bastard deserved.

That made it about right, by me.

The metallic clunking of the engines shook the foul air now. Dee held his staff up, and I saw the sloping ramp, its concrete cracked and weed-grown; but it could have been the stairway to Heaven. 'There lies your way,' he said. 'But I would not take my leave of you in these noisome depths. I shall join you for a moment upon the marches of your strange future.'

When we emerged into the air it was still crisp night, and the stars were glittering cheerfully, considering what was rising up to them. I noticed the noise at once, even over the chug of the pumping gear. The hum and buzz struck deep in the ears, the beehive drone of modern life. Especially the bits of it I kept nicking.

'I regret I shall never see this world of yours, with all its wonders,' said Dee wistfully. 'But still more so that I shall never again enjoy your company. Fare you well, my boy, and fall not back into your old ill ways. There is more of good in you than many I have heard called honest and esteemed. I cannot now give you the rewards you were promised, for all your toil, but here is a trifle in token.' He passed me a pouch, which clinked interestingly. 'Ah, and this is a letter also, from my lady Jane, and from – ahem! –

Mistress Joan. Would you credit it, they made me swear it should not be opened in my presence. Ah, womanish as ever!' He chuckled fondly.

So did I, for different reasons. Not that different, come to think of it. 'You look after yourself, too. I mean, I'm not saying give up on the angels, OK? Just the mediums. If someone says they've picked up a message for you, well, you could ask why the angels don't deliver it directly. Look at it this way – the medium *is* the message!'

Dee thought a moment, then nodded. 'Most profound, my boy; most profound. Well, this is our parting, I fear. Come clip me now!'

Being embraced by a man is not exactly my idea of fun; I had some close shaves in the nick, being small, blond and young. Still, it was the way in Dee's time. Old Loew had done it too, and at least Dee didn't have oil and garlic in his beard. Loew's was like a salad.

Apart from all that, as I watched Dee lead the patient ponies plodding away back down that nasty slope, I realised I was going to miss them both. They hadn't approved of what I was, but nor had they screamed, or preached, or patronised – much. There was something to be said for the religious approach. Maybe I ought to try it one day, if I could find something I believed in – First Reformed Seventh-Day Ferrari Fetishists?

More likely Hell on Wheels, Maxie.

I stood there a moment, feeling very lonely. Then I opened the envelope, and read it in the dim glare of the sewage farm's lights. There was a letter, and if you want to know what it said, you mind your own business. Besides, I've no idea what her standard of comparison was, anyhow; though something suggested it was more than just the other two. Or maybe that was Joan's expert opinion. But there was also a ring, and a very nice one too, gold with a blue stone. At least this wasn't going in the hockshop, no matter what.

Mind you, I'd said that about my watch, and the old man's too. Even true champions and flame-bodied lovers have to eat.

The purse had gold in it, nice bright, new Austrian thalers that any expert would recognise on sight – as a forgery, because they were that new. I knew a bloke who could take care of that, though it'd be a fresh experience for him ageing something genuine. All told, I probably had at least a grand's worth here, at collector's prices. And sitting waiting in my little roof-nook hideout, if the rozzers hadn't happened upon it – and I'd bet dollars to doughnuts they hadn't – was another sweet, sexy fifty times that.

My ears practically rang at the thought of it. I needed a drink to celebrate this. And where better than the Wheel? Lots of places, since you ask; but at least it was nearby, and that's always a good point in a bar. I could have another go at getting around Poppy – or rather, over. Or under. Or wrapped around, or all of the above, choose one from each column. Maybe I could show her Jane's letter as a reference.

The thought buoyed me up so much I practically floated along the path back, even without external power. It took longer on foot, and seemed to have developed a few extra turnings since I'd last passed that way, but I kept the Wheel firmly in mind. It didn't seem to be so very long before I came in sight of the village outskirts, and saw over the thatches, against the greying sky, the pointy poplar stand which marked the pub.

Greying. Sod. They'd probably all be still in bed, and I'd have to wait for my drink. Still, maybe I could catch Poppy in her nightdress, or better still out of it. I sauntered down the path, hopping over puddles and kicking stones like the eight-year-old I probably am. After everything I'd been through, the place almost looked like home. I strolled into the village, hearing the cocks crow and smiling benignly at the scrubby watchdogs that yapped at me from their tethers.

What did all-purpose Ye Oldes have for breakfast? Bread, of course; eggs; bacon; sausages, surely. Maybe not coffee or tea, though; but I could face beer. Mulled, with spices, to take the chill off. I'd earned it, after the things I'd been through, after the first awful night I'd taken that path. Maybe Fisher would be there, and I could tell him just what I thought of him and his advice. You could see the path from here, at the crossroads ahead, winding up the hill there, where those idiots were waving . . .

Oh.

Right at the top of the path, at the brow of the hill, lounging there as if they'd been waiting.

Oh, *shit*.

The crossroads lay between me and the pub. At the speed they moved, they could buzz down it in a moment and stuff me before I'd taken two steps across.

One of the women cupped her hands to her mouth and shouted. '*Going somewhere, Maxie?*'

I blinked. The voice was hers in pitch, but the accent was that of the jolly black guy. And he'd made almost the same movement. I was hypnotised, rat by snake; only this rat was more than commonly resentful. '*You!* ' I screamed back. 'We exorcised you bastards! We cut you off! You can't track me, you can't tempt me any more! Where'd you bloody bubble up from?'

'Not the same sewer as you, *señor*!' This time it was the Oriental guy; only the timbre was female, and the words sounded like the Spanish woman.

'Don't get rid of us that easy, Maxie!' called the blond man mockingly. 'Cut off – huh! Why sweat it? We brought you here, we found you here! All we had to do was drift back'n just hang around. We knew we'd get you, sooner or later. Sooner it is, too. Gotcha now – and we're not gonna lose you, not this time, not nohow. So why not make it easier and come talk like a civilised citizen?'

He'd started the speech; but the Oriental took it over somewhere, seamlessly, and it finished in the black guy's mouth, smiling as ever. I was beginning to understand at last, and it chilled my blood horribly. 'Civilised? I talk to citizens with names! I don't even know yours! I don't know a damn thing about you!'

They weren't even bothering, any more. They just laughed – the same laugh, from mouth to mouth and back again, and sounding bigger, somehow, than all of them put together. 'Go on!' I shouted furiously across the dawn breeze. 'You think you've got me?

Then no reason you shouldn't tell me your names, show me yourselves – all of you! Who're the hidden ones? Who's the real power behind you, the real face? Which of you was first?'

'*First?*' The laugh was huge and horrible. It seemed to shake the sleeping thatches and draw them in towards it, sucking them inward. A burst of baby squalling arose from behind one banging shutter. 'There is no first! There was no first! Why should I remember, why should I know or care? I know only the now, and the next! There is only *Me*!'

'Then what d'you want me for?' I screamed, into the windy echoes. Leaves whirled up around my head, dust stung my face. 'Why won't you bloody leave me alone?'

The laugher was cold. 'Because you have tasted Our power, Maxie! Because We know you will not resist it, not in the end!'

'You bloody wish! But why me? Out of all the bloody Spiral, *why chase me*?'

That did it. I understood then, even before they said anything; and they seemed to sense it, because they laughed that laugh again. 'Because you are not of the Spiral, Maxie! Because *We* lured you out of the Core! To be Our bridge, Maxie, Our conduit! Our vessel, Our vehicle into a world that's unprepared for Us, that cannot guard against Us! And through you, *in* you, We'll grab life by the throat – not just the Spiral's shifting shadow life, but to the Core!'

'You *bastards*!' I was vaguely aware of the hot tears streaking my cheeks. 'You utter frigging bastards! You want to . . . take me over, don't you? To ride me! To *steal* me! Like a bloody car!'

And didn't that raise a laugh. 'You have stolen yourself, Maxie! If you'll not come to Us, We'll come down upon you! You drank of Our wine – *you're Ours for the taking!*'

It was more like an animal roar – a bestial one, certainly. The figures on the hillcrest seemed to lean together, straining like the landscape, as if I was watching it in a deforming foil mirror. It was nothing at all like computer animation, like morphing; nothing nice or fluid. It was a sucking, straining distortion that drew faces and limbs together into a vast, inchoate vortex, a whirling hor-ror in which, for an instant, an individual feature would still be seen, stretched to a thread of familiar shape or colour. The bellow thundered across the dawning sky, and the poplars bent.

'Come to me, Maxie. My name is *Legion!*'

Out of the vortex the face took shape in a sudden bulging thrust, the nightmare face as I'd seen it, but solid now, no longer made of writhing human outlines – or at least you couldn't see them. And it was vast. It was a wolf's face, a bat's, a man's, a hairy predatory vision of every animal fear, lifting hot and steaming above the hillcrest. Through the boiling mists beneath its body rose, manlike, hulking, yet hung about with the same reeking, matted fur. And above its shoulders, vast as the hill itself, black wings hunched upward to blot out the dawn.

I wasn't hanging about to criticise. Religious I'm not, but that shape straight out of the universal sub-conscious struck directly down from eyes to legs, with the barest bypass to my brain. I was already running as its great arm reached out, racing the black waterfall of shadow the clawed hand sent sweeping ahead of it, down the hill to the crossroads.

Run, or – no, not die. I'd guessed what I had to fear down there, and it wasn't death, nor hell neither. But the terror of it sang down my legs and turned my tendons to red-hot wires, my lungs straining, my heart drumming. As I ran I felt a sullen tremor in the earth, one of those awful footfalls I remembered so clearly, and the sky flared green at my back. The crossroads opened out before me – and blackness swallowed them, the last spilled dregs of the sinking night. I screamed, I suppose; I took the crossing running, and as my foot touched it I leaped. It was like leaping an open freezer; a deadly chill breathed around me, sickening my stomach, riming my hair.

Then the stony path slapped my worn shoe soles, and I was through. Shadow was all it was, the shadow of the reaching arm and not its substance. Vast and slow the thing itself reached out for me, cable sinews tautening one claw-tipped finger; but I was through, away and running for the Wheel. Running madly, screaming for Poppy, running like a man possessed – or one about to be.

I fell, more than once, rolled in the dust and hardly felt it, springing up again and shrieking as the shadow touched the walls and trees around the sleeping houses. Once, twice the ground shuddered at one of those fearful footfalls, slower than before but massively weightier, a mass no obstacle could stop. It felt like about a century before I reached the pub wall and swung around it. I scrambled over the low fence without even breaking stride. The door was shut, locked and barred maybe, but I was damn near ready to run right through it, toon-style.

I didn't have to. It opened as I thrashed through the clawing rosebushes and on to the lawn. It opened, and there was Poppy herself in cap and shawl and long white nightgown, candleholder in one hand and a gnarly broom upheld in the other. I flung myself at her feet, unable to run another stride. Why, I didn't know; what could she do or anyone, against that monstrosity? But this was all the safety I could think of. I babbled, I screamed, I don't know what sense I made; but I didn't need to.

The arm of blackness lay all across the village now. The thing hung vast in the sky, its shell of ghastly green glare rippling against the greyness. The arm that cast the shadow reached down towards the straining thatches slowly, effortfully, as if the air was turning thick and sticky as syrup, but horribly unstoppable. Towards us it stretched, it strained; but it was so vast it would reach us all the same, and soon. The nearer it reached, though, the less clearly I saw it, somehow. I thought my eyes were going out of focus, but it was the thing itself, the fringes of its ratty fur blurring and shimmering, edged with prismatic rainbows as if I saw it through a cheap lens.

I knelt at Poppy's feet, my breath wheezing into tortured lungs, too weak even to clutch her legs, and she reached down and put a protective arm about my shoulders. Her very steadiness made me aware how I was shaking. I knew why. I understood only too well what that thing was.

What had Loew guessed? Men who'd made themselves into the image of demons. He'd been right, up to a point. Not demons. *A* demon.

A blend. A merging, a composite monster made up of its own victims, drawn in by the very strength it gave them. Until drawing on that strength made them more and more a part of it, until all but the shell of their individual selves was lost, dissolved in the greater self-image. An Arcimboldo portrait, Faust and Mephistopheles in one.

Even from that vast height those narrow eyes were fixed on me, flaring red, piercing, hungry – a hunger I could feel, a hunger for the individuality I had and it hadn't, for all its compounded power, the thirst of minds whose own lives had long ago been lost and dissolved, to live again through another. Not just the few I'd seen, the eight or so; those shadowy figures behind them had only been a glimpse, all that could be seen of the ones that had gone before. A symbol almost, of a vast queue of victims winding off into obscurity.

And it would have me soon like all the rest, walk in my shape, but with all that vast, invisible crowd trailing along after me like the segmented body of some enormous worm. Like all the rest, only worse, because through me it could walk in the Core, in the world I knew, a wild possibility reaching in from the shifting chaos that was the Spiral, tearing open the gates of probability to let loose all hell. A demon unleashed, to violate every law there was, natural or otherwise – my demon, Maxie's Demon.

Through me, for as long as I lasted. Until I was hollowed out and burnt up, until I was so broken to the insanely fragmented wills behind me that I no longer had a will of my own. Until I joined the head of that queue, that horrendous body, and went snaking away with my fellow shadows to rope in some other poor wretch, on the hooks of his own weakness.

The wolf jaws parted, and between the stained sabre teeth the long tongue lolled and slavered, dripping foam that boiled into nothingness. The reaching claw seemed to quiver with massive effort, as if it was hooking in the universe. The reek from the fell grew thicker. Even the grass around me seemed to be straining upward in answer to that summoning claw.

Poppy's wide lips set in a pout of obstinate defiance. 'Oi! Shoo! Be off with you! Nasty great thing!' She brandished the broom indignantly.

The very sight of her started me laughing helplessly. I sprang up, and the slight effort seemed to float me right off the ground in that pull.

'You get out of it!' I shouted, though I could hardly breathe, and my lips slurred the words. ''S'not you it wants!'

'It's everybody, moi dear, in the end! Can't be standing for that, now, can we?'

She was right. Suddenly I felt very strange. I was still afraid, I was bloody terrified – but I was also icy calm.

If it was going to get us anyway, suddenly it didn't seem that important. If it was inevitable, it didn't matter; what mattered was how. All the more reason not to take it lying down. Or whimpering, for that matter. Maybe something like that happens to soldiers in wars. I could almost believe the sergeants in the war movies shouting, 'What d'you wanna do – live for ever?' Because you don't get brave when you think like that – but you do get angry.

The monstrous finger stretched out to me. I stretched a couple back, and added a juicy Italian gesture for good measure. 'You want me?' I screamed. 'You sure? I'll give you bloody indigestion! A century's worth! I'll run you ragged!'

It sounded even limper than that, believe me. A fart in a tornado would have had more effect. But it made me feel a bit better. It would have been nice if that claw had even faltered in its long, slow thrust, but it didn't.

'Get inside, Poppy!' I repeated, hoarsely. 'If it gets any nearer—'

The girl actually giggled. 'Never you fret, moi dear! This ol' place ain't so very easy overset, oi can tell you! There's been worse than that hereabouts in moi time and before it—'

'Worse than *this*?'

'Oo yes, and never yet – oh, *there* you is! We was wonderin' what was keepin' you, wasn't we, moi dear?'

Fisher.

Fisher, in a dapper green jacket and tan slacks that made me want to weep, because they were the first normal clothes I'd seen in what felt like a century, the first token of a world where things like this didn't happen. Fisher, striding out of the door past me with only the swiftest glance, and not an ounce of fear or hesitation in his step.

Fisher, not alone. Two women with him. Two awesome women, glowing with life, who almost made me forget the monstrous thing overhead. One dark, short-haired, sleek as an otter and as quick, with eyes that snapped and glittered in a strong-featured spearhead of a face. I knew her from the magazine, his wife, but wearing some kind of uniform now, grey, with chain mail at the shoulders, and swinging an awesome sword at her hip.

The other, taller yet, wore a sword too, a massive, basket-hilted thing. Her blonde hair foamed like a waterfall over broad shoulders and a blunter, more sensual face, just the heavy side of pretty, but with a wry half-smile that mirrored a glint of wisdom in the eyes. Her tight, dark T-shirt and leggings, in some kind of fuzzy midnight moleskin stuff, left a lot of tanned skin bare. Even in the shadow it glinted golden over her whipcord muscles, as if by the stored radiance of tropical suns.

And if all this seems like funny things to be noticing with the end of everything coming in at zero feet – well, you haven't seen them, that's all.

'Alison, Mall, stand by him!' snapped Fisher, lounging out on to the lawn and standing, leaning on his stick, staring up at the living stormcloud above. The wind whistled about him, and the poplars bent low. The gate rattled and the sign swung and creaked within its frame, slowly and ponderously, as if the Wheel itself really was swaying in the balance of fate. I saw the vast eyes shift then, the red flares turn from me to him. He nodded quietly, as if acknowledging or accepting something.

And this time the claw really did falter.

Fisher moved almost faster than I could see. The stick in his hand sprang upwards with the suddenness of a fencer's lunge, and stretched as it sprang, striking like a snake. It was a spear, a huge one, a white wood haft with a black tip glittering—

The sky hammered. For an instant I thought Fisher was struck by lightning; but the lightning struck upwards, earth lashing fire at sky as if to revenge the centuries of natural punishment. The spear spat steely light into the black form above, and the light lanced out and branched, beating against the matted beast fur. The demon reared up, flailing, and howled like a hurricane. We all staggered, and clapped our hands over our ears.

Except Fisher. He stood like a statue, with the cold light pouring from the thing in his upraised hand. Blue afterimages seared my sight. The black claw blazed like a welding torch. Snaking lines of sparking light raced spitting along the arm and burst in crackling fire across the gigantic body. The fur stiffened and bulged, and seams of actinic blue-white burst out. The thing shook violently, the wolf head jerked back and was suddenly enveloped in the awesome blinding blossom that welled out from within.

From eyes, from throat, from nostrils the white beams shone against the smoke, utterly blotting out the green glare and the red. Then the agonised muzzle was enveloped in the fireflower, and the whole vast creature burst apart in midair. Light flooded the sky, and the landscape stood out stark and colourless as the glare leaped from horizon to horizon, as if to bleach the universe a uniform white.

Then there was no monster, no dismembered fragments, only human bodies whirling in a pale tornado vortex that seemed to hurl them outward as they reached its margin. They were alive; they flailed their limbs frantically. But one by one they were gone in an instant, leaving one alone at the heart, one that hung in the air an instant and came plummeting down like the loser of a dogfight, smoky trail and all, right down on our heads. I ducked, but it went tumbling over and down into what must be the margins of Willum's field.

A hundred-foot fall, at least. I winced as I heard the thud.

And suddenly there was the first trace of warmth in the grey sky, and all the birds were singing. Fisher lowered his walking stick and leaned on it with a satisfied air.

'Well,' I remember saying, though my own voice sounded tiny and hollow in my ears, 'no wonder *he*'s made a few killings in business!'

The women who flanked me snorted. 'He did that first,' said his wife. 'The rest came later.'

They were both looking at Fisher, and that suited me very well. I ducked down, and was one step away from scuttling off when two hard hands descended on my shoulders. 'What, just slipping away, Master Maxie?' enquired the blonde cheerfully.

'We can't have that, can we?' purred the brunette. 'Not the hero of the hour! Steve is simply dying for a word with you.'

'Hero' would have been more encouraging if I hadn't been reminded of a cat dabbing at a mouse. If Steve was dying for anything to do with me, he didn't show it. He strolled back, quite unnecessarily smoothing down his hair, and pecked the brunette's cheek lightly. 'Well, that'll stop him laughing in church, eh?'

It hadn't been laughing the way I heard the

expression, but Fisher was evidently the decorous type. It didn't stop him giving Poppy a squeeze, dirty devil. 'Sorry we had to get you up, Poppy, but if we'd shown ourselves sooner he'd have been away like spit off a hot stove. We had to lure him as close in as possible – thanks to our little bait here.'

'*Bait*?'

He gave me a cool look. 'Afraid so. Since you were in the way, you might say.'

I surged up, only to be thrust down again by those impossible hands. 'You lousy bloody bastard! You set me up for this! Right from the start! You sent me up that bloody road, that night!'

He scratched his immaculately shaven neck a moment. 'If you remember, I did suggest you'd be a lot safer heading back to the junction. I knew It was trying to lure someone in, someone who would suit It – or Them, or whatever you like. Naturally It was drawn to Dee and Kelley's little experiments. They opened a way for It, closer in to the Core; and that alerted me. That was why I'd been hanging around here lately, hoping I'd get a lead. That was why I warned you, that night.'

'You could have been a bit bloody clearer!'

'What, said a ninety-foot hairy demon was after your backside? You'd really have believed that on top of everything else, wouldn't you?'

'So you just let me walk out into . . . into . . .'

'Oh, no. Nothing like that. Not unless I had to, anyhow. But you're fast on your feet, Maxie my boy. I was on your tail that night, but I hung back too far. You got away from me, and blundered right on in. When It appeared, I was too concerned about you to

deal with It immediately, and It backed off before I
could reach It. Then you did a runner. Ever since
then we've been searching. We almost got you with
the cops, and back in Prague. We had a little trouble
with the watchmen there, but Mall and Alison
actually hove in sight of you—'

I sank down, groaning. The women with swords –
not the demon's creatures at all, but these two
Amazon bitches.

'Yes,' he said severely. 'And you'd have saved
everyone a lot of trouble if you'd only hung on.
We'd have settled Kelley's hash easily enough.' He
tapped his shoe with his stick, and I flinched.

'I wish you wouldn't do that,' I muttered. I'd as
soon see someone tap-dance on an A-bomb. Maybe
I'd done Brother Edward another favour, at that.

Fisher grinned. 'Anyhow, by the time we tracked
you down again you were on your way home, so it
seemed simpler just to let the thing come after you.
We needed to get It in really close. You were never in
any real danger, though.'

'Huh!' was about the best I could manage. 'Look,
since you're so bloody communicative, I suppose
you wouldn't mind just telling me who you really
are – and why the hell you're mucking about
anyhow? What's happened to that – to them—'

'Me? Just another eccentric billionaire,' he said, a
little absently. 'But on the Spiral you rarely stay just
one thing long. And like you, I've got powerful
contacts. As to what's happened – to the people who
made that thing up, you mean? Back where they
came from, back to the moment in time where that
thing first got its claws into them. As if none of

this ever happened. Those were pretty desperate moments, though, mostly. They weren't very nice people, any of them; they needed the demon's power to become what they wanted to be, and you saw what that looked like. The last of them, anyhow, the ones still individual enough to take on any real shape. Thugs and no-goods writ large. They split up because they could push deeper back into the margins of the Core that way, and because they looked less alarming. But they were only really shells for that thing. The one you could never see clearly, the one who started the process, who began sucking others in.'

'I suppose I felt that. That there was something really weird or inhuman about them, anyhow.'

Fisher's wife nodded. 'You would. You're bright, and you had strength enough to resist what they dangled in front of you. They hadn't. Most of them are on their way back to the gutter or the gallows now.'

'Not all,' said the big blonde, shaking that mane of hers. 'One there is I know does well by her vices, and dies rich and in good name none dare question, a pillar of Mother Church.'

Fisher shrugged. 'Well, it happens sometimes. I've no control over it, thankfully. My life's complicated enough as it is.'

'Jesus, you think you've got troubles?' All this talk about gutters and gallows had brought everyday life back with a rush. 'What about me? The cops still think I'm Mr MacManiac! And if they don't get me Ahwaz will – and will anyway, if I end up in jail! I'm screwed!'

Fisher shook his head. 'No, no – that isn't the case at all. Look, I need a drink and some breakfast, and I'm sure you do – but come along with me a moment. Let him go, Mall. Poppy, ladies, you'll excuse us for a few minutes? And maybe scare up some bacon and eggs?'

'I wish you hadn't mentioned that drink,' I grumbled, trotting along beside him and his infernal long legs. He swept around the pub and back along the path to the junction. 'Couldn't we have it first?'

'This'll only take a minute. You see there?'

Oh God. He was pointing that stick over the gate into Willum's field. And yes, I certainly did see, though God knows I didn't want to. You couldn't miss it, not with that smoke or that smell.

I swallowed. 'I don't think I want any bacon. That was—'

'Yes. Your demon. The man who began that creature, who started the whole fearful thing off, its heart and driving will that began using his powers to swallow others, up and down the very length of the Spiral itself.'

I looked at the black, flattened thing in the margins of the field, spread out like a charred starfish. 'I never saw his face. I never will now, that's for sure. Who was he? Where'd he come from?'

'I've no idea.' Fisher leaned on the gate like any city slicker playing the rustic. Any minute now he'd start chewing a grass stalk. 'He could have been anybody, couldn't he? A secret policeman. A guard at an extermination camp. A serial killer. A religious fanatic, or a tribal one, a nationalist. A terrorist leader. A gang boss. An ideologue, even, who never so much as stained his hands, yet killed and enslaved more than all the rest put together. Maybe he was born long ago, maybe he hasn't been born yet. Does evil need a single name? Let him stand for all of them. But he must have been a pretty accomplished son of a bitch even before he discovered the Spiral and moved out on to it, drifted gradually outward towards the Rim. Good and evil there, they become absolutes in themselves. So he changed, and grew, and moved back again, in a new form – a heightened form. As they always seem to.'

He sighed. 'And so it ends. Because he was hungry for new experience, for a new link back into the Core. Cruising up and down, looking for new people to live through, and gradually take over, and use up, and absorb. All subject to him, all becoming part of him, till in the end they just faded into his memories; and in time he forgot them. Pretty good likeness of a demon, wouldn't you say?'

I nodded. 'But why me?' was about the best I could manage.

'Why anybody? He was casting about for somebody from the Core. He got you and Kelley; he preferred you. Maybe he thought you had more brains and talent. I'd say he was right. He thought you were special enough to take a risk on. I'd been after him for some time, but he was clever, he never came close enough to the limits of the Spiral, and his power with it. He could always get away. You drew him too far, and I'm grateful; and it's given you your reward.'

He reached down and plucked a grass stem. I twitched it out of his mouth. 'What sodding reward?

What're you flaming well rabbiting about?'

He nodded towards the field. 'This. A car wreck, with an anonymous burned body beside it, origin unknown. It could have been you, the man who stole the car. It still could be.'

I gaped at him. 'Don't be daft. OK, no finger-prints, maybe, but the Filth have still got dental records, tissue-typing – they'll know it's not me!'

'But do they know who you are?'

'Listen, it'll be all around Soho by now! Waxie Maxie sent out to lift a Ferrari – oh.'

He grinned. 'Got it now? Knew you were smart. The cops don't know who Waxie Maxie is, or was once. They don't have any records filed under that name. They have a dead man they won't be able to identify, so they'll assume it's this Mr W.M. And the others who know it isn't, Ahwaz and so on, they'll probably assume you got it on the marshes with the rest. But they won't be in a hurry to prove that to the cops, will they?'

I leaned on the gate and held my head. 'What then? So I'm dead. What do I do? Where do I go?'

'Anywhere you like.' He patted me on the shoulder. 'Don't you understand? Did Ahwaz know you by your real name? Did anybody? It really is Waxie Maxie that's dead here. You're shot of him at last, and all the debris that went with him. The petty villain's gone. All that's left is—' He paused, and squinted at me, and took a deep breath.

'—Julian Everard Maximilian von Arnim de Bel-vere Hastings Ferris – *whew*! – who made a minor mistake so long ago everyone's forgotten. And, incidentally, your conviction for that's scrubbed off the record by now. So even that can't be used against you.'

I'd done a lot of gaping lately, but never better than that. I couldn't speak, I couldn't even form a coherent thought. All I could do was gawp at him with my face hanging out.

'So,' he chuckled, 'congratulations, Mr Ferris. All you have to do now is decide how you're going to start your new life. And you're a bright enough lad for that. In fact – don't take this wrong, but I think we could probably find some room in C-Tran for somebody with your education and, er, street smarts. Clerical, certainly, but maybe something more interesting. How about PR? Or marketing?' He looked me up and down a moment, and a slight shadow crossed his face. 'Marketing, definitely.'

And of course it was just exactly then that my pride started to act up – never when I really need it, of course. 'A job. Well, thanks. With somebody always knowing who I am, of course. Somebody always keeping just the tiniest bit of a weather eye on me. Watching my timekeeping, checking my expense sheets, counting my petty cash.'

'Afraid so,' said Fisher. At least he was honest, a virtue I've always liked in others. 'Up to a point, anyhow; and for the first few years. I've a business to run. But you can't expect to get away without some penalty, at least. Think of yourself as walking wounded. With a scar that'll gradually heal. That's a lot luckier than some.'

I looked at him, and I thought. He didn't seem to be in any hurry; but then nobody did, in this strange place, a halfway house between worlds. Except me, and maybe that had been my mistake. 'Look,' I said at last. 'I'm grateful. I appreciate – well, everything. I can't pretend I'm not being pulled, hard; and I know damn well I don't want to go back to being what I was. But, well, I've always made other people's mistakes, if you know what I mean – from my father's onwards. Now there's just me, and I've picked up a bit of street smarts, as you say. Whatever I do, however it turns out, I'd better make my own way, clean. Maybe I won't do as well, but . . .'

I shrugged.

So did Fisher. 'I thought you were going to launch into "My Way". Well, suit yourself.'

'That's what I can do now, isn't it?'

He smiled, and nodded. 'The offer's open if you want it. Give my people a call. Feel like some breakfast now?'

'No thanks.' I jerked a thumb over the gate. 'I've rather lost my appetite. And besides, I think the sooner I'm out of here, the better. Give my love to Poppy, will you? And respects to your wife and the other – lady. And you . . . Christ, you really dumped me in this, didn't you?'

He grinned. 'I own cars. And I did save your hide, in the end.'

'Yes. So thank you, too – you bastard.'

'Don't mention it – you thieving little git.'

We grinned, and I scrambled over the fence. The hiss of a scythe stopped me in my tracks. That psychotic Willum had appeared from somewhere and, apparently oblivious to the smoking corpse, begun hacking away at the grainstalks. There never seemed to be any fewer of them.

I turned back to Fisher. 'What's he really cutting?'

Fisher munched a fresh grass stem. 'You don't want to know. Believe me, you *really* don't.'

I picked my way through them gingerly, and waited till I reached the fence to make a rude gesture at Willum. He looked up, and tapped his scythe meaningfully. Hastily I clambered through, and was nearly flattened by an early-morning bread truck. Back home with a vengeance.

Only not quite. How? I thought of standing there sticking out my thumb, till I heard the sirens. There were at least three cop cars flocking to what looked like the remains of a gruesome car crash in the central reservation. I recognised the red door that lay to one side, and decided not to look any closer. Time's complicated enough as it is. Besides, I was still allergic to cops.

And that brought back my dilemma. I really had been pulled this way and that, but by a factor even the mighty Steve Fisher didn't seem to know about – that fifty grand in the chimney stack.

If the cops hadn't found it yet. If they weren't staking it out. If Ahwaz wasn't keeping an eye on things.

Maybe if I waited – but then it might be discovered. Maybe if I went at once – then I might be nabbed. I didn't dither too long, though. Speed would be the essential, that was clear. In, then out, fast; and heigh-ho to a whole new life.

The trouble was still how. I had all that dosh waiting. I had at least a grand's worth of gold in my pocket. But any modern money, not being in a purse, had rolled out under the general stress of events, and I couldn't offer a taxi-driver pure gold thalers; I'd like to see him make change, for a start. I should have touched Fisher for my fare, but I wasn't going back, not with Willum in the way. So how?

I strayed thoughtfully across the junction, looking around and wondering. Even a basic bus fare was out of the question. People I tried to panhandle referred me politely to the cops, or not so politely. I wasn't the hitchhiking prospect I'd been, not the way my clothes looked now. But I had to get back, had to.

I looked around. Almost without thinking I'd strayed into the service station car park. It was filling up quite well already, considering the hour. Just the sort of time I liked – had liked, once. Plenty of choice, plenty of cover, nobody especially alert after night driving. A good time for lorry hijacking, too; but that wasn't my main line, I needed backup muscle for that. Better stick to what you know, for just this one last time.

And the target was obvious, a low, open sports four-seater, a type I knew; its deliberately antique lines concealed a mighty fistful of V8 performance. Under the cover of its neighbours I slithered up alongside it, crouching down, peering over into the seating well. This was a beautiful model with a ritzy interior, sleekly styled period door handles, animal-esque hood ornament, the lot – just the kind of wheels to whisk me on my way.

As a loan, of course, just this last time.

And nothing to hold me back but a couple of alarms and an immobiliser – a few seconds' work, even without my trusty Swiss Army knife, the

Autoverbrecher model. A tracker, too, probably – hard to find, but what the hell, by the time they locked on I'd be long gone. I took hold of the door handle – and screamed.

It was wet, it was hot and it had teeth, and they clamped down on my fingers, hard. I only just managed to tear my thumb free from the horrible little demon head it had become. Then, as I staggered back, clutching my ballooning thumb, I was horrified to see that hood ornament rear up, with the morning sun flashing on its chromium claws and teeth, and spring down lightly on to the tarmac. Barely in time I bolted for my life, with the little monster ripping away at my trouser legs, snapping at my ankles and snarling in a shrill, metallic squeal.

Oh, sure, it was logical enough when you thought about it. This was the nearest car park to the junction, the Spiral was bound to still have some effect, I couldn't be expected to remember Steve Fisher drove a Morgan. But why, of all the cars in the universe to break into, did I have to pick on that one?

It'd be cameras next, honestly.

APPENDIX

IT HAD BETTER be pointed out that Maxie's views on people, police, places and life in general are like icy roads – safest taken with more than a pinch of salt. In any case, they don't necessarily represent those of the management.

Prague

The city of Prague has been described as the Crossroads of Europe – which might well explain why Maxie gets so tangled up in it. It seems to have given birth or shelter to more extraordinary characters, both real and fictional, than almost anywhere else. Sometimes it's hard to tell which is which. Is it the hapless Gregor Samsa whose outlook Maxie so radically rearranges, in Chapter 8? Selling insurance was certainly Samsa's job; but the appearance and manner belong to his creator, Franz Kafka – who, somewhat unexpectedly, was a cheerful, even arrogant extrovert, a snappy dresser and ladies' man. It was only through his subconscious, perhaps, that the city's shadowy alleys wound and twisted their wormtrails.

They may also have played a part in the story of Emilia Marty, *née* Elina. She was nominally created by the Czech fantasist Karel Čapek, inventor of the term *robot*, in his play *The Makropoulos Case* – more famous as Janáček's brilliant opera. But in her eerie, timeless allure she too is something of an archetype, an embodiment of the spirit of the city.

The Emperor Rudolph II, on the other hand, who supposedly brought about her fate, was entirely real. His portraits, including the weird ones by the painter Arcimboldo, depict a jolly, rubicund face, but with an underlying sensuality and cold slyness no flattery can conceal. He was a great ruler in his way, devoted to arts and pleasures, and – for his time – remarkably broad-minded and enlightened, impatient of church dogma. He was also fascinated by any kind of unusual knowledge or research, and, as was common in his time, he lumped serious scientific research together with outright magic and sorcery. It was said that he encouraged the Jews because of their kabalistic magicians, but it was their financial facilities he really valued.

Rudolph's Prague may have been slightly more tolerant than Maxie found it, but Jews still had to wear distinctive yellow circles and endure scorn, assaults and occasional pogroms. Nevertheless many of them managed to grow rich – not least by financing the Emperor – and raised some fine buildings in the Jewish Quarter, which survive to this day. Only thirty years later the first Jew was elevated to the nobility, and they increasingly became an integral part of the city, and one of the largest communities in Europe. Ironically enough, the Nazis, who finally wiped it out, also carefully preserved the Jewish Quarter's buildings, to create a museum to a 'vanished' race.

Among these is the Old Cemetery, *Stary Zidovsky Hrbitov*, in which stands the grave of another real person, Rabbi Loew. He is remembered as a wonder-worker, and people still insert written prayers for help into the crannies of his tomb. His seat in the oddly named Old-New Synagogue is still marked. Whether or not he really was a kabalist is unknown; but legend says that the Golem itself is still concealed somewhere about the building. If so, some dedicated restorer is in for a surprise.

The Hussites, briefly encountered in Chapter 8, were a fierce religious and nationalist movement in fifteenth-century Bohemia – now the Czech Republic. They began as followers of Jan Hus, an influential church reformer who was, as usual, burned at the stake. Under his successors they fought the Holy Roman Empire to a standstill, and, while they were faction-ridden and often gorily fanatical, they were the founders of Czech national identity. They bulk as large in the national consciousness as Washington and Lincoln for Americans, Bruce and Wallace for the Scots, or for the English Churchill and . . . Bobby Charlton?

Doctor Dee

Also entirely historical are the most improbable characters of all. Maxie is not the most reliable witness, but they, and their wives, and their tangled relationship, seem to have been very much as they appear here. Dee was famous in his lifetime as a scholar and a magician, and may have been the model for Shakespeare's Prospero. He was born in 1527, the son of a London wine merchant, and studied at Cambridge, and at Louvain and elsewhere in Europe. The seventeenth-century chronicler John Aubrey had Dee described by people who knew him: 'He had a very faire cleare Rosie complexion; a long beard as white as milke; he was tall and slender; a very handsome man . . .'

He was unquestionably one of the greatest scholars of his age, whose mathematical work helped to advance sciences such as navigation and astronomy, and sought to systematise astrology and magic in the same way. He was a genuine genius; but nobody knew it better than he did. He was, to quote another chronicler and fellow-astrologer William Lilly, '. . . the most ambitious person living, and most desirous of Fame and Renown . . .' He believed that kings and rulers should be guided by the wisdom of distinguished scholars – with, of course, appropriate honours and rewards, which he was not slow to demand. He appears to have treated the angels in much the same way; the invocation on page 208 is taken from his own records. He also had another weakness, all too common in geniuses – an utterly naïve, irrational streak, which they will defend with all their brilliance, often to the point of self-deception, and with an angry contempt for lesser intellects who somehow won't share it.

Queen Mary engaged him as an astrologer, then jailed him for predictions she didn't like. This smoothed his path with Elizabeth I, on whom he made a considerable impression. She called him her philosopher, and under her protection and patronage he assembled an immense and famous library at his Mortlake home, visited by notables from all over Europe. He married, as his third wife, one of her young ladies-in-waiting, Jane Fromond. Increasingly, feeling the limitations of ordinary knowledge, he began to explore what would now be called divination and mediumship, to get in touch with higher powers. Various willing 'scryers' flocked to take advantage, among them, sometime in 1581, one Barnabas Saul. A year later, apparently worn out inventing clever enough angelic messages, Saul fled. Three days later a young man, one Edward Talbot, introduced himself to Dee with an account of Saul's shady past. One suspects that word of a vacancy had got around in certain circles. He too began to 'scry' angelic visions in Dee's equipment, producing much richer, wilder and more scholarly revelations. Dee, delighted, immediately engaged Talbot at the high wage of £50 a year plus board and lodging. Their association survived the discovery, a year later, that 'Talbot' was actually one Edward Kelley.

Edward Kelley

According to Aubrey's contemporary Anthony Wood, Kelley was an apothecary's son, born near Worcester in 1555. As Talbot he had studied at Oxford, possibly with another magical scholar, Thomas Allen, but had dropped out under some unspecified cloud. He had since been convicted of forgery, for which he was sentenced to have his ears cropped in the pillory at Lancaster; he had also been involved there in disinterring a corpse for necromantic rites. Early in Dee's service he married the widow Joan Cooper, apparently unhappily; he later blamed his choice on the angels. There is no description of Kelley, only one engraving of unknown origin; it shows an impressive but hard-faced man with flowing hair and beard – possibly to cover his notched ears.

Kelley had an obvious interest in Dee's success, and the angelic messages he transmitted began to feed the good doctor's ambition, steering him away from the English court to his Polish admirer, the prince Albrecht Laski. It was under his patronage that in 1583 Dee, Kelley and their families set out to impress Europe.

Rulers such as Stephen Bathori of Poland and the Emperor Rudolph received the pair royally at first, partly because Dee exaggerated his influence with Elizabeth, because he represented a new thought free of Church restraints – and because of Kelley's impressive alchemical demonstrations. An eyewitness account, by Sir Edward Dyer, survives of him heating base metal in crucibles together with a mysterious 'powder of the Stone' – the famous Philosopher's Stone, presumably – and appearing to produce gold. Lilly and his fellow antiquary Elias Ashmole record others. Unfortunately, in 1586, Kelley, perhaps trying to ingratiate himself with the Emperor, delivered a tactless angelic message to the Papal Legate in Prague. An attempt was made to lure the pair to Rome, no doubt for a fireside chat about heresy. When that failed, Rudolph was pressured to arrest them. Dee and Kelley hastily retreated to a noble admirer's country estate, but in 1589 they returned briefly to Prague, to mend fences with Rudolph. The Emperor knighted Kelley; Dee was more or less ignored. Elizabeth twice sent an envoy to recall them, but to Dee's chagrin she too was more interested in Kelley's potential.

What happened then is not clear – except to Maxie; but Dee and Kelley split up. Dee returned to England in grand style. Elizabeth gave him an academic post, but he lived expensively, with eight children to educate and a large household. Kelley remained behind, probably unwillingly, and was imprisoned in the tower of Zerner Castle. Dee tried to get Elizabeth to have him released; but in 1595 Kelley fell from the tower window – officially while trying to escape – and died of his injuries. Dee's diary records the news without any comment.

In 1605 Jane Dee died of the plague. When the magic-hating James VI and I came to the throne Dee's prosperity finally dwindled, and in 1608 he died. Lilly records that in his last years, looked after by one daughter, Dee was so poor that he often had to sell one of his precious books to buy dinner.

Aubrey records Dee's son Arthur, by then a successful doctor, remembering that as a boy he 'used to play at Quoits with the Plates of Gold made by Projection in ... Dr Dee's lodgings in Prague, and that he had more than once seen the Philosophers' Stone.'

Steven Fisher

The mysterious Stephen Fisher tells his own story, along with much more about the Spiral, in the cycle of books that begins with *Chase the Morning*, and continues through *The Gates of Noon* and *Cloud Castles*.